FILTER THIS

Sophie White grew up in Dublin and has a first-class honours degree in Fine Art from the National College of Art and Design.

After moving to New Zealand in her early twenties, Sophie went on to train as a chef while there and worked in the French Alps for several years before returning to Dublin in 2012.

Sophie began her writing career at age twenty-seven, when she started writing a weekly column 'The Domestic' for the *Sunday Independent*'s *Life* magazine. After the birth of her first child, she became a full-time writer, penning reviews of both books and restaurants, cultural commentary and interviews for a variety of Irish publications, and her first book *Recipes for a Nervous Breakdown*, part-memoir/part-cookery book, was published in 2016.

Mother of Pod, the successful podcast she hosts with Jen O'Dwyer, was launched in January 2018 and they launched a second podcast with Cassie Delaney, *The Creep Dive*, in January 2019.

Sophie lives in Dublin with her husband and two sons. *Filter This* is her first novel.

Instagram: @SophWhiteWrites
Twitter: @SophWhiteWrites
www.sophiewhite.info

Also by Sophie White
NON-FICTION
Recipes for a Nervous Breakdown

Sophie White

Filter This

HACHETTE
BOOKS
IRELAND

First published in Ireland in 2019 by
HACHETTE BOOKS IRELAND

1

Cataloguing in Publication Data is available from the British Library

Trade paperback ISBN 9781529343311
Ebook ISBN 9781529343328
Audio ISBN 9781529343403

Typeset in AGaramond by Bookends Publishing Services, Dublin

Printed and bound in Great Britain by Clays Ltd, Elcograf, S.p.A

Hachette Books Ireland policy is to use papers that are natural, renewable and recyclable
products and made from wood grown in sustainable forests. The logging and manufacturing
processes are expected to conform to the environmental regulations of the country of origin.

Hachette Books Ireland
8 Castlecourt Centre
Castleknock
Dublin 15, Ireland

A division of Hachette UK Ltd
Carmelite House, 50 Victoria Embankment, EC4Y 0DZ
www.hachettebooksireland.ie

For Mary

Author's Note

I was a late adopter of Instagram. I joined at the end of 2016 and was immediately enthralled by the epic pageantry of the everyday to be found there. Instagram is an amazing space on the internet – it's beautiful, it's motivational, it's fun and it's funny. I've made friends there and found pockets of brilliant women doing exciting, interesting things. Like Ali in the book, I too sat in a sick room for many years. And like Ali, I scrolled to escape. It was very soothing. Here was a time-travelling app that could deliver me from this painful drudgery to another reality: like mine but better. After my dad died, I remember being struck by the oddness of 'returning' to Instagram and this strange life where I performed a sort of public diary on the internet.

Filter This is in no way based on real people or real events though people have, it has to be said, done much crazier things on the internet than any described in these pages. *Filter This* is not a critique of the people who earn their living on Instagram. Nor is it a rallying cry to unplug or disconnect – I'm nearly at five thousand followers, lads, I'm too close to quit now! It's a story about denial. About how attractive, but ultimately destructive, it can be to simply put a filter on everything and disengage from the hard stuff.

Prologue

18 months earlier

'Oh my gaaawd, you guys! The big day has finally arrived. I have been dreaming about this moment since I was a little girl ...'

Ali closed the front door behind her and ventured further into the hall. The peppy voice, which was coming from the kitchen, didn't match their dingy house. It definitely didn't sound like someone who'd be hanging out with Liv, Ali's best friend and housemate. Dumping her bag by the hall table and chucking her coat on the stand, Ali peered into the kitchen.

'First things first, I've got to take you all on a tour of the

1

vendors without whom this magical and momentous day would not be possible.'

Liv was feverishly taking notes at the kitchen table in the cramped room, her phone propped against the fruit bowl in front of her.

'The Aperol Fizz bar has been generously provided by the Cocktail Boys – because we all know mama needs her pep to par-tay.' The woman on the screen gave a slightly randy wink to the camera and slapped her own ass.

'What are we watching?' Ali pulled up a chair to join her friend.

'The disintegration of society,' Liv muttered. 'AKA Instagram.'

'Ah, is this essay research?'

'Yep. I'm thinking there's actually so much more to be said, though, it may even be enough for a research master's.'

'Oh my god, gals!' Liv was interrupted by the intensely blonde, intensely polished woman in the phone. 'Would you look at this flower arch made by my fave pal @EmmasPetals – isn't it ah-mazing? There's a discount code for all my followers at the moment. Just use "MamasMiniMadams" at checkout for 5 per cent off all orders. And don't forget to follow Emma – she is just so inspiring.'

'Whoa!' Ali laughed. 'Just to clarify, Emma's a florist, right? Like, she hasn't found a way to eradicate thrush or anything?'

'They all talk like that.' Liv grinned. 'Everything is "amazing" on there. Or "empowering".'

As if on cue, @MamasMiniMadams was back. 'The amazing team from @EmpowerGrooming gave me my intimate grooming for this incredible occasion. They're all about empowering women to feel our best and most hair-free on our big days.'

Ali mugged. 'I do feel empowered when I shave my pits. Love how she hasn't even mentioned the lucky groom yet.'

'Oh no, this isn't her wedding day,' Liv corrected. 'It's one of the mini madams' First Holy Communions.'

'Shut up!' Ali laughed.

'Seriously.' Liv picked up the phone to tap back a few Stories. 'Look, here's the little bride of Christ here. In custom Vera Wang, no less.'

'Jesus!' Ali whistled at the sight of the little girl mincing up a red carpet leading to a festooned marquee. 'This shindig is mega. It's like *My Super Sweet Sixteen* only with more rose gold and selfie sticks.'

'And sponcon,' Liv added. 'Every scrap of this thing is being paid for by brands. It is one long exercise in pluggery.'

Ali held the phone closer, peering at @MamasMiniMadams' highly choreographed entrance to the party at the top of a sweeping staircase, her white dress managing to be both gigantic and highly revealing. It looked like a fairy tale. She looks like she's moving through a dream sequence, thought Ali. 'Why is she so blurred?' Ali glanced at Liv.

'Oh, she's filtered to fuck.' Liv shrugged. 'How was work?'

'Grand, the usual madness. Every scene ran long and Stephan made one of the extras cry. I'd better change – I'm heading up to my dad.' Ali returned the phone and headed to her room.

❖

3

Ali sat on a bench at the edge of the car park of the nursing home where her dad lived. She had to go in. She'd been fannying around on her phone for ages, staving off the inevitable. It was so hard to go in there these days. He didn't know her anymore and answering his confused questions was unbearable.

'And, tell me, have you worked here long?' he asked her the week before. 'I have a little girl who looks a little like you.'

I'm that little girl, Ali wanted to scream, but she'd long given up correcting him. It was futile.

A WhatsApp from Liv dropped in, providing welcome distraction.

Thought you'd like an update on the Super Sweet Communion Extravaganza. The Carter Twins are now doing a set. 😁

Attached was a screen-recording of the Instagram account from earlier.

Ali shielded the late afternoon sun from her phone screen. @MamasMiniMadams was wearing a different dress from earlier – Do people do outfit changes at Holy Communions? – and was being fed champagne by a Carter twin while the crowd whooped and hollered. Wow, that escalated.

'Here's my mum and dad!' @MamasMiniMadams indicated an attractive couple in their sixties slow-dancing among the chaos of the kids, all high off their tits on giant doughnuts, and their tipsy, well-heeled parents.

Everyone looks so polished. Ali glanced down at her own grungy tee and faded jeans. And not just the people – their whole world gleamed. The clip ended on the Carter Twins being urged to 'Take it off' by a rowdy crowd. The Aperol Fizz had evidently gone to their heads.

Absentmindedly, Ali checked Instagram on the app store. 'Like, capture and share moments ...' announced the app description. 'Express yourself by sharing your day, the highlights and everything in between.'

Highlights are pretty thin on the ground for me, Ali thought ruefully as she hit the Download button. A few taps and she'd set up a new account – @Ali_Jones. She hit the camera icon in the top left corner of the app and glanced around the car park, checking she was alone, before holding the phone up to her face. It was like a mirror. She could see her tired eyes and the beginnings of a spot on her chin. Behind her the sign read 'Ailesend Dementia Care Home'. She swallowed – Insta-grim more like.

She messed with the little buttons on the bottom of the screen. One gave her kitten ears and heavy eyeliner. Another bathed her in a celestial glow. The next button set off a beautiful wreath of pink flowers blooming about her head. Her blotchy skin was transformed. She still looked like herself, but as seen through a prism of perfection. The filter showed blooms at the edge of the frame, obscuring the sign just past her right shoulder. She turned her head this way and that but neither her flowers nor her new-found perfection slipped even for a second.

She snapped the picture.

It looked good.

1

'Get up!' Ali was startled awake by Liv huffing at the door. 'It smells like underboob sweat and curry chips in here.'

'Name a more iconic duo!' Ali shouted, grinning at her housemate's retreating back as Liv stalked back down the hall towards the kitchen. Ali shook off the fug of sleep and was hit with the fug of ... well, herself basically. Sitting up slightly, she took in the room brimming with shite, a pale January morning leaking in around the brown velvet curtains, and then noticed a deeply unnerving, moist sensation.

'Ick ... what the f—?' Her left hand felt weird and she realised she'd fallen asleep with it partially submerged in a tray of curry chips, while in her right hand was her phone, of course.

'Gah.' She carefully retracted her hand and held it aloft, away from her and the, admittedly, already fairly gross bed sheets.

With her right hand, she hit the Home button and impatiently keyed in the security code (all the same number for ease) and assessed her updates since she'd last checked at about 1 a.m. Three new followers, 180 likes on the #selfcare yoga post she only dimly remembered putting up last night and one comment from Dee, which basically didn't count. Dee was a sweet girl from the wardrobe department at work, but she just didn't seem to get that she and Ali were not friends.

Ali threw the phone to the end of the bed and flexed her fingers. 'The phone claw' Liv called it whenever Ali complained about her stiff fingers.

'Is it a sign that perhaps clutching your phone in a vice-like grip while sleeping is not the healthiest of behaviours?' asked Liv in the voice she used when she was pretending to be joking but was, in fact, deadly serious.

Liv had taken up sending her links to articles like 'How to Break up with Your Phone' in the last six months. To prove a point, Ali had begun to make a big deal of leaving her phone charging in the kitchen at night. Though this display of abstemiousness had necessitated the purchase of a decoy phone with matching cover. Expensive and probably indicative of an even bigger problem that Ali didn't feel particularly keen to explore further. And anyway, decoy phones aside, her Instagramming was a fairly innocent little pastime.

'It's not a big deal,' she'd argued with Liv only the evening before as they watched *Cold Case File* for the umpteenth time while Ali absentmindedly stroked the phone like a beloved pet, one eye on her feed and one eye on the TV. 'Instagram is pretty and it's fun.' It was also something that seemed to be paying off, however slowly – she was closing in on nine thousand followers. The same could not be said for her attempts at playwriting since finishing college, which had just been wall-to-wall rejection and left her feeling utterly worthless.

After Liv had ambled off to bed, Ali'd lain alone in her room with the phone propped on the pillow facing her – the stories of beautiful girls with perfect lives washing over her – when she'd felt the familiar spike of upset puncture her trance-like state.

Emma O'Brien, a fashion blogger from Cork, was getting ready for the Rebel Gin event – an event Ali hadn't been invited to. I have the same amount of followers as her, Ali thought, peeved. She hit Emma's smiling profile pic to bring up the girl's account. 'Hmm – 11K followers. That's up from a month ago …' An hour passed and Ali, completely engrossed in a deep Insta-dive on Emma, had barely noticed. That was when she'd gone for the chips. And bought the wine.

'It is Tuesday after all,' she'd reasoned when her body veered almost of its own accord towards the Esso garage for a bottle of white. 'I'm days from cracking 9K followers – that's worth celebrating.'

The wine had stirred a bit of optimism (the first few glasses always did) and that's when she'd put out the yoga mat, crystals and candles for her #selfcare post and slurred out a few thoughts in the caption about looking after yourself and practising mindfulness.

Now, remembering the optimism of the previous evening, Ali retrieved the phone, reminding herself that one of her #goals was to be more mindful of the good things and three new followers and 180 likes is no bad feat. Consulting the time – 7 a.m. – she soothed her mounting anxiety: lots of people would be barely up yet. Speaking of, she needed to get going. She had to have coffee with the mothership, Mini, at 8.30 before she needed to get into the TV station for work.

Ali was a production assistant on *Durty Aul' Town*, the top and only soap opera in the country. When she'd taken the job to get a foot in the door, as her drama-studies tutor in college had suggested, she'd assumed it would just be short term while she figured out her plan. Then quite rapidly three years had slipped by and she'd gotten no closer to the writers' room, and the more time she spent adjacent to a career in TV and theatre, the more she wondered if it was what she really wanted after all.

She hauled herself out of bed and sat on the side, carefully avoiding the now empty bottle of Sauvignon lolling on the floor and setting the chip tray down alongside it. She frowned at her greasy hand, holding it away from her before wiping it on the carpet. The carpet's minging anyway, she figured.

She hit the search function on Insta and entered 'S', prompting the app to supply her with the name 'Shelly Devine'. Ali opened the profile (Shelly Devine, 255K followers: Happy wife of @DivineDanDevine, mama to @BabyGeorgie, Loving the

9

journey but the juggle is REAL!) and checked on the last post. The picture showed a pristine Shelly with soft dark waves cascading over her shoulders captioned:

That fresh hair feeling, Thanks @BinnyK @Copenhairgen #FreshHairDontCare #blowdry #feelgood #selfcare #haircare #influencer #iger #dubliniger #dublinigers #dubiger #dubigers #shellyisdivine #BlowinOutTheCobwebs #LolAtLife #lovelife #TakeMeNowMrDevine

The post, barely an hour old, already had 5,736 likes and 54 comments. What must that even feel like? Ali wondered. She hit Home and opened the Notepad app, selecting one of her docs in progress, 'Shelly stats'. She updated the info then reverted to Instagram, liked Shelly's selfie, added 'You look amazing' and hit Post. Ali slumped back against the pillows but then, feeling troubled, abruptly snatched up the phone once more. She frantically unlocked the screen and brought up the post of Shelly's irritatingly immaculate face again. Hunched over the phone, Ali found her comment and hit Delete. She retyped 'You look amazing' and added seven exclamation marks and a heart-eyes emoji. She hit Post again and settled back against the pillows.

Ali scrolled through Shelly's feed absentmindedly while she engaged in a few minutes of deep, gut-churning loathing towards Shelly Devine. Ugh, she's so basic – why does everyone love her so much?

Ali frequently wondered who the 255K followers even were.

'Who even likes this? It's so vanilla,' she raged as she scrolled obsessively over coffee, lunch, dinner and on her pillow at night.

Ali's own meagre following had been building steadily since she'd joined last year but it was an uphill battle. She'd tried every trick in the 'how to become an influencer' book but thus far her biggest fans seemed to be her own burner accounts (@JamieC, @SheilaMalloy and @KerryConnor) who, combined, had about sixteen followers but were frequent and enthusiastic commenters on all of Ali's pictures.

Coming up in a few months was the social media event of the year, the Glossies, where Ali had hoped to be nominated for Best Newcomer but really, at this rate, she'd be more likely to be hit with another bout of cystitis than make a splash in the influencer pool in time for it.

Just then, a new post dropped into Shelly's feed. The pic showed a radiant new mum Shelly cradling her baby, captioned:

#tbt when @BabyGeorgie was the most perfect baby and I was bathed in all the new mum love vibes, and #blessed with the most wonderful breastfeeding journey thanks to NaturPro9400 the #supplement with the most effective blend of vitamins to promote milk supply and bonus (!) it does wonders for your hair and nails too, ladies. #spon #ad #NaturPro9400 #workingmama #collab #brandambassador #supplement #lovethis #workwithshelly #georgiedevine

Georgie Devine was only three but she had her very own Instagram account (189K followers) and endorsement deals and was brand ambassador for several well-known products including, somewhat bafflingly, a de-icing agent for cars. At least, I don't have to sell my baby on Instagram for a bogus supplement, Ali thought cattily.

Leaning in and peering closer at the picture, Ali could see it looked like Shelly had done a bit of photoshopping on a little rash on Georgie's cheek.

Then Ali felt mean. She couldn't blame Shelly for cashing in on that sweet baby dollar; you have to work with what you have in this game. The problem was Ali didn't have much by way of aspirational fodder for Insta.

She lived with Liv, who'd been her best friend since Ali had mistaken her for a foreign-exchange student on day one outside St Margaret's secondary in Killiney.

'Where are you from?' she'd asked the small girl with dark hair, brown skin and headphones around her neck.

'Bray,' Liv had responded flatly.

'Ah.' Ali had been thrown.

'We have Indian people in Bray, like.' Liv was sarcastic.

'Yeah, alright. I'm not a racist.'

'You just assumed I was foreign!'

'Well I'm not the biggest racist here then.' Ali indicated the other kids in uniform awkwardly milling, waiting for the doors to open at 8.15. 'I'm talking to you, at least.'

It was a gamble, but luckily Liv had laughed and that had been that for them, friends ever since. Though, while she loved her,

Liv wasn't much of a one for Prosecco boomerangs. Ali usually called on Jess, Clara and Kate, their school gang, who were much more up for nights out, though irritatingly they'd all coupled up in recent months and were forever making arbitrary trips to Ikea with What's-his-name-again and staying in for takeaways and Netflix.

You're twenty-fucking-five, Ali wanted to scream. You're supposed to be out making the most of your youth. Though now at the midway point, Ali felt her twenties had been a bit of a dud thus far. A useless degree in Drama Studies and English and a ropey economy meant *Durty Aul' Town* was the only thing between her and all-out failure, aka an unpaid internship. Writing was lonely and hard and when her Insta started to take off with her #wellness posts, selfies, carefully curated #OOTDs and behind the scenes posts of #TVlife on *Durty Aul' Town*, she'd switched her focus almost instantly.

She saw so many other girls being plucked from Insta to go on to TV-presenting gigs and modelling gigs, getting book deals, make-up deals, tan deals – surely it would get her somewhere, even if she wasn't exactly sure where she wanted to go right now. It could only be a matter of breaking in. She made sure she went to all the media events in town, trawling for freebies to open on her 'gram and being snapped for the social pages.

Liv liked going out, but her tastes ran more to pints and experimental instrumental metal gigs than anywhere the influencer crowd flocked. If Ali wanted to do a selfie when they were out, she'd practically hide rather than face Liv's ribbing.

Anyway she much preferred staying in with Liv. Watching crap TV and offering their own sarky commentary was more fun.

They'd moved in together during the second year of college. The house had belonged to Liv's granny and looked and smelled accordingly but it was close to Dublin City University, where Liv had studied sociology and psychology and, after a year's break, had now plunged into a two-year master's in sociology with a view to pursuing academia. Social media was, in fact, her area of research. Ali had a major trek out to work and her mum's house on the south side, but Liv's parents charged them next to nothing, plus it was close to Ali's dad, Miles.

She waded through the sea of clothes that covered most of the carpet towards the far corner of the room, where she'd fitted a small section of pale laminate wood-effect flooring on top of the frankly offensive brown carpeting that Liv's granny was so devoted to – it covered the floor of nearly every room in the house including, most creepily, the bathroom.

Ali cleared the faux-marble-topped dressing table in her 'Insta-studio', swept a face wipe over her face and scrubbed at last night's smudged eye make-up. She switched on an enormous ring-light mounted to the wall to her right beside a large round mirror and appraised her face. The lasting effect of Esso wine meant her wide brown eyes were looking more than a little bleary and her dirty-blonde hair which fell in waves past her shoulders was attempting to form a single giant dreadlock. She consulted the time – 7.20. Better get going. Mini was never late and it'd be a terrible shame to cut into her berating time.

She whacked in some eye drops and began the lengthy hair battle. Ali's face had come good since the days when the boys at school had called her a 'fugly dog'. She'd had a pretty intense awkward stage spanning about a decade – who didn't? And options for self-improvement were limited back then; you couldn't just filter yourself into oblivion in every pic. After such a shitty adolescence, Ali saw her creamy skin and high cheekbones as a form of karmic redistribution.

Of course, the definition of 'pretty' had changed drastically, even over the last couple of years, and Ali, like most of the influencer crowd, had made some subtle improvements. Her top lip had always seemed a little thin so she'd had it filled last year – which meant, of course, that her bottom lip definitely looked a little thin so she'd plumped that one up as well. A little filler in the cheeks and Botox around the eyes were all pretty standard but lately she'd been more and more concerned with her nose. It was more prominent than she liked, though that would be a different level on the surgery scale. Filler you could do on a lunch break but noses were an undertaking.

Liv, naturally, did not approve. 'You're looking more like that crazy cat face lady by the day,' she'd erupted when she found Ali scrolling through #newnose on Insta one morning.

Mini hadn't even mentioned the little adjustments. Either she thought they were an improvement or she was too preoccupied with work to notice. Mini Riordan was a key player in the Irish art scene – her gallery, Ait Art, represented the biggest artists and she chaired about a million boards. Plus Mini had Miles, Ali's dad, to deal with, who they would no doubt be discussing over this coffee. Ali grimaced at the prospect.

Ali propped her phone up on the dressing table and hit View All on the Stories function while she moisturised her skin and began hurriedly painting her face.

'Hey guys!' A peppy, faux-American-by-way-of-Dublin-4 accent squealed out of the phone. 'I'm so sorry I haven't been on for a while …'

Ali scoffed. 'You were on last night, Laura! I think we can survive without you for a couple of hours.'

'It's been a crazy morning …' Laura continued earnestly.

Already? Please. Ali rolled her eyes.

'I've been visiting Pegasus Pilates and it just clears your head, ya know? I can't wait to tell you how amazing it's been for my day so far …'

Yeah, yeah your day's already amazing. It's not even fucking 8 a.m., Laura, chill out. Laura (a wannabe MUA from Shankill, 11,374 followers) had had a breakthrough lately and had started doing sponcon with a beauty subscription service, Bellabox Ireland, which was fairly major, and Ali couldn't help it: she was jealous.

What did she have? Ali glared at the eerily flawless face filling the phone screen. It had a touch of the uncanny about it – it looked very close to human but also unnatural in a way that was hard to put a finger on. The filter had blunted the things that would have rooted the face in reality – things like normal unevenness in texture and skin tone, things that are suggestive of actual human flesh. Also the stripy, clunky shading and a heavy hand with the highbeam gave Laura a distinctly tigery look. I mean, really, thought Ali, if you're claiming to be a professional make-up artist, there's no excuse. But still, tiger face and all, Laura was doing well for herself.

The problem was Ali didn't have the kind of commercial USP that would elevate her in the scene. She did the twenty-something thing, chatting about her Tinder dates. She did a bit of beauty, a bit of skincare, but she didn't have any really good hook. Her content was a bit unfocused – like her life, she sighed. Why does everyone go on about your twenties? If this shitshow of crap jobs and no money are the best years, I wanna get off.

It definitely didn't help that everyone else seemed to have it together. There were, of course, Instagrammers who didn't go in for the Insta-bullshit, they kept things a little less rose gold on there. Posting funny videos and cool stuff. She followed several who used the app to show their creative work and campaign for causes they believed in. They were completely themselves but the fact was that Ali figured she had even less to offer being her real self on Instagram.

Laura was now prattling on about her plans for spoiling her dad on his birthday in a few days. 'Are we all just major daddys' girls?' she'd written in pink over a pic of Laura and a middle-aged man in matching charity-run tees. Ali abruptly tapped forward on the Stories until the dad chats were done.

Glancing around her dismal room, her gaze came to rest on the Christmas card she had made and then neglected to hand over when the appointed day had arrived a few weeks earlier. What was the point? Miles wouldn't know what she was giving him. Christmas, birthdays and Hallmark holidays were the bleakest of all the days she'd spent by his bedside.

What did they add up to now? Three Father's Days since he'd known her name. Three depressing birthdays. 'We'll help you, darling,' Mini'd say, holding a small cake and bravely making it through 'Happy Birthday'. Ali'd leaned forward and blown out his candles while Miles stared at the wall, his empty eyes never registering their presence in the room. Then they sang the family favourite 'Oh Why Was He Born So Beautiful', the song Miles used to strum along to on his old ukulele.

She now kept the ukulele beside her bed and ran her fingers over it every night, pressing the strings he used to pluck during singsongs at her parents' raucous parties. When one of the strings broke last year it took a month for her to finally replace it, feeling the loss so sharply it took her by surprise. Now the ukulele had one new string that Miles had never touched and Ali had lost another precious piece of her dad.

For his fifty-eighth and fifty-ninth he'd sat up in his chair in the nursing home and wordlessly accepted proffered morsels of the cakes Ali'd stayed up late the night before baking. By the last one, sixty, he just lay on the bed, still staring but by now unable for food that wasn't puréed. Mini and Ali had eaten that cake.

As Laura breathlessly extolled the virtues of an early-morning Pilates session, Ali snapped back from the airless room at Ailesend Home where even now, as she sat in her bedroom and put on her make-up, Miles was trapped, suspended in some terrible limbo. Ali paused in her involved make-up routine and pressed her fingers to her eye sockets – it was here that she felt the unbearable pressure building any time she thought of Miles and, by extension, Mini.

Most of the time, Ali and her mother were at war, engaged in a decades-long battle of wills. Mini was never satisfied with her only child. Or at least it seemed that way to Ali. They'd been fighting forever, hence Ali's eager departure at twenty to live with Liv in Grannyland. The house was a godsend, as Ali couldn't have afforded to rent properly back then with just a job in her dad's old restaurant in town a few nights a week. Miles had been starting to show signs of forgetting, and a few weeks after she'd moved in with Liv they got the diagnosis. Early onset Alzheimer's. Ali had debated moving home, but she got on better with her mother with a bit of distance, and Miles wasn't so bad back then – at least not at first. By the time two years had passed, they had to move him to a home.

In generous moods, Ali reminded herself that Mini didn't mean to be hypercritical – she just rarely had an opinion she didn't voice. Ali's hair, her clothes, her Leaving Cert subjects, Ali's insistence on wearing peach ('very unflattering, darling') were all an affront to Mini.

However, when they sat side by side in Miles's bleak little room with the stack of adult nappies in the bedside locker and the hopeless stench that no amount of Jo Malone candles could cover, Ali felt close to her mother. But no one welcomes that type of closeness – she'd rather they were out shopping and having the kind of mother–daughter fun that she could at least mine for Instagram.

Ali swallowed hard and shook her head slightly in a bid to dismiss the dark thoughts that could gather so quickly like clouds on some inner horizon. She began to apply the first of many layers of light-reflecting base to her now-primed skin. Make-up had come a long way since her teenage love affair with Juicy Tubes and glitter mascara. Now even the plainest girls had so much scope for improvement with contouring and highlighting. Some of the influencer wannabes took it to ridiculous levels, using their original features as the mildest of suggestions as to where their eyes, lips and noses began and ended, shading in unwanted chins and reshaping their most unfortunate features with expert blending of light and dark. In the pics on their feeds, it was flawless. It didn't work in person, though. Often Ali would meet a fellow wannabe in the pleb pen at an event and the girl would be unrecognisable. So much can be done with a bit of highlighter and a knack for angles. Ali didn't quite need that help which was why, she was sure, the influencer game would pay off for her.

She had a toe in the fame pool with her TV job, and she kept its details vague to the other Insta-mavens – not wanting to reveal that she spent much of her day just enacting the whims of the megalomaniac series producer, Stephan. She also got invited to the media ligger events where everyone shouted in each other's faces about how busy they were while sipping champagne from mini bottles through a straw and tried to get selfies for their feed with the big fish like Shelly Devine.

Speak of the devil! Now Shelly Devine's beautiful face filled the phone screen. She looks like another species, thought Ali glumly. Shelly played a minor character on *Durty Aul' Town* and even at 6 a.m. calls she looked perfect. Her dark hair, pale skin and grey-blue eyes were a striking combination, and even dressed down in her uniform of skinny jeans, boots and boyfriend blazer, she looked worlds away from the other influencers. On set, Ali was constantly checking herself in an effort not to come on too strong whenever they crossed paths.

'Good morning, Shell-Belles!' Shelly was beaming into the camera. 'I'm going to take you through my morning routine in a few minutes but first I just had to show you the absolute best guy in the world …'

The camera on Shelly's phone switched to front cam as she began to creep through a textbook Celtic Tiger pad, ridiculously plush cream carpets stretching in every direction. She kept up a running, whispered commentary about the 'state of the place' as she made her way upstairs (past some obscenely cringe studio shots of 'her lovelies' – the lucrative Baby Georgie and the Divine Mr Devine).

A manicured hand eventually pushed open a door to a darkened bedroom strewn with chocolate-coloured fur throw pillows. A couple of scented candles flickered improbably – who lights those ever, never mind first thing in the morning? – on the bedside tables. The camera panned to the chiselled torso of a sleeping

Dan Devine, covered from the waist down with a light sheet. Ali was watching with interest (it'd been a while) when Dan started awake. There was a truncated exclamation – 'The fuck are you do—?' – from the absolute ride who, Ali knew from extensive stalking, was 'in finance'.

In the next Story, Shelly, now back downstairs, was fiddling with the Nespresso, making coffee for 'Mr Devine'.

'He's a grumpy bear in the morning …' She laughed lightly into the phone, the spotless kitchen gleaming in the early-morning sun behind her.

Ali looked up momentarily to cast her eye around her own decidedly more grim surroundings. It was a granny house and there was only so much you could do with it. Though even the light in Shelly's world looked cleaner. The light seeping around her own curtains (brown, of course, Granny standard issue) was murky and the air in the room felt heavy. Heavy like you could chew on it. Ali's eyes roamed the small space, the crumpled bed, the grubby sheets and several old takeaway bags from last weekend on the floor crowding the side of the bed.

Another bottle of Sauvignon (this one only nearly empty) stood on the top of the white plasticky chest of drawers, the kind every eighties child once had, complete with half-peeled-off stickers. The wine was no big deal – it wasn't even finished. Then she flashed on the empty bottles stashed in the drawers beneath. She hadn't gotten around to the recycling in weeks. 'I'll do it … when Liv's not around,' she murmured.

Ali finished her face, roughed up her hair so that it was just the right level of dishevelled and launched the camera app on her phone. She hopped back over to the bed, flicked on the ring-light she had screwed to her bedside table and slipped under the sheets, careful to move any curry-chip detritus out of view of the phone lens. She cleared her throat a couple of times, practising a husky, sleepy voice: 'Morning, babes, morning, bitches, namaste, babes …' Giving the frame of the shot a final check, she hit Record. 'Aloha, ladies, how's my Insta-fam? I can't believe I am such a slob this morning …'

She exhaled heavily at this, managing to both sigh and pout at the same time – it was a textbook Insta-face meant to appear adorably weary.

'I have a crazy day of meetings and appointments ahead so I need to kick this booty straight into my morning routine. The first thing I do is a little journaling to record my positive intentions for the day, then I'll do my sun salutations and enjoy my fave breakfast proats. The recipe's down on my feed – you guys have got to try it. Chat later, babes!'

Ali posted the video to her Stories and headed for the kitchen.

2

Liv was eating toast and frantically highlighting her notes when Ali slumped into the cramped kitchen. It was a heavily linoed space. Liv's granny had apparently liked her orange faux-tile lino so much she'd not only covered the floor and backsplash with it but also the chair seats.

'Morning.' Liv paused her highlighting to take Ali in. 'Can I just say this,' she indicated Ali's *RuPaul's Drag Race* levels of make-up, 'is somewhat at odds with this.' She waved the same hand over Ali's grotty PJs.

'Yeah, well.' Ali laughed. 'You should see what I'm up against. They all look demented.'

Liv was still watching her and Ali suddenly felt conscious of the state of her pyjamas and her unwashed hair. When had she last washed it? Dry shampoo was a wonderful thing but you could become overly reliant. The pyjamas were white cotton, or at least they had been until relatively recently. Now, however, there was a yellowish tinge to them and several ominous-looking marks of indeterminate origin and one unmistakable stain. Curry sauce. Ali shifted slightly and tried to twist the stained cuff out of view.

'Ali, eating curry chips in bed …' Liv ventured, her tone deliberately light '… is probably a sign you're hitting rock bottom.'

Ali laughed and smoothed her hair, then, noticing her hand, which was practically two-tone, the consequences of a mildly drunken fake tan application, she crossed her arms, hiding the offending hand from Liv's scrutiny. There should be a warning on fake tan – something like 'don't tan when tipsy'.

'Don't be crazy, I'm grand. I'm better than grand, I'm great.'

'Are you really, Ali?' Liv looked concerned and she was doing her 'real-talk voice'. 'You've gone deep into this stuff lately. Fake tan and things. And, like, I can understand you wanting a distraction with everything with your dad …'

'Liv.' Ali cut across her, smiling a little too hard – she found it tough to cope with people bringing up Miles. Just the week before, she'd run into Marcus, her dad's old business partner, in the street near where their restaurant used to be – two years ago Mini and Marcus sold Frederick's, formerly a Dublin institution, and it had been converted into an artisanal coffee roasters. Just seeing Marcus, a person she so closely associated with her dad, had caused the now familiar unease to erupt in her belly.

'Gosh, Ali,' he'd begun falteringly, 'you look so like him.' Ali could feel the pressure behind her eyes then and she'd felt like running. Sometimes being faced with the sadness of Miles's vast circle of friends and acquaintances was worse than being faced with Miles himself and the horror of his decline. Even with Liv, she hardly spoke about him anymore; it was easier to pretend that nothing was wrong.

Ali tried to shrug the thoughts away. 'I love you, Liv, and I'm fine. I'm just having breakfast!'

'OK, OK. I just don't get why you're so in thrall to the tiger people. You slag them but you're also morphing into them – you see that, right?'

Ali reminded herself not to get so defensive. Liv just didn't get the Insta thing. It was a bit of an out from all this trouble with Miles and it was hardly hurting anyone. It was true that teenage Ali had been vehemently opposed to fake tan, but people change. What's a bit of fake tan and filler these days? She was hardly lying about anything important – it was just what it took to even be in the running among these girls.

Ali pulled a dark slate tray from the cupboard above the microwave and set it down on top of Liv's notes.

'Hey!'

'Shhh, I won't be a sec.' Ali clicked on the camera on her phone and began arranging rose-gold cutlery, a mason jar of some kind of oat concoction that she had made god knows how long ago and a few stems of dried lavender on the tray. 'I don't slag them, and I'm not morphing! It's a game, just a fun game. Insta is a viable career now. People make the jump from Insta to TV and modelling and all kinds of things these days.'

Ali grabbed a bag of spinach from the fridge, blended a few handfuls with water in the Nutribullet and decanted it into another glass jar, then added a red-and-white striped straw from her stash in the cupboard.

'How are you going to get from Instagram to writing, Ali?' Liv asked.

Ignoring her, Ali carefully lined up the shot and snapped about fourteen pics. Liv observed, silently sipping her coffee, until Ali had finished and then she burst out laughing.

'For fuck! Will you please make a fresh oat thing for tomorrow? I don't wanna know what's growing in here.' Liv gingerly examined the greying concoction. 'Surely that doesn't look good in the pics.'

'I can fix the colour in post.' Ali shrugged as she tossed the green 'juice' down the sink, while tweaking and captioning her post:

Wednesday power proats and a green juice for NAILING this day. Hope everyone is feeling as excited as I am for the coming week. I've got some amazing #secretprojects in the works and loads of #werk to get through before the #Glossies launch party tomorrow night 🏃 🍾 👗 💃

#getyougurl #healthyaf #proteinpow #proteinpowered #DiscoverUnder10K #DublinIger #IrishInfluencers

Ali hit Post, chucked the phone on the table and returned the tray and various accoutrements to the cupboard. As Liv smoothed her notes, Ali casually nicked her coffee and finished the cup. 'I'll make more.' She laughed at Liv's outraged face. 'So what's on the agenda today? Any chance of a lift to coffee with Mini? She's down at something in the RHA Gallery and I said I'd come in on my way. I can't be arsed bringing the car – there's never any parking at work.' No need to tell Liv that last night's wine was probably a bigger problem than the lack of spaces. Ali filled the kettle and began assembling her customary breakfast concoction (stale croissant stolen from the work canteen, stuffed with a few slices of cheese, crushed flat and squashed into the toaster).

Liv glared pointedly at the breakfast ritual. 'This is why we nail through toasters,' she remarked, accepting the new coffee Ali proffered with elaborate mock deference. 'You're such a messer. And, yes, I will drive you in the complete opposite direction to where I'm going because that is the dynamic that has emerged in this friendship. I'm leaving in five, though.' She started gathering her stuff as Ali began the daily process of extracting the molten hot croissant complete with lava-like melted cheese out of the toaster, burning herself in the process.

'Every day.' Liv shook her head, laughing.

'It's hotter than the fucking surface of the sun,' yelped Ali as she finally managed to transport it (stringing cheese still attached to the toaster) to a plate. 'Right, meet you in the car, two minutes.'

❖

In the car, Ali fiddled with the heat. 'Bloody freezing. Why can't we just make a global decision about January – just axe it altogether, something like that?' she muttered, then noticed Liv's glum face. 'Is it getting to you too?'

'I've got the thesis-adviser meeting,' said Liv as she merged lanes and joined the early-morning traffic heading south across the river. She drew in a breath and continued in a doom-laden tone, 'With Emer, like.'

'Oooh.' Ali bit her lower lip. 'Is that gonna be …?'

'Insanely awkward? Fuck, yes, it is.' Liv gripped the wheel tightly. 'We haven't spoken or texted since the whole Solpadeine incident.'

'Riiight,' said Ali. 'I'm so sorry, darl. I still feel like that was all my fault.' Ali had, after all, had the wine already open when Liv had arrived home from a disastrous party at Emer Breen's house. The fifty-something Emer was an eminent member of the sociology faculty in DCU and was 'the spit of Connie Britton' according to Liv, who immediately fell for her. They began dating around Halloween but in secret as Emer was very concerned about appearances and had only recently divorced from her wife, also on the faculty. Liv didn't mind them being low-key but then Emer had barely contacted Liv over the Christmas holidays and at this party, a week earlier, Emer had pretty much ignored her and then ended things when Liv cornered her in the utility room.

'No, no,' Liv continued her lament. 'I'm twenty-five years old, I should have known it wasn't a good idea to mix Solpadeine and wine.'

'Yeah, I'd say it's a pretty significant red flag to be, like, actually dissolving it in the wine,' said Ali, remembering trying to get the phone off a very sloppy Liv in their living room.

'Why did I tell her I loved her?' Liv moaned.

Ali felt helpless. At the next set of lights, she pulled Liv into a hug, patting her head. Liv kept her shiny dark hair cropped short and partially shaved on one side. It suited her dark skin and liquid eyes. Liv's mum was Indian, which Ali'd envied as long as they'd been friends – Liv was gorgeous.

As Liv drove on, Ali remembered the dipshits in their year who'd put on a ridiculous Apu from *The Simpsons* accent whenever she'd raised her hand in class. It was probably because they all fancied her but it wasn't easy being made to feel different, especially as a teenager. Liv once came in with her mehndi still on her hands after a cousin's wedding and Simon Verdon had said horrible, ignorant things about Liv being dirty. Ali had always been quick with vicious put-downs, which shut them up, and Liv was far too proud to show how much it got to her.

That was the Liv–Ali dynamic all over, really. Ali could always be relied on for an emotional outburst and the ever-restrained Liv would hold back, reserving action until after she'd made about a million pro–con lists. This was why it felt strange to Ali to be consoling Liv about something stupid she'd done herself – it was usually the other way around. Though it wasn't stupid to fall in love – it was Emer Breen's fault for screwing around with her student and then freaking out and back-tracking.

'It'd be bad enough just sitting in a room with her after I sent her that WhatsApp recording of the St Vincent song we used to love.' Liv flinched at the memory. 'But it's gonna be an even bigger shitshow because the first chapters of my thesis are due in three months and I'm supposed to finalise the title today. You know, the thesis title that I haven't even nailed the wording of. So maybe just murder-suicide us both right now, please.'

This had been a plan B between Ali and Liv ever since they'd first sat beside each other in Ms Devally's form room on the first day of First Year and Ali had dropped a tampon which Liv, in her haste to pick it up, accidentally kicked into the middle aisle of the class.

'Oh Jesus, you can just murder-suicide us right now,' she'd muttered to Ali, who had unexpectedly broken into peals of laughter. Then Ali had sauntered casually right out in front of Sam Waters and Dave Keeling, the hottest guys (though admittedly they were thirteen at the time) in class 1DY, and retrieved the glowing white bastion of teenage embarrassment as the whole room watched in varying states of disgust, disbelief and, in Liv's case, pure unadulterated awe.

'I would genuinely be happier with a death pact than having coffee with Mini right now,' Ali sighed as Liv pulled up around the corner from the gallery and put the handbrake on. 'Look, you didn't do anything wrong, Liv.' Ali turned to hold her friend's gaze. 'Emer is the one who should be embarrassed. And she's crazy to let a young hot bitch like yourself get away.'

Liv tried to laugh. 'You better go – Mini will be waiting.' Like clockwork, Ali's phone roared to life with 'Mini Calling'.

Ali grabbed her bag and hopped out of the car.

'If you come across an idea for a sociology thesis title on your travels, send it my way,' called Liv as she pulled away from the kerb.

The phone was still ringing. I'm two fucking minutes away, thought Ali, but when there was no let-up, she finally hit the green key and Mini Riordan's forceful voice burst forth, per usual already mid-flow.

Mini didn't really do conversational preambles – she preferred launching straight into the third or fourth sentence in any given conversation. 'Hi,' another person might attempt to open with, but Mini would already be miles down the conversational road, bitching about some idiot journo who'd gotten an artist's name wrong or some such. It had a destabilising effect on whoever was on the receiving end. Ali suspected this was precisely Mini's intention, as it meant keeping everyone on the back foot – most especially her one and only daughter.

'I've got to get to my next appointment by 9 a.m., Alessandra, and I cannot—'

'I am literally walking through the doors,' Ali shouted over her, startling the older man behind the coat desk. 'And I'm not even late yet!' she added.

'Well, I appreciate that,' Mini replied. 'It was more of an anticipatory "where are you", I suppose! I'm down by the counter. Please hurry on now – we need to discuss a few developments.'

3

Shelly Devine was trying to stifle a giggle as she filmed a video of her husband sleeping, tangled in Egyptian cotton sheets in their huge bed. He moaned lightly and turned over as Shelly hopped up to get a better angle.

'What are you doing?' he muttered groggily.

'Oooohh, someone didn't get home till late last night …' said Shelly, narrating her video.

'What the fuck! Take me off your fucking Instagram,' Dan roared, realising what she was doing.

'Relax – it's a video on the internet.'

'No, it's not, it's our lives all over the internet.' He'd turned away, pulling the sheet around him. 'I really am getting tired of the whole SHELLY thing. It's embarrassing. You're embarrassing me and you're embarrassing yourself.'

'Dan!' Shelly didn't know what to say. She was just trying to be playful, to get a bit of fun back into the equation. Though, truthfully, her social media analyst, Amy, had told her to include more of her husband on her Insta. ('The plebs like the whole hot-husband thing so try and do more stuff with Dan in it, especially topless Dan,' Amy'd advised, obviously thinking of the poolside snap of Dan in Speedos that had garnered 13K likes the previous summer.)

Dan rolled back over, checked the time on his own phone, got up and started getting ready. 'I handle huge deals all day in work – how can I expect people to take me seriously when my wife is filming me doing funny noises for Georgie or trying to fix the dishwasher?'

'Don't be silly – no one is thinking about it like that,' Shelly said soothingly and reached out to him, her gorgeous Mr Devine.

'And I fucking hate that "Mr Devine" bullshit. You sound pathetic. If anyone knew the absolute BS you and Amy cook up in your "office" while I'm paying a full-time fucking babysitter for Georgie, making up a fake Instagram account for me so that I can leave sycophantic comments on your pictures, ugh.' He shook his head. 'How many followers does @DivineMrDevine have now?' he asked stonily.

'It's 53,000,' said Shelly quietly, sitting on the edge of the bed. 'You're doing some sponsored content with Toyota at the moment. Don't call me pathetic, please.'

Dan looked down at his wife and his face appeared to soften slightly but he looked detached. 'You've changed so much, Shel. When I married you, you wanted to be a serious actress. You had real ambitions. I can't even believe that you take this shit seriously.' He indicated the phone, clutched as always in her right hand.

'Screw you, Dan.' Shelly formed the words quietly but confidently. 'You're a snob – this just offends your Malahide sensibilities. I'm having fun with this and I enjoy it. And my followers need me. I get messages every day from the women I'm inspiring and empowering.'

At this, Dan did the worst possible thing: he laughed. He walked all the way out of the room laughing and that hurt. How had it gotten to this point? They used to be good together, didn't they?

Shelly returned to the kitchen, her stomach roiling. She'd already been up at 6.30 quietly puking in their en suite, running the taps so Dan wouldn't hear.

She posted the first video of Dan to her account just as Amy breezed in, breakfast roll in hand. The smell was like an assault on Shelly's already sensitive gag reflex and she immediately leaned forward and threw up in the kitchen sink (Belfast, naturally – it would have cost a fortune but she'd agreed a few #spon posts of Baby Georgie having her bath in it and the sink people had fallen over themselves to give it to her).

'Eh, gross.' Amy was clearly less than impressed with her boss's gastric greeting.

'Sorry,' came a slightly echoing response – Shelly was still head-in-sink waiting to make sure there wasn't any more to come. 'I'm just feeling a bit sick.'

'Yeah, I'm getting that,' replied Amy, who had hoisted herself up on one of the high stools around the marble-topped peninsula ('Nobody gets islands anymore – it's all about the peninsula now – they're so much more … London!' as Shelly had enthused on her house-tour video commentary) and was surveying her boss impassively.

'What?' Shelly wiped her mouth and spoke carefully, still uncertain if she was finished puking. She saw her assistant's pretty green eyes widen.

'Wait, wait, wait,' Amy said emphatically as she held up her hand. 'You've been skipping your run lately. And you ate a pastry-based canapé at the Great Lengths Hair Extensions dinner the other night.'

Shelly knew she'd never stood a chance hiding it from her but, even for Amy, this was a fast rumble. She leaned in for another vom just as Amy gasped, 'O-M-fucking-G, are you up the pole?'

Shelly had hired Amy two years before. She was a gifted manipulator of the various vagaries and whims of the Instagram algorithms. Shelly had created a good foundation when she began Instagramming just after Georgie was born, but by the time the little girl had turned one, the SHELLY brand had become a micro industry and more than she could manage by herself. Amy was also a far better strategist. Whereas Shelly had essentially stumbled into this strange new breed of success, Amy knew how to play the game, and since her arrival reach, engagement, opportunities and profit had grown exponentially. She was, however, not even remotely on-brand herself.

Amy was slight – she could probably pass for twelve though she was actually twenty-six. She'd grown up in the Liberties with her mum and dad and four brothers, which maybe contributed to her staunch refusal to take any crap from anyone. She had two sleeves of vivid tattoos snaking up each skinny arm and meeting across her shoulder blades. More flowers and birds and mythological creatures adorned her calves and thighs, and Shelly was forever reminding her to cover up at the various events Shelly made paid appearances at. Amy Donoghue, it seemed, was confident enough in her indispensability to flagrantly ignore this instruction.

She adjusted the vintage cat-eye glasses perched on her elfin face and immediately launched the app she used to track Shelly's schedule. 'When's the due date? We have so much to organise.'

'I'm not officially pregnant,' Shelly managed to splutter, slowly straightening back up. 'Well, as in I am but I haven't even told Dan yet. It wasn't quite part of the … em … plan,' she whispered.

Though was that really true? Shelly wondered.

While Dan had been categorical about not wanting another child, ever since Georgie had turned three Shelly had begun to yearn for another baby. That's not to say that she'd done this on purpose. Of course not. She might have been a teeny bit careless with her pill a couple of times (Dan didn't even take part in contraception efforts) but she hadn't gone behind his back or anything … Though whether Dan would see it that way was another story. Things had been tricky between them. Dan didn't exactly take SHELLY seriously as a real business.

She tried to ignore his snarky comments, but last night as she'd been arranging the table for a dinnertime post for Georgie's Instagram ('Delicious dinner with mommy and daddy thanks to @organicbabynomnom #eatgreenbabyorganicbaby #growingstrongbabies #spon #ad #georgieisdivine #shellyisdivine') he'd been derisive.

He'd just arrived in from work and was leaning against the peninsula ('It seems odd to have it jutting out from the wall like this – can we not just get an island?' had been Dan's take when renovating the light-filled kitchen extension) and swigging a bottle of Tiger.

'What are you whoring the poor child out for tonight? A crate of own-brand baked beans, a hotel break in Kilrush?' He'd said it like he was joking but Shelly could hear the tightness in his voice.

'Dan! God! They're actually organic sweet potato fries and kale pesto and Georgie's loving them.'

'Right.' He'd looked sceptical and then announced he was heading out with some of the lads from work.

He'd come back at 3 a.m. Shelly hadn't been able to sleep and heard his fumbling progress through the darkened house and up to their bedroom on the third floor of the sprawling detached house in Portmarnock they'd bought five years ago, the year they'd married. Luckily, Georgie was a heavy sleeper and so didn't even stir as Dan walked into at least three pieces of furniture en route to the bed.

'What are you talking about "not part of the plan"?' Amy

was frantically tapping things into her phone and apparently ignoring the potential fallout of Dan Devine learning that he had unwittingly impregnated his wife again. 'It's a feckin' brilliant plan! The SHELLY Instagram enjoys a major boost in engagement whenever we re-share pictures from when you were pregnant. Any post of you holding Georgie or #TBTs you've done to when you were preggers the last time has done wonders for the brand. In short, the plebs—'

'Followers, Amy!' interjected Shelly, horrified.

'Sorry, OK, the followers love Shelly with a belly,' Amy finished with a satisfied grin. 'I need to completely overhaul the Q1 Insta strategy, like, yesterday!'

'Well, I'm not telling Dan yet. I need some time to think about this. Anyway, I'm only a few weeks gone – there's no need to be changing anything just yet.' Just then a Calendar Alert pinged on Shelly's phone. 'Have you scheduled the baby announcement reveal already?' She couldn't help but smile at Amy still feverishly tapping things into her phone.

'I'm just throwing things in – don't get caught up in exact dates just yet. I'm only trying to get a structure on this rollout, a loose timeline in place,' Amy muttered without even looking up. 'We want to get the absolute maximum out of this foetus. The baby buck is mega – way bigger than it was even three years ago when you were having Georgie. Back then any decent SMA would've been advising clients to downplay the mother angle but tides have changed on that – the whole mumfluencer buzz is mega now. And we're gonna fucking own it.'

Shelly laughed lightly and then, hearing Dan's footsteps on the stairs, quickly ran the taps to clear the sink of any incriminating vomit. Dan had already had one go at her this morning – he could not find out about this right now. Not yet.

He came into the kitchen carrying Georgie, and Shelly pasted a smile on her face.

'Mama!' Georgie reached for Shelly and Dan deposited her into Shelly's arms and started pulling pages out of his laptop bag.

'Hello, sweet baby! You slept well.' Shelly nuzzled the little girl's neck.

'Peppa,' Georgie shouted.

'No, not till later,' Shelly said firmly, smiling.

'Peppa! Peppa! Peppa!'

Amy looked positively pained at the noise emitting from the child and consulted her phone while Shelly tried to calm Georgie down.

'Peppa. I want Peppa!'

'Marni's on the WhatsApp, she says she's two minutes away,' Amy shouted over the child's chanting.

Georgie immediately switched to shouting 'Marni' and, despite Shelly's attempts at distraction, there was no let-up until Marni, the French minder who'd been with them for two years, walked in the door – at which point Georgie jumped down from Shelly's arms and ran to the girl. Shelly tried to ignore the pang she felt as Marni swung Georgie up into her arms.

'Let's go and pick out your outfit, bébé!' They headed upstairs, Georgie whispering excitedly in Marni's ear.

'Thank Christ,' Dan snarked. 'Someone nearly had to do some parenting there. I have a call in two, so if you could just keep it down out here,' he said and headed into the room off the kitchen where Shelly and Amy usually did the flat lays.

Shelly slumped back against the peninsula. It wasn't even nine and she felt like crying.

Amy remained buried in her phone – she had a knack for invisibility whenever things were awkward between Shelly and Dan – but a message from her on Slack dropped into Shelly's alerts proclaiming the jam-packed day officially underway.

Pro-milk sponsored breakfast post – if you're still so intent on this foodie angle, though you know my feelings on it, then we've got a car coming at 10 to bring you to set.

Shelly sighed. At least Amy had no interest in talking things out – it made things a bit more straightforward. Theirs was a strictly feelings-free relationship.

She began arranging Pro-milk (a dairy-free protein-enriched milk substitute) products on a tray. Amy thought the food blogging was a bit unglam for SHELLY but Shelly was keen to cut back on posts with her daughter in them and she wanted to diversify. Plus *Durty Aul' Town* wouldn't go on forever.

The show had been good for her when she and Dan had moved home from London, even if it was a bit of a come-down compared with what her RADA friends were doing. Though Plum, her bestie who kept her up to date with all the old crowd, loyally pooh-poohed this notion.

'No one's "made it", Shelly. Delia's doing guided tours of the London Dungeons playing a Victorian hooker with a heart of gold, Matt's got an eczema ad in the works and Edwina's already jacked it in and tossed off to Surrey with the prerequisite banker and baby on the way.' At this, Plum abruptly shut up, having inadvertently described nearly exactly what Shelly'd done on graduating from RADA.

Plum didn't get it – people needed security. Shelly hadn't had a deprived childhood by any stretch, but when she'd arrived at RADA at twenty-one, she'd realised there was a whole other level of wealth that, growing up with her hard-working parents in Kimmage, she didn't know the first thing about. When she'd been introduced to Charity, Plum's posh mother, she'd made gaffe after gaffe – or at least that's what it felt like. Charity and Plum loved her and never made anything of those blunders (Shelly cringed remembering how she'd described the family's country house as 'shabby chic') but Shelly had felt painfully aware of their differences as the months and years passed.

She got out the faux marble board and steel cutlery and added them to the tray of props as she thought back to when she'd finished drama school. The possibilities had seemed endless. She and all her London friends were working shitty part-time jobs while they put on their first plays and traipsed around to auditions. On weekends, she'd head to Plum's parents' country place, which was like something from an Evelyn Waugh novel. Her London friends were all kind of broke but in reality everyone had a safety net, except Shelly.

Her parents had been ecstatically proud of her acceptance to RADA and open-minded about her acting ambitions. Jim had a permanent, pensionable job in the tax office and Sandra had stayed home with the children, but they'd both been active in the local choir and loved helping out on the school plays when Shelly and her sister and brother, Serena and Johnnie, were the all-singing, all-dancing O'Brien kids. They'd encouraged Shelly when she decided to pursue acting after being in Dublin Youth Theatre, and while they helped her set up in London, they couldn't pay her rent while she threw herself at every part that came up.

The winter after they finished RADA, the London crew were going skiing and, knowing Shelly couldn't afford the trip, a few of them, presumably at Plum's insistence, clubbed together to pay her fare.

'Don't even facking bother trying to say no.' Plum was adamant. 'The whole trip would be a dud if you weren't there. You can borrow Mummy's old ski suit and we'll all be too pissed on vin chaud to notice how ridiculous you look.'

It was a life-changing trip in that the host, Dave, whose parents' chalet they were all crashing in, had brought his friend from work. An Irish guy. Dan Devine. They'd all met sleepy-eyed in the airport and Dan was all but presented to Shelly.

'Someone for you to play with!' Plum said, winking.

'Racist,' said Dan with a twinkle that muted Plum momentarily.

Shelly laughed and joined in. 'Yeah, what, just cos we're both Irish we're going to hang around together? What, are you gonna quarantine us?'

'No, you're gonna hang around together because you're both shit skiers. And that's because you're Irish,' laughed Plum.

'Definitely racist,' Dan whispered to Shelly. 'Don't mind them, they'll be shit at the après.' He gave her a wink and Shelly excused herself immediately to go to the bathroom and check what her face was doing at this ungodly hour.

Plum followed her. 'Dan's fit. Dave says he's a rising star in the office.'

Shelly was still jangling from the encounter but she was intent on playing it cool. 'Well, I dunno if I'd have much in common with a City boy, no offence to you and Dave.'

Plum grinned. 'You don't have to marry the guy!'

Famous. Last. Words.

When Dan had showed up he was everything Shelly wanted: gorgeous, confident and on his way to a good career, her ticket to a more comfortable life, and they adored each other. At least, Shelly thought they had. In the early days, Shelly pulled out all the stops. She never wanted to slide into that complacent drudgery she'd seen in other couples. She always made an effort with Dan, never slobbing around in trackies or grotty T-shirts. Even after they were practically living together in Dan's apartment, Shelly was careful to never let the side down.

As she considered how things had changed, she arranged the dairy-free, wheat-free, refined-sugar-free muffins that their personal cook, Donna, had prepared last night on the dark slate plate she'd selected and added it to the tray. Where other couples seemed loose and comfortable with one another, a kind of formality remained between Dan and Shelly. The small things she'd chosen to ignore about Dan at the beginning – his slight lack of regard for her own ambitions, his ambivalence towards her family – seemed to magnify with the passage of time. After Georgie was born, it was obvious that Dan saw his daughter primarily as Shelly's responsibility. And he was definitely not too thrilled with the enormous profile SHELLY had earned in the last couple of years.

Of course, he liked the influencer thing when it suited him – he'd loved the trip to Lapland to see Santa last month. Shelly was verging on feeling defiant when a wave of nausea reminded her just how far from having the upper hand she was at that particular moment. It was hard to separate the nausea of early pregnancy from the nausea of panic: the two had merged to provide a constant uneasy feeling that had been the backdrop to all her thoughts since seeing that positive pregnancy test four days ago.

Shelly distributed some Pro-milk into little jugs. She was feeling conflicted about the baby herself. She hadn't had the easiest of times with Baby Georgie – she suppressed a shudder remembering those terminally long nights pacing the floors with the red-faced screaming little thing, fearful of waking Dan up. That screaming little thing had frightened Shelly and in those early days her antipathy towards the baby had settled deep in a secret, shameful part of her. It wasn't right to not love your baby, was it?

It had been a bleak and lonely time, not at all what Shelly had thought being a new mum would be, and she'd felt betrayed by what she suspected was all pretence on social media. However, it was a pretence she was soon participating in, posting pics of her baby on Insta. She was too afraid of what it meant that she wasn't in love with her new life as a one-woman dairy to be honest with anyone about it. Putting pictures on Instagram where everything looked perfect and happy made things feel … not perfect and happy exactly, but safer somehow. And then @ShellyDevine had really taken off for her.

Much later, Shelly had gone to the GP and been prescribed antidepressants for the gnawing fear that the doctor called postnatal depression. Part of Shelly suspected that this longing for a second baby was rooted in wanting a do-over on motherhood, to do the baby thing and get to feel it the way others seemed to. It was shaky logic upon which to pin such a major event, but other people had more than one baby. It wasn't an outrageous thing to want, was it?

And maybe it would draw them closer, her and Dan. Shelly consulted Donna's instructions on how to decorate the muffins and sprinkled some cinnamon over them. Dan would come around, she felt. It was all a matter of how she couched the news when she told him. She just needed to find the right way and the right time. She lifted the tray into the flat-lay studio, careful not to make too much noise as Dan was wrapping up his call.

'Yep, yep,' he glanced up at her and then turned away, 'I think we need to push the McLoughlin account 2018 review out to the end of next week. The numbers will look healthier and that gives us a bit more time to put together the new investment opportunities presentation … Grand. See you then.' Dan hung up and started clearing his files off the huge central table over which hung studio lights and a tripod for shooting overhead shots.

'Sorry, I'll get these out of your way, had to get that call done before Damien left the Melbourne office.' He seemed to be over his earlier strop and was being polite enough. Maybe, Shelly thought, it'd be a good time to broach the Daddy Bears' Picnic event. It was in three weeks' time and the PR company running it was a major SHELLY client. They'd brokered deals with premier brands that, in turn, poured major money into the various SHELLY accounts, and it was crucial to show up looking like the family they purported to be on Instagram.

'I was thinking it'd be nice to do something as a family soon.' She set the tray down and began arranging the jugs and muffins under the lights. 'The Lapland trip feels like ages ago.'

'Yeah.' Dan had one eye on his emails but seemed to be listening.

'I was invited to this really cute event in a few weeks' time. It's in Shanaghan House – it's called the Daddy Bears' Picnic and there'll be food and games for the kids. Perfect family chill time,' she added.

'Is it?' Dan put his phone down and, leaning his hands on the table, stared across at her. It was hard to read his expression. 'Is it family chill time? Or is it a work obligation?'

'Well, it's a bit of both, I suppose,' Shelly said slowly, hand-picking her words.

'I see.' Dan's face was impassive and his tone flat. 'Can I ask you – you're an actress, right?'

Shelly didn't like where this conversation was going. 'You know I'm an actress.' She folded her arms.

'Uh-huh, and do you get paid for acting out bullshit storylines? Cos I don't.'

'Dan!' Shelly blinked rapidly to ward off furious tears. She was too scared to point out that actually all the money earned with @ShellyDevine, @DivineDanDevine and @GeorgieDevine went into their joint account. 'Why do you have to turn every little thing into a fight?'

'Why do you have to turn everything into a photo op, a bit of sponcon for your Insta?'

'I don't do that,' Shelly said weakly. Goddammit, this had gone way off script.

'Don't you?' Dan slung his bag over his shoulder. 'Thanks for the invite but I think I'll spend my quality time with my daughter off-camera. You should think of doing the same.'

He walked out the door, his parting shot still ringing in Shelly's ears.

4

Mini was poring over her iPad when Ali took the seat opposite her in the little café. They were the only customers at this time of day – it was much more of a lunch spot.

'Hi, darling,' she muttered, not looking up. 'I'll just be one moment,' she added, holding up a long, elegant finger that boasted an almost architectural-looking ring; her other hand, Ali noted, was bare. Where was her wedding ring? Mini's hair was immaculate in her trademark blunt steel-grey bob and her red lipstick was pristine. She wore a white tuxedo shirt-front under a corseted jacket. Despite a cutesie name, Mini always looked severe. An interviewer had once described her look as 'malevolently chic', which Mini had loved.

Mini had never looked or acted like any of the mums at school.

It was another thing she and Liv had bonded over. Liv's mum, Myra Anand, was a psychologist, a reiki practitioner and the author of eleven bestselling books on sex, family and relationships – including one in which she graphically detailed Liv's conception, *The Untold Orgasmic Joys of Middle Age*. Liv's older siblings, Lex and Nella, were now in their late thirties – she was an afterthought baby. 'The menopause ignited something of a sensual fervour in me,' Myra had written in *Untold Orgasmic Joys*. It came out the year Liv turned sixteen.

The waiter appeared, mercifully dispelling any lingering images of an orgasmic Myra Anand, and Ali ordered a coffee.

'Right.' Mini slapped her iPad cover closed. 'How are you getting on? Still working on *Dirty Ole Dublin*?' Ali was certain Mini got this wrong endlessly on purpose.

'Yep,' she answered, tight-lipped. 'It's going great.' It wasn't a lie as such. She just had a policy of pretending to Mini that *Durty Aul' Town* was her dream job to minimise lectures – not that this worked.

'Alessandra, you're stagnating. I can see it.' Mini sighed.

'I'm not stagnating – *Durty Aul' Town* is perfect. It's a foot in the door and it gives me lots of time to work on my other projects.' Ali could hear herself parroting her college tutor, though she doubted anyone would count her Instagram as a 'project'.

'You got that foot in the door three years ago. I remember Miles was delighted – he was obviously more far gone then than we realised.'

Ali fought the desire to challenge this remark, remembering

her aunt Eleanor, Mini's only sister, urging her to give Mini the benefit of the doubt when she came out with this kind of thing. 'She doesn't mean to be so harsh. It's her way of coping,' Eleanor insisted. 'Cut her some slack.'

Well, no one's cutting me any slack, Ali raged silently. Maybe I need a bit of slack. He is my dad after all.

'Where's your wedding ring gone?' Ali wearily changed the subject, discreetly checking the time. Almost done.

'That's actually what I wanted to talk to you about.'

'Oh?' Ali raised an eyebrow, prompting Mini to lean closer.

'What have you done with your eyebrows? They look ridiculous.'

'Jesus, Mum. This is the way everyone wears them now. It's called high definition.'

'Well, they're doing you no favours. Anyway, that's not why we're here, although maybe they should be on the agenda. Should we be staging an intervention – that's what they call it, right?' She cackled to herself.

Mini's idea of a joke had always been pretty cutting but in the last few years, with Miles being so sick, the humour in her remarks had ebbed away entirely. Miles had always softened Mini; he had also united her and Ali. Without him their family just didn't work. It wasn't even a family – just two people who couldn't seem to last a conversation without a fight.

Ali rolled her eyes. 'I actually have to go to work too, you know.'

As if just remembering why they were there, Mini looked serious suddenly and even a little nervous, which was definitely strange.

'So I've been wanting to tell you something. I've been thinking for a while now about maybe going on a date … with a man … who is not your dad.'

This was not what Ali had been expecting. And then as she began to feel engulfed by the information, she realised she also didn't think she would care so much about something like this.

'You can't go and date. He's not dead, Mini.' Ali could hear her voice rising but she couldn't stop it. 'What are you going to do, bring your dates to visit him in Ailesend?'

Her parents had always been so together – she couldn't picture her mother with someone else. They were a team, an unlikely one but a team nonetheless. They'd been something of an 'it' couple back when Miles was still centre of the floorshow at Frederick's. It had been a hub for the Dublin theatre and art scene with Mini and Miles at the heart of it.

Ali had loved working there during college, back when she thought she wanted to be a playwright. After Miles had started to get sick, everything about that world had reminded her of him. He'd performed in theatre productions in his early twenties in Cork before moving to Dublin in 1984 to pursue bigger roles. Miles had worked in restaurants between acting gigs and had eventually become sidetracked by the business.

'You're not a widow, Mini,' Ali pointed out flatly. The ethics of this seemed seriously dubious. 'You could at least wait till he's dead to go on dates,' Ali finished bitterly.

'It's not dates plural. It's just one date,' Mini argued. 'You can't possibly understand what the last few years have been like for me. Your dad wasn't supposed to be lost to us at sixty. I wasn't supposed to be this odd widow-like creature. I'm lonely, Alessandra. I don't want to be alone – I want companionship. I still travel all the time and it's no fun without your dad. It's not just intercourse, you understand.' Ali suppressed a shudder at this but Mini was on a roll. 'I need a partner, not just sexual gratification.'

'I get it, I get it,' Ali cut across her, realising 'I get it' sounded like she was granting her permission, but anything to make Mini cease and desist with the sex talk. 'Look, if you want to go on DatesForTheDecrepit.com that's your business. I just don't want to hear about it.'

'Darling, I have to tell you about it. This is Dublin, there'll be talk.'

'Why would there be talk?' Ali narrowed her eyes. Mini shifted about, fiddling with the cover of her iPad.

'It's Marcus.' Mini crossed her arms and faced Ali with a resigned expression.

'Oh, what the fuck, Mum!'

'I didn't plan it and nothing untoward has happened yet. We just realised we have developed feelings for each other and want to pursue it.'

'Dad's business partner.' Ali shook her head. 'No fucking wonder you're worried about gossip.'

The waiter, presumably sensing the tension, tentatively approached the table, set Ali's coffee down and swiftly fled back to the safety of the counter.

'Anyone else, Jesus, Mini – date him for fuck's sake.' Ali jerked her head at the waiter, who looked positively frightened and dropped behind the counter, pretending to be doing something on the floor. The café was way too empty for this kind of confrontation.

At this moment 'Oh Superman', Mini's supremely pretentious ringtone, started up and she pressed her earpiece to take the call. Mini would take a call in the middle of a funeral. Ali sometimes felt she'd spent her life watching her mother talk to other people.

'I'm in the middle of a meeting, Erasmus, what is it?' Mini avoided Ali's glare while she listened to her assistant, who took the phrase 'long-suffering' to new levels. Erasmus was more soul-sapped than long-suffering as he babysat the various artists Mini represented and obeyed every whim of Mini herself. 'They're all as psychotic as each other,' Mini interjected wearily. 'Tell him to return the baby immediately. He's too old and he's not making enough money to still be carrying on with this *enfant terrible* shiteology.' She hung up and offered a single word by way of explanation. 'Edmund.'

Edmund was a performance artist Mini had been repping for years and had ruined practically every party Miles and Mini had ever thrown in their house. He once arrived wearing a young nude man draped around his shoulders and insisted on keeping him in the spare room where all the other coats were thrown on the bed. The other guests had been unhappy about a naked stranger rolling around among their clothes, a fact Miles patiently tried to explain to Edmund. It was all a moot point anyway as the guy, who Edmund later admitted he'd met on the bus, took off into the night wearing a four-grand fox-fur coat with several wallets stuffed into the pockets.

Mini hung up and reached for Ali's hand. 'These nails are disgusting, darling. They can't be hygienic.' She held the middle finger, examining Ali's multi-coloured fake nails.

Ali took her hand back, twisting her still-pointed middle finger up, and carefully stood, giving her mother the finger at close range all the while. It was incredibly satisfying even if it looked ridiculous. 'I'm going to work. You may not think my job's important but they will notice if I'm not there.'

❖

On the bus to work, Ali pulled out her phone. The tension that always amped up when dealing with Mini could usually be tamed by some calming scrolling. Checking in on her posts was like doing a scratch card. She opened the app with the buzz of anticipation. The protein-breakfast post was raking in the likes – a few hundred! Including one from Shelly herself. Whoop. Getting the follows from bigger accounts was important so other people would see she was doing well. She went through the comments, replying to each one individually – engagement was key to boosting her account.

As the Georgian buildings of the city centre gave way to the starker dual carriageway, Ali updated her Stories with chat about her day ahead. She tried to make her job sound more exciting than it was, hashtagging everything with #werk and #TVlife, but the reality was she was a lowly production assistant at the mercy of Stephan and the actors, many of whom were total knobs. She'd even been in college with one, Seamus Rourke, who never missed an opportunity to highlight how differently their careers were panning out.

'It's still so weird that you're, like, a runner, isn't it?' he'd said the day before when she came to get him for his scene. 'I always thought you wanted to write plays and stuff.'

The ping of the bus nearing her stop interrupted her thoughts. She grabbed her bag, hopped out at the TV station and headed towards Studio 4, where today's scenes were shooting.

Inside the studio was hectic as usual. *Durty Aul' Town* was shown four times a week and getting episodes rehearsed, shot, edited and aired was a daily shitfight. Four scenes into the day and Ali found herself beside Terry, the show's head writer, as they watched Stephan storming around the set of the town's fictional pub, O'Mahoney's, while crew scattered in every direction trying to look busy and avoid him.

Stephan raged around, spittle flying as he bitched people out of it for the slightest misstep or goof. He was most unpleasant but fun to watch, Ali thought, as long as he wasn't directing his ire at her. He'd been series producer of *Durty Aul' Town* for twenty-seven years and it seemed to have gravely affected his mental health. He terrorised people indiscriminately, from the make-up artists to the show's oldest and longest-running stars, Yvonne Lawler and Eric Vaughan, who had appeared on the pilot episode as the couple who owned O'Mahoney's. It was, in fact, Yvonne who was the source of Stephan's current tantrum.

'Jesus,' Stephan screamed mid-scene. 'This cannot go on. Can we do something about Yvonne's face? Please. It's giving me the creeps. She looks like the aul' one from *Titanic*. Trevor, check the lighting, will you? Or actually, fuck it, Yvonne, just face the other way – that's right, luv, back to the camera. Thanks. Thanks, pet.'

Stephan, Ali believed, deliberately cultivated his reputation for being an arsehole. He strutted around in his uniform of black drainpipe jeans, black polo neck and old Doc Martens, smoking rollies and generally trying to act like a badass Tarantino-type despite being a fifty-something TV producer who had only made one show in his entire career. When younger up-and-comers came on board to join the writers' room or operate cameras, Stephan's desperation to impress was an embarrassment.

'Christ,' muttered Terry beside her. 'The poor woman is nearly seventy.'

'Ali?' Shite, Stephan was roaring her name now. 'Ali? Where the fuck is Ali?' Stephan was standing dead in the centre of the set – if he'd bothered to turn his head slightly to the left, he'd spot her.

'Stephan! What can I do?' Ali scurried into his eyeline, digging in her pack where she kept the day's running order, scripts, Stephan's CBD oil, more heavy-duty medications and snacks. 'Sandwich? Are your sugars dropping?' Stephan had recently gone keto, which was making *Durty Aul' Town* an even more trying work environment than usual. Ali pulled out the lump of cheddar cheese sandwiched between two rashers that catering made specially every day.

Stephan snatched it up without a word of thanks and strode off to berate some other unfortunate and Ali returned, rolling her eyes at Terry. All the crew bonded over Stephan's bonkers ways.

'I'm not sure he actually gets the keto thing.' Ali grinned. 'So did you, eh, have a chance to look at that thing I sent you? I know you probably didn't, I know how busy you are …'

Months ago, Ali had done a spec script for *Durty Aul' Town* for a storyline for Imelda, Shelly's character, but it was hard to find the time to corner Terry. Plus she wasn't totally sure she wanted to hear the feedback. If he hadn't been chasing her to offer it, it was probably not glowing.

'Ah, I did, Ali. Sorry – as you say, the pace around here … It can be really hectic in the writers' room.' Terry was looking awkward and Ali decided on the spot that, with everything that had already happened that morning with Mini's burgeoning love life, maybe she didn't need this buzzkill.

'Look, no worries, it wasn't right. It's cool.' She tried to smile.

'Ali, you could be solid. I think you just need to give it more work. The scenes felt a little, I dunno … mannered. Maybe it's coming from college. You did theatre, right? TV's a different animal. Also I just felt, you know, if Imelda's dad was getting sick – her reactions seemed a bit off. Wouldn't she be more upset?'

'Well, maybe she's just handling it a bit differently. Maybe she doesn't know how to handle it. But yeah, no, you're right.' Ali started backing away – she didn't want to get upset on set. 'Um, thanks, Terry. Thanks for reading it.'

'Ali, these things take time. There's nothing instant about making a career in writing. Keep sending me stuff.' Terry was smiling kindly and Ali couldn't take it. Still backing off while trying to smile, she stumbled over some huge camera cables and, thankfully, at that moment Stephan called for a five-minute break.

Ali went to the loo and took the opportunity to pop on Insta. It was like a little mental massage. She knew Terry wasn't wrong. She'd been writing less and less in the last year. The things she wanted to write about were just too painful and then her Insta had started taking off and it was more fun and easier racking up likes than wordcounts.

Her post had a new comment:

@Janet_pics: You're so dedicated, Ali, no wonder your skin's so gorgeous. I need to start juicing more. What do you put in yours?

Ali smiled and turned her front camera on to take a selfie. She angled the phone above her but not so much that you could tell she was taking a piss. The light was so nice. She sucked in her cheeks slightly, touched her tongue to the roof of her mouth (a tip from Kate, who swore it killed any hint of a double chin), pouted heavily and snapped a few options – thirty-six for safety. As she edited the pic in FaceFix she had to admit her skin was good, but definitely through no efforts of her own, plus @Janet_pics had never actually seen her skin unfiltered.

Ali finished prepping the pic then googled a green juice recipe and pasted it into the Instagram caption.

So many people have been asking about my skin, and while I think it's mostly genetics, here's the green juice recipe I swear by. #greenlife #skinfluencer #DublinIgers #DiscoverUnder10K #Juicing #HealthyAf

Instantly the likes started rolling in. Selfies do well but you can't be seen to be doing too many or people think you're too up yourself. Ali sighed. It was a delicate balancing act.

She finished up in the loo and headed to make-up, where Shelly would need escorting to her next scene.

In the make-up chair, Shelly was scrolling on her phone. She looked up and smiled as Ali jogged towards her.

Ali was nervous around Shelly. She was so perfect-looking and Ali was afraid of coming across as desperate.

'Hi!' Shelly smiled, putting the phone away. 'Are we set?'

'Yep, Scene 36 down in Imelda's living room.' Ali picked up Shelly's script and water bottle and they headed down to studio.

'So how are you? All going well with your account?' Shelly was always polite but a bit distant with Ali and she sensed that Amy, Shelly's assistant who often hung around set, did most of the likes and comments on Ali's posts that purported to be coming from Shelly.

'Yeah, great, really looking forward to the Glossie Awards launch tomorrow night! Any excuse to get dressed up.' Ali smiled, ignoring Stephan's shouting in her headpiece about where the fuck were they. Ali tried to maximise these moments to ingratiate herself with Shelly. She held the heavy door to the studio open for Shelly and ushered her in, helping her over the spaghetti junction of wires and shielding her from various crew bustling past as they made their way around the back of the set.

'Oh, I know.' Shelly smiled. 'There's actually a really exciting new element to the awards this year,' she whispered conspiratorially.

'They've got a wild-card nomination that will go into the Influencer of the Year category!'

'Seriously?' Ali's eyes widened. 'So just anyone could be picked?'

'Well, I shouldn't tell you but they'll be announcing it on their social tonight so no harm. Basically, anyone who wants to be in the running for the wild card just needs to post an #OOTD tomorrow and the winning OOTD will be announced at the launch party! It's an initiative to boost up-and-comers. They're actually letting me judge the posts!'

It seemed a bit much that the woman in contention for Influencer of the Year was permitted to essentially choose the wild-card entry for that same category, but then what wasn't irritatingly incestuous and nonsensical about the whole Irish Insta-world? And in a way, it could work in Ali's favour. Shelly Devine would never crown a winner among any of the upper mid-level influencers, whose clout she most likely genuinely feared. Ali's non-threatening just-under-10K followers would be much more acceptable to Shelly. Plus, she actually knew Ali existed, unlike the other faceless nobodies.

'That is so exciting, Shelly, wow! Oh my god, it would just make my life to get that wild card!'

'Well, you've got the heads-up on it anyway.' Shelly winked and tapped her nose. 'No 'gramming that now or I'd be in major trouble.'

Shelly continued onto set as Ali considered the news. Getting that nomination was a long shot but a long shot Ali'd been waiting for, a chance to get some notice and seriously up her Insta profile.

5

The next morning Ali began her Insta prep early. It was still dark out and the heating hadn't kicked in yet as she sat in front of the ring-light, smoothing serum over her face. She was feeling super-positive about the wild-card nominations – this was the boost she'd been looking for. If she could just nail a spot in the Glossies everything else would fall into place. *Glossie Life*, the best-read women's mag in the country, would be promoting her account; the other influencers would know who she was. It was going to be huge. She'd even swapped shifts with Ruairí, one of the other PAs, so she'd have the whole day off to prepare.

She'd also put Liv on notice, WhatsApping her the night

before. She might hate Insta but Ali's #OOTD shots had come on in leaps and bounds since she'd first started haranguing Liv to photograph them. Liv had replied:

I'll do it but no lengthy location scouting, Ali. I am chained to my desk. Emer gave me an extension for the purposes of salvaging my thesis, not shooting 450 different options of you doing hip-pops and trying to 'find the light'.

Yesterday's meeting with Emer must have gone OK – maybe an unanticipated upside of being screwed (literally) by your tutor was that they didn't really have an option but to give you an extension when you needed one.

Ali brought up her profile as she blended her foundation. Really, she wasn't doing so bad for only having been around for a year. Nearly ten thousand was not terrible by any stretch. And she would surely double that by the time the awards came around in four months' time. If she nailed the post today.

Interrupting her thoughts of 20K followers and Glossies glory, Ali's phone buzzed to life and the words 'Mini calling' began flashing.

Ali felt sure no good would come of answering this call but her mother had a hold over her, a kind of nefarious force that meant Ali felt compelled to hit the green button.

'I know you're still mad at me so, believe me, I wouldn't be asking if I didn't absolutely have to, but there's been a disaster with Edmund in Paris and I have to get over there and do some damage limitation. Miles's consultant is coming by today and one of us has to be there, and since I'm already on the plane, I'm afraid you have to, darling.'

At this Mini drew breath, giving Ali just about long enough to catch up with the fact that her whole day was being hijacked by her mother.

'But, how're you calling if you're already on a—' Ali tried to cut across her.

'You'd swear a visit from the consultant,' Mini steamrolled on, 'who we effing pay a private fee to, by the way, was akin to a sighting of the messiah for all the advance notice we get. Anyway, anyway, anyway, you're going to have to get up there, Alessandra. And the worst part is there's no exact appointment. It's like a DHL delivery – he's coming between 10.30 and 4.30. You're so good – let me know what he says. Bye, darling, thanks, thanks, bye, bye, bye.'

'But—' Ali tried again, however the call had already ended. 'How about "Are you free today, Ali? Would you mind going up to your dad, Ali?"' she hissed venomously at the silent phone, which then buzzed back to life, giving her a fright. It was Mini again, as though she'd heard Ali's words.

Ali hit Accept and Mini's voice rang out once more. 'I've forwarded you an email with questions for the consultant.' Then she was gone again, no hello or goodbye.

Ali felt like crying. The day had kicked off to a great start. She'd prepped outfits, and even nicked a roll of coloured paper the evening before from one of the studios at work to use as a backdrop so her outfit would really pop. Now she felt completely ambushed. It was hard work sometimes just getting into a good mood and then trying to preserve it. How would she do the Glossies wild-card post now?

She placed the phone on her dressing table and tried to compose herself. A single two-minute exchange with her mother was basically the equivalent of cardio and Ali's heart was pounding furiously. The slight queasiness she experienced any time she had to visit her father in the nursing home was also kicking off in the pit of her stomach. Frustrated, she brought her fist down on the table, causing her phone to jump. It hurt a lot. And somehow that felt better.

'Ali?'

She started at the sound of Liv outside the door. 'Yeah, yeah, come in,' she said, trying to sound normal.

'Are you OK?' Liv poked her head around the door, squinting as she peered into the semi-darkness.

Ali felt a shiver of slight self-consciousness – she really should tidy up; there were empty Bulmers cans on the floor right by the door. She hoped Liv wouldn't look down. 'All good, just Mini completely screwing me as per usual,' Ali said, laughing lightly, hoping to distract Liv from the state of the place. 'She says I have to go up to the home and sit there all day waiting for the consultant to come by, probably just to say all the stuff we already know.'

'Aw, Ali.' Liv made to come over for a hug but luckily caught her foot on a partially concealed bag on the floor and stumbled, the threatened hug mercifully scuppered. Ali was relieved – it was harder to keep it together when people were nice to her about Miles.

'It's fine, I just need to figure out how I'm going to do this outfit of the day pic.' Ali started gathering up bits of clothes and make-up and stuffing them into a bag.

'What? You're still …?' Liv looked mildly disturbed. 'Maybe you just need to go and be with Miles and, you know, focus on the important stuff.'

'This is the important stuff too. Hey, will you come with me for a bit and just take a few shots? It'll only be an hour, I promise.'

'Ali. Do some sponcon in a nursing home? That's a bit … dark, like, isn't it?'

'It's not sponcon – I wish.' Ali laughed. 'Come on, please! There are no good mirrors there to do it with myself.'

'Eh …' Liv looked deeply uncertain. 'It seems creepy as fuck, no?'

'It'll take literally two minutes – nobody'll notice even,' argued Ali, pulling on jeans and a jumper over her stained pyjamas.

'Well, I'm really sorry but I'm glued to the desk today, remember? I told you I have to go back to Emer today.'

'Sure look, grand, I'll swing it one way or another. Maybe I can ask one of the nurses.' Ali swept the contents of her dressing table into a large make-up bag.

'Is that a joke? I feel you've drifted far from reality here!'

'You don't understand. If I can just get this wild-card entry it'll be a springboard to the next level.'

'You sound brainwashed,' Liv said flatly. 'And I feel like you're ignoring your dad—'

'Liv!' Ali's voice momentarily hit a higher register before she collected herself and tried to breathe slowly. 'I'm not ignoring him. I don't mean to ignore him. Look, this is a healthy outlet for my creativity.' Ali was trying to reassure herself as much as she was Liv. Liv didn't understand the terrible guilt she felt any time she thought of Miles. 'Good luck with Emer and stay strong. Remember, she made a huge mistake ditching you – you're a hot bitch and she's old as fuck! I'll see you later and don't forget to like my outfit of the day pic!' Ali did some jokey air kisses, grabbed her bag and headed down the hall and out to the car.

Ali spent the drive to Ailesend enthusiastically bitching on speakerphone to Kate and layering on ever-more-bonkers amounts of contour crayons when stopped at traffic lights. Kate was the only one of the school gang who was in any way interested in the Insta-world. She was hatching her own Insta-takeover that would come into effect whenever Darren/Dave/John (was it bad that Ali couldn't keep track of the various boyfs' names?) coughed up the ring. Kate had recently secured the handle @ShreddingForTheWedding and was set on capitalising on her #WeightLossJourney to the tune of a sponsored wedding.

Nothing mad, she'd pointed out, just a mid-size boutique festival-vibes wedding with glamping and strict Coachella dress code. Darren/Dave/John had actually already proposed in an impressively elaborate spectacle comprising a rowboat, a string quartet and fireworks. However, Kate had dispatched him to improve on the ring (a perfectly nice solitaire) and tone down the proposal. 'It's all about the bride-chillah this year,' she'd scolded him. 'I can't feckin' Instagram this *Pride and Prejudice* reenactment – the proposal aesthetic needs to match the wedding, which will be Norfolk bohemian with desert influences.'

Ali wanted to be supportive so hadn't pointed out that the bride-chillah theme seemed strongly contradictory to the 'shredding for the wedding' buzz. It seemed likely that Darren/Dave/John would be returning with an improved ring any day now.

'So have you seen the Crystal Doorley pics?' Kate's voice sounded gleeful.

'No! Spill,' demanded Ali as she inched forward in the morning traffic. She felt better already, even with the unscheduled Ailesend visit taking up most of her day off. With the Glossies wild card she actually felt like she had a purpose. Maybe she could do Insta-content up at Ailesend more often – it'd be a good use of the time there.

'So you know how Crystal never shuts the fuck up about being so totally natural, and never uses tan and only uses products that are cruelty free? Well, someone sent vintage posts of hers to Bloggers Uncovered showing her coming out of some tanning boutique – so much for all natural,' Kate brayed.

Bloggers Uncovered was an anonymous account that specialised in calling out the lowly crimes and mid-level misdemeanours any influencers might be engaged in.

As Kate read captions from old Crystal Doorley Insta-posts in which she had foolishly gloated about being able to tan naturally, Ali mused on the wedding and what would be her inevitable relegation to the singles' table. Relationship content was a pretty un-mined area for Ali. She hadn't had a serious boyfriend since college, she'd wasted most of her degree mired in an angst-ridden on-again off-again relationship with Harrison – a tortured thesp she'd met in Players. In the last year, she'd briefly seen a guy called Ian who worked in lighting on the show but things had been busy, with long days on set, visits to Miles and attending any and every PR event in a bid to keep her perfect record of appearing in the diary pages of every Irish glossy intact.

When he'd said he was heading to Oz, Ali wasn't too perturbed. She even got a good couple of weeks out of the wine memes and inspo quotes the 'break-up' provided her. She did a bit of online dating here and there and made sure to get loads of shots for future use, to post on those nights in with Liv when nothing was going on but a bit of Netflix and Scroll. The guys were grand for a 'gram but she couldn't say she was that interested in them – she had a habit of writing them off for the most minor of infractions. One guy kept using the phrase 'bantz' while another was a big fan of recounting his exploits with 'the lads' and after a while Ali, bored of his shite, began keeping count of how many times he used the word 'lads'. This became a useful barometer on future dates. She now had a ten-'lads'-and-you're-out policy, which apparently ruled out huge swathes of the males on Tinder. The fact was it was hard to like people. And maybe Tinder just wasn't the place to find funny, enlightened men – though there had been that vaguely promising one a few weeks ago, Sam. If only it hadn't ended so disastrously ...

Ali navigated the traffic in the weak winter sun as Kate

continued to gleefully relate the ins and outs of Crystal's public shaming.

'Now there's this hilarious voicenote doing the rounds from some girl saying Crystal's all-natural body scrub gave her some fungal rash.' Kate was giggling away. 'I'll send it on to you.'

Viral voicenotes were the latest gossip craze. They spread faster than HPV, and even though many had been exposed as hoaxes, they were still good for a laugh. A recent one about a well-known politician going on a Tinder date blew up so much his department had to release a statement refuting the claims. About twenty people had sent that one to Ali in the space of ten minutes.

Kate now segued into talk of her impending engagement. 'We're going to do it in the farmers' market. I'm just trying to find the perfect collarless cheesecloth shirt for Paul …' Of course, that's his name! thought Ali triumphantly, Paul. 'And I need to get the mani done and probably put on a few more pounds still.' For the wedding-shredding plan, Kate reckoned she needed to be coming from a 'slightly heavier place', as she put it, so 'the emotional arc would have more impact'.

Ali could see the turning for Ailesend and cut in. 'Darl, I've gotta go – I'll see you at the launch tonight. Keep me updated and remember "carb diem"!'

Ali tapped the phone to end the call and swung in through the large stone entrance that led to a long tree-lined drive up to the nursing home. It was always quiet here and a certain hopeless quiet always seeped over Ali too as she neared. Coming here to the grim place where the man who'd taught her to swim and drive – and, yeah, occasionally annoyed the crap out of her with his corny jokes – now lived was hard.

At the end of the avenue was a mostly empty car park. Ali nabbed a space and took a breath. Ailesend could suck her down on the best of days and she couldn't go there today. She stuck in her headphones and delivered a little self-talk: 'The wild-card nominations are a one-shot thing, Ali. Stay focused.' She hit the Instagram icon then opened the front camera, gave her face a quick check and started a Story.

'Hey Insta-fam, I have the most amazing project in the works – I just can't wait to share it with you. I'm heading in to a top-secret appointment, but let's just say that it's going to be epic.'

Ali replayed the Story, appraising her look and delivery. Ugh, she sounded bloody constipated. She deleted the Story and began again. Many attempts later and it still didn't sound quite right. She was about to hit Record once more when an incoming call interrupted the shoot. Mini. Oh, fuck. Ali checked the time – 10.45. That couldn't be right. She hadn't been trying to record the same Story for forty-five minutes, had she? Mini would freak.

Grabbing her bags, she hurriedly rejected the call, jumped out of the car and recorded her exciting-announcement Story one more time. She hit Post and started towards the main entrance, sending a rapid-fire series of one-line texts to Mini, giving the messages the urgency of a telegram, assuring her that she was just arriving at Miles's room.

Mini responded 'Fine' and Ali slowed down, relaxed again. She signed in at reception and made her way down the hall to the ward where Miles resided, as a couple of DMs pinged in from followers excited about her exciting news.

Ali had only begun the exciting-news thing fairly recently. She'd endlessly watched other influencers liberally breadcrumbing pending news and announcements, envious that they had such exciting and exclusive projects in the pipeline. Then she began to twig that she rarely noticed any of the announcements panning out. Some months later, they might post something with a caption trilling about how delighted they are that they can finally reveal … whatever the hell it might be. That's when Ali started lashing up the odd announcement Story (never a post, as that would be more trackable) and enjoying a little contact buzz, knowing that somewhere some other girl was jealous of her fabulous meetings and exciting projects.

She clicked into the first DM – *'Hope you're OK, hun?'* – and was puzzled. Ali stopped just short of the entrance to Miles's room and replayed the Story. Shit, shit, shit. Just behind her chattering face was a sign pointing right for St Bridget's Ward. Feck, feck, feck. Ali's mind raced – they'd all think she was getting work done.

Ali went back to delete the Story but it already had over a thousand views (stats that would usually delight her). Sometimes a deleted Story was worse, people could be very quick on the screen-grabs. When an influencer drunkenly posted Ali'd immediately send a screen-grab to Kate before the girl sobered up and deleted it. Screen-grabs in WhatsApp groups were like cigarettes in prison, a form of currency to barter with your friends. Or, for more committed bitching, to post on Rants.ie threads – which obviously Ali would never do. Someone could be screen-grabbing this Story right this second.

Just then the door to Miles's room swung open and Tabitha, one of his nurses, came out. On seeing Ali clutching the phone to her chest and looking stricken, Tabitha's face shifted from smiling to concern. 'Ali, are you OK, dearie?'

'I'm fine, I'm fine.' Ali squeezed past Tabitha's immense boobs and into her dad's room, eyes darting, her mind frantically scrambling for a solution. 'Hi Dad,' she chirped at the figure lying prone in the bed. 'I'm just popping to the loo.'

She ducked into the bathroom that adjoined her dad's room, studiously avoiding looking at all the depressing paraphernalia: wipes and latex gloves and worse.

She should say something on her Stories to explain or distract. But what?

6

'OK, Glossies launch tonight – we need to talk strategy.' Amy was perched, her highly decorated legs entwined, on a high stool in the corner of Shelly's walk-in-wardrobe-cum-office. Amanda, Shelly's full-time make-up artist, was priming Shelly's flawless skin on a neighbouring stool.

Amy hit a wall-mounted keypad beside her and a projector screen descended from a hidden compartment in the ceiling above the opposite wall. She aimed a slim silver remote at a projector perched on a discreet shelf above her head and the screen of her own laptop appeared across from them, displaying an infographic representing several mid-level Irish influencers.

Shelly shifted a bit to peer around Amanda, who was now

applying muddy brown stripes to her cheeks, forehead and down the sides of her nose.

'Go easy, Amanda,' Amy instructed, frowning at Shelly's face. 'We've got M&S sponcon up first at 11 a.m., so just low-key, everyday-mam-in-the-park vibes but with a touch of SJP, OK? Save the Kardashian homage for touch-ups tonight before the launch.'

Shelly caught Amanda's eye and gave a jokey little eye-roll, nodding towards Amy. Shelly was paranoid that one day Amanda would go rogue and spill on all the goings-on behind brand SHELLY so she always took pains to keep her onside, especially when Amy was being … well, Amy.

'So, let's talk wild-card nominations.' Amy carried on tapping away at her spreadsheet on the iPad. 'We need to nail this. Too many lame choices and it'll be obvious you're trying to limit the competition, but we don't want anyone who's too good. I've put together a shortlist here for you to look over – obviously, I've got a pretty good handle on these girls. They're the usuals, uncontroversial, all under ten thousand followers, blonde, low appeal in terms of sponsored-content deals, apparently unable to put together an outfit without minimum five Penneys items—'

'I love Penneys,' chimed in Amanda. 'It's great for a few bits.'

'No shit, Amanda,' said Amy without looking up.

Shelly jumped in. 'I know, Amanda. I'm addicted! Where would we be without Penneys? Sure this is Penneys.' Shelly smiled, tugging on her silk shorties PJ set – it wasn't, it was Calvin Klein.

Amanda pinched some of the silk between her fingertips. 'Well, you can always tell it's not the real deal up close,' she admitted.

Amy was flicking through the first few outfits posted by the more eager wannabes. 'Jesus, here's a terrifying ensemble,' she exclaimed as Dawn O'Connor, a fitness blogger, appeared on the opposite wall in shiny PVC thigh-high boots, a red kilt, white shirt and shiny PVC baker-boy cap.

'It's a look,' said Shelly, careful to be diplomatic.

'Oh my god, LOL,' Amy burst out as the next wild-card wannabe's #OOTD post appeared.

Shelly flung a dark look in Amy's direction. 'I like it,' she said loudly, drowning out her assistant's scoffing.

Amanda paused in her blending and turned to assess the latest offering. 'Is it a bit … revealing? Does she have it on wrong?'

Amy was shaking her head. 'It's a nightmare – she must have it on backwards or something. There's a lot of vadge on show there.'

Shelly laughed in spite of herself, but then was hit again by another wave of nausea. Any time she seemed to relax even for a minute the nausea was back – like a pesky reminder that her life was heading for a terrible collision. Amy continued to flick through the slideshow, keeping up a harsh commentary and occasionally noting down 'potentials'. Amanda was carefully working away, shading and highlighting. Shelly closed her eyes.

Maybe the best thing to do was get away with Dan for a few days and do the reveal in a nice relaxed, luxurious setting. She had a backlog of invites from practically every exclusive hotel in the country. Amy kept any and all perks on a spreadsheet for reference any time there was a date night or mini-break on the horizon. All they need do was pick one, get Georgie sorted and hit the road.

Maybe Dan would be happy with the news? Maybe another baby was what they really needed to be more like a real family? A sharp prick wrenched Shelly out of the reverie; Amanda was tidying her brows. But the prick served as a necessary reality check – after all, Shelly realised, no marriage in history was ever improved by a new baby.

'Marriages have to survive babies,' her own mother had joked in the hospital the day Georgie was born. 'Ah yeah,' her dad had agreed, cradling the hours-old Georgie. 'We were in the trenches for a long time there but it'll pay off now when you're all wiping our arses in a couple more years.' Her parents had chuckled at that, while Dan practically flinched – he did not get her dad's humour – and Shelly had felt the anxiety rear up. Dan had never made much effort to fit in with her family. In the early years, when they'd come home visiting from London, they'd sometimes stay with either Johnnie or Serena, her brother and sister, but Dan never made much of an effort with them and then she'd felt weird about being there. She knew they thought Dan was a snob and as time passed Shelly drifted apart from them. Especially after Serena went to Canada and Johnnie had kids. She still sent him and Mairead tickets to the panto and other bits of free swag she thought they might like, but it was mainly to make herself feel better.

She knew she was different to the old Shelly who Johnnie'd

bailed out of trouble with their parents when she was caught drinking as a teenager. She acted different and she definitely sounded different. Johnnie once said he was sick of the act she put on in front of Dan. It had really stung, more so because she knew he was right. In London, she'd somehow taken on a bit of a persona and it didn't quite match up with the pre-Dan Shelly. Had she known even back then that she and Dan were not a good fit and just tried to be what she thought he wanted? It was not an idea she enjoyed investigating, and she tucked it away to the back of her mind. They needed to make their marriage work and that was just that. Too much depended on it. Shelly took a deep breath. It would all be better after she told Dan about the baby and brought him round to the idea.

Where to go for the baby announcement? Laurel House was an option and Dan would love the oyster bar. But even thinking the words 'oyster bar' was a torment with this nausea. Of course, she'd need to take care of the requisite Instagramming while they were there – there is, after all, no such thing as a free luxury mini-break – and that could potentially piss Dan off. He just doesn't get that it's work, she thought.

Maybe she could have Amy do it remotely. She could record a few generic having-a-lovely-time posts against a neutral backdrop and send pics on the sly when they were down there, then Amy could do all the faff of uploading them.

'OK.' Amy clapped her hands. 'Amanda, this is gorge,' she said, waving her hands in the general direction of Shelly's face. 'You're off the hook now until touch-ups around 5.30 – that cool?'

'Fab.' Amanda gave Shelly's face a final once-over.

Amy was busily tapping away on her phone. 'Mail me the list of products used with corresponding Insta-handles. And don't just guess them like last time, Amanda – that's just sloppy and gives me more work to do.'

Shelly and Amanda exchanged furtive smiles and Shelly gave her a little encouraging wink as she headed out the door. It was great to have Amy do the delegating, really. Any correcting or unpleasantness with the personnel, Amy handled like a pro and Shelly didn't have to get her hands dirty. It meant that PRs and stylists never bitched about her – they could all moan and rail against Amy while Shelly's nice-girl vibes remained perfectly intact.

'OK, real-talk time.' Amy began taking snaps of Shelly's finished make-up. 'Look left,' she commanded. 'Suck in your cheeks. So my top three recommendations for wild cards are Grace O'Mahoney, Dara Stoney and Sinead Worthing. They're all the perfect blend of nice and potentially useful.'

Shelly took in the profiles of each girl as Amy outlined their stats and prospective uses. Grace O'Mahoney (9.5K followers) did PR for some luxury brands – 'Could cough up some nice gifties for us,' commented Amy. Dara Stoney (just over 10K followers) was a stylist and art director who created shoots for the country's biggest magazines – 'It'd be good to get you into more fashion editorials, enough of this "at home with" stuff. Dan's never up for it anyway,' said Amy, never one to waste time on tact.

Shelly sometimes felt uneasy about the endless machinations and quid pro quo nature of the Insta scene, but it was a grimy world, and this was how it just was sometimes. Anyway, the girls would be delighted – it's networking not bribery, reasoned Shelly. At this she had a sudden thought. 'Wait, what about that girl on the *Durty Aul' Town* crew?' She searched her brain for a name, clicking her fingers. Aisling? Alex? 'I was talking to her yesterday …'

'Ali?' Amy looked sceptical. 'You already liked one of her posts yesterday morning, so you're set on that front. Plus she's doing better these days – you don't want her actually giving you a run for your money!'

'But she has a hand in the production schedule and you know what a killer the early-morning calls are …' Shelly hated sounding grabby and Imelda wasn't getting many scenes lately but, still, 5 a.m. on set was a bitch.

Amy looked dubious as she flicked her fingers over the phone screen, checking the GlossiesWildCard hashtag. 'She hasn't actually posted for the wild-card entry yet.'

'I told her yesterday and she was definitely into it.'

'OK, I'll suss that and give her the nudge re call times at tonight's launch.'

'Thank you.' Shelly smiled. Amy worked for her but sometimes it felt like the reverse.

'Fine, I'm bumping Sinead then.' At this Amy's phone buzzed in her hand and she hopped down from the stool. 'Right, outfit-of-the-day time for us – we've got some sponcon Stories for your

M&S partnership and we also need to pencil in some Georgie Stories for this afternoon, numbers are dipping. I'll ring Marni.'

Shelly flinched at this – it was all so bald, carting Georgie in and out of her life as needed. So much was scheduled in every day – she was at work, after all, so she needed childcare – but then staging quality time with her daughter for the SHELLY account felt terrible. Sometimes in bed at night she'd look at the account, full of posts about #MamaDaughterTime and pics of her looking adoringly at the little girl and the guilt would start to choke her.

'It's no different to mums at the office all day,' Shelly would think, trying to assuage her anxiety. But she knew she was different. Those women would probably have given anything to be home with their kids, while Shelly had practically run back to work after Georgie. She loved her little girl … but the lonely, long days of early motherhood had scared Shelly. She was certain she would never take to it, that nothing would feel normal again. The doctor said depression but Shelly suspected she was just a shit mother, just wasn't cut out for it. When she returned to set she was relieved to be free and that made her feel even worse.

Amy stormed over to the wardrobe and flung it open. Flicking through the assorted blazers, she selected a blush one from the new M&S collection and thrust it at Shelly. 'Try it with the Acne jeans,' she commanded. 'I'll see you downstairs.'

7

The bathroom adjoining Miles's room was a place Ali never went into if she could help it. It was a large windowless wet room with a showerhead in one corner, a sink and a raised toilet with bars for patients to hold on to. In there, there was an ever-present danger of encountering some new fresh horror of his disease and now, pacing frantically, she was assailed by the depressing accoutrements of decline – nappies, urine-sample containers. 'Just don't look closely,' she counselled herself. She needed to address the problem at hand.

More DMs were dropping in from eagle-eyed followers who'd spotted the sign for the ward and assumed she was in hospital.

'*Oh, exciting! Are you trying out the ear lobe lipo we were chatting about?*' asked @LauraOD.

'*If you're in for fillers, get 2ml, with 1ml can't see any difference TBH. They'll try and argue but stand your ground,*' advised @makeupmadam119.

'Ali?' Tabitha called from outside the door. 'You dad's ready for his lunch – will I give it to him or do you want to?'

'OK, OK,' called Ali. 'I'll do it. Leave the tray and I'll be right out.'

Ali flicked on the camera and smoothed her hair. 'Hey, lovelies, thanks for the DMs. A few of you guys might have gotten the wrong end of the stick there. I'm not getting anything done and I'm totally fine – I'm just working on a little surprise coming in a few months. Big kisses!'

There, that's fine, thought Ali, hitting Post.

She slipped back out of the bathroom and went over to give her dad a gentle kiss on his cheek. 'Sorry, Miles, Instagram dramz!' She smoothed his hair. 'How are you?'

Miles lay flat on his back, a sheet draped over him. Ali had a slight fear of her dad's body now. She didn't like to think of how frail he was beneath the flannel pyjamas he wore. He was extremely thin. 'The Slimming World gang would be so proud – you're, like, Victoria Beckham-thin, Dad!' Ali's feeble attempts at humour dissolved in the oppressive atmosphere. Miles's brown eyes were open but trained firmly on the opposite wall. He didn't appear to even register her presence in the room. The doctors said he might have some cognition but how much was anyone's guess. Based on this, Ali tried to chat to him as much as possible and fill him in on what was going on in her life, but she couldn't get over a persistent and unpleasant sense that he really had no concept of where he was or even what he was anymore.

Ali wasn't sure which thought was worse: that he had some consciousness left but couldn't communicate with them, or that there was nothing left of his mind and all this chatter was slipping into a terrifying void where the spark and flow of his neural pathways had once twisted and turned. The locked-in theory gave Ali nightmares. She frequently dreamed that Miles was back but he wasn't the charming, loving jokester he'd always been: he was an angry, malevolent being who was raging with her. After these dreams, she always felt vulnerable, as though exposed as the shitty person she'd always suspected herself to be.

Being a good daughter was just so much work. She often looked at her fellow visitors and wondered at their incredible reserves of love and patience. They seemed relaxed and at ease, like compassion and care came easily to them. She tried to touch her father, to hold his hands and stroke his cheeks, but deep down she knew the truth was she was scared of touching him and she hated this about herself.

She never had the guts to ask Mini if she suffered this frustrating spiral of self-hate. Ali suspected Mini would not be good at alleviating Ali's guilt, and she certainly didn't want to invite Mini's analysis – mainly because, more often than not, her analysis sounded distinctly like criticism. There was a lot of 'you never' and 'you always' and, TBQH, who needed that?

After pushing open the windows and taking a few deep breaths,

Ali pulled up a chair to her dad's bed, raised its head and assessed the lunch spread.

'I'm not gonna sugarcoat it, Dad, it's pretty fucking bleak today. By the looks of it we've got a pre-masticated mélange of vegetables, some meat-related product and a gravy of indeterminate origin. Quality-wise, I'd say we're talking mid-seventies transatlantic-flight meal with an extremely depressing caloric-pumped pudding for dessert. Aesthetically speaking, let's just say there are more appetising sights on offer when googling "untreated haemorrhoids".'

Ali watched Miles closely, searching for a reaction, any glimmer, no matter how tiny, that he'd heard her. Nothing. She loaded a fork and brought it to his mouth. Even though his gaze never shifted, he accepted the bite and even chewed and swallowed. This seemed confirmation enough that Miles was gone from her – old Miles would never have accepted such a hideous meal.

Once his bites had started to slow, she carefully tipped some of his thickened drink into his mouth and wiped his face. The gloopy beverage was supposed to prevent fluid going down the wrong way and potentially causing pneumonia, which could be serious for her dad. Or a way out, Ali would often catch herself thinking on particularly bleak days.

'I have to take a picture for this thing I'm doing,' Ali announced. It sometimes felt awkward talking to Miles. She'd seen other visitors showing their loved ones pictures on their phones or reading aloud from the newspaper but it felt somehow pointless. Maybe she and Mini were just too cynical – not that she particularly liked admitting that she was like Mini in any way.

Ali turned on her Spotify and hit Play.

'I made you a new playlist.' She smoothed Miles's hair, which was longish, the way he'd always worn it, and still a lovely shade of blond with just a hint of grey. He still looked like himself in lots of ways. At sixty, he was younger than many of the nurses and doctors who looked after him and, apart from being so incredibly thin, and his complexion, which was now a troubling shade of grey, he still looked a lot like his old self. Ali couldn't quite remember when all the problems had started, which seemed ironic given the diagnosis Miles finally got at fifty-five. Alzheimer's. A particularly cruel flavour: early onset.

The first signs were so innocuous that Ali and Mini worried they might've been missing them for ages. Forgotten words, buying the same CDs over and over, pouring milk on his porridge and then going to do it again and again until Mini or Ali would stop him. When he sang around the house, gaps in the lyrics appeared that he filled with nonsense words. In time (so, so quickly, really – early onset advances rapidly, the doctors explained) the songs were all nonsense and you had to listen carefully to hear the beautiful melody still buried beneath.

'I didn't put any of your prog rock shite on there,' Ali warned as the reedy voice of Neil Young trickled into the room. The sun had rounded the building and light was pressing against the curtains. Ali pulled them back and the room instantly brightened, though the dreary atmosphere remained.

Sophie White

She checked her phone for the time – 2 p.m. Better get going – she didn't want her post to be too early in the day and get buried by all the rest, but she couldn't be too late either. Ali set to work, pulling out the gear she'd brought for the #OOTD picture. She smoothed a pale-green floral print dress and hung it on the back of the wardrobe. She felt a familiar sense of calm descend as she plotted the post – Instacalm they should call it, she thought.

Ali chattered along to Miles as she unpacked the rest of her clothes. 'The brief said "show your own unique flair", which some Instagrammers have taken to mean "show your own unique flaps"! Anyway, I just need to do a gorge shot of my chosen outfit, and if I get picked I'll get a wild-card entry to the Glossies' Influencer of the Year award, which could be an amazing springboard career-wise.' Not that Ali really knew what her career goals were anymore. She flashed on Terry's kind expression of the day before – her script was too 'mannered'. Ali pushed the thought away, things are depressing enough without dwelling on that. She glanced over at Miles. His eyes were staring slightly upwards and his mouth was hanging slightly open – it was a face that looked mildly mocking, which reminded her of the old Miles in a funny way. He would've been pretty amused by some of the more ridiculous Insta-antics.

'Don't scoff,' Ali said with faux indignation. 'It's a big deal! The Glossies have the power to put an influencer on the map. It's the launch tonight and then the wild-card nominee has two months to make their mark. Maybe even win. We could be talking tan brand ambassador, maybe a coffee-table book, cosmetic collaborations, seriously!'

After trying a few different looks, Ali settled on a floaty midi navy dress covered in tiny stars and some perfectly battered ankle boots. She looked delicate and feminine. It wasn't the most Insta outfit, but she reckoned the gamble might pay off – she would stand out from the crowd purely by dint of covering up a bit.

She grabbed her phone, which was now playing Fleetwood Mac's 'Never Going Back Again' – fitting, given her Stevie Nicks-inspired look.

'I'll be back – I just need to find someone to take my pic. No offence, but I'm not entirely convinced you'd manage it.' She blew a kiss over her shoulder and slipped out the door.

Ali headed down the corridor scouting for the right person. She passed lots of residents she recognised and then rounded the corner towards the nurses' station. She toyed with the idea of asking one of the care team but it seemed inappropriate. Tabitha was there doing paperwork. She loved Tabitha – she was in her fifties and had three teenage sons at home in Manila and somehow, in the last two years of coming to Ailesend so often, her presence had practically become more comforting than Ali's own mother's.

'Ali?' Tabitha hadn't even looked up. 'Everything OK?'

'Yep, all good. Dad told me to tell you lunch was horrendous and he's ready for his G&T whenever!'

Tabitha laughed and continued with her work.

Ali ploughed on down the custard-coloured corridor, the rubber floors squeaking underfoot, as she looked for someone closer to her own age who could be trusted with photography duties. She turned left down another corridor, which led to the courtyard with a little garden that hardly any of the residents on this ward were well enough to visit. Until about a year ago, Miles had been able to walk with help but now he was stuck in bed.

The walls of this corridor were lined with child-like artwork that some of the more compos mentis residents had made during art therapy. The effect was weirdly reminiscent of a primary school. She often wondered if the Ailesend board was made up of sadists. Sometimes it felt like they were trying to compound the misery of the place. Her thoughts were interrupted by a feeble voice.

'Help me … help me … help me.'

Ali shivered slightly. She was outside John Mahon's room – he was another early onset patient like her dad. Suddenly the door opened and a hassled-looking woman in her thirties rushed out, nearly colliding with Ali.

'Sorry,' she said.

'No probs, I know the feeling.' Ali smiled gently in what she hoped was an understanding manner but the woman's brow furrowed. 'Oh,' Ali went on. 'You know, when you've done your bit and then you're all, like, "Wah, get me out of here!"' Ali flailed a bit in an attempt to mime escaping, but the woman looked less than impressed with the insinuation that she was fleeing.

Ali frantically started to backtrack. 'Sorry, I didn't mean that you're dying to go – just me. Like, I love my dad but when I'm leaving I'm just so relieved, ya know?' At this the woman's face softened.

'Sorry … I do know what you mean,' she admitted quietly.

'I'm Helen. I've just moved home from the UK. That's my dad.' She gestured back to the closed door. Another 'help me' came from within and Helen flinched. 'The doctors say it's a reflex – he's not distressed. They think it's more like a needle skipping on a record.'

'Jeez,' Ali muttered. 'You got really unlucky in the Alzheimer's lotto. Of all the things he could be stuck on saying.'

'Yep.' Helen sighed.

'At least my dad doesn't say anything.' Ali laughed bleakly. 'Imagine if they were all like, "Don't you leave me here, you fuckin' bitch!"'

Ali had a habit of saying the wrong thing when she was nervous. And from the look on Helen's face, this was the wrong thing. 'Oh my god, I'm so sorry. When I was a kid, my mum used to say, "Some things are inside thoughts." That was an inside thought.'

To her surprise, Helen actually laughed a little. 'That was the most inside thought ever! I know what you mean, though. Some days in here are just so shitty, if you didn't laugh you'd cry. Or scream. Or throw something.' Helen looked tired but a little more relaxed too.

Ali smiled and frantically tried to think of how best to introduce the idea of the photograph without seeming weird. 'Will you take my picture?' she eventually blurted. Helen looked surprised. You need to give a reason, thought Ali. 'For a … souvenir.' Jesus, maybe not that reason. 'Sorry, not a souvenir … what I mean is … my aunt sent me this dress and I want to send her a pic of me wearing it.'

'O-K.' Helen was clearly a little dubious.

Ali edged past her towards the courtyard. 'Maybe down here where it's a bit brighter?'

It was chilly in the courtyard as Ali quickly shifted an overflowing ashtray off the table and out of the way of the shot. She took out her phone and reapplied her lipstick in the screen then handed it over to Helen with a list of directions for the composition.

'We really need to get all of me in shot here, and don't be afraid to let me know if I should suck my tummy in or whatever. You tell me what's working.'

Ali arranged herself leaning back against the wall, one leg straight, one leg bent, revealing the thigh-high slit in the dress. She arched her back slightly and pulled her features into one of her practised pouts.

'How am I looking, Helen?' she called. 'More leg?'

'Well, maybe less, if anything. It's for your aunt, you said?'

'Don't mind that. We need sexy but not too raunchy.'

'Do we?' asked Helen, looking baffled. She took what looked to be a couple of lacklustre snaps and stooped to gather her handbag. 'Look,' she said, 'I really need to be going … Eh, hope your aunt enjoys these.'

'Wait, but I wasn't ready!' Ali glanced quickly down at the phone. The last shot was definitely not a goer – she was fixing her knickers, for fuck's sake. She went after Helen, who had already headed back inside and was striding back up the corridor. 'Helen, come on, just a couple more – I need to get the angles better.'

'No!' Helen wheeled around and looked reproachful.

'Whatever this is for, I'm not into it. Frankly, it seems in bad taste posing here.' She gestured around vaguely. 'It's really not the place.' On cue, John Mahon started up again and Ali burned with embarrassment.

'No, you're right. Sorry, Helen. These are actually perfect. Gorgeous. Thanks for the help. Nice meeting you.' She slipped past Helen and hurried back towards Miles's room feeling Helen's eyes on her the whole way.

Back in her dad's room, Ali slumped against the door. Miles hadn't moved so much as a finger in the time she'd been gone.

'Well, that was a shitshow,' she huffed, flicking through the pics as she settled on the side of Miles's bed. 'Oh god, I look like some middle-aged auntie drunk at a wedding in this one,' she sighed, holding the phone out in Miles's general direction. 'It'd make you appreciate Liv. She complains about doing it but she actually makes me look good.'

A quick search of the Glossies wild-card hashtag over on Insta threw up some of the other wannabes who'd been quick out of the gate with their entries – in the case of one poor unfortunate, so quick as to have apparently put the dress on backwards. Ali peered closer – the slinky strappy number was borderline pornographic. If this was the competition, she could probably go with the thong-extraction pic and do fine.

A knock on the door startled Ali. 'Yes?' she called, chucking the phone on to the side table and grabbing Miles's hand, attempting to look like a loving daughter. She hated being caught on the phone while visiting.

'Ms Jones?' A smiling face peered around the door. 'It's Dr Walsh. We met at the ward Christmas carols a few weeks ago.'

Ali suppressed a shudder at the memory. It had been one of the more spectacularly grim afternoons in Ailesend. She had refused to put a Santa hat on Miles and after horsing into the mulled wine stormed – quite clearly completely plastered – out into the car park and cried. Not her best moment. And this greeting presented a further unsettling development – she did not remember meeting this woman.

'Yep.' Ali smiled tightly as Dr Walsh shut the door and settled herself in the chair across from Ali's seat on the bed. 'Great night that was. Juxtaposing crippling degenerative disease with festive cheer is always a winner.'

If Mini had been there, Ali would have been getting a kick, but Dr Walsh just smiled vaguely and pulled a file from her bag.

'So,' she continued briskly, 'your dad is responding really well to his treatment.'

Ali raised an eyebrow and looked from Miles to Dr Walsh. The silence stretched on, the only sound being the grind of the pump for the air mattress Miles needed to ward off bedsores.

'"Really well"?' Ali's words cut through the silence. 'Is this what's considered the clinical definition of really well?'

Dr Walsh's cosy smile dropped and she crossed her legs, slipping on her more businesslike veneer. 'Ms Jones, my responsibility is to take the measures necessary to keep your father comfortable and minimise the risk of further infection. That last infection has weakened him considerably. He's finished the last course of antibiotics and we are doing everything we can to keep him stable.'

'I know, I know,' Ali muttered quietly. 'I've heard this before. It's just that … he has no life now. You wouldn't leave a dog in this state. It's just—' Ali swallowed. She could feel her throat tightening as she strained not to cry – she hated to cry in front of people. Finally she got the words together. 'It just feels so cruel,' she finished.

'I know, Ms Jones. But there's nothing we can do. I have my responsibilities.' Dr Walsh launched into a detailed report on how perfectly and exactly to the letter those responsibilities were being carried out. Ali nodded in all the appropriate places, trying not to give in to the urge to scream.

The details droned on and Ali picked up her phone and started flicking before she even realised what she was doing. It was like a nervous tic. Thankfully, Dr Walsh, still talking, was leafing through her file and hadn't noticed. Ali fumbled helplessly, trying to shut off the screen, which had frozen on the pornographic image of the strappy-dress wearer. Of course, this was the moment Dr Walsh chose to look up.

'Sorry, sorry, I was just checking the time … I just have a work thing on today,' explained Ali, finally shutting it off.

For the briefest moment, Ali toyed with asking Dr Walsh to do the pic, but one look at her disgusted face told her that would not be a good idea. All of a sudden, Ali felt a wave of defeat crash over her. It was hard enough coming here and feeding Miles and pretending he could hear her without some bitch making her feel bad for picking up her phone for two seconds.

For the rest of the meeting Ali steadied herself and listened, even asking the odd question from Mini's email. Finally Dr Walsh began gathering her things. Ali tentatively cleared her throat – she had one more question but it felt somehow stuck.

'How long do people really stay like this?' she asked, her eyes fixed on the floor, blinking rapidly, trying to keep the tears at bay. 'How long can he live like this?'

Dr Walsh sighed. 'It could be weeks or months. He's so young, maybe even years. I'm sorry, I can't give you a better answer.'

Ali slumped back on the edge of the bed and watched the doctor closing the door quietly behind her. One part of her felt guilty for asking that question in front of her dad, while another part insisted there was nothing of him left now. A tear hit the back of her hand and snapped her back to the present.

She walked to the mirror on the opposite wall. No crying now, Ali. She gently wiped her eyes and took a long, slow breath. She had to look good for this pic. She stood back and considered the mirror; it was a large square full-length one. Maybe it would do? She could draw the curtains; they were a simple sheer fabric that would diffuse the light quite nicely. Her eyes came to rest on the figure in the bed. The bed would be in shot.

Ali pursed her lips as she reviewed her options. There was nothing in the room to block him. The wardrobe was bolted to the wall. She caught herself considering the blanket covering the lower half of the bed. She could almost hear Liv's voice inside her head. 'That's dark, Ali,' she'd say. Ali dismissed the idea and turned back to the mirror to check just how much of the bed would be visible. Maybe a bit of FaceFix would do the trick? If she could remove a blemish or shave whole chunks off her body, she could probably fix the background easily enough.

Opening up Insta, she could see a ton of DMs from her followers. The sight of the little glowing icon in the top right corner started a pleasant glow in the pit of her stomach that then radiated outwards. They were probably all wondering what she had planned for the Glossies. She felt a little giddy – it was the same feeling she got seeing the likes and comments rolling in on her posts. Checking the time, she decided to save them for later. It was good to draw out these little treats, and she needed to get a move on – there were only two hours to get home, spruce up and make it to the Glossies party. She ducked her head out the door of the room and checked the corridor. All clear. She took the pic, did some editing, covering the background as best she could, carefully added the #GlossiesWildCard and hit Post.

8

After a quick stop-off home, Ali'd spent the taxi ride to the Talbot fixing her make-up and chugging gin from a 7Up bottle and was only getting around to checking her DMs as she walked across the reception area.

Oh my gawd ... someone's working on something exciting alright! Congratulations!!! @AndreaH

Ali STOP! What IS this? Are you saying what I think you're saying? @AnnaDelaney1

I am so excited for you! I have three and it's the best thing I ever did. @Sally_anne123

Ali was baffled. She stopped just short of the red carpet leading into the ballroom, which was nearly as glammed up as its occupants. The ceiling was covered in a layer of gold balloons, the ribbons dangling a few feet above the guests. Waitstaff bearing trays of Prosecco and canapés were coming in a steady stream from the kitchen, though they rarely got more than a few steps into the room before being ambushed, their trays emptied in a matter of seconds.

She was about to check her Stories to see what on earth they were all talking about when a photographer from one of the magazines waved to her.

There was an accepted hierarchy of people who attended these events. At the lowest rung were the mid-level wannabe influencers all scraping to get their pictures taken and appear in the social pages of *Hiya* and *Glossie Life* magazine. Next up were the journos who were ostensibly there to mop up the free booze and finger food. The celebs (or Zee-lebs as the PRs called them) came next in the pecking order. Given there were really only about six bona fide celebrities on the island, this set were a motley crew of reality TV stars, GAA players and the occasional British soap star doing a paid appearance. The PR people were top of the food chain, given that they organised the events, controlled who was sent the best freebies and generally had the most dish on everyone in the room. The photographers had a similarly impressive command of the gossip and generally strolled around looking amused at the proceedings, dispensing scandal to select favourites among the crowd.

'Hiya, Ali,' Davey, the photographer called out. 'Will you do one on the red carpet for me?' In Dublin, they got the red carpet out for pretty much anything – she'd walked a carpet at a Tupperware launch at Poundland last month.

'Only if you take one for my Insta,' Ali called back.

'Sure, be quick.' He grabbed her phone. 'I think they're about to start any second – they brought Shelly in a minute ago.'

Ali scrambled onto the red carpet and fixed her dress, a black backless tulip-shaped mini – a choice that was backfiring, as the pic on her phone confirmed when Davey returned it. She frowned; it was bunching quite a bit on her tummy.

'Yeah,' Davey counselled over her shoulder, 'if you're doing a voluminous silhouette, it really works best in colour. In black it loses definition and you wind up just looking like a lump.'

'Thanks,' Ali said, mildly affronted. 'You're a pro at this, I suppose.'

'Ah, see it all the time – don't worry, your legs look smashing.' He grinned. 'The hashtag is GlossiesLaunch, by the way. You'd better lash that up on Insta quick or they'll kick you out – no such thing as free Prosecco.' He winked, handing her a glass from a passing tray.

Ali gulped about half of it back as she pushed through a crowd of girls all screaming, 'You look ah-maz-ing' at each other near the door. As she squeezed further into the crowd, she brushed against the upper arm of a tall redhead and became momentarily glued to her due to the sheer quantity of Mahogany Minx she'd applied. 'Sorry,' muttered Ali, unpeeling herself. Where was Kate?

At the far end of the room, a small purple stage backed by silver curtains had been erected. Flowers flanked the stage, which supported a podium and three small plinths where shortly Shelly's chosen nominees would take their places, ready to battle it out for the wild card.

Ali finally saw Kate at the other side of the room and mimed texting on her phone. She quickly WhatsApped *'See you after, good luck'* to Kate and found a spot on the left just as the lights in the packed function room dimmed. The crowd hushed as the music amped up. A spotlight found Blake Jordan, flanked by two male dancers, at the back of the room and followed him as he strutted towards the stage to Lizzo.

Ali quickly flicked back to her red-carpet snap and filtered the pic. It wasn't the greatest but social media managers took note of people who didn't hashtag the fuck out of every event and were known to blacklist for the slightest oversight or infraction. She hesitated briefly over the wording – maybe she should acknowledge the bad angle? – before settling on the caption: 'Please excuse what is apparently MATERNITY wear 😊 Wish me luck in tonight's #GlossiesWildCard comp' and hit Post.

The editor of *Glossie Life* magazine was by now welcoming Blake Jordan to the stage: 'Ireland's answer to Graham Norton everyone ...' The room erupted in applause. Isn't Graham Norton Ireland's answer to Graham Norton? wondered Ali. Blake grabbed the microphone and with breathless, reverential tones began to explain the genesis of the Glossie Digital Influencer Awards.

'We all know it's the biggest event in the Irish social media calendar – oh, except maybe when Gemma McCarthy gets the puppies out for a rare sighting. Hi, girls!' Blake wiggled his fingers at Gemma – a well-endowed influencer, looking stunning in a plunging evening dress – who pretended to scold him then laughed and blew him a kiss.

'The Glossies is an incredible opportunity,' he continued emphatically, 'for the brightest lights in our industry to celebrate their stellar successes across digital campaigns, product development and charitable works and to showcase their unique skills. Categories will include Best #Nofilter Selfie, Best Insta-Stories, Most Gas, Most "Authentic", Best Weight-Loss Journey, Best Couples Goals, Most Inspiring Influencer and Best Brunette Influencer … LOL, that's a joke – sure I know ye're all "blondes".' Blake smirked while doing air quotes as the crowd laughed appreciatively.

'Of course the most coveted award on the night will be Influencer of the Year – last year it was a close race with the Divine Ms Devine beating the gorge Ms Gemma by only a tiny margin.' The spotlight found Shelly just off-stage who, prepped for the moment, was smiling and clapping in Gemma's direction.

'Our reigning queen, Ms Devine, joined the board of the Glossies, who, as you all know as of this morning's little announcement, devised an incredible new element this year to help springboard the career of one lucky mid-level Irish influencer.' Blake paused to let the drama of the moment play. Hundreds of expectant faces were trained on the envelopes he now produced from inside his tux jacket.

'The brand new Glossies wild-card entry competition is an opportunity for a relatively unknown influencer to be plucked from obscurity and given a chance in the big leagues.' He was carefully enunciating each word, looking meaningfully into the tense faces in front of him at the foot of the stage. 'The chosen wild-card entry will be supported by *Glossie Life* magazine to reach a wider audience. But it's not just a case of a few shout-outs and reposts and wham, bam, spank you, ma'am – no!' He was becoming more animated with every word. 'The wild card must deliver on the content to have any chance in this race.'

The crowd – most of whom were holding phones aloft to capture the moment – held their breath. The lights dimmed until all but a tiny spotlight illuminated the first wild-card envelope.

'In this envelope, I have the name of the first nominee on the wild-card shortlist hand-selected by none other than Shelly Devine herself. She's been tirelessly trawling the GlossiesWildCard hashtag – that's right, Fidelma, she was looking at your manky bathroom.' Blake pointed at a blogger to the left of the stage. 'Who takes an OOTD in the bathroom, I ask you? Only joking – I loved your dirty knicks on the towel rail in the background. Penneys, hun?'

The blogger gave him the finger and laughed uproariously. 'Three for a fiver,' she called out, giggling.

Turning deathly serious again, Blake continued. 'If I call your name, come up and take your place in history – aka one of the three platforms to my left.' He winked. 'Don't take a selfie or call your mam.' He gave a little wave to his own mother, Teena, just off to the side of the stage – a bit of an Insta-celeb in her own right, thanks to her son. 'Shelly will join us to announce the wild-card finalist. Then we'll all skull some bubbles and be up for our proats and 5 a.m. power Pilates … 2019 – would ya be well!'

He produced a small rose gold letter-opener and carefully opened the envelope.

'Oh. My. Gee. Our first wild-card nominee is Grace O'Mahoney!'

The crowd clapped as warmly as they could muster, hair extensions whipped in every direction as the assembled looked for the lucky nominee. The spotlight found Grace crying and hugging her friend – who only began to reciprocate when she noticed all eyes were suddenly on them. Grace was wearing a floor-length shimmering green leopard-print dress and enormous Gucci earrings. Ali knew Grace vaguely from Instagram – she was in PR foremost but also had amassed a pretty big following on Insta in the past year.

Grace took her place on the most prominent, centre plinth. 'Well played,' thought Ali.

Blake gave a run-down of Grace's myriad social media achievements ('We love your clean-eating posts, Grace – who knew you could, or would want to, make a Snickers out of dates, bee pollen and coconut water?') and then turned back to the crowd, who immediately fell silent.

'Our next nominee is a major up-and-comer on the Insta-fashion scene. She regularly styles the covers of our fave mags, including *Glossie Life* magazine – but no nepotism here,' he quickly added. 'Dara Stoney, you big ride, get up here!'

Whoops and whistles rang out as Dara Stoney made her way through the crowd blowing kisses and took the plinth on the right.

Ali began to feel a bit glum in the face of so much confidence and body contouring. She didn't stand a chance, she thought bitterly, and downed the rest of her glass, already scanning for another tray-bearing waiter.

Her outfit-of-the-day pic was a pretty poor effort if the scrolling images being projected on the back of the stage were anything to go by. Snap after snap of the other entries, all perfect shimmering bronzed legs and abs, were playing on a loop and, sure, some of the FaceFix work was a bit heavy-handed but, still, Ali's own pic was infinitely worse.

As Blake Jordan chatted on about Dara Stoney's talent with a selfie, Ali slipped her phone out to confirm just how shite it was.

The outfit was good but given that everyone else had gone for quantity over quality in the flesh stakes, maybe the Stevie Nicks hippie vibe had been misjudged. It looked like she was trying to hide a 'problem area', as Mini would say. She had also done a sloppy job editing the background to hide that she was in a care home. She could just about make out the ghost of her dad's hand in the frame behind her right elbow. FFS. The DM notification glowed red, showing thirty-six unread messages – she still hadn't had a chance to check her Stories to see what they were all on about. Thirty-six was a lot for Ali.

She tuned back in to Blake Jordan long enough to ascertain that he was in the middle of an anecdote about a mishap involving himself, a well-known and volatile Irish panto star and her pet iguana and not about to announce the third nominee just yet. She opened her DMs and began flicking through the messages.

Oooooh, I see those pee pots, are you in Holles St, missus? @MaggsieLolz

Oh my god, Ali, are you in the Holla?! How far gone are you? @ClodaghH

When're you due, hun? You're gonna love it. @SlimminWorldHun

I'd know those toilets anywhere LOL! I have the best antenatal Pilates instructor, you HAVE to go. @JennzerOD

Ali felt the kind of potent panic that starts in your toes and sweeps up and through your entire body – what the fuck were they on about? They seemed to think she was pregnant. Sketchily she glanced around and then opened her last few Stories.

There in the background of her last Story were enormous stacks of urine sample containers and nappies and her smiling away, shiteing on oblivious. Ali raised the volume just enough to catch what it was she'd said.

'Hey, lovelies, thanks for the DMs. A few of you guys might have gotten the wrong end of the stick there. I'm not getting anything done and I'm totally fine – I'm just working on a little surprise coming in a few months. Big kisses!'

Working on a little surprise … uh oh. That did sound a bit off in the context of what looked like a hospital bathroom with piss jars in the background. Feck, feck, feck.

She'd have to fix it the second they announced the winner. Shit. What a crappy fucking day. A waiter passed and she swooped in for another Prosecco. Tilting the glass to her mouth, she was suddenly aware that Belle McGinnley, a brand consultant who had a fashion blog on the side, had appeared by her side, smiling.

She leaned in. 'You'll have to go easy on the old bubbles, I hear,' she whispered conspiratorially. 'I saw the Story and I was, like, "Is she hinting at something?" I wasn't sure but then I saw the post! Congratulations, mama!'

'The post …?' Ali lowered the glass and brought up her feed on her phone. The red-carpet pic with the stupid quip about maternity wear had more than five hundred likes and a ton of comments congratulating her. Ali gasped. Jesus, this was loads more engagement than she usually got.

Spying the phone over her shoulder, Belle murmured, 'Oh yeah, they love a good pregnancy journey. When I was expecting Emmerdale, I doubled my following.'

At this Ali, who had been about to explain the mishap, stopped. 'Doubled?' she repeated.

Belle nodded emphatically. 'Best thing I ever did.' She smirked. 'Well, I mean, obviously Emmerdale is the best thing that ever happened to me. But she's also the best thing that ever happened to my Insta!' She winked and then clamped her mouth shut, realising the final shortlisted wild card was about to be announced.

Blake Jordan, clearly revelling in his duties, waved the final envelope. 'I've just learned from my Insta prowling that our final wild-card wannabe has had a pretty big day already today ...' He paused, pressing the envelope to his pursed lips. The silence seemed to intensify with each passing second. Every girl in the room wanted to be on that final plinth. Ali was feeling jangly – she wanted to neck the last of her Prosecco but Belle was still right beside her and thinking she was up the duff. As Blake wrung every last bit of tension from the moment, Ali consoled herself. It was just some people on Instagram – she'd be able to smooth it over and then just go quiet for a few days and nobody would remember.

At last, Blake exhaled dramatically. 'Phew, sorry for that pregnant pause there! Though our next nominee knows all about that ... Please welcome Ali Jones and her "little surprise" to the stage!'

Ali felt the blood drain from her face. What the holy fuck was going on? Fuck, fuck, fuck, fuck, fuck. The spotlight found her and the crowd had turned as one heavily-contoured-and-not-entirely-friendly-looking entity to look at her. Ali flung a wide smile across her face and swiftly shoved the Prosecco glass into her tote bag.

The crowd applauded dutifully – they seemed sapped of their enthusiasm now that the last spot had been nabbed.

She made her way forward, trying to quell the storm of anxiety rising with every step. Maybe no one had noticed. Maybe she could just gloss over it. Maybe he wouldn't mention it again.

As she reached the stage, Blake boomed, 'Someone help her up, for god's sake – a woman in her condition can't be leaping about.'

Two waiters rushed forward to manhandle her awkwardly onto the plinth, one somehow managing to pull up her skirt in the process, while the other knocked the bag from her hand – out of which naturally fell the hidden glass, sloshing Prosecco everywhere. This was not quite how Ali had imagined this moment of glory would play out. While one waiter smoothed down her skirt, the other passed her bag back and dumbly held the glass out towards her. She smiled coldly at him until he finally got the message and withdrew the incriminating evidence. Ali wanted to kick them both. Absolute fucksticks.

'So, Ali, you're having a big day!' Blake mimed a pregnant belly, winking.

'Yeah,' said Ali, feeling her cheeks starting to burn.

'Are you excited?'

'Yep.' She nodded, staring out into the crowd and wondering what the actual fuck she was doing. Belle's voice seemed to be whispering in her ear once more: 'They love a good pregnancy journey. I doubled my following.' Doubled. Double!

'Double …' Shit, she'd said that last one out loud.

'What?' Blake was clearly exasperated with her monosyllabic answers.

'I'm … ehm …' Ali felt like she was teetering on the edge of something momentous. This was a bit more than lopping off chunks of her arse with FaceFix or lying about #DateNight and

#proats. But then again, she deserved this. Things had been sucky and look at how many people had liked her maternity-wear post.

The silence had gone on for too long – it was now or never. The whole place was staring at her, waiting for her to speak.

'Ali, Ali?' Blake clicked his fingers in front of her face and then shouted at her crotch. 'You dilating, hun?' The room erupted in hysterical laughter.

'Sorry, sorry! I was saying I'm gonna ... ehhh ... double in size, LOL!'

Blake looked irritated at her lack of cooperation on the bantz front and was clearly unimpressed with her belated and poor effort. 'Yes, well, anyway, we have our fab finalists and now to select our wild-card winner and the micro-influencer who'll get the chance to become a mega-influencer, please welcome our favourite mega-influencer herself, Shelly Devine!'

Ali's heart was thumping. What the fuck are you doing, Ali? screamed Rational Brain. There had to be two hundred people in the room – any one of them could find out she wasn't pregnant. On the other hand, pregnancy content would be about a million times better than sitting-around-the-depressing-home content, which was the way her life felt like it was going right now.

Shelly hugged Grace and Dara, then when she came to Ali, she gave her an extra squeeze and whispered, 'It's such an exciting time,' giving her a kiss on the cheek.

For a split second Ali pictured bump shots and packing the hospital bag and really did feel a warm glow of excitement in her tummy. Almost without thinking, she placed her hand on her belly and smiled back at Shelly. 'You're glowing, ya know,' Shelly enthused.

She took the microphone and began a long account of how hard it had been to narrow the list down to these three 'extraordinary women'.

Ali looked around, finally taking in that she had made it to the stage. So many times she'd been in the crowd at – or worse, not even invited to – these events and now here she was on the other side. The niggle of anxiety was still scratching at her. 'It's a very big lie' that prick of a Rational Brain insisted. It was a lie that was underway now, reasoned Ali. It wasn't her fault everyone took her up wrongly.

'And the wild-card finalist of 2019 is … Ali Jones!' The room erupted. 'Follow Ali's Glossies wild-card journey on her Instagram account, @Ali_Jones, and we can follow her journey from bump to baby there as well.'

Shelly went to hug her new rival but stopped upon seeing her face. 'Wait, are you OK?' She looked concerned.

Ali had blanched at the mention of the word 'baby'. Oh god, somehow with all the pregnancy talk she'd forgotten that key element. A baby.

Shelly peered at a pale-looking Ali before turning back to the crowd. 'Well, enjoy the bubbles and the nibbles and thanks for joining us for this gorgeous evening.' Shelly hustled Ali off the stage. 'Are you feeling alright? When are you due?'

Ali was still reeling from the B-word. 'Ehm … yes, I need to figure that out still,' she replied, slightly dazed.

Shelly looked bewildered but before she could answer, an excitable PR burst into the conversation.

'Ali!' She hugged and kissed her on both cheeks. 'Mags McEvoy. I rep Baby Got Bump, a gorgeous new maternity-wear line. Have you got any ambassador deals in the works yet? We'd love you to consider us for your maternity wardrobe – how does a lunch meeting sound?'

Ali's anxiety began to recede at the mention of 'ambassador deals'. 'Well, it's all still pretty new,' she began. Ali could see Kate just beyond, trying to get to her through the throng.

Just then another PR swooped in. 'Congratulations, Ali! I'm Penny from Classy Communications. One of our clients, Baby Bazaar, would love to set up a meeting to discuss how best our two brands could coalesce, integrate and define a mutually beneficial goal.'

'Eh …' Ali was still sorting through the individual words of that rather baffling sentence when she was spirited away by two official-looking women.

'We need some shots for the social channels and then Emily, our social manager, will do a bit of chat for the Instagram, OK?' said the taller of the two, steering Ali towards the red carpet.

Ali turned back, trying to find Kate in the crowd. 'Sorry! Call you later,' Ali mouthed when she finally spotted her friend, an oddly sour expression having invaded her heavily made-up face. Kate just nodded and disappeared back into the throng.

As the crowd parted before her, Ali could feel envy radiating off the girls she passed, girls with more followers than her but it was Ali about to be interviewed. Being at the centre like this was intoxicating – though maybe that was the Prosecco on top of all the taxi gin. Ali snuck a look at her phone and gasped at the rate that messages, comments, likes and new followers were pouring in.

'OMG.' She stopped dead, her head still buried in the phone.

Amy Donoghue, Shelly's assistant who had been following behind, caught up with her and leaned in to check out the screen. 'That'll be the baby boom.' She smirked, falling into step with Ali as they resumed walking towards the red carpet.

'Jeez, hardly,' said Ali, disbelieving.

'No, seriously,' insisted Amy, glancing back to make sure Shelly was following them. 'I've seen this before – they just love a baby bump. Between this and the wild card, I'd say you're poised for big things in the next few months. If you play it right.'

Ali chewed her bottom lip nervously as they reached the red-carpet area where the two organisers were arranging the photographs and beckoning Shelly forward.

'We'll do you after, Ali. Then everyone together,' called the taller one.

'Why the face?' Amy whispered. 'What's the problem?'

Ali, frankly, didn't know where to begin. 'Well, it's … eh, the news … is very new … I haven't exactly told anyone yet.'

'Never mind that.' Amy waved away Ali's concerns. 'Believe me, I know how this thing works.'

'How?' It was well known that Shelly's genius right-hand woman eschewed every platform herself. 'You don't even do social media.'

'A doctor doesn't have to be sick to treat people.' Amy grinned and Ali caught the subtle implication. Apparently, Amy reckoned they were suffering a sickness. Jeez, she doesn't know the half of it, thought Ali. Or maybe she does. She glanced at Shelly, wondering for the first time if everything in the perfect camp Shelly was exactly as it seemed.

'The main thing,' Amy carried on, 'is to eke out every last #bumpshot and #pregnancyjourney and #blessed moment of this thing.'

'Yeah ...' Ali felt buoyed by these words – she could almost see all the cute posts arranged in a montage in her mind. It would be so nice to have something, well, nice to put on Instagram. Her thoughts returned briefly to the grim task of photoshopping her dad out of her Insta-post earlier, the pic that had won her a place on that stage, but quickly she shook herself free of the unpleasant memory. You do what you have to do. This pregnancy was gonna be fun, she resolved.

'Oh and Ali?' Amy had her phone out and was now snapping pics of Shelly being photographed, gesturing impatiently at Shelly to adjust her head. 'Find the light,' she called, then turning back to Ali she added, 'Can you do something about Shelly's call times? They're very early. I know she'd really appreciate it. You can do that, right?'

'Sure, of course,' Ali said quietly as she felt a little squirm of angst in her tummy. Was that why she'd picked her? Everyone was now absorbed in Shelly, who was turning this way and that so the photographer could capture every perfect inch of her. A group of Insta-fans were gathered, held back by a velvet rope, phones in hand to capture the divine Shelly.

'You look ah-ma-zing, Shelly' seemed to ring out on repeat. What must it feel like to be loved like that? It suddenly struck Ali as incredibly unfair. What did Shelly have?

'Ali, is it?' The photographer was sizing her up and beckoning her forward.

She carefully stepped onto the red carpet. She saw the faces of the girls frantically posting every second spent basking in Shelly's presence.

Thinking of Mini and her date with Marcus and the blank eyes of her dad earlier that day, she thought, Fuck it, suddenly feeling defiant, maybe even a little reckless. I'm gonna make the goddamn most of this chance. I deserve something good to come my way.

She slipped in beside Shelly, placed one hand where her supposed bump was going to be and smised for the camera.

9

Shelly felt deflated the day after the wild-card announcement. It was nearly 8 a.m. when she woke up to find the house quiet. Dan must've left as soon as Marni arrived – she came early on Fridays so Dan could hit the gym before work.

Shelly seized the moment to snuggle further down into her pillows. This is what counts as a lie-in in my life, she thought ruefully. It was a rarity. Georgie favoured the scream-in-Mama's-face 6 a.m. wake-up call. Dan must've gotten up with her. Shelly tried not to dwell on this but the thought immediately made her edgy. She could never tell with Dan if the lie-in, if you could call it that, was given out of consideration or if he was actually off somewhere raging because he'd had to get up with Georgie.

Even if she did do her fair share, Dan always seemed to act like the martyr.

Was everyone's marriage never-ending one-upmanship over who was doing the most parenting? Shelly was convinced Dan had a leader board in his head to keep a running tally of how many trips Shelly went on, how many early calls she had to do for *Durty Aul' Town* and how many bedtimes she missed because of launches she needed to attend. It drove her crazy. Suddenly she became aware of a shadow in her peripheral vision.

'Jesus!' Shelly started at the sight of Carlson, her personal trainer (his name had definitely been Carl at some point – he was from Ringsend, for god's sake – but he'd adopted the 'son' to stand out on Insta), standing at the bedroom door with hands on hips.

'What the eff is this doing here?' he brayed, brandishing a banana peel.

'I needed a snack,' Shelly said defensively.

'A snack, a snack. What have I told you about thick-skinned fruit? Why not just stuff a Mars bar down your neck?'

'I came in late last night and was a bit hungry ...' Shelly attempted to defend herself.

'Late? Late!' Carlson was getting extremely red in the face. 'First you eat a fucking banana, and now you're telling me it was a post-6 p.m. banana feast! Shelly, I cannot work with someone who is not committed. You're wasting my time, you're wasting your own time.' He flung the banana peel on the carpet. 'You can drag your ass out of bed, pick this up with your teeth and give me a three-minute plank while you're down there.'

Shelly had eased the duvet up to conceal her smile during Carlson's rant. She attempted to nod in a serious fashion.

'Are you laughing under there?' he roared.

Luckily, at this moment Amy appeared behind him.

'Sorry, it was me.' She had a hand raised in a gesture of culpability. 'I let him in. But I didn't know he'd mainlined 10 grams of creatine already.' She pretended to give Carlson a soothing shoulder massage as she added, 'And I did not tell him about the banana.'

Carlson shrugged Amy off and clicked his fingers at Shelly. 'She did tell me you're duffed up again, though, and just so you know,' Carlson pointed an accusatory index finger in Shelly's direction, 'I'm not accepting that as any class of excuse for skipping training or gorging on thick-skinned fruit. Now up – we're doing legs and arms today.'

Carlson stormed downstairs towards the second-floor weights room and Shelly slipped out of bed reluctantly. Her lie-in had been cruelly snatched from her, meaning she was not in the mood for anything right now. The early pregnancy tireds had begun in earnest and she felt like she was trying to walk underwater while wearing a suit of armour. She also felt pissed off with, well, everything.

'Maybe don't tell any more people about my little situation?' she sniped at Amy, who handed over her morning glass of lemon water and followed her into the adjoining bathroom where she perched on the bath while Shelly washed her face. She didn't look even remotely concerned that she'd pissed her boss off.

'Carlson had to be told.' Amy shrugged. 'He'd be screaming at you for not doing all the core moves. Anyhow, it's not safe to not tell your trainer you're preggers.'

'Still, I can do it myself, Amy.' Shelly could feel the low-lying rage that had plagued the early months of her first pregnancy returning and taking up residence. What was with her? Even Carlson's ridiculous tirade hadn't cheered her up for long. Sometimes she was like this after big influencer events. Being around all the fans could be draining – not to mention chatting to the other influencers: that was another game of perpetual one-upmanship. She always came away feeling like she wasn't doing enough for the SHELLY brand. Hazel was doing an app, she'd said. Do I need an app? wondered Shelly.

Also, she'd felt almost jealous at Ali Jones's news. Which was crazy. She was bloody pregnant herself – there was zero reason to be jealous. Still, she envied the uncomplicated life Ali probably led. It was all so easy when you were young and didn't have so many people relying on you. Ali probably wasn't endlessly second-guessing herself or wondering if she was doing the right thing. Or if she'd married the wrong person. The thought stole across Shelly's brain unbidden and she quickly tucked it away, filing it under 'Things Not To Be Dwelt On' deep in the recesses of her mind.

Amy was already tapping away on her phone, going through the schedule for the day, while Shelly pulled on her workout gear.

'Today is swag day,' Amy said in a bored voice. 'So I'll be getting on with unboxing and what not.'

Swag day used to be a major slog in the early days of SHELLY. It had been amazing when Amy had first come on board and taken over unboxing the daily onslaught of freebies. On swag day, while Shelly did her workout or ran lines for *Durty Aul' Town*, Amy would repaint her nails nude, ditch the industrial-looking rings she favoured and put on Shelly's wedding and engagement rings. Then she'd film her hands unboxing everything, so all they needed were generic reaction shots from Shelly and a few bits of ooohing and ahhhing audio, and Amy could cut it together for Instagram. It was the perfect solution – there was, after all, only so much Shelly to go around and, a couple of minor continuity glitches aside, it worked perfectly.

'We have a beauty lunch in the Dax,' Amy droned on. 'And then it's on to that charity afternoon tea. I have your speech in Drafts – I'll forward it to you to familiarise yourself. Amanda will be here at eleven for hair and make-up so you can cast the eye then. I've also pencilled in some park time with Georgie at 4 p.m., which will be perfect for that #realmom campaign we've got running next month with the VitaPro supplements.'

Shelly nodded along as she texted Dan:

Hey Boop, I'm sorry I missed you this morning. What do you think of trying for a little break away just the two of us? How're you fixed workwise? We could head away Monday for the night? My parents would love a couple of days with Georgie ...

Shelly carefully read over the wording and took out the apology, changing it to *thanks for the lie-in this morning*. Amy was still hectoring about various commitments coming down the line as Shelly reconsidered 'Boop' – it was a pet name that dated back to their early days, but maybe in light of their run-in yesterday morning, he'd see it as manipulative.

'So as I was saying,' Amy continued, 'I think it's paramount that we bump the pregnancy reveal up as soon as possible.'

'Wait, what? Amy, no. We agreed we'd wait. I'm asking Dan to pencil in a night away right this second.'

'Well, sorry, Shelly, that may have been all well and good yesterday but that Ali Jones thing was big news last night. Brand managers are already putting campaigns together for the year and, frankly, she is a pretty exciting prospect for them. She's young, she's new, she's fresh. I'm concerned she's gonna clean up in terms of partnerships. All that'll be left for you will be some haemorrhoid cream sponcon.'

'She has a fraction of my following, Amy. I really don't think she'll be much of a threat.'

'Well, you're being naïve in that case.' Amy remained infuriatingly blasé, absorbed in tapping away on the phone. 'She may have a fraction of your following but she's also a fraction of your age.'

Shelly rolled her eyes. 'Nine years, Amy.'

Amy shrugged. 'Also the micro-influencer thing is becoming a much more attractive option for brands – the engagement is higher with a smaller following. Shelly, you know that.'

She glared at Amy, who serenely held her gaze, raising her

eyebrows and looking completely unruffled. The most annoying thing was that she was right – she always was. Shelly felt mutinous, *Am I being bullied by my own assistant?*

'When were you thinking?' Shelly finally asked peevishly.

'As soon as you sign off on the post, boss.' Amy flicked through the phone and brought up a picture of Shelly taken at an event a couple of days ago. It was an #OOTD pic, and she looked good. Amy had captioned the pic:

Dress by @HouseOfFermina; shoes by @louboutin; bag by @Zaraofficial and BUMP (that's riiight, Shell-Belles!) by the one and only @DivineDanDevine. #HereWeGoAgain #pregnancyjourney #instabump

'Cute,' said Shelly sullenly. 'Look, I know we need to get this out there, I just –'

'Can't tell Dan?' offered Amy.

Shelly bristled. They never talked about Shelly's marriage but she could see Amy meant no malice – she had a look that was hovering about as close to sympathetic as was possible for Amy to muster.

'Look, I'm saving the post in Drafts so it's ready to rock as soon as you sort your shit out with Dan,' said Amy in her best I'm-trying-to-be-reasonable-and-you're-not-making-it-very-easy-for-me voice. 'But I am strenuously advising that you launch this sooner rather than later. Now you'd better get down to Carlson before he fully gives himself an aneurysm.'

'Fine.' Shelly left Amy to her unboxing and jogged downstairs. She paused outside the door to the weights room and could hear Carlson griping away inside.

'Now she's fucking late. Thinks she can maintain an Insta-bod with a few acai bowls, a bit of Barbie foot and FaceFix – she's starting to believe her own bullshit.' He sounded breathless and Shelly figured he was lifting while bitching – his Lift 'n' Bitch method, which most of the influencers swore by. He was completely mad but he was also discreet and had a good understanding of what the Insta-life demanded.

'You can't shift a mom gunt with a few green juices,' he carried on. '"Oooh, Shelly, how do you stay in shape? What's your secret?"' He mimicked the daytime TV host who'd asked her this very question last week. '"Oh gosh,"' he'd switched to his breathy Shelly impression, '"I don't do anything. No diets or training. I'm just running around after Georgie all day, you know." Ha! Laughing my fucking ass off.'

He's batshit, thought Shelly as she pushed the door open and prepared for some light torture.

10

Waking up late the morning after the Glossies launch, Ali momentarily forgot what an insane time she'd had the night before. She fumbled for her phone, groggy and confused. And queasy. It was 9.20. Work in two hours. Ugh. They were starting late to shoot late. At least it was Friday – *Durty Aul' Town* rarely shot on weekends and she and Ruairí, the other PA, took turns doing any bits required. He was up this week, TG. Ali flopped back and tried to sort out the blur of the previous night.

Queasy was her normal morning sensation but it wasn't the usual anxiety queasiness – usually inspired by garage wine, late-night Insta-scrolling and ill-judged Mystery Bags (her local chipper's take on the ubiquitous Spice Bag). Instead this was an excited queasy, Ali realised. It was surprisingly pleasant.

The launch party came rushing back to her in a series of thrilling flashes. The fug of so much fake tan and hair product combined with body heat incubating in a poorly ventilated room. Ring-lights, selfie sticks, Proseccos, her name being called and then scanning the sea of bitter-looking Instagrammers as she stood onstage while Blake Jordan, *the* Blake Jordan, interviewed her. Shite. The excited queasy was rapidly being supplanted by the more familiar anxious queasy.

Something ... not brilliant had happened that was tempering the excitement.

Suddenly the memory of Blake Jordan miming a pregnant belly veered into her head. She'd had a bit to drink but she hadn't been drunk drunk. Surely not drunk enough to tell everyone she was ...

'Oh my god,' she whimpered as the worst Fear of her life hit her like a battering ram.

She launched herself under the covers, clawing through the sheets until she felt the comforting shape of her phone. She heaved herself up and crouched over the screen. She opened Instagram and gasped when she saw the sheer volume of notifications. Three and a half thousand new followers overnight.

Three thousand five hundred and thirty-fucking-six.

She attempted to steady herself as she refreshed her feed, unable to believe what she was seeing. The DMs were rammed. Too many messages to read. Ali started feeling shaky. At last she'd get to do one of those Stories she'd watched influencers do countless times. The ones where they said they'd had so many amazing messages and were trying to work through their inbox and hoped to reply to everyone soon.

Ali could feel a bubble of pure, unbridled glee filling inside her. She bounded off the bed and landed smack on some crunching object hidden beneath last night's dress. 'Fuck,' she yelped in pain and then a giggle escaped her lips. 'Oh my fucking god!' She giggled uncontrollably. This is what they meant when people said they were beside themselves. She wrapped her arms around herself, feeling like if she didn't restrain herself physically she might take off from sheer delight.

'Fuck, fuck fucking fuck!' She felt like dancing or singing or screaming. Shit, this was bad but also, fuck, this was amazing. She checked her phone again – ten more followers in the last couple of seconds. 'Oh my god,' she squeaked.

She looked at her last post. Ooops – looked like she'd already made it official. The pic (posted at 1.15 a.m.) was a positive pregnancy test with a very poorly spelled caption thanking everyone for their kind wishes. At least she'd put every pregnancy-related hashtag known to man on it and tagged more than fifty key accounts.

Drunk Ali's pretty on it, she thought admiringly. But how did she get so drunk? She paused in her gleeful self-hug and waded back through the night's memories. She'd left the Glossies before 11 p.m., unable to drink any more Piss-ecco due to her fake pregnancy.

Of course, the pink champagne. She was given a huge hamper of goodies as she'd left, including a bottle of pink champagne, and she'd celebrated the main way she knew how these days – slugging the bubbles from the bottle in what she figured was a kind of rakish and decadent vibe and scrolling on Instagram with one eye squeezed shut the better to focus.

She had a couple of flashes of meandering around the kitchen trying to make toast. Had Liv come in and shouted at her? Eek, yes, that sounded familiar.

Then it hit her. Liv. Quite possibly the biggest spanner in the pregnancy plan – if she could call it a plan. Shite.

The euphoria of becoming an overnight social media phenomenon was beginning to subside and the well-earned and clearly unavoidable hangover was making its way towards her. It was an onslaught as inevitable and unrelenting as an approaching high-speed train.

Ali crawled back on to the bed and eased herself into a semi-recline, pulling a heavy book over to rest on her face – this (along with a shneaky can of G&T) was Ali's tried and tested hangover cure. Something about the weight pressing down, pushing back on the pounding in her skull, was a relief.

'Or you could just not drink, ya know,' muttered Rational Brain. 'Mnam nanh manah mana.' Ali aped the voice then felt momentarily sheepish. Is it a good idea to be mimicking the voice inside your head that's trying to be sensible? Well, Rational Brain just didn't get that sometimes wallowing in a pure, delicious hangover was just what you needed. Besides, she'd earned this – she'd won the wild card, after all, she deserved to celebrate.

Rational Brain tried to point out that she always 'deserved' wine, whether she was celebrating some minor Insta win or comforting herself after a bad day sitting with Miles, but Ali drowned out those uncomfortable truths with some immensely satisfying scenes from last night.

Just then her reverie was interrupted by her phone buzzing in her hand. She nudged the fourth Harry Potter up slightly to peer at the screen. A message.

I just saw your post, we need to talk. Call me ASAP.

She squinted at the contact name. Tinder Sam.

Ali sprang up in a move that was far too athletic for her current banjaxed head. The book fell to the floor straight into the tray of curry chips still languishing there from two days ago. As she contemplated the grim sight of the book partially submerged in curry sauce, her right hand began to buzz again.

Ali froze.

'Tinder Sam calling …' The screen heralded the incoming call in a way that, to Ali in her sensitive state, felt distinctly gleeful – though perhaps sensing judgement from an inanimate device was edging dangerously close to paranoia.

Ali held the phone at arm's length lest Tinder Sam detect her presence. She didn't want to end the call in case he could tell that she'd rejected it. Though in fairness she'd already rejected him pretty brutally IRL. Ali felt her cheeks burning at the memory. Poor Tinder Sam.

They'd hooked up about six weeks ago, at the start of December, and from his message, it seemed he'd MacGyvered his way into thinking her pregnancy post had something to do with him. While Tinder Sam seemed adept at basic arithmetic, he clearly wasn't thinking this through – they'd used a condom, for god's sake. Ali didn't allow rogue mickeys near her unsheathed. The date had been a memorable one for several terrible reasons. It had started on a good note, in that Tinder Sam appeared to tick all the boxes in terms of what Ali required from a Tinder date.

'*Beautiful but dim,*' she'd texted Liv just ten minutes in. '*In short, perfect!*'

Liv had texted back some vague bemoaning of Ali's refusal to give guys a chance or even pick one that might have a few words of sense to string together, which Ali disregarded, instead plunging into the pitcher of margaritas Tinder Sam had already ordered.

She had arrived at the burrito place in town first, affording her a good chance to appraise the merch from a distance when he arrived. He was well over six foot, lean but not overly muscular, with a sweep of dark curly hair. The whole picture was pretty appealing and his clothes weren't completely mortifying either – this, however, struck Ali as slightly suspicious. Did he have a girlfriend? Not that Ali cared all that much – she thought of Tinder as a kind of orgasm dispenser. ('It's like a servicing for your vagina!' she'd told Liv brightly the first few times she'd swiped. 'It scratches an itch. You're never going to actually like anyone on there but it serves a purpose.')

As he approached, he raised a hand in greeting and an intriguing stretch of toned torso was revealed along with a teeny glimpse of boxers. They looked like SpongeBob Squarepants boxers – which probably ruled out a girlfriend. As he came closer she could make out a smattering of freckles across his nose, which was weirdly endearing, as was the awkward way he put his hands straight into his pockets after his initial wave, as though he was suffering from wave-regret. He was pretty cute.

As he made his way through the Friday-evening post-work crowd, Ali had felt a pleasant flutter of nerves at the thought of what he was taking in about her at this very moment. She was wearing a short leather skirt with an old Ramones T-shirt and flat gladiator sandals. She'd actually spent so much time on pre-date Insta-content (it was important to wring as much as possible out of these opportunities) that she had only just had time to lash on the prerequisite fake tan and was concerned that it was still a bit sticky. She tugged her skirt down and returned his wave.

She'd deduced from his profile on Tinder that he liked music, films and kite surfing. This revealed exactly zero, as every single guy on there listed almost an identical round-up of hobbies. His pics were the usual barbecue pic, some snaps from his year in Oz, his San Diego J1 – that kind of thing.

Ali had said yes to his offer of a date deep in a wine fog a few nights before. At the time it seemed like some human contact and affection might be a good idea – Liv had been away doing some wholesome activity with her running buds and Ali had drifted into a slightly unhealthy routine of solo wine and *Room to Improve* (a guilty pleasure of hers).

'*I love your profile pic*,' his message began.

Ugh, not a very promising opener, thought Ali, peering at the phone. Who was this guy? A quick flick through his pics and she had to admit he was pretty attractive. He had exactly the kind of nerd-level that Ali liked. Nerds had gone mainstream, which was a boon for nerd-enthusiasts like herself. She called them Therouxs (after their leader, Louis) and they were a rare find in the wild like this. She'd screen-grabbed his profiler and sent it to Liv, who got back to her within seconds.

Oooh, a Theroux – what's he doing on Tinder? I thought there was a mandatory order that male Tinder-users needed a baffling devotion to protein powder and a minimum nine gym selfies. If I was on a man-jag I'd nab him this instant!

Ali had swiped right but maintained a careful disinterest, as she always did these days. It was a personal policy not to take Tinder too seriously. She didn't hold much hope of finding anyone she actually liked on there, and she didn't really have time for dating in earnest – mostly it just gave her something to do and a bit of #datenight content. The guys had largely been a let-down. At the beginning, she used to get excited for every date, thinking this'd be the one straight out of a Zooey Deschanel movie, but usually the dates more closely resembled a crap episode of *Nationwide*: stiff conversation, chemistry non-existent, often with a bizarre focus on livestock – though this was perhaps a specific trait of Irish Tinder. And yet there she was wading into the murky, potentially venereal-disease-ridden water of Tinder once more …

Ali's hand buzzed again. It was Tinder Sam – again – bringing her back from the unfortunate night she and Liv had affectionately dubbed the Tan Ram. Jeez, he's freaking. Maybe I should be freaking? You should be freaking, insisted Rational Brain.

Still ignoring the persistent buzzing, Ali sat on the bed and tried to think. In a way it was too late to do anything – it was already out there. And besides, the Glossies were only a few months away. She could just roll with it and figure out what to do then. She could go on a big trip; she could say she'd been a surrogate. She could style it out. Influencers often talked about projects that never materialised and people didn't grill them on every little detail.

Mini would never find out – she was old school and completely allergic to Instagram. And besides, she was so focused on her stable of artists that most of the time it was like the rest of the world didn't even exist.

Liv would have an opinion, that's for sure. But maybe Liv's opinion didn't fucking matter, Ali thought, feeling defiant. The Glossies was big for her, and Liv didn't understand how bleak things had been since Miles had gone downhill. Well, maybe she did, but she didn't know what it was like sitting with him day in, day out while everyone else was off living their stupid best lives. She deserved to have a bit of fun, and Liv would have to get on board.

Tinder Sam seemed to have given up for the time being, though a couple of messages dropped in imploring her to ring him as soon as possible. Ali took the opportunity to check back in with her rapidly growing following. She gasped. Four hundred more in the twenty minutes since she'd last checked. The bump effect was real.

Ali slipped into her Gmail and found 181 new messages. Whoa, usually the inbox was a barren wasteland of spam, random newsletters she'd forgotten to opt out of when buying stuff and the odd invite to a launch party. She and Kate usually pooled their resources when it came to getting in to these events. They had a loose agreement that they'd tell each other about any invites they received (most likely through some bureaucratic mishap on the part of the PR interns).

Kate had the edge as she did phones in one of the PR agencies, Keane Eye Branding, and Ali knew she didn't always divulge when something good was on. Then a pic of her with some Five-Digit influencer (this is what they called the upper mid-level ones who'd broken the ten thousand followers mark) would be in the social pages and Kate would be sheepish the next time they talked. But Ali always let it go – it was a cut-throat game and she couldn't begrudge Kate whatever machinations she was working. Ali had a few of her own, after all. She suddenly realised with renewed glee that she had now entered the upper echelon of the Five-Digit crew.

She scanned the subject lines of the emails. 'Ambassador opportunity', 'Maternity Brand Proposal', 'Pregnancy supplement campaign', 'Invite: Spa opening', 'Invite: Babymoon in Killnavan Lodge', 'Invite: Pamper Mama Weekend'. Fucking hell, this was how those 'grammers seemed to be on a perma-holiday. A babymoon sounded very nice, she mused – just then the phone started up again. An unknown number this time. Ali, like every normal person, had a deep-seated fear of the unknown number.

She hit Accept and held the phone slightly away from her ear in a bid to remain non-committal in the face of whatever dastardly cold call this might be.

'Hello,' she ventured.

'Ali, hi, hi! How are you?' The voice had the manic quality of someone accustomed to dealing with and managing people. It was the voice of a person required to be nice and tolerate bullshit in a professional capacity. In a word: PR.

'I'm Holly from Green, Hilliard and Mason PR.'

Bingo, thought Ali.

'You must be overwhelmed this morning? Everyone is talking about the Glossies wild card! And of course your fab news. I'm just following up on an invite I sent you a couple of hours ago. I know you must be inundated, so I thought I'd just give you a ring. We're doing the most adorable event in a few weeks' time in the grounds of Shanaghan House. It's a real family destination and I'd love to introduce you to Siobhan, their brand manager, a good person for you to know! It's going to be gorge. They're transforming the grounds into a kiddie wonderland and there'll be a marquee so it'll be really cosy. It's called the Daddy Bears' Picnic. It's just so sweet to get all the dads involved ... So are you in? You and your other half, I mean? The dads are essential, as we all know!' She laughed.

'Ehhh ...' Ali tried to gather her thoughts, which Holly appeared to take as a lack of enthusiasm.

'It's a really exclusive event,' she hurriedly continued. 'The goody bags are fab. I know there's some Crème de la Mer in there.

133

And all the gang is coming – Hazel, Polly, even Shelly.' She listed the preeminent Insta-mums, doling each name out like a form of currency – which, of course, it was.

Hazel, Polly, Shelly and Ali had a certain ring, thought Ali. It'd be a chance to get in with the mums that mattered. The lack of a baby daddy was a bit of a stumbling block, though. As if on cue, at that exact moment, Tinder Sam dialled in on the call waiting. She considered his name as the phone flashed and Holly could be heard continuing the hard sell on the Daddy Bears' Picnic. Maybe she should see what he had to say. A 'daddy bear' (ick, by the way) could lend the whole thing a ring of truth. And he hadn't been terrible. If it hadn't been for the whole tan-cident she might've responded to his follow-up texts, but she'd reckoned he was just being polite. Trying to save her from being embarrassed about what had happened. Or worse: that he had a thing for scat. Ugh, even just the word 'tan-cident' was giving her a full body cringe. The call waiting stopped flashing and Ali made a split-second decision.

'You know what,' she interrupted Holly mid-flow, 'count me in – it sounds fun.'

After hanging up, Ali regarded the missed calls from Tinder Sam. He was probably bricking it, thinking she was about to land him with a baby. The best thing was to meet him and suss him out. Maybe she could mine him for a bit of baby-daddy content and cut him loose. Easy.

'Can't talk right now but wanna meet Monday night and we can chat? It's all good – don't stress,' she WhatsApped.

Ali lay back on the bed and switched over to Insta to check out some of her new followers. @HolisticHazel, one of the biggest Insta-mums, was among them. Amazing. Ali grinned, imagining herself in the VIP area of the next Insta-event. Her reverie was broken by Liv barrelling into the room, and Ali scrambled to look marginally more together and not completely hungover.

'Ali, what the fuck?' Liv was breathless, brandishing her phone.

'Hey—' Ali began, momentarily wondering if she could maybe just let Liv believe the story too, before Liv cut her off with a mocking dramatic reading of the typo-filled post Drunk Ali'd written.

'"So excited to officially announce my *pegnancy*",' Liv read in a scathing voice.

OK, clearly trying to fluff it with Liv wouldn't be an option, thought Ali.

'Blah blah blah hashtag blessed,' finished Liv, glaring viciously at her. 'This is the most fucked thing you've ever done.' She tossed the phone on the bed and crossed her arms. Ali felt a spike of fear at Liv's face. Her jaw was set, her expression stony and Ali instantly felt her buzz evaporate. 'This isn't just fake breakfasts and bullshit posts about mindfulness, Ali.'

'Look, it's not that big a deal,' began Ali, bracing herself for Liv's onslaughts. Liv rarely got angry, which of course gave her anger, when it did occur, a frankly terrifying weight. 'I mean, it is a big deal. I know, I know. I just mean that I didn't intend it to happen.'

Ali launched herself out of bed and straight into damage

control, invoking everything from how humiliating it was being up on stage to how hard it was with Miles being so sick. Ali could feel Liv's fierce rage wilting, even though her eyes narrowed slightly when Ali mentioned Miles. Ali continued to grab at anything within reach to make Liv understand.

'Before I knew it, it had just taken off and I didn't know how to go back on it – it'd be too humiliating to own up to it now.' Liv sat on the end of the bed looking at the floor while Ali delivered her pleading statement, pacing in front of her. 'It just feels so good, all these people saying nice things and having something to look forward to.' At this Liv's head snapped up and Ali instantly wished she could call those last words back.

'There's nothing to "look forward to", Ali.' Liv shook her head in disbelief. 'Are you becoming delusional right now? Do I need to have you sectioned?'

'I didn't mean that.' Ali had not been prepared for this conversation. She needed to buy time before trying to get Liv onside. 'Look, it's happened now.' She tried for a soothing, more reasonable tone, something that made her sound like a person in control. 'I'm just going to let it play out for a couple of months, just until the awards are over. Then things'll die down, and people will forget.'

'Ali—' Liv was interrupted by Ali's phone buzzing among the bed sheets.

Saved by Tinder Sam. She'd better answer him. 'I have to get this,' Ali told Liv, turning slightly to shield the conversation from her.

'Ali, you're freaking me out – why didn't you answer my calls?' Tinder Sam sounded like a man on the edge.

'Hey, yeah, I know, it's been mad – but don't worry, you don't have to do anything. We'll sort it all out. Let's just talk on Monday – I'm in the middle of something. No more calling now, and I'll see you at Grogan's at six on Monday. OK?'

'OK, it's just … I mean … how are you, like—?'

'OK, byeee.' Ali cut him off before he could ask any more questions. Ones that would be considerably harder to answer.

'Who was that?'

'Ehm, it was just,' Ali stooped to check her face in the mirror and tried to sound casual, 'Tinder Sam.'

'Tinder Sam?' Liv looked bewildered, then obviously a little internal arithmetic meant the penny dropped. 'Stop. He thinks this has something to do with him?'

'Well …' Ali bustled about the room avoiding Liv's eyes and starting to get dressed for work.

'Ali!'

'I'm going to meet him on Monday and we'll talk everything out.' Ali was keeping it deliberately vague – she didn't even know what she was going to say to him yet.

'Do I need to remind you of a little something called the Tan Ram?' Liv was starting to look amused in spite of herself.

Ali groaned. 'Stop, I'm trying not to think about it.'

It had been the perfect date until things got messy – in the most literal, visceral sense. All had been going well. Dinner chat had been nice. Tinder Sam appeared to be some kind of office man – Ali had checked out of the conversation for a few key moments, mentally wording the Insta-post she was going to sneak off to the bathroom to upload, and missed the whole job explanation. He had a nice smile and a good sense of humour. By the time the second pitcher had been ordered, Ali was set on hooking up.

They'd headed back to Tinder Sam's place in Rathmines, even doing a little light hand-holding as they strolled down the canal. Ali took a few surreptitious shots for the 'gram and was pleasantly buzzed from the booze and the promise of what was to come. Other loved-up couples were meandering along the path and Ali was struck by how they too must look like that. Young. Happy. Normal. These were not things Ali associated with herself, and it felt more like she was trying it on for size than really living it. Tinder Sam was asking her about her family.

'Let's take a selfie!' she interrupted brightly – she didn't want to kill the mood with any information that might lead him to the dreaded Sympathetic Head Tilt.

He laughed and bent his head towards hers for the picture. At the last moment, he turned his head and went in for the kiss. The move was definitely a bit lurching and awkward but Ali had to hand it to him – top marks for catching her off-guard. And mega marks for delivering what was practically a white whale in the Insta-world: a kissing selfie that didn't look totally staged and cringe.

The flat was in the basement of a fairly manky Georgian house. Guys' flats always let them down, she'd observed, following Tinder Sam through a dark, narrow hall and into a dingy front room. There was always a *Reservoir Dogs* poster or some naff Bob Marley pic and an underlying smell of Bovril. Not that her own bedroom was much better. She rounded the doorframe and came face to face with a tie-dyed purple marijuana-leaf wall-hanging with Bob's face emblazoned in the centre. On the far wall hung a framed (framed?) picture of Al Pacino. Bingo, thought Ali.

They started kissing on the futon (of course it was a futon) and it was very, very nice, Ali had to admit. Even more than his broad shoulders and the way he could pick her up and pull her on to his lap, his smell appealed to Ali in a way she'd never experienced before. He wasn't drenched in some hideous man-perfume called Grunt or Machete – he just smelled good. She pulled his T-shirt over his head and he looked up at her grinning shyly, which was cute as fuck. He seemed a funny mix of confident and boyish. He put his hands on her waist and pushed her top up a bit, stopping just under her breasts, his fingers edging in to that sensitive place. His left thumb wandered further up, grazing her nipple through the cotton of her bra.

'Where's your bed?' whispered Ali.

Tinder Sam hopped up enthusiastically and pulled her into the back room, which was extremely basic. How do guys live like this? Ali wondered. White built-in wardrobes lined one wall, a double bed butted up against another and a single depressing light bulb dangled overhead. Tinder Sam had undressed faster than anything she'd ever seen, his shyness apparently gone the way of his clothes. She liked this lack of self-consciousness. It was kind of unexpected. He unzipped her skirt and pulled her knickers down. He was good at this. Ali giggled slightly but then gasped in surprise as he kneeled and started to tongue her. Fuck, he could be a real potential, she thought, just as her eyes raised and locked on a deeply disturbing sight.

Hanging on the wall opposite in this supremely monastic room was the single interior-design decision Tinder Sam had made in his bedroom. A *Love Actually* poster. Jaysus. What is that about? Tinder Sam was still doing lovely things, but now Ali was consumed by the unnerving thought that Tinder Sam liked *Love Actually* – liked it so much he had procured a poster and hung it proudly in his room.

There's not much worse that could be on a boy's bedroom wall, reflected Ali sadly. Maybe a message written in blood like 'I want to eat your face'? That would certainly be a red flag too. Though at least something like that would suggest a somewhat original mind with discerning tastes, but *Love* Fucking *Actually*? That's a hard no from me, thought Ali sadly. Better just sex 'n' go.

And this was when things started to go really downhill. As they were finding their rhythm, and Ali had managed to momentarily forget Tinder Sam's bizarre predilection for shite romcoms, a strange slippery sensation was kind of thwarting the movement. Initially Ali thought maybe Tinder Sam was a sweater but then realised his back was dry and the moistness was mainly in the legs and crotch area. Ali snuck a look and recoiled. What the fuck?

'It was like a dirty protest,' she'd wailed, filling Liv in later over tea and stress-biscuits in the kitchen.

Liv was laughing so hard she was unable to speak. She'd leaned over and peered under the table at Ali's legs, which were indeed a mess, streaked with unsightly stripes of darker and darker shades of brown.

'It. Was. Everywhere.' Ali had covered her face with equally muddy brown hands that must have suffered some contact dirty protesting and was speaking through her fingers. 'The sheets. Me. Him. Ick. It was an ick-fest.'

'A shitemare.' Liv nodded in sympathy. 'At least it wasn't actual shite,' she offered by way of consolation.

Ali looked up – her hands had left even more brown streaks on her face. 'This is the point I've hit with Tinder dates? "Well, at least I didn't shit myself!"' she said in a faux-happy voice.

This started Liv off laughing again. She wiped her eyes, gasping for breath. 'What happened? What did he do?'

At this Ali buried her head in her hands once more. 'It was a new tan, Chocolate Starfish …'

Liv snorted. 'Where do they get these names?'

Ali ignored this and continued, 'I'd put it on right before I left and I didn't rinse it off cos I was late and I didn't think it'd matter. Anyway, once we got started with the, ya know, business time, well, it was very hot and –'

'Moist?' supplied Liv and they both cringed in unison. 'Moist' was their most hated word.

'There was just a lot of … flesh-slapping, ya know,' Ali went on, wincing at the memory of Tinder Sam's face when he'd looked down. 'Anyhow, the whole thing must've, like, activated the tan and it was all lubey and sweaty and brown. Ugh. It was the worst.'

'What did he do?'

'Well, he finished.'

Liv snorted at this. 'Amazing, guys can overcome anything at that moment. You could probably have shown him a picture of a headless torso and he would've just kept at it. Did you finish?'

'Nope, I literally said "sorry about the sheets" and fucked it out of there. And now I must go to bed and pass away from mortification.' Ali'd grabbed a final few stress-biscuits and trudged towards the door

'Yeah.' Liv had nodded sadly. 'Maybe give yourself a little rinse beforehand,' she offered with a slight smirk.

'Fuck you.' Ali had chucked a biscuit at her. 'I know it's funny but it's also such a shame – before the whole *Love Actually* thing and the bed shitting, he actually seemed pretty cool …'

'So did you hear from him since the date then?' Liv's voice brought Ali back to the present and gave her a glimmer of hope. Perhaps Liv's curiosity about Tinder Sam was outweighing her pissiness about the faux foetus?

'No, he DM'd me and even tried to instigate a chat a couple of weeks later but I just couldn't bear to talk to him. I was too morto.'

'But if he didn't have a problem with the Tan Ram, then no big deal, no?' Liv persisted. She was clearly sufficiently distracted from the fake pregnancy for the time being, thought Ali, relieved.

'If he didn't have a problem with the Tan Ram then I don't really know what to do with that.' Ali laughed.

'Oh, you reckon he's ... scatty?' Liv raised her brows and pursed her lips.

'Shut up!' said Ali. 'Look, maybe I was too quick to write him off and now, well ...'

'You need a fake baby daddy,' finished Liv. 'Gotcha. All I can say is this will be a disaster. I am honestly concerned for your mental health and I'm going to go Google "psychotic break symptoms" right now.'

'Thanks for the show of support,' Ali retorted.

'Oh, I'm sorry, you need my support during this very difficult fake crisis pregnancy?' Ali knew Liv had dropped the outrage, at least momentarily, by her tone, which was still kind of stern but a little playful too. 'I. Am. Here. For. You.' Liv adopted the emphatic rhythm of an American reality TV star. 'Whatever you need. Rub your feet? Steal you a baby? I am on it. Perineum massage?'

'Eww. What even is that?'

'Worst fake pregnant lady ever, Ali. You need to do your homework.'

'I will,' insisted Ali, by now poised to head for work – she didn't want to leave Liv unsupervised in her room, but she remained stubbornly seated on the bed.

'You're not even going to ask how the thesis extension went, are you? This is how it always goes. Everything is more important than my academic stuff. I wrote that my last paper was being published in the WhatsApp group and there were tumbleweeds.

Then Jess is all "that Tinder guy came on my tits" and it's like an emoji exploji. Now even a fake baby is stealing my thunder.'

'Sorry, sorry, sorry – did you settle on a title for the thesis? Has Emer still not mentioned the messages?'

'Yes and no.'

Ali took a moment to sort those answers. 'Great, so she's ready to move on and ignore your demented Solpadeine-fuelled outburst.'

'Yep and I am going to continue aggressively pretending I don't care about her until I actually somehow don't. That works, right? Wanna know what my thesis title is? I think you might relate ...'

From Liv's wily little smirk, Ali sensed this was a trick question, but she needed to wrap this up and get over to the station. 'Go on.'

'"Fear and Self-Loathing in the Insta Age: A Cultural Analysis of Why a New Generation Would Rather Live a Lie than Face Reality". That's not too close to the bone now, is it, Ali?'

'No.' Ali started herding Liv towards the door. 'That is not what I am doing here. Look, just keep me out of it, please. I have to go. I'll see you later. Domino's? Cheesy Crust?' Ali was deliberately invoking their fave to get Liv back onside.

'OK, you're buying. If you don't want me to out you as a foetus faker, that is – hey, this whole thing has a pretty sweet upside for me,' Liv exclaimed faux brightly as Ali gave her a final friendly shove out of the room and down the hall.

Ducking back in, she grabbed her bag, laptop and phone, snapped a quick #OOTD for the 'gram and slammed the door behind her.

11

Over the weekend Ali'd kept a low profile. Liv had gone very quiet on the matter of the pregnancy, which was freaking Ali out more than anything. She'd become increasingly annoyed as the days passed without Ali resolving the issue and now a stony silence was reigning over breakfast. Ali couldn't even bring herself to do a proats Insta-post while Liv sat sullenly across from her.

'What are you up to today?' Ali tried.

'I'm going to UCD to meet a PhD student who is writing a thesis on the selfie. I'm hoping she's going to supply some quotes for one of the central chapters.' Liv didn't even look up from her day planner as she spoke and Ali nervously fiddled with her toast. She couldn't deal with Liv being angry with her – Mondays were depressing enough.

'Ah, cool.' Ali nodded.

'I suppose you want a lift to work? Is that why you're bothering to ask?' Liv fixed Ali with a bitchy smile.

'No! I always ask what you're up to. Please don't be like this.'

Liv stood suddenly and started shoving her planner and notes into her bag. 'I just can't believe you've let the whole weekend go without fixing this thing. And you're going to meet Tinder Sam tonight and say what?'

'I don't know yet.' Ali faltered. 'I'm going to work that out today. Kate's coming down to work over lunch and we're going to make a plan.'

'Does Kate know the truth?'

'She doesn't need to know. She's just gonna help me with the Insta-strategy – the bump journey and stuff.' Ali squirmed a little – she knew how it sounded.

Liv looked stunned. 'So you're actually going ahead with this?'

'Just for a couple of months, just until the awards, and then I'll figure it out. I'll say I was a surrogate or something. It's not hurting anyone.'

'Isn't it, Ali?' Liv replied starkly before leaving the kitchen, quietly shutting the door behind her.

❧

Ali spent the morning in studio, coordinating scenes, and then settled into one of the empty prefab offices just behind the fake Ballyknocken main street that served as background for all exterior scenes in *Durty Aul' Town*. It was the perfect place to work for an hour, as the rest of the day would be spent filming an outdoor scene in which John Jo, the resident troublemaker played by her old college 'chum' Seamus, would be dealing some cocaine to the youths of Ballyknocken ahead of a disco in the community centre that was serving as this week's dramatic climax.

She sent Kate a voicenote with directions for where to find her and pulled out her laptop. She'd spent the weekend replying to the PRs offering money for branded content, setting up meetings and feverishly researching the 'mumfluencer' thing. Just what the hell did they do? How much was too much? A browse on the hashtag 'bumpjourney' quickly told her nothing was off-limits.

She marvelled at how lucrative kids-as-content seemed to be. Insta-mums at Disneyland and on cruises, snaps showing improbably perfect houses filled with improbably perfect children. Here was an English Insta-mum in her exquisite bathroom in Somerset bathing her baby in a claw-footed bath of milk infused with Earl Grey and lavender sponsored by Twinings. Jaysus, thought Ali. Further investigation uncovered only more bonkers iterations of the same pristine and perfect scenes of motherland.

She knew she needed to be smart about this bump thing. It had to play out perfectly. Not a single scrap of bump content could be squandered. After her little fact-finding mission, she realised that every step of the #bumpjourney had to be engineered to within an inch of its life. At least not actually being pregnant would make all this considerably easier, thought Ali, observing the #bumpshoot of an American mumfluencer who had arranged her artfully nude, heavily pregnant body into an aerial yoga pose.

Some of this shit would be hard enough to manage when you weren't growing a whole other person inside you.

She brought up a Word doc and started to lay out a timeline for the next nine months. She added the date of the Glossies, Thursday, 28 March, and calculated that she'd be roughly fifteen weeks pregnant by then. A bit of image searching told her there'd be no need for bump padding at that stage. Women showed at different stages, according to BumpAndMama.com, and often first-time pregnancies wouldn't show until five or six months. Bingo. Ali began adding other key dates, consulting the website's month-by-month pregnancy guide – first doctor's appointment, first scan. She was getting into the swing of this and feeling productive and excited. She couldn't wait to do her first #bumpjourney post.

When had she last felt this good? A memory surfaced instantly. It was a memory she usually pushed away – it hurt too much to go there – but today, feeling this good, she felt safe to remember.

It was three years ago, the day she got the job on *Durty Aul' Town*. She'd cycled out to her parents' house in Seapoint. It was early May and the days were stretching, filling – it had seemed – with possibility. Their house, the house she'd grown up in, was the last in a row of five Georgian villas set down a lane below the coast road just south of the city. These houses were special, each painted a pale pastel – pale green, blue, yellow, peach and, theirs, the last in the row, dove grey. The sea was so close, waves practically lapped at the gates. All summer long, day-trippers could be heard marvelling, 'Imagine living here,' and that evening Ali missed it.

She'd swung her bike through their gate and practically collided with Miles who was trooping barefoot down the path in just swimming shorts with a threadbare maroon towel slung over his broad tanned shoulders.

'Hey!' His greeting was warm and ever-so-slightly tinged with a vagueness that had become a familiar aspect of his speech. You wouldn't notice if you didn't know him; if Miles's voice had not been the soundtrack to your life, you wouldn't hear it. Ali heard it and had to suppress a flinch every time. He hugged her and then, gripping her shoulders lightly, stooped to her level, smiling, seeking her smile in return. Ali recognised this for what it was: a stalling tactic.

Miles was about fifty-seven at the time and had been diagnosed eighteen months before. In that time, he had become adept at fudging the lapses and gaps in his memory. His acting days had come back to help him play his final part: himself. She smiled back. His were the same wide, hooded brown eyes that she possessed.

'My pal.' He grinned. That'll do, Ali'd thought. He knows my name – it's just not coming this second. He'd always called her 'pal' or 'Ali Pally'. 'Coming for a dip?'

'Yep, hang on, I'll grab a towel.' Ali hopped off the bike and leaned it across the gate to keep Miles from continuing on to the water. It wasn't necessary, just a precaution. Miles had a companion for when Mini was out working, Dominique, and she was probably just inside.

Ali started back up the path, spying Dom waving at the bay

window to the right of the front door. Ali waved back and headed up the stone steps and into the hall. The evening sun was still streaming into the garden at the back of the house onto which Mini had added the light-filled glass cube mandatory in all south Dublin homes of the wealthy, but Ali preferred the rest of the house, which had mostly retained its unruly, slightly wonky floorboards and mildly maritime mood.

As a kid, crouched at the base of the large bay windows on either side of the front door, you couldn't even see the front garden or the narrow road in front of the house, and Ali had pretended to steer the house over choppy seas to the tongue of land across the bay. On this evening, Ali had crouched in the fading glow of the hall, rooting through the trunk by the foot of the stairs. She'd grabbed a rough, cardboardy towel, pulled her jersey dress – under which she wore her togs – off over her head and hung it on the end of the banisters. She kicked off her trainers and headed back out the door towards the sea and sky.

She and Miles had swum a lazy, companionable breaststroke out to the far buoy and back. It was amazing that Miles still seemed so confident in the water. He no longer drove or cooked, he couldn't deal with the Sky box at all, he asked the same questions over and over, but every day of the year he still planted his feet firmly on a smooth flat rock that Ali – and the others on the terrace – called Miles's Rock. He paused to absorb the moment, raised his arms to make a V, bent his knees and bowed his head.

Ali didn't like to wonder about how frightened he really must be. What happened when everything became unmoored inside your head? What did it feel like to scrabble after your thoughts and memories as they fled in every direction? And the harder you tried to grasp it, the harder it was to hold on to your life. It was so unfair. When Miles dove in to the sea he seemed at home, for a while at least.

Ali told him about the new job and Miles even fetched up some stories from his theatre years, when he'd acted with people who'd gone on to be the biggest names in Ireland's entertainment industry. He knew one of the older actors on *Durty Aul' Town*, and though he didn't get his name, he did remember a funny story about how, when they were young, the guy had been in a show and had stolen the toaster and kettle from the props department every night to bring to his bedsit and then brought them back into work every morning.

After the swim, they'd gone in to eat and then Ali buzzed home, leaving Miles safe with Dom until Mini got back. It was a perfect night. Nothing had happened, as such, but those were the good days, as Ali learned later. The days we ignore will be some of our happiest, Ali had realised, since life had become considerably more eventful and more painful. She hated thinking about that day for a whole host of thorny reasons. Revisiting it was like plunging a hand into brambles. She felt bad for being impatient with Miles's searching for words, getting names wrong as they chatted, for not staying and helping him to bed, for being too scared to deal with the reality of their situation, for leaving it to Dom. For the fact that they had Dom in the first place. She should've moved home and been the one to take care of Miles. But trying to sort through the regrets was pointless. Ali emerged from the memory, swallowing hard to combat the tears that threatened.

Good things, Ali, think of good things. She picked up her phone to check on her still-growing following. As she flicked over the notifications, each little heart and new follower felt like a little hit of joy pulling her back to the present and easing the ache inside.

'Ali!' Kate flung open the door of the prefab. 'You dark horse, or should I say broodmare!' She leapt over, her long brown curls bouncing, to give Ali a hug and a kiss. Then she flung herself into the neighbouring chair. 'I cannot believe you told Instagram before you told me. Well, actually, maybe I can.' She giggled. 'How many followers are you on now?'

Ali, grinning, handed over her phone.

'Oh you fucking betch.' Kate's green eyes widened. Her lashes were so long Ali could practically hear them rustling when she blinked. 'This is deadly. I am so glad you called. I've picked up so much working at Keane Eye and with launching @ShreddingForTheWedding. First things first, we need to brand this fucker. I hope you don't mind me saying, the pregnancy announcement was a bit haphazard.'

Ali nodded regretfully as Kate carried on sternly. 'There's no more room for sloppiness. Marian Keane's first rule of branding is don't play in someone else's backyard. This pregnancy journey has to stand out and be uniquely yours. Any thoughts on a hashtag? You need something catchy. And maybe change your handle to reflect the new direction your Insta's taking – at work we always advise clients to do that.

'Well,' Ali consulted her notes from the weekend, 'Shelly used #ShellysBelly during her first pregnancy. It's pretty good – sounds kind of cute and cosy, relatable. I was thinking Ali's Pally? Or Ali's Little Pally?'

'Booze to Bump?' Kate offered, winking. 'God, no drinking for nine months. And a baby at the end. It's mad, isn't it? I didn't even know you were seeing anyone.'

'Well, it was just a hook-up.' Ali was uncomfortable – it was the first time she'd had to lie directly to someone. 'Nothing goes with "Ali",' she moaned, to change the subject.

'Muhammad Ali? Momma Ali? Would anyone get the reference?' Kate wondered. 'Does the reference even make any sense?'

'Ali or Nothing? Ali Baba and the Forty Thieves? I'm just typing random words now.'

'Wait! Ali Baba. Ali's Baba! It's perfect. #AlisBaba! Ali's Baba and the 40 Weeks.' Kate clapped her hands.

'Yesss.' Ali deleted the dross and retitled the doc 'Ali's Baba'.

'Nailed it.' Kate grinned. 'So have you told your mum?'

'Eh no, she's very busy with work so I might leave it a while.' Ali tried to look busy, flicking through the open tabs on her browser.

'God, speaking of: what are you going to do about work? It's just so massive!'

Ali ignored her and pulled up the article on branding she'd bookmarked on *Medium*. Turning the screen towards Kate she said, 'This says lead with the story not the product.'

Kate nodded sagely, once more invoking her boss. 'Marian says "define your narrative". It's so important. Are you bravely going it alone? Were you "trying"? Or are you going to come clean about the hook-up? It's super relatable. Plus what's your aesthetic and tone gonna be?'

'I actually put together a Pinterest board last night, hang on.'

Ali handed the phone to Kate and she examined the various Insta-posts Ali had pulled together. 'There seem to be two kinds of preggers bitch on the 'gram,' Ali explained. 'The yummy-perfect-elaborately-staged-bump-update-shots-mummy or the more warts-and-all here's-my-pregnancy-acne vibe.'

'No offence, but I'd say you're slightly more the pregnancy-acne gal,' Kate said.

'Thanks.' Ali grinned. 'I think I'm going to go with visual perfection with occasional revelations about slight discomfort or giggling references to getting "chub rub" and eating "all the doughnuts" for relatability purposes.'

'Some well-placed "brave admission" of anxiety or something like that would also be a good shout down the line,' added Kate.

Ali added 'brave admission' to the schedule. Just then she heard the unmistakable approach of Stephan outside the prefab.

'Ali? Ali!' Stephan was roaring. 'You, where the fuck is my PA?' She could see him through the window shouting at Jay Darcy, one of the biggest radio presenters in the station, clearly not recognising him – or not caring.

'Shit.' Ali scrambled to put away her stuff. 'I have to get out there. WhatsApp later?'

'Yep, I'll slip out in five – don't worry.' Kate threw a couple of air kisses her way and hung back so as not to be spotted as Ali headed out the door.

'Ah, there you are.' Stephan was red from the raging. 'You realise you are holding up an entire crew and cast right now?'

'I'm sorry. I was on break and then I lost track of time.'

'Oh yeah, shitting out another spec script for Terry, were you?'

'No and eww.' Ali could feel colour rush into her cheeks. She hadn't asked Terry to keep quiet about her writing but she definitely didn't think he'd tell Stephan.

'Don't be cheeky, young one.' Stephan stepped close to her. 'You're on your last chance here. You swapped shifts with Ruairí last week without a word to me, which is not part of procedure. I am trying to bring dramatic, timely and relevant stories into the homes of middle fucking Ireland. Every day I walk in here and I elevate the medium. Do you think that's easy? With fuck-all budget and pissy little wans like you fucking around taking breaks and getting ideas above your station?'

A huge chunk of the cast and crew were standing outside Bernie's Bets, one of the fake shopfronts, watching her public humiliation. Of course, Seamus was there doing a Sympathetic Head Tilt. Ugh. Stephan was walking back to the set, already having moved on – that was how little Ali meant around here. It was just one of many dressing downs he'd likely dispense throughout the afternoon. No one ever stood up to him because he was such a lunatic. He had no qualms about firing people on the spot and right now, thinking of her growing following and the offers of sponcon and partnerships rolling into her inbox, Ali felt reckless.

'Stephan?' she called after him quietly.

He turned, looking peeved. 'Still intent on delaying us, Ms Jones?' he sneered.

'Sorry for holding up the "art",' Ali replied. 'I just wanted to know were you always such a prick, or is it just since you can't get your dick hard anymore?'

Gasps and stifled giggles rippled through the assembled cast and crew and Ali smiled sweetly at Stephan, who stormed over to Ruairí.

'Call security, get this lying little bitch out of here.'

Ruairí hurried off, looking stunned.

'Excuse me, Stephan?' She was done now, might as well enjoy it. 'Helloo-oo? This lying little bitch still has a few things of yours.' She delved into her pack and began tossing his keto snacks and various meds towards him. 'Although I don't know why anyone would need Viagra at work.' She shrugged innocently and chucked the pack straight at him just as security arrived to manhandle her off the lot.

That was fun, she thought. Probably the most satisfying moment of my life. And she owed it all to Insta!

12

Ali settled herself on the bus into town, still glowing from the showdown with Stephan. Who'd have thought she'd leave work on the day of being fired feeling so invigorated? It was still too early to head into Grogan's to meet Tinder Sam but maybe she'd browse the shops. Though easy on the spending, she thought, at least until the first Insta-deal came through. She checked her balance. Hmmm, maybe I should've looked at this before calling Stephan a floppy-dicked prick? A little over a grand. She'd just paid rent so at least that was sorted. It'd be OK – she thought of the money she'd get for the folic acid post she'd accepted that morning. €500 to tell her now nearly twenty thousand followers how much she loved Follan's Folic Acid!

She plugged in her earphones and brought up Shelly's Insta-story. A nice little distraction was in order. Never mind telling strangers about supplements, she had no clear plan of what she'd be telling Tinder Sam later, and a little holiday in Shelly's banal, beige world was always oddly comforting.

Shelly was on a holiday of her own, apparently, in a plush hotel room overlooking the ocean, giving a spectacularly dull tour of the various seaweed shampoos and volcanic body scrubs.

'If only all Mondays could be like this. Mr Devine and I have decided to treat ourselves to a little impromptu staycation in the gorge Ballinahagh House. Ballinahagh House boasts beautiful sea views, world-class restaurant The Eden Bush and also has bar food available in the family-friendly Cockles and Mussels lounge ...'

Ugh, the plugging is just too much sometimes – she sounds like she's reading straight from the press release, thought Ali, skipping forward a couple of Stories. Now Shelly was on the balcony zooming in on a distant figure strolling down at the water's edge and talking some nauseating shite about her gorgeous husband.

'Fucking hell, we get it, he's a ride – just put it away,' murmured Ali, forgetting she was on the bus. The older woman beside her scowled at her and Ali laughed. 'Soz, but she never stops going on about him and, like, he's daytime-TV hot at most!'

The cranky woman turned back to the window and Ali resumed her Stories. The next one showed a selfie with the distant Dan Devine in the background, captioned 'my heart'. I'm actually gonna vom in my mouth now, thought Ali. Why is he all the way over there if you're so in love?

Suddenly it occurred to her, perhaps for the first time ever, that these were real people. Inside her phone they all seemed so distant and abstract. She flicked back to the selfie with the tiny figure in the background turned away. Shelly was radiant as per usual: her dark hair was twisted into an artfully careless side plait; her make-up was subtle – her big blue eyes, high cheekbones and full lips didn't need much help. But peering closer, was there a hint of tension around the mouth? And she looked a little wan. Trouble in the beige kingdom? wondered Ali, who couldn't help but feel a dark, cruel little shiver of pleasure at the prospect. Stop it, Ali, she admonished herself. There's a word for that – schadenfreude. Or just plain old bitch. Ali put away the phone, pulled herself up and headed to the front of the bus – her stop was next. She had two hours to figure out what to do with Tinder Sam.

❖

Shelly was frantic as she dashed around her huge suite with its wrap-around balcony overlooking a desolate beach. She consulted the list Amy had sent her. The bathroom-products tour was done and the various necessary details regarding Ballinahagh House. Amy had the dinner pics taken care of – the hotel publicist had sent shots of the food directly to Amy to caption and post while they were eating. Dan had huffed his way through many a free high-end dining experience because Shelly had to take a few snaps for her channels, and Shelly needed to keep him sweet before dropping the baby bomb. He'd been pretty wary of the trip when she'd proposed it in bed on Friday night.

'I'd rather pay for a nice hotel and it just be us, babe. All this play-acting for the 'gram – it's embarrassing.' He'd been in a more reasonable mood than the day before and she didn't detect a derisive tone, rather the tone of someone a bit worn out.

'I promise it's just going to be us,' she'd said, moving closer to nuzzle his neck the way he liked. She and Amy had engineered every last detail so that, bar a few teeny bits of housekeeping, Shelly could be totally focused on Dan while Amy did the Insta-updating remotely. Though when she thought of all the trouble they were going to just to keep Dan sweet, she felt irritated. Lots of people would enjoy this kind of thing but Dan seemed unwilling to either enjoy it or accept that it was work.

The phone buzzed on the marble-topped table beside the enormous bed. Amy on the WhatsApp reminding her of the dress she needed to plug for the #DateNightOutfit pic. She didn't want to give Dan any ammo about her being glued to Insta so her plan was to take the picture now, before they went for their couples massage, and save it in Drafts, then post it discreetly later (7.30 p.m. according to Amy's schedule). She checked the time. Dan had been gone for forty minutes, which meant he'd be back any second. Better hustle.

She flipped open the top of her weekend bag – the source of the first fight of the trip (if you didn't count Dan complaining about coming in the first place, which Shelly chose not to). The bags were from Louis Vuitton and they'd had to do a couple of pictures with them before leaving to drive the forty-five minutes to Ballinahagh House. Dan had erupted in front of Amy, which was rare for him.

'I'm not posing with this man-bag,' he'd said scathingly. Amy looked unfazed but Shelly felt uneasy. Dan sounded kind of homophobic the way he was saying man-bag – it was mortifying.

'Don't then,' snapped Shelly. They quickly did some shots with Shelly that Amy would upload later.

'I'll sort the man-bag thing,' muttered Amy. 'Don't worry.'

Shelly had said goodbye to Georgie, who was staying with Marni until Shelly's mum came to collect her in an hour or so. She could see Amy discreetly filming the farewell and Shelly cringed a little. What kind of life had she opted into?

They'd got into the car – one they didn't pay for: it was #gifted by the car company, not that Dan would ever complain about that. He'd been excited the day they went to pick it out a year before. They'd probably be getting another model in a couple of months. Shelly buckled up as Dan chose some obnoxious throbbing bass music for the drive. No 'what would you like to listen to?' Nothing. Shelly had waved to Georgie out the window and felt a stab of guilt.

She loved her daughter, but for some reason she was forever stuck in a loop of guilty feelings about her. Just like right now. She felt happy to be getting a little break and a chance to spend time with Dan, but then she felt bad about being happy at getting a break away from her darling girl. It was exhausting. Did other mums feel this? She didn't really know the yummy Insta-mums like Hazel well enough to ask them, and Plum only had her stepkids who she only saw on weekends for comparison. Also, she was keenly aware of the role Georgie played in the appeal of SHELLY the brand. Was it exploitative to feature her on the various SHELLY platforms? Especially when she was such a terrible mother?

'All mothers think they're terrible mothers,' her own had advised when Shelly sought reassurance, but it didn't take away the wretched feeling that seemed to haunt her every interaction with Georgie. Sandra thought she was too hard on herself. She'd come with her to the doctor and held the tiny Georgie, just a few months old, while Shelly went in and tried to explain the bottomless fear that seemed to engulf her whenever she was alone with the baby.

After, when her Instagram began to take off, Sandra was encouraging but still worried about her. 'You don't have to be the perfect mother,' Sandra had reminded her as Shelly posed with the baby for a picture. 'Just be present, that's all I was.'

Sandra couldn't know that even that made Shelly feel bad. She worried constantly that she was most present for her daughter when it was for Instagram. She felt fraudulent, the captions, now mostly penned by Amy, braying about how much she adored motherhood felt like a terrible lie.

Now she idly picked up her phone to see that Amy had already posted the video of her saying goodbye to Georgie to the Shelly Insta-account.

Need to squeeze in every last hug – gonna miss my girl so much while we're away basking in 5-star luxury in @ BallinahaghHouse.

Jesus. And now she was bringing another baby into this bizarre pantomime. Speaking of which, she needed to get this #DateNightOutfit snapped before Dan returned and she'd have to hide the phone.

Date night and I am loving my outfit from @oliviascloset. Feeling so blessed to be sharing this rollercoaster adventure of a life with the @DivineDanDevine. The last few years have been such a joy, with the arrival of @BabyGeorgie and the launch of my footwear line, writing my first lifestyle book INSPO FOR EVERY DAY and, of course, by my side through every incredible achievement was my husband. We've snuck away for a couple of loved-up days in the tranquil surrounds of @BallinahaghHouse.#love#family#datenight#DateNightOOTD #DateNightOutfit #irishinfluencer #irishmama #mumfluencer #secondhoneymoon #WinterBreak

Shelly checked the pic over one last time. She wasn't as good as Amy at FaceFix. She erased a spot on her chin – presumably soon to be joined by many more, the bloody joys of pregnancy acne – and shaved a few centimetres off her waist. The dress was actually gorgeous, lilac, which suited her dark hair, and kind of twenties style. It was short, heavily beaded and plunged low in front, which was working nicely with the early pregnancy boob job she was currently enjoying – pity they were so sore to the touch. Dan would surely want some action tonight but the thought of anyone coming near her in her current state was deeply unappealing. Still, wearing this flirty little dress, showering Dan with all the attention and having sex would definitely set the scene for Baby Bomb.

Did other people have to work this hard with their husbands? It hadn't been so hard at the beginning. They'd travelled and stayed in glamorous hotels and partied with their friends, though the group had started to shift and drift, as was the way with these things. And Dan had been looser then – old Dan would definitely not have been uptight about a few pictures on the internet. Though old Shelly had been very different too. Old Shelly probably wouldn't have done anything Dan didn't a hundred per cent approve of. So maybe that's what happened. She changed and he couldn't deal with it.

Yep, relationships were hard work – but what if only one person was trying?

Shelly gave the retouched pic a final filter to bring up the highlights and give the whole thing that all-important glow of perfection. She regarded the girl in the picture, who was now a few times removed from the woman sitting in a borrowed dress in all-the-strings-attached luxury waiting for a man she used to adore unquestioningly.

She hit Save in Drafts, ready for later, and then quickly took the dress off. The weight of it slipping to the floor was oddly satisfying – here was something substantial in this invented world of hers. Costume change. She pulled on the bathrobe and put her hair up into a topknot. She slicked a little serum over her make-up to give her a fresh-faced no-make-up-but-still-frankly-perfect look – another minor deception from Amy's arsenal of tricks – and turned the camera on.

'Shell-Belles! We are just basking in this gorgeous reprieve from the Georgie-juggle – you know what I mean, mamas! We love them but sometimes you just need some mummy–daddy time.' She winked. 'We're just about to hit the spa to get some majorly needed chillaxation in, if Dan Devine would ever get a move on!' She raised her voice as if trying to be heard by some nearby pesky husband. As if they had a playful, easy relationship. She posted the Story then did several Boomerang takes to get the exactly right, perfectly adorable eye-rolling one, over which she typed:

What is it with men taking AGES to get ready? And they think WE'RE the bad ones!

Check. Filter. Share.

Great! With the Dan and Shelly Show done, she was now ready to spend time in her actual marriage.

Shelly stashed the phone, filled the bathroom sink and began to take off the sticky serum and her layers upon layers of make-up. Out of nowhere the tears began. I can't be crying. Shelly pressed her manicured fingers to her cheeks, automatically trying to suppress the swell of sadness, dread and exhaustion – then she remembered that she didn't need to be on camera for the rest of the night so red puffy eyes didn't matter.

She sank to the edge of the bath and gave in to the tears. The relief was profound. She didn't quite allow the sobs that were threatening to boil over – that just wasn't her style and she needed to keep an ear out for Dan, who'd be back any minute. He'd notice her blotchy face. Shelly had never been a subtle crier and he'd be grumpy that she was in one of her 'moods' – not that he'd even acknowledge it. She'd bet her life on him not so much as asking if she was alright. A little thought wormed its way in. Do I even like him anymore?

Shelly squeezed her eyes shut, attempting to dodge the question even though it was coming from within. A small part of her was starting to admit the answer to this was probably not. But life felt like it was steamrolling ahead and any attempts to change course or dismantle what she'd created – Shelly's Perfect Life – seemed impossible. Instead she sat having her very contained, economical cry and then washed her face as soon as she heard Dan come in.

13

Ali stood in the side passageway of Grogan's and peered round the door into the pub. Tinder Sam was there sitting in front of a pint surrounded by the weary Monday-night crowd. Seeing the pint made Ali want a pint. Damn this fake pregnancy, she thought, slinking back into the passageway to stall the inevitable awkwardness for a few more minutes. It was really going to make things tricky. What else was she not supposed to be doing? She'd have to do a Google deep dive at some point. In the meantime, what the actual fuck was she going to say to Tinder Sam?

For the last few days, she'd only had to agree with people thinking she was pregnant, like Kate and the PRs who'd been inundating her. Except for the drunk Insta-post – which happened in a blackout and therefore, according to Ali's Rules for

Life, didn't count – she hadn't had to launch the info on anyone yet, especially someone who was presumably going to be very unhappy about it.

She'd wasted the bus journey scrolling the Dublin Insta-mums' pages, stealing their pregnancy memes to repackage for her own use later – after all, she'd no idea what kinda shite pregnant people would relate to – so she still didn't have an opener prepped for Tinder Sam. As post-work punters squeezed past her into the pub to get in from the cold, Ali tried a few opening gambits on for size in her head.

How about: 'Hey, Tinder Sam! What's your last name?' Jaysus.

Or 'Tinder Sam, will you father an imaginary baby with me so I can score some free swag and rack up those sweet, sweet likes? I'll give you any of the freebie make-up products that match your skin tone!'

Maybe say as little as possible, thought Ali, or just back out right now.

The backing out did seem like the most sensible thing to do. What if he freaked? Or didn't believe her? The problem was that Ali kind of liked the excuse this gave her to see him again. She'd liked him. If it hadn't been for the *Love Actually* thing and ruining his bed, she probably would've texted him back. He was a ride. Ali was just leaning forward to sneak another look at him when a huge figure barrelled round the door and straight into her.

'Fuck.' Ali was flattened on the sticky floor of Grogan's side passage, arguably the most vom-anointed stretch of ground in Dublin. Tinder Sam's stricken face was peering down at her.

Well, that was the opening gambit taken care of.

'Ali! Oh my god. Are you OK? Jesus, I didn't see you. I'm so sorry.' He pulled her to her feet and then, leaning close, whispered, 'Should we go to the hospital? What do you do if you have a fall? Oh god, I can't believe I did this.' Tinder Sam looked ashen and Ali felt a wave of sympathy. Poor guy. First he hears he's got a fake baby on the way, now he thinks he's hurt the fake baby somehow.

Ali found herself thrown by the sudden proximity of Tinder Sam – she'd forgotten about that vaguely intoxicating aura of his – and took a hasty step backwards.

You can't actually get with him, she reminded herself, he's the fake-baby daddy. He'd pulled out his phone, his dark hair falling into his face as he scrolled in agitated manner. Ali felt a spark of irritation. What the hell's he checking?

Tinder Sam's concerned face looked up. 'The app says it's fine – the baby is really well cushioned in there.' He awkwardly indicated her tummy. Then a tentative smile broke on his face. 'It says the baby's, like, the size of a pea – that's so cute. We should call her Sweet Pea until we, ya know, get to meet her. I deffo think it's a girl!' It was probably the most tender moment the side passage of Grogan's had ever known – were it not for the light gaslighting taking place, of course.

And never mind gaslighting – what the hell app was he talking about? Tinder Sam took her hand and led her through to the pub, gently settling her in a booth. He seemed to be interpreting her slightly bewildered manner as a result of her fall and was looking worried, offering, 'Tea? Decaf coffee? Juice? Though juice could be a bit acidic on the tummy – is the morning sickness passing yet?'

'Eh, ehmmm, yeah, no, I'm fine. With the vomming, like. I'll have a Diet Coke.'

'Is that OK for the baby? I use Diet Coke to clean bike parts.'

'It's fine,' said Ali a little sharply – she needed him to go away for a minute so she could get a handle on the situation.

'Sure, sure.' He backed off a little. 'Hormones are a bitch, right?' He winked very cutely.

'OK, I get it, you've googled pregnancy. Well done. You're top of the I-banged-a-random-girl-and-now-I'm-supposed-to-be-the-nice-guy class. Get the drinks and we'll talk.' She shooed him away and he ambled off to the bar, grinning.

He didn't seem remotely put off by Ali's bitchiness – rather he was amused by it, which she remembered from their date. It was part of what got her back to his depressing flat in the first place. Usually guys didn't really get her. If she was being catty or bitchy, they never seemed to cop that she was joking. Tinder Sam had been entertained by her cutting remarks about a bad date unfolding at a nearby table where the guy was eating chicken wings with a knife and fork ('Well, he's got a date with his own hand later – no way she'll be boning him now,' she'd remarked).

This whole encounter was already way off-script. Tinder Sam's intense hotness was really disconcerting, for one thing. For another he was not responding to the news of her impending apparent womb-fruit with the appropriate horror and insensitivity associated with males of a certain age and demographic. He didn't seem pissed off at all – if anything he was being really nice about it. It was fucking weird.

He'd downloaded an app. This was a level of commitment that she could never have predicted. Phone storage was the scourge of millennial existence. Ali could not truthfully say that she would download a not-completely-essential app if the life of another human being depended on it. 'He made space for me on his phone' was the 2019 equivalent of 'he gave me a spare key'.

All of this would be amazing if she actually was gestating his bastard child. She remembered Kate getting pregnant off some stranger penis in college and the Stranger Penis had been utterly obnoxious when she'd informed him. From the get-go, she'd been planning to terminate the pregnancy, but he still took the conversation – that she'd had with him out of courtesy – as an opportunity to shame her and insist he couldn't be the father.

While it was hideous for Kate, it had served as inspo of sorts for Ali – she'd been counting on Tinder Sam being similarly dickish. Her plan had been for him to want nothing to do with the baby. She would say that was fine, and she would never bother him for anything in exchange for a few shots for Instagram of him posing as an adoring boyfriend and father-to-be, albeit with a fake name (she was planning on saving this element for after he agreed to the first bit).

Him actually wanting to be involved and, worse, being excited about the prospect was, frankly, scuppering her. She'd been intending to blackmail him into participating, therefore retaining control over the plan. Him playing an active and willing part just seemed dangerous. She really needed to keep him at arm's length, she thought, watching him make his way back to the table, especially given how hot he was.

As he settled himself across from her, Ali delivered a silent micro pep talk. Ali, she sternly told herself, get the fuck over it, this is business. Stop looking at his shoulders and very, very nice arms, and smile and nice face.

'So …' Tinder Sam was smiling across at her. 'Can you believe the due date? I mean, crazy or what?'

Ali blanched. 'I have to go. For a minute.' She stood up abruptly, grabbing her bag and knocking over a stool in the process. 'I need some air. Stay here. Don't come after me,' she said, sounding way more bonkers than she'd intended.

He held up his hands as if to say 'who – me?'

Ali hurried outside to the cobbled street that was already beginning to fill with people clustered around the heaters, smoking and drinking pints. Liv was not the ideal person to be burdening with this stuff, she thought, but there was absolutely no one else.

She pulled up WhatsApp and embarked on a garbled voicenote: 'Liv, he fucking knows the due date. I don't even know the due date. He's into it, which is weird. It's weird, right? And even worse he's hot, way hotter than I remember. This was not the plan.'

Anxiously, Ali sent the voicenote and stood watching as the tick went blue and she pictured Liv listening in the library – at this time she was usually working late in college – shaking her head and rolling her eyes.

Ali felt jangly all of a sudden. This was advanced-level lying, way bigger than a caption on Instagram. She was basically lying directly into Tinder Sam's face and it didn't feel good. Liv's response appeared in the WhatsApp thread; Ali hit Play and put the phone up to her ear.

'The due date, wahey, that's some advanced mathsing out of Tinder Sam – he could play a brilliant but tortured mathematician who exclusively communicates ideas by writing on window panes and falls for Jennifer Connelly. Tangent, but I for one am worried about Jennifer. She's starring in the new *Top Gun* sequel, it seems like a cry for help ...' Ali laughed in spite of her mounting anxiety – that was the most Liv response ever. The voicenote continued. 'Anyway, TBH I'm not seeing the problem with this. It sounds like everything is going great, oh wait, except, hang on ... Isn't that a fictitious baby you're gestating there, Ali?'

Suddenly the sound went funny – Ali could hear Liv fumbling with the phone and then distant voices. Ali strained to make out what was being said.

'I got your email, Liv, and I do think you're much more engaged with this idea. It's timely and provocative. I can see it in print – if you give it the work.'

'Yeah, I'm really glad you like it. It means so much to me that you're into it ...' At this, the woman – who Ali now realised was none other than Emer 'Still Has It at Fifty' Breen – interjected.

'Liv, that's not what this is about. You can't be doing this for the wrong reasons. Trying to win my approval will undermine the rigorous research this paper is going to require. If you're trying to impress me because of whatever shared history we may have, well, that would be perhaps an indicator that you need another adviser.'

Ali scowled – she sounded like a fucking robot. And Liv, if the impassioned 'No, I'm not even thinking about us at all, I swear' was anything to go by, was still firmly in the throes of Emer-mania.

The voicenote ended there. Poor Liv. Emer had been Liv's first serious relationship, though Ali had wondered if it was all a bit too much on Emer's terms. Liv had been touchy any time Ali had suggested this and, given Ali's track record with guys, she didn't exactly have much to offer in terms of advice. This was probably the first 'second date' she'd had in a year and, obviously, certain elements of the encounter would probably preclude it from being considered a bona fide date. At this, Ali's focus snapped back to the situation at hand.

She flicked into the Insta app and noted her following had swelled by another few hundred. In her notifications she spotted that she'd been included on a list of Hot New Mamas-to-Be to Follow on Instagram from Notions.ie. This thing was getting bigger, whatever about what telling Tinder Sam might mean. The fact was she was in now. Plus, given her performance on set today, she was relying on Insta for a lot more than a few freebies now – she needed this to pay off. A few deep breaths and Ali headed back in to Tinder Sam.

14

'Oh my god, Shelly! I love you!'

Shelly looked up to see a girl, about twenty-something, phone-in-hand, standing by their table.

'I am fully wearing the Shelly Contour Palette right now.' She leaned further in to the table, turning her head to better display her expertly applied make-up and Dan, who'd been tucking into a huge steak, dropped his cutlery with a pointed clatter and folded his arms.

'I have your book too, I love it, read it every night. And I'm wearing the Shelly Corn Protectors right now!'

At this Dan snorted and Shelly winced. She knew she'd been right not to tell him about that particular brand collaboration. It was a couple of years ago, just before Amy had come on board and devised clearer guidelines for the company.

Shelly smiled. 'I'm so thrilled to hear you like, well, everything. Your contouring is fab.' She was uneasy – it made her realise how little she was ever out with Dan anymore. She hadn't had to do a meet-the-fans moment in front of him in a long time and it made her extremely self-conscious. Also, she was petrified this random gushing girl would ask him something related to his Instagram which, while he was aware of its existence, was a serious sore spot.

Amy had been adamant about setting it up, but Dan had refused to so much as engage in a debate about it. The argument had seemed to be at something of an impasse until Amy (without Shelly's permission) emailed Dan a twelve-month profit projection of @DivineDanDevine's potential earnings and he grudgingly acquiesced. His participation was minimal – brands were happy to be associated with Shelly in any way, and they rarely minded that Dan wouldn't talk about the brands in Stories and, for the most part, just posed in the distance with whatever product was writing the cheque. As part of the agreement, Shelly would usually give them a mention too to sweeten the deal. Between them, the Devine family had virtually every demographic in the market covered.

'Your dress is gorge – where's it from?' The girl's brow furrowed slightly. 'You haven't posted it yet, have you?' She was rapidly tapping on the phone, apparently checking her Insta even while Shelly was sitting right there.

'Ah no, thanks for reminding me – I must pop the date-night outfit up.' Shelly smiled.

'Oh, it's date night, is it?' Dan's tone was unmistakably snarky but the girl didn't seem to notice.

She turned to him. 'Oh my gawd, your poem on Valentine's Day. I died. Died. I sent it to my fella and was, like, See – this is a Valentine's Day post!'

'Right.' Dan's jaw was set and Shelly tensed.

'Well, if you don't mind, we're trying to squeeze in a little bit of us-time here …' Shelly was careful to keep her tone light – the followers could quickly turn nasty if they sensed you were trying to move them on.

'Of course, your mum's minding Georgie for the night,' she said, still apparently not getting the hint.

'Mm-hmm.' Shelly nodded. Dan had resumed eating. Loudly. Shelly knew how to get rid of her. 'Will we do a selfie?'

The girl's face lit up. 'Yes!'

Dan's eyes bore into her as she leaned her head in to the girl's and smiled for the camera.

'OK, well, it was—' Shelly began wrapping up the encounter but the girl clearly had other plans.

'Do you not want one for your feed?'

'Ehhh … OK.' Shelly took out her phone and snapped a quick shot of the two of them.

'I wasn't ready! Go again.'

Shelly shot Dan a pleading look. 'I'm sorry,' she mouthed but Dan just kept chewing furiously. Shelly took another pic, which the girl peered at.

'Can you just tidy up my jaw a bit? And just take, like, an inch off my arm there.' Shelly paused and the girl looked impatient. 'In FaceFix, like – here, let me do it, it won't take a sec.' She grabbed the phone and quickly tweaked the image. 'There, now you'll tag me, won't you? I'm @KellysKlobber – I'm a fashion blogger too!'

'Oh, amazing, I must check out your blog. It's been so nice to meet you.' Shelly was firm, giving her two air kisses. 'Have a lovely night, Kelly.' She squeezed her wrist and managed to give her a gentle push away from the table. Kelly, looking delighted with the encounter, wandered back to her table, where several couples were sitting, craning their necks to look at Shelly and Dan. Shelly gave a little wave and Dan laughed.

'The queen waves at her loyal subjects.' He shoved the last bite of steak into his mouth sullenly.

Shelly stiffened. She wanted to tell him to cop on and stop being so over the top. However, she was keenly aware that they were on show here in the dining room, surrounded by couples chatting and enjoying the view over the ocean and the cliffs to the right of the bay. There was a winding path up along those cliffs where Shelly planned to suggest a walk tomorrow. She'd tell him about the new baby there. It would be private but not so private that Dan could go completely apeshit either. Unless he went all out and gave her a push. Shelly nearly laughed out loud and Dan spotted her smiling.

'What?'

Seeing an opportunity, Shelly decided to try to get him back in a good mood. 'Oh, just the corn protectors – I'd completely forgotten about that collab. What was I thinking?'

She could see Dan relax slightly. He laughed and then they were both laughing and it felt really good. Shelly felt a pang for the early days. He leaned forward. 'That girl, though, Kelly's Klobber!' This started them off again and the tension seemed to ease.

Dan stood. 'I'm just going to the jacks – wanna see about dessert menus?' Shelly nodded and watched him head off. She asked a passing waiter for the dessert menu and pulled out her phone to post the outfit pic from earlier. She kept one eye out for Dan as she searched the drafts and selected the post – she didn't want him catching her on the phone. The waiter dropped off the menus and started clearing the plates just as she hit Share. She stashed her phone back in her bag as Dan came back into the dining room. She smiled brightly at him as he sat down.

'So, I thought we might go for a walk tomorrow?'

'Oh yeah?' Dan was scanning the dessert menu, distracted.

'Yeah, just to get some time together. Alone. Just us.'

Dan had put down the menu and was looking at her with mild amusement. The look could be interpreted as mocking, but maybe that was part of their problem as a couple – their marriage had become a vicious cycle of perceived slights, defensiveness and no real communication.

'I am aware of the meaning of "alone",' said Dan. 'I'm not the one who struggles with that concept.' He glanced down at Shelly's right hand that was empty, conspicuously so. No phone at dinner. Dan's phone was out on the table between them, but his phone hadn't become some symbol of their dysfunction. Shelly's, on the other hand, was like a mistress – a rarely referred to, nefarious entity lingering in the marriage. It was buzzing away in her bag against her leg, purring like a loving pet. She could feel it vibrating with notifications, likes and adoring comments on her date-night outfit. Telling her she was beautiful and lucky. That her life was something to aspire to, that she and Dan were goals.

'Have I taken my phone out once?' Shelly could feel her blood rising. It was the same argument over and over, so familiar now that they didn't have to do the extended dance of accusations and recriminations to build the rage from minor hurt to all-out fury. It was as though at the end of each fight the rage did not diminish but remained coiled, ready for its next round, burning as brightly as it had the last time Shelly had shoved it away.

'You're the one struggling with this – you can't deal with my success. Have I so much as looked at my phone since we've been here?' demanded Shelly again. Then she checked herself, imagining a hundred Instagram Stories capturing a meltdown.

'Shelly, has it occurred to you that I go on about this because I care about you?' Dan was being quiet, doing his I'm-so-calm-and-reasonable Dan thing, which usually annoyed Shelly. Now, however, she really looked at him and any scathing tone was gone. He looked tired and a little sad. 'I'm not jealous of your free swag and being accosted by sycophantic twenty-year-olds over dinner. I'm worried about what all this has done to us, to Georgie, to our family. To you. It's not healthy, turning your whole life into this sideshow of perfection.'

Shelly was sitting ramrod straight, her hands gripping the sides of her chair. She felt very hot all of a sudden.

Dan looked drawn. 'I do want to salvage this.' He reached a hand across the tablecloth. 'I think we can.'

'Salvage it?' Fear gripped her – had it really gotten to this?

'I don't think I want to stay married to the two of you ... to Shelly and SHELLY.' Dan was choosing his words carefully. 'I want my daughter to be a kid for as long as possible, not playing "selfies" and saying she wants to be a YouTuber when she grows up.'

'You don't want her to be me, basically.'

'You're not even you anymore. I know you don't like to hear this but you've changed. Old you would've mocked this.' He mimed preening for a selfie. 'You playing you in some Facebook version of your perfect life is a complete waste of your talent, Shel.'

'It's Instagram – how after all this time have you not got that?'

'How after all this time have you not got that it isn't even real?' Dan flared up and Shelly glanced around nervously.

'No one's looking, Shelly. No one cares. You're just some person in their phone that they watch – believe me, you're not impacting them in any profound way.'

That stung. How had the evening gone so badly off track? They were supposed to be getting on. She was supposed to be prepping Dan for tomorrow's baby reveal. God, she sounded like one of Amy's Google Calendars. This dinner had, in fact, been labelled 'groundwork' on the schedule. And right before they'd come down to dinner, her phone had pinged with a reminder set by Amy – 'Objective: fluff Dan'. If Dan ever saw some of that stuff ... Shelly shuddered inwardly.

In the early days of SHELLY, Dan had treated it as an amusing hobby. Starting the account had been an attempt at a way out of the post-baby sadness, and he'd initially been happy that she was up and about, putting make-up on again and apparently no longer crying every day. When it started to gain traction, he was genuinely happy for her, if a little confused. He often asked her why she wasn't going after more auditions and instead spending all her time meeting with brands for partnerships and doing ads for reconstituted-ham-related products, but he hadn't been judgemental about it. Not then at least.

Shelly could feel the evening rapidly slipping out of her control – she needed to get him back onside. 'Will you share the chocolate bombe with me?' she asked tentatively. 'Please, Dan.' He knew she was pleading for more than a dessert split.

He sat back, shoulders sagging. 'It's not the time for this.' He seemed to be speaking to himself as much as to her. 'One bombe, two spoons.' He smiled over at her. 'We can talk more tomorrow.'

The table buzzed abruptly – it was Dan's phone. He glanced at it.

'The lads' WhatsApp,' he said, picking it up. 'Aidan's got some new gym idea and he's pestering everyone for money.'

Shelly watched him scroll and felt her own right hand twitching in longing – she was dying to see her own phone. Even though every post was a winner, it was still a bit like playing a game, and seeing likes and comments from other top-tier influencers gave her a nice little buzz. She was trying to get in with some of the UK influencers. That was a big pond and Amy was cooking up lots of plans for breaking in to the Insta-club over there. She noticed Dan laughing and shaking his head. 'What?'

'Oh, nothing. Just a few of the lads messing, saying you're pregnant.'

'What?' Shelly felt a nervy swoop in her stomach. How on earth?

On hearing her tone, Dan looked up, his brow furrowed. 'What's wrong? They're only messing.' He watched her face and his eyes narrowed. The silence stretched between them. 'They're messing, yeah? Shelly! What the fuck – are you?'

'Ehmmm …' Shelly bit her lip – panic was coursing through her from the pit of her stomach to the tips of her fingers. How could they know? 'What are they saying?'

Dan thrust the phone over at her.

Aidan: Whopper news @Dan. Didn't think you had it in ya (again!)

Lex: Yeah, Maire just told me. Congrats, man! Two! You're fucked now LOL. No more golf weekends.

Mark: When's Shelly due? Will you still make it to Primavera?

Dan: Shut up, you pricks. Shel's not preggers. LOL, I think I'd know.

Seeing Dan's response made Shelly feel sick. How had this happened? How'd Maire know? She barely knew Maire. Just then another response appeared in the group.

Aidan: Eh, check your wife's Insta, dude 😁

Fuck. That stopped Shelly cold. The date-night-outfit post had been in Drafts. Amy's pregnancy announcement had been in Drafts as well.

Dan's hand was outstretched, waiting for her to hand back the phone. She was frozen. He couldn't see that last message.

'Give. Me. The. Phone. And tell me what the hell they're talking about.' Dan's voice was cold and eerily calm.

Shelly couldn't find the words. 'Ehm. Will we step outside for a minute?' She tried to stall for time.

Dan reached across and seized the phone. He took a second to catch up on the last message. He looked up. 'Instagram.'

The word was like a bullet. Shelly slumped in the chair, afraid to even reach for her bag. The vibrating felt menacing all of a sudden. A sweet purring pet turned malevolent.

'What have you done?'

'I … I don't know, Dan,' Shelly said helplessly.

'Are you duffed up?'

Shelly winced and dodged the question. 'I don't know what they're talking about.'

'Well, do you wanna check?' he spat.

Shaking, Shelly grabbed her bag, pulled out her phone and brought up Instagram: The latest post had 48,000 likes, thousands of comments. Stats that would usually thrill her but right now she felt unsteady; the world was off-kilter. The pregnancy announcement was there at the top of her grid. She could feel the tears coming. Dan would never believe this had been an honest mistake. He would say it was a deliberate manipulation to strong-arm him into accepting this pregnancy. She gripped the phone hard. Should she delete it?

'Show me,' Dan commanded.

Shelly felt precarious. Delete it and he'd never see it – maybe that would make it easier to smooth it over. He wouldn't have the visual, the wording to throw at her.

'Show. Me.' Dan was losing it. Nearby diners had clearly become aware of the storm brewing at their table. To their right, a group had stilled, cutlery poised above plates, obviously straining to hear.

Shelly checked the time – nearly twenty minutes since she'd posted the pic. If it hadn't been reported there'd be time to delete it. It wasn't the perfect solution but it would at least prove to Dan that she hadn't done it on purpose. She quickly googled her name. The top six results were reporting her pregnancy announcement. The will to manage the situation ebbed away instantly – it was futile. She flicked back to the pregnancy announcement post and handed the phone to Dan, keeping her eyes down.

'Dan.' Her voice was small and beseeching. Tears were gathering on her lashes, ready to tumble forth. 'It was an accident.'

Dan pushed his chair back from the table in a rush of fury. He pulled the phone closer to his face, disbelieving. The dining room was now watching with open fascination. Shelly could see Kelly's Klobber out of the corner of her eye. Was that a phone in her hand?

'Which part was an accident, Shelly? Huh? Which part exactly was an accident? The part where you fucking got up the pole against my wishes? Or the part where you completely humiliated me and told the fucking world about my baby before I knew about it?'

Shelly had nothing to say. Literally nothing. She felt sick. She gulped in air and gasped out some words. 'Please, Dan …' She covered her face.

Dan crouched down beside her chair and she felt a flash of hope, extinguished just as quickly when Dan snarled into her ear. 'I'm leaving right now, Shelly. Don't follow me. I don't want to see you, talk to you, breathe the same air as you. You can come back the day after tomorrow as planned. I'll talk to the solicitor.'

He stood, chucked her phone on to the table and walked out of the dining room, a sea of dropped jaws in his wake.

Shelly gathered her things. She needed to move. Now. She hurried through the dining room, keeping her eyes down. Once she made it to the hall, she swerved right and broke into a run. She dialled Amy but no answer. She reached the ladies, which was mercifully empty, and barricaded herself in a cubicle. She whispered a frantic voicenote explaining what had happened and the scene in the dining room and sent it off to Amy.

A couple of agonising minutes passed before Amy rang.

'We're going to be fine, Shel.' Hearing her assistant's voice was incredibly soothing. 'Where are you right now?'

'In the ladies beside the dining room.'

'OK, first things first: containment. Time is of the essence. We can't have anyone getting on to Notions.ie, stirring up shit. You stay right where you are. I need to make some calls. Do not leave the bathroom – lock the door and don't come out no matter what happens. I will call you right back.'

Amy hung up and Shelly sat down on the lid of the toilet. Flashes of Dan raging in the dining room returned, assaulting her. What did he mean 'talk to the solicitor'? He couldn't be planning on separating after one slip-up? Though it hadn't been just one slip-up exactly – more a series of unhappy days smoothed by mundane distractions like birthdays, anniversaries, dinners and TV. And the distractions had worked less and less as they had drifted apart.

The phone rang. Amy. Thank god for Amy.

'OK, I've dealt with the onlookers.'

'Do I want to know how?' ventured Shelly, sniffing and trying to calm down.

'I've spoken to management. They made an announcement, comping everyone's meal and night's stay in exchange for sensitivity in the matter.'

'Oh my god,' Shelly breathed.

'There's just one guest who was present that they couldn't locate. She must have slipped out just after you. Kelly something. Don't worry, we'll find her and neutralise her. It's not a problem. Put it out of your mind now, Shelly. You need to rest up. We need you on form tomorrow. We don't want a whiff of this detectable on your social channels. Dan will come around and when he does we want the narrative to be in place for him to step back into. The concierge told me Dan left the car park five minutes ago so you're good to go back to your room now. The night manager,

Sean, is waiting outside the ladies to escort you. Lie low, order breakfast to the room in the morning and I'll be down by 10 a.m. to get you out of there.'

Shelly hung up and went out to Sean, who smiled kindly and, without a word, brought her back to her empty room, Dan's belongings gone. She collapsed on the bed and cried hopelessly. She felt ransacked by the events of the evening. She turned off the lights and, in the dark, scrolled through the likes and comments on her bump post. The squeals of 'congrats' and 'suits you' and 'you look beautiful' soothed her like a morphine drip until she eventually fell asleep.

15

'So what are you? Some kind of pregnancy enthusiast?' Ali was watching Tinder Sam giddily inputting her details to his app, iBump, as they strolled away from Grogan's. It was after 11 p.m. and they'd been chatting for hours.

'Yep, I trawl Mumsnet like most guys do Pornhub,' Sam deadpanned. 'What? Is it really so hard to believe that I'm excited about my baby? Right, what else do we need to put in here?' He squinted at the app. 'We have your due date, obviously ... what are the chances, like?' He smiled up at her.

'Yeah ...' Ali wasn't so sure about his delight in the fact that their hypothetical baby was due on 9/11 – if anything it seemed to spell disaster. 'D'you not think that's, like, a negative? Maybe we should just move it by one day. No one'll realise.'

'But it was a huge moment in history, Ali.' Tinder Sam was apparently stunned that she wasn't considering it some kind of serendipitous timing.

Was he some creepy type who admired terrorists for their, like, tenacity? Or argued in pubs about how the Third Reich's infrastructure had been pretty solid if you just discounted all the genocide?

'It was an unimaginable tragedy,' he continued, 'but the heroism of everyday people and the way the city pulled together and all those people calling their loved ones from the planes.'

'Riiight.' Ali flashed back to the *Love Actually* poster. Evidently he was a pathological emoter. He looked like he was blinking away tears.

'Anyway, I'm not an enthusiast about random pregnancies … just this one!' Then to Ali's horror, he went in for a belly kiss.

She intercepted his bump assault, literally pushing his face away with her hand. Jesus, she was tempted to get pregnant just to get out of the awkwardness of this situation. 'Eh, it's very sensitive,' she lied.

'Are you getting stretching pains? Cramps? Has there been any discharge?' Tinder Sam's concern was sweet if a little gross. He seemed unaware that half of South William Street had just heard him question her about her discharge – a woman sitting outside the painfully hip cocktail place they were passing looked close to throwing up.

'Shhh.' Ali was giggling in spite of herself.

'What? Discharge?'

Ali, laughing, cocked her head at the disgusted woman clutching her martini.

Tinder Sam rounded on the smoking pen of the bar and spoke directly to the woman. He was a good head taller than the glass that surrounded her and the twenty or so other cocktail swillers, vaping and scrolling on their phones. Ali didn't reach the top of the partition and shrank even lower. Oh god, what was coming?

'Are you shaming my girlfriend for her vaginal discharge?'

'Oh Jesus,' muttered Ali, trying not to laugh and praying there were no Insta-mavens among the group.

As one, the assembled vapers took on the look of studied avoidance adopted by all humans when confronted with erratic behaviour of any description.

'Discharge is a perfectly normal function of a healthy vagina. We've just been conditioned by porn culture to expect vaginas to be groomed like some thoroughbred pet. Well, no more, I say. She is growing life inside her!' He pointed at Ali, who waved helplessly and pulled him away.

'OK, OK, you can drop the woke-man act,' Ali scolded.

'Their faces, though!' Tinder Sam looked delighted with himself.

'Yeah, yeah, you're great. Vaginas everywhere are applauding you for defending their right to discharge.'

'What does an applauding vagina sound like?' he asked, completely straight-faced.

Ali started to laugh and then was struck by a thought both pleasing and unnerving. She was enjoying herself. Like, really enjoying herself. She was having as much fun as if she was out pissing about with Liv – her barometer for all people, not only dates. Before Ali could delve further into the murky territory of whether or not she even could, never mind should, enjoy herself with Tinder Sam, a person she was lying to on a scale even she found troubling, he grabbed her hand and pulled her close. That smell. It was intoxicating, intoxicating enough to make her forget about *Love Actually* and the fake foetus and his abundance of feelings regarding 9/11. Tinder Sam leaned in and brushed her lips with his and then buried his face in her neck, breathing deeply.

'Fuck! You smell so good,' he whispered in her ear, sending shivers (literally shivers, like in a Danielle Steel novel) down her spine. Ali allowed herself to sink into his kiss. It was all getting out of control, she thought vaguely as a not-altogether-unpleasant feeling of vertigo swooshed through her.

'What's the deal with sexing a pregnant person?' he whispered.

Ali smiled, trying not to flinch at the P-word. 'What does your app say?'

Tinder Sam took out the phone, his cute little brow furrowed as he scrolled. He surfaced and said with a solemn look on his face, 'Pregnant women require regular vaginal servicing of a sexual nature.'

'Fucking ewww,' Ali squealed, batting him away.

'I'm sorry, Ali, it's the rules.' He advanced on her. 'To promote healthy discharge.'

'No. More. Discharge,' Ali shouted, startling several people in the vicinity and giving herself and Tinder Sam a fit of giggles that lasted all the way up to Stephen's Green.

They got a taxi and without any debate headed towards Rathmines and Tinder Sam's basement. Ali was hyper alert to the proximity of Sam – maybe it was time to drop the Tinder prefix? – and the anticipation and anxiety were mingling to produce a heady atmosphere in the back seat. Was he even aware of it? She stole a look. He was staring straight ahead, apparently lost in his own world. It was weird to think of herself as a character in someone else's life. What did Sam know about her? She was Ali: she took pictures of her food, had wavy, dirty blonde hair and brown eyes? Lived with her friend Liv. Had, at least as far as he knew, a little blueberry-sized amalgam of their two bodies growing inside her. How could he be so fine with all that?

'Are you going to stare at me all the way there?' He was still looking dead ahead but a half-smile played around his lips.

'Calm down, I'm not staring at you. You've just got stuff on your face,' Ali retorted and turned to look out the window.

They were crossing the canal, the city lights reflected in the dark water. It was so nice to really take it all in, Ali thought. Usually she was hunched over her phone looking at someone else's pic of the canal with the night sky above and enhanced by a filter. Her thought was interrupted by Sam taking her hand and, to her total shock and considerable alarm, she felt sudden tears gather. How long since she'd held someone's hand like this? Or at all. She held the cool, dry hands of her father, which was indescribably hard to do for some reason, like holding something unbearably hot. It took a lot out of her to hold Miles's hands, which is why she most often sat by him holding her phone instead.

I am lonely.

The thought disturbed Ali. So she soothed herself, turning her focus to thoughts of her growing following, and marvelled at how nice it was to hold Sam's hand. It'd make for a great post, though asking for a hand-holding pic would be the fastest way to break the moment.

'Come on … why're you not staring at me anymore?' Sam was faux whining. 'Tell me I'm pretteee!'

Ali grinned. 'That's the last thing you need.'

They pulled up outside the battered Georgian house. It looked completely different now, bathed in the First Proper Date Filter. Tinder Filter had left Ali with a distinctly grotty impression which she was now reframing as bohemian.

Once through the door, they attempted the kind of passionate, on-the-move fumble always shown on TV, which naturally ended in a painful collision with the hall table, and neither of them undressed in any significant way.

Ali looked at Sam's black skinny jeans wedged halfway down his legs and laughed. 'We'll need to surgically remove those, I'd say, c'mon.' She led the way, pulling off her jumper en route to the *Love Actually* shrine that doubled as Sam's bedroom. Sam kicked off his trainers and shuffle-hopped after her, cupping his junk.

She flopped onto the bed to enjoy the spectacle of him trying to get free of the jeans – he is so cute, she thought. At last, he kicked them clear and raised his arms in triumph. 'The boner is unleashed!' he roared.

'Well done, it's a very nice boner.' Ali grinned.

Sam pulled off his faded T-shirt and came towards her, gathering her into his arms and kissing her neck. He pulled off her top and her breath caught as he started licking her nipples through the lace of her bra. He's just so good at this, she thought as he parted her legs and started to push into her. Ali moaned but suddenly Sam stopped.

'Maybe you should keep it down,' he whispered.

'Eh, I'm not even being that loud.' Ali was testy. 'Besides I was just trying to be encouraging for you,' she added.

Sam laughed. 'Yeah, yeah,' Then his grin disappeared and he turned serious again. 'Look, it's not the neighbours or anything – it's ... eh ...' He cocked his head down towards her stomach.

'Oh for god's sake, sex is fine with a baby in you, have you literally never watched a movie? The guy always says this and it's fiiine. C'mon, do the thing you were doing.' She leaned up to nuzzle his ear.

He began to move into her once more then paused again.

'I know the geography is all fine, I know the baby isn't being tortured by some creepy game of whack-a-mole with my dick, but they can hear in there and research says development starts very early.'

'Sam! Please shut up.' Ali wrapped her arms around him and kissed him.

'Okay we can google it after, let's just be quiet, if we can.' He kissed her back.

❖

As Sam got tea on – she wished she could suggest some wine – Ali looked at the pictures on his living-room shelves and texted Liv.

Gonna stay with Tinder Sam, see you tomoro X.

The pics were of little Sam pretty much at all times surrounded by women of various ages but all united by a familial thread of similarity. Liv replied in textbook Liv-fashion.

O-kaaay. Seems weird. Bye.

Sam appeared bearing mugs and with chocolate digestives under his arm.

'Is this your harem of bitches then or what?' Ali indicated the pictures.

'Ha. Yuck. No. I have a lot of sisters. And aunts.'

'And mothers?'

Sam placed the tea on a low table made – student-cliché style – from some bricks and a pallet.

'Ah no, Mum died when I was small.'

'Oh fuck. I'm sorry for bringing it up. Shite.'

Sam laughed. 'No, don't be, I love talking about her. I was seven when she died so I remember her, but I think talking about her really helps that. We talk about her all the time – my sisters, my aunts. My dad, before you ask,' he added with a smirk, 'was never really around. I think I was two when he left. He actually lives in Dublin but we don't see each other. Or, well, we do in that really awkward Dublin way. It's not a good town to not see people. I saw him once in the queue for a gig but I'm not even sure he recognised me. But anyway, yeah, Mum – that's her in the middle one holding me – she was brilliant. She was a nurse, loved singing, was always bawling me out of it for shit I'd do! Fucking scary when she wanted to be. She actually got a clot in her brain and that was that – she was in work but she died within minutes and they couldn't save her, the fucking irony!'

Ali sat down across from Sam. 'I am so sorry that happened to you.'

'Yeah …' Sam gazed at the biscuits sadly before coyly venturing, 'How sorry?'

Ali's eyes narrowed.

'Like, would you say you're give-Sam-a-blow-job sorry for me? Or just dry-hump sorry?'

'Chancer.' Ali laughed. 'And might I add: creep. Dead-mother-card-playing sicko.'

Sam naturally looked thrilled with himself. Then added solemnly, 'It's what she would've wanted.'

Ali threw a sofa pillow at him in response. 'What are we watching so?'

Sam chucked the remote over to her. 'It's such a weird one, isn't it? The what-they-would've-wanted thing. Like, surely what they would've wanted would be not to be dead. And if that was out of the question, as it appears to be given our current biological limitations, then what they certainly wouldn't have wanted would be people carrying out meaningless traditions, like burials and funerals, in their name. I swear I heard someone say, "Get the antipasti platter – it's what she would've wanted" before my mum's funeral, and I was like, "Joan, you just want the antipasti platter. If you've got some kind of cured meat agenda here just be upfront about it and stop using my dead mother to procure your precious cold meats."'

Ali laughed and felt an unfamiliar urge to share something of her own experience. 'Yeah! I suppose I know what you mean. My dad's not well – he lives in a home – and whenever I go to visit him the nurses are always on about, "Oh, he's having a great day today," and I just want to say, "Really, Sheila? This is what you consider having a good day?" Like, how far do your standards have to plummet before you believe that lying in an adult nappy on an inflatable mattress to prevent bed-sores constitutes a good day?' Ali laughed nervously. 'Sorry, I never talk about this stuff. I never feel like people will understand. And sometimes it is just kind of funny, in a completely hopeless way.'

Sam smiled. He looked understanding but there was no sign of the dreaded head tilt. 'What's wrong with him?'

'He was diagnosed with Alzheimer's when I was younger and now, well, it's probably easier to just go through what's right with him. He's breathing – that's pretty much it,' Ali finished flatly.

Sam went over and gathered Ali in his arms. Pressed against Sam's soft T-shirt, she allowed herself a few silent tears.

'Fuck you, Sheila, you stupid bitch!' announced Sam. Ali

laughed in his arms but he didn't let go all at once. 'What'll we watch?' he asked.

'Ehm …' Ali sat up, smoothing her hair and surreptitiously wiping her face. 'I like really hideous true-crime shows.'

'OK, perfect, we're watching *Frenemies: Loyalty Turned Lethal.* You'll love it.'

Ali was impressed that Sam didn't even need to check Netflix for this totally spot-on suggestion. He was full of intriguing surprises.

16

'Don't worry, the dust has settled and none of my eyes and ears have mentioned anything.' Amy was trying to get the perfect candid of Shelly contemplating a cup of coffee, 'Shelly Blend' by Coffee Culture, but Shelly hadn't stopped fretting for the two weeks since the Dan meltdown in Ballinahagh House. She was convinced at any moment that Deborah Winters, the social diarist at Notions.ie, would twig some hint of the story on the wind and do a devastating exposé.

'The hotel definitely rounded up everyone who was there, right?' Shelly clutched her cup of vile instant coffee and struggled to look anything other than how she felt, which was queasy and anxious, amid the plush perfection of her living room. She sat in the centre of a sprawling cream-velvet couch artfully strewn with throw pillows of various shades of beige and silver.

The throw pillows were hilariously impractical; several were made of some type of high-end chainmail, while others were satin and difficult to sit on without sliding off. The tall windows, flanked by beige satin curtains, looked out on the garden, where Georgie was being read to by Marni. Lately, in an unfortunate case of toddler mispronunciation (or so Shelly hoped), Georgie was calling Marni 'Mammy'. We must make sure the next au pair's name doesn't bear any resemblance to 'mammy', 'mum' or 'mummy', thought Shelly. Then, noticing Amy hadn't answered her question about the hotel, she added impatiently, 'Well?'

Amy aimed the camera. 'What? No! No one knows. Do your laughing-to-yourself-looking-down-and-slightly-to-the-right thing.' She snapped about thirty versions of that pose. Shelly knew she was not making it easy for Amy today – she'd have some amount of work to do in post on Shelly's under-eye bags alone.

'That's not what I asked,' Shelly said in an imploring voice. 'I said did the hotel definitely get hold of everyone who was there? To explain the importance of discretion?'

'OK, let's try holding the cup with both hands and looking up to the left and laughing at something funny someone over here has said.' Amy waved in the direction of a corner of the room empty but for a large built-in TV cabinet. 'Yep, we tracked down everyone.'

Shelly obliged with the fake-laughing but still felt troubled. 'Even that Kelly girl? I saw her with her phone out.'

'Yep.' Amy was adamant, though Shelly detected a little uneasiness. However, Amy was already on to directing the next shot. 'OK, last pose, cup the coffee and close your eyes like you're really savouring it.'

Shelly obeyed and immediately wrinkled her nose. 'Ugh, it's foul.'

'Caption-wise, I think we'll go with something more along the lines of "that moment in the morning when I can enjoy some quiet contemplation and feel huge gratitude for being given the opportunity to design this incredible blend #ShellybyCoffeeCulture".' Amy smirked.

'Oh god, seriously, I'm gonna be sick. Again.' Shelly sprang from the couch and barely made it to the end table. Cutting her losses, she aimed for a vase of fake flowers. With Georgie she'd been sick for the first twelve weeks. Nine weeks down, three to go. At least none got on the carpet. Marni could clean up the flowers. That's what you get for being Georgie's new 'mammy', Shelly thought darkly.

She headed down the hall to the bathroom, feeling bad for thinking such a horrible thought. Marni should clean the flowers because minders are supposed to do a bit of housework, not as some kind of punishment for showing up and enchanting Georgie with her big Disney Princess eyes and endless time for playing unicorns and whatnot. Shelly tried to convince herself that she would love to be playing unicorns and sticking glitter to stuff all day long but she had to work – especially now that Dan was sleeping in the Seomra in the garden and their marriage appeared to be hanging in the balance.

In the bathroom, she brushed her teeth and ruminated on the weeks since their return from Ballinahagh House. She'd arrived home to an empty house and learned from her mother-in-law that Dan and Georgie had gone to stay in her in-laws' holiday home in Sligo. Shelly was bereft. She had known in her heart that things hadn't been right between them for some time, maybe even since Georgie'd been born, but she'd calmed herself with articles about marriages having fallow periods and had even begun to believe her own Instagram narrative. How could her marriage be in trouble? Sure, there was a picture of them kissing on holiday right there on the grid (never mind that picture was taken three years before and being rolled out now as 'fresh' content by Amy).

She'd obviously worked hard to save face on her social channels, keeping up with her #spon commitments and doing posts that didn't require her daughter or husband as props. Though there were only so many #metime #selfcare baths one could take to fill a feed. And with Dan's words about her 'sideshow of perfection' echoing in her head, it had started to feel weird taking a bath for some me-time while Amy sat cross-legged on the floor, taking pics, horn-rimmed glasses pushed up on top of her head, and briefing her on forthcoming collaborations and updating her on what the other mumstagrammers were bringing out next. Podcasts, online stores, lifestyle magazines à la Oprah, a range of branded DIY tools, guest 'curating' the Aldi Special Buys, and on and on. Amy was adamant that the next SHELLY project be huge and, frankly, the thoughts of it all exhausted Shelly.

Dan and Georgie had returned a week later and Shelly felt things settle into a new normal of separate beds and civility. It was not a normal that Shelly liked. She felt she hadn't had a chance to get a handle on the situation – there'd been so much on. Just yesterday Amy had brought the presentation for Q2 2019 to Shelly's dressing room during her nail appointment.

'Introducing Shelly's Grow and Glow Pregnancy Roadshow!'

'No,' Shelly had responded flatly and they'd been bickering about it ever since.

Amy hadn't seen Dan since the baby reveal had gone awry so it was easy for her to ignore that the SHELLY house of cards was dangerously close to collapsing. That very day they were about to attempt a subterfuge that went far beyond anything they'd ever tweaked in FaceFix. It was so bad Shelly felt another wave of nausea gathering pace just thinking about it. It was worse even than the time Shelly had posted a pic of a random baby she'd found on the internet when Baby Georgie was going through an unfortunate plain stretch as an infant.

'Shel?' Amy called from the other side of the door. 'The Dans are here.'

'Jesus,' Shelly muttered, giving her clammy face a quick once-over in the mirror. 'Is this too far?' she asked her reflection. They were due at the Daddy Bears' Picnic in an hour's time and were in dire need of a 'daddy'. Amy had lined up some Dan-a-likes for the Instagram coverage. Shelly felt deeply uneasy about the scheme but, as always, the SHELLY juggernaut was a law unto itself.

Amy had been emphatic. 'We cannot miss this, Shelly. I know you think you're safe up on your pristine pedestal at the top of the Insta-mummy shit pile, but, believe me, there are about a million wannabes just dying to topple you and they're not afraid to get a little dirty in the process. Ali Jones is going from strength to strength – people are loving her budding romance with that Sam guy, she's playing the whole knocked-up angle remarkably well for an amateur and her body isn't as wrecked as yours. When you two shit out these babies, she'll be bouncing back a hell of a lot quicker, so the best you've got to work with here is consistency and class. Green, Hilliard and Mason are massive – we need to show them you're bankable. And that means showing up with a daddy bear and doing your nice girl thing. This world is moving very fast, Shelly – we need to adapt to keep up. In a few months SHELLY could be considered the untouchable heritage brand of the mumstagrammer scene – the Dior to Ali's Isabel Marant – or it could be old hat. It's up to you.'

Shelly agreed to the Dan-a-likes. And now they were streaming into the house like an odd parade of smart-casual clones. Shelly followed the identical haircuts as they made a left into the living room.

There were six almost-Dans to choose from and Shelly found a mad thought stealing through her mind: I could just let Dan go and pay one of these guys by the hour forever. The convenience of the proposition was verging on tempting. She'd go on date nights not having to hide her social media updates. Bringing out the phone mid main course wouldn't set off a tsunami of sighs and clipped words for the remainder of the evening. Almost Dan wouldn't give a shit about her phone – he'd be too busy watching the clock, counting down till he could knock off and head back to his real life.

'OK, fellas, line up.' Amy was herding the men around, demanding they turn this way and that. 'We need to get a read on what you'll look like on the phone from a distance, so could everyone do that, please?' Some of the Dans were looking a bit perplexed. 'Yes, that's right,' Amy called encouragingly. 'Put your phones up to your ears. Good boys.'

'What's, eh, this gig for?' asked one of the Dans, who was using his hand to mime a phone.

'Confidential,' snapped Amy, moving down the line, turning the Dans this way and that.

Shelly hung back. She couldn't bear to be too hands-on in this humiliating process. Amy joined her.

'Chatty Dan's talking into his hand,' she remarked, arms crossed.

'I can hear you,' he huffed.

'I don't care,' Amy called back. 'He's got a shitty attitude,' she said to Shelly, making no effort to lower her voice. 'And a flat ass.'

Chatty Dan looked incensed.

'We should wrap this up,' muttered Shelly. 'I vote second from the left.'

'Yeah,' Amy agreed. 'His tan is actually a better match with yours, tonally speaking. I always thought Dan's was a bit clashy. And he's actually taking the fake phone conversation seriously.'

Indeed, this Dan had gone quite method, channelling his inner Joaquin Phoenix for the assignment and conducting a heated conversation with his wallet. He concluded with the devastating parting words, 'Well, I don't care what you think, Mum,' snapped the wallet shut flip-phone style and spun around with a flourish. 'And ... scene.'

The other Dans grudgingly applauded and Amy immediately started shouting them down. 'OK, thank you, gentlemen. We're going with James Franco here but thanks for joining us today and I'll notify you if we require a stand-in at any date in the future.'

A stand-in for a stand-in, thought Shelly ruefully. What fresh hell is this?

Of course, the way things were going with Dan it didn't seem like such a remote possibility. They'd reached something of a détente regarding the @DivineDanDevine Insta-account. Shelly and Amy would be honouring any outstanding contracts previously agreed upon and then phasing the account out altogether. The Daddy Bears' Picnic was a bit of a grey area as it wasn't strictly #sponcon, but Amy was trying to close a big deal with Green, Hilliard and Mason and didn't want to rock the boat by not showing up with the prerequisite daddy bear in tow.

'What Dan doesn't know, Dan doesn't know!' she had exclaimed as she tapped furiously on her laptop, loading the calendar with fictitious Dan Devine brand contracts. 'So long as we lash them in and save the doc, we can keep brokering deals. If it comes to it, you can always argue in court that they'd been agreed prior,' she finished triumphantly.

Shelly was verging on awed by the sheer commercialism of it. She knew it was gross to be continuing to milk Dan during this rocky patch, but on the other hand, they would resolve this soon enough and it'd be madness to throw away all that they'd built with @DivineDanDevine. Amy was right – as long as they could explain it down the line, there was no need to be rash.

Shelly reflected on this as they gave the new Dan a spruce in the dressing room. Amanda, NDA signed in advance, was having trouble with the brief.

'You want him to look like your Dan – why?' She looked from Amy to Shelly to Almost Dan blankly.

'The "why" is not important, Amanda.' Amy was tapping the steel toes of her Doc Martens against the legs of the high stool she was perched on, illustrated legs crossed spaghetti-like. 'Just give him a few more greys in the temples and darken the under-eye area – he's supposed to be stressed at work.'

'O-K.' Amanda dusted Almost Dan's hair with leave-in shampoo and began smudging bags under his eyes.

Almost Dan peered over at Shelly. 'So where's this thing on, then? Is this how you usually get dates?' He was smiling playfully. 'I love you on *Durty Aul' Town*.'

Amy hopped down from the stool, yanked her glasses off her head and shoved her face right into Almost Dan's, eyeballing him. 'What are you doing?'

'Eh, nothing.' Almost Dan shifted awkwardly. 'Just doing the small talk. First-date stuff,' he added shyly.

'This is not a first date, FFS! You're already married.' Amy was scathing.

'We're married?' Both Almost Dan and Amanda looked stunned at this news.

'Ugh, I'll explain on the way after you've signed the confidentiality agreement. You done, Amanda?'

Amanda gave Almost Dan a final once-over with a bit of powder and stepped back, looking concerned. 'Yep, he's good to go,' she said quietly, biting her lip.

'No need for that face, Mandy, it's all under control.' Amy gathered her various phones, checked Shelly's face ('More highlighter and concealer on the bags,' she snapped) and began marching them out the door.

The car journey was taken up with explaining Almost Dan's role. As they neared Shanaghan House, Shelly pretended to be preoccupied with her Insta while Amy put Almost Dan through his paces.

'What are you to be doing at all times at this event?' she drilled.

'Be on my phone,' he said quickly, miming the phone using his wallet.

'Use your actual phone,' Amy barked.

'Yep, sorry. Got it.'

'What do you do if someone comes over to you at any point?'

'I do the I'll-be-off-in-two-seconds gesture,' Almost Dan held up two fingers in the universal symbol, 'then turn as if I'm talking and scurry away.'

'OK, good. Maybe try not to scurry. Real Dan's not a scurrier.' Amy glanced at Shelly. 'You OK?'

'Yep,' Shelly lied. She was so nervous she felt paralysed. Was this madness? What if someone noticed? She tried to remember if any of the Insta-mums had ever met Dan in the flesh. Even if they hadn't, just anyone getting close to this Dan could be a problem. Amanda's skills did not lie in subtlety and Almost Dan's face was looking a bit too made-up – was that highlighter on his cheeks?

'It's too late to worry now, Shelly,' Amy answered her thoughts. 'We'll get in and get out. Quick distant photo op. Show face, but not too much. And we're home free.'

The taxi pulled into the car park of Shanaghan House. Straight away Linda of @LindasLittlePrecious (3,008 followers) was jogging alongside the car. 'Shelly! Oh my gawd, it's been forever!'

'Get on the phone now,' Amy scream-whispered at Dan while Shelly rolled down the window and offered Linda her hand, which Linda immediately clasped on to. 'Dying to catch up.'

'We'll just park.' Shelly smiled tensely, trying to let go. Linda's grasp was strong but Shelly managed to shake her off, retract her hand inside the still-moving car and roll the window back up.

'See you in there,' Linda called, slightly winded from jogging.

Once parked, Amy, spotting Shelly's alarm, immediately began outlining a detailed plan. 'Everyone calm down – that was an unexpected ambush there by Linda Whatever-her-name-is but soon as we're in, it'll be grand. Dan, your main objective is, at all times, to keep your distance. Skirt this perimeter fencing.' Amy had brought up a schematic of the large country house and grounds on her iPad. 'Stay on the phone, be low-key. Shelly, just do the "oh, Dan's so in demand but he couldn't miss this" line and move the convo on. Easy.'

Amy consulted her phone. 'OK, Marni and Georgie are arriving in three.' Amy had brought in a separate-cars rule eighteen months ago when Georgie had had an unfortunate spill on a dress on loan from a boutique Shelly'd been working with. Shelly was always stressed that someone would spot them at one of these events doing the handover of the child. Some days she could reason herself out of it with a stern reminder that she was a working mother, ergo she had childcare. It just so happened that her work required occasional cameos from her daughter.

'Muma! Muma, Muma, Muma!' Georgie's squeals pierced her rumination. Shelly slid out of the car and was nearly floored by the loving ferocity of the child's greeting.

'Muma, Muma.' Georgie wrapped herself, koala-like, around Shelly's leg and launched straight into the kind of high-pitched, meandering, occasionally surreal monologue that three-year-olds specialise in. 'We went in the garden and I saw a budderfly bringing toast back to the babies at home. Then the budderfly made her babies babycinos and they all made cake. And then, and then,' she was gasping out the words, trying to hold Shelly's focus, 'then Mammy bought me here ...'

'Marni,' Shelly interrupted sharply. 'It's Marni, sweetie, not Mammy.'

'Marni,' Georgie said carefully then, losing her place in the spiel, noticed 'Dan', who'd just emerged from the car followed by Amy. 'Who's that? He looks like Dada.'

'I am your dada,' Almost Dan said cheerfully, to which Shelly and Amy hissed 'Shhh' in unison and Marni, having just ambled up behind Georgie, exclaimed, 'What!'

'Nothing, nothing,' Amy said. She glared at Almost Dan, who made a big show of appearing to take a phone call, only serving to exacerbate the weirdness of the situation.

'Georgie, please don't run ahead like that – there could be cars, *chérie*,' Marni admonished gently and Shelly tried not to think about the fact that the child immediately detached from her leg and relocated to the minder's.

The entrance to the Daddy Bears' Picnic was mobbed with Insta-mums, PRs and a few sullen-looking photographers who'd drawn the short straw in terms of photocalls. Elsewhere in the city, models in bikinis were posing with outsized objects and here they were in a pit of screaming kids and their trussed-up mums and bored dads.

Shelly steeled herself on the approach. Just past the imposing entrance to the main house was a photo area, an archway of cascading faux flowers under which arriving families were posing with a man in a bear costume before entering the manicured grounds of the house, where a marquee filled with picnic tables had been set up. Waiters circled bearing hot chocolates and Prosecco, while face-painting and games for the kids were in full swing.

'Shelly!' A pretty young woman with a severe bob was waving her over to the arch. 'Holly from Green, Hilliard and Mason PR, welcome!'

'Hi, Holly, so nice to see you again – you're looking gorge. New hair?' Shelly couldn't remember ever having clapped eyes on Holly but this was generally a safe opener.

'Aw, thanks. I was really unsure about it at first.' Holly ran a hand self-consciously over her shiny mane.

'No, it's gorgeous on you!'

'And this must be Georgie?' Holly leaned down to admire the little girl's cupcake-shaped tote bag. 'Stylish just like her mammy.'

'Her name's Mar-ni,' said Georgie, correcting her.

'Ha, shhh,' Amy interjected, stepping in front of the child. 'You never know what they're on about.'

Holly smiled, straightening up. 'Would you mind popping over to our teddy bear to do pics for the social pages – you and, of course, Mr Devine …?' Holly was craning around Shelly to see 'Dan', who was lurking just behind and already on the phone. He was twisting this way and that in an effort to keep his face partially hidden – from the look on Holly's face the effect was coming across more odd man than busy man.

Amy quickly took control. 'He's on to Asia, huge deal going down, but he wouldn't miss this for the world. We'll get the pics snapped and obvi we'll do lots of shouting about this gorgeous venue on the SHELLY profile and Dan's and on @BabyGeorgieDevine, of course – the audience over there is solidly middle-income families, your target demographic.'

As the photographer encouraged Georgie to smile for the camera – a born pro, she didn't need much coaching – Shelly felt a bit more chill. As soon as they wrapped this bit up, Almost Dan could get on with keeping his distance.

Behind the photographer, a small crowd was gathering. Anxiety tugged at Shelly but, she reminded herself, it wasn't unusual – people flocked wherever she went. She'd be doing selfies for the next two hours if she didn't have Amy here to do her bad-cop routine and usher people on. She waved to the women, to the visible delight of several.

'Just a couple more, Shelly,' called the snapper. 'Can you get yer man there to turn around a bit more? I'm only getting profile.'

'That's his good side,' Shelly joked to distract.

On her right, the guy in the bear costume seemed to be saying something. 'Hey, Justin, mate! How are ya? What're you doing here? How's the acting going?'

Almost Dan, hearing his real name, put away the phone and gave the bear a friendly hug.

Shelly was still smiling, hoping they'd wrap it up before anyone noticed her husband was apparently friends with the man in the giant bear suit.

'Darren – that you? Fuck's sake! You're down on your luck, bit of a far cry from Jack Reynor, no?'

'Well, at least I'm getting paid to be here! This your family?'

'Nah, I'm actually getting paid for this gig too.'

At this Shelly whipped around. 'Dan,' she said pointedly. 'Stop the chit-chat, let's get this shot and go.'

She gripped Almost Dan's arm and turned back to the photographer, smiling. Through gritted teeth she muttered, 'Just look down like you're laughing at something I'm saying so they can't see your whole face.'

Tensely she surveyed the crowd. They were smiling vacantly, and no one seemed aware of anything amiss.

'Just look at me, Shelly, thanks.' The photographer clicked away.

She fixed her smile but in her peripheral vision she spied a strangely familiar figure. She flicked her eyes over. It was hard to be sure without turning to see but it looked like that Kelly girl from the hotel. Was she holding up a phone?

'Great, just one more …' Snap. 'And we're done.' The photographer lowered the camera and Shelly zeroed in on the spot over to the right where she thought she'd seen the girl, but there was no one. Had she imagined it?

Aware of the crowds waiting expectantly for her, she pulled

Almost Dan in and whispered, 'Give me a goodbye kiss on the cheek and then you can get back on the phone.' She was mortified but the whole show needed to look right. 'Thanks,' she added, barely able to look at him – what must he think?

Almost Dan gave her a peck, headed off towards a waiter distributing jelly sweets, grabbed a handful and stuffed them into his pocket. Shelly watched as he held the phone up to his ear and shouted, 'Asia, it's me, let's get back to that money deal.'

She suppressed a shudder and turned to her followers.

After the selfie session, Shelly took Georgie over to where the Insta-mum squad were gathered in a roped-off area by the rose garden – their children, being fielded by a fleet of minders, grandparents and bored older siblings, were scattered nearby.

'Shelly!' @HolisticHazel greeted her by remaining seated on her cashmere picnic blanket and firing a couple of lacklustre air kisses at her while Polly jumped up to embrace her enthusiastically. It was a weird set-up with Hazel and Polly. They cultivated a friendship to a certain extent, tagging each other, commenting on each other's posts and making a big show of building each other up in worthy blogposts about women helping women, but at the end of the day Shelly, Hazel and Polly were the three biggest fish in a very small pond so the undercurrent of envy and competition was never far from the surface.

Hazel was a former singer. She'd had some degree of success in the early 2000s with a single called 'Everybody's Gonna Party', then she'd disappeared from view only to re-emerge ten years later on the Insta-scene, remade as a bona fide earth mother, dripping in children and extolling the virtues of very, very expensive natural hair and skin care – her own line, natch. Her beautiful home was floor-to-ceiling hessian, attractive for the 'gram but itchy as hell, Shelly thought any time she went over there.

Hazel's online persona was one of Zen equilibrium with a great eye for a flat lay; in person she was a complete megalomaniac with an unending appetite for bitching. Polly, on the other hand, was sphinx-like with her views, never committing an opinion to the record in case she'd be held to something. She had two little boys and a devotion to crafting that was impressive or suspicious, depending on how much one really knew about the behind-the-scenes machinations of Instagram. Amy insisted there must be a sweatshop of poorly paid minions responsible for Polly's exquisite output.

'Great news re the impending bump! That's going to be so good for engagement.' Hazel smiled coolly.

'Eh, yeah, I suppose so,' Shelly said, trying to seem like she didn't totally catch Hazel's meaning.

'Oh, come on, Shelly,' she continued impatiently. 'You know it! If my body wasn't so wrecked from so many natural deliveries I'd still be at it. Financial reviews of the years I was growing my babies were just incredible. We might still do a bit of fostering – that's a corner of the market that's pretty untapped, though I think there're privacy issues with those kids. Still, always ways around these things – a little tasteful pixelation, perhaps.'

'Hazel.' Polly looked rightly disturbed at this idea.

'Oh, drop it, Polly. I'm just thinking out loud. Anyway, I'm so flat out with the new app it'll be a while before we can really get back to working on the family – in development terms, I mean.'

Hazel made Amy's shady activity seem mild in comparison. Before her sixth child was born she'd casually mentioned that she'd arranged the pregnancy so her due date would fall in summer because summer bumps 'performed better' on Instagram. Just then, Hazel's summer bump, named (shock) Summer, ran past heading to the charcuterie table, leading Shelly to notice something of a stir over at the entrance.

'What's going on?' Polly asked.

Hazel turned to see, looking quizzical. 'Weird, we're all here already.'

'Hazel!'

'Shut up, Polly, we were all thinking it!'

'It's that newbie, Ali Something – the one with the wild card for the Glossies,' Polly murmured.

'Ah yes, the bump rival.' Hazel fixed her piercing green eyes on Shelly. 'It's going to be very hard to compete with a young, pert bump like that. You're due around the same time, yes?'

God, she missed nothing, thought Shelly.

'Ha, you're too much, Hazel!' Shelly feigned breezy. 'I actually know Ali – she's a great girl. She used to be in production on *Durty Aul' Town*.'

'Mm-hm.' Hazel sounded sceptical.

'They're coming over …'

Shelly craned to see Ali and a tall guy wending their way through the marquee.

17

Ali was nervous at meeting the Insta-mums and parading Sam around her new Insta-life. He'd seemed a bit confused over the last few weeks whenever she'd update her Stories in front of him or get him to take a picture of her outfit.

'You don't really sound like the real you when you go on there,' he'd said.

'Yeah, well, no one's very interested in the real anything on Instagram,' she'd replied.

Entering the Insta-world of an event like this seemed particularly surreal with Sam in tow. There were women everywhere talking into their phones.

'It's just so fab to get some quality time together as a family,'

@LindasLittlePrecious shouted into her iPhone to their right while just beyond, her husband looked bored on his phone and their little girl had taken off her own soiled nappy and was hitting other children with it.

'It's like *Black Mirror* in here.' Sam snorted with laughter and Ali struggled to hide her own giggles. He rounded on her, holding her upper arms and smiling as though he'd hit on some brainwave. 'Hey, I have an idea! How about when we have our kid we actually look at it from time to time.'

They both glanced back at the family – Linda and the husband were still bent over their phones, while baby 'Precious', apparently despairing of her distracted parents, was wearily putting her own nappy back on.

'Careful now, don't be all smug,' Ali warned. 'Liv's sister has kids and she says the phone's a sanity saver, only thing keeping her from running away in the dead of night, according to Nella.'

'Ali! So great to see you, and this must be Sam.' Holly had descended and was already air-kissing him. Ali was glad of the interruption. As much as she and Sam were getting on well, she couldn't quite quell the creep of unease in her stomach whenever he brought up the baby.

'Hi, Holly, this is all gorgeous. And, yes, this is Sam.' Ali was getting used to having an unwitting partner in crime for this whole thing and, well, life in general.

Sam, Ali had to admit, really grew on a person – even Liv liked him, sort of. This was good, as he'd been staying over loads over the last couple of weeks, like a real boyfriend. It was tricky for Ali, though, as she'd had to seriously curtail her single habits, not to mention clean her room.

When she talked about Sam on her Stories, her followers lapped it up – it turned out that introducing Sam and laying out the whole one-night-stand story had been inspired. It was a millennial fairy tale for the ages. Blending the 'pregnancy journey' with the 'newly loved-up couples goals' narrative effectively brought together two huge audiences and had rarely been seen on Instagram before. Her following had soared to 57K in the last three weeks, with couples content often matching the bump-journey stuff in terms of likes and comments.

She was finding her niche in a way that she never had in the old days. She'd introduced a regular diary-style show on her IGTV called *Ali's Real Talk* in which she voiced her apprehension at the changes coming in the next few months. She'd even been commended for her 'refreshing honesty' on the Notions.ie's Insta-watch column. In her chats about going from 'terminally single' to 'playing house', she of course omitted the biggest habit she'd had to curtail: her drinking. With Sam around more and a fake pregnancy well underway, her boozing had virtually evaporated by necessity, and she didn't like how much she missed it. It was making her analyse the wine-love far more than she cared to. Still, Sam's hand in hers at night, instead of the glass, was nice.

'I'd love to intro you to Polly, Hazel and Shelly – they're congregated in our little unofficial "VIP" area?'

'Oooh, are we "VIPs"?' asked Sam, mimicking her air quotes and winking.

'Ha, LOL,' said Holly and turned to lead them over to the Insta-mums who were sitting apart from the crowd while their children scampered nearby.

Sam sniggered and Ali shot him a meaningful look. 'Zip it, Tinder,' she whispered urgently, employing his pet name to make sure he knew she was being serious but wasn't angry. 'These are the mums who run this whole scene. I need to get in with them. I presume they hate each other but on the grid they are BFs and I need to get in on that.'

'Hazel, Polly, Shelly! I'm not sure if you gals know each other but this is Ali from @AlisBaba, and Sam, her daddy bear.'

'Hi!' Sam waved. 'Listen,' he turned to Holly, 'what does a bear have to do around here? Shit in the woods?'

'What?' Holly was alarmed.

Ali groaned. 'He thinks he's being funny.' She noticed with relief that Shelly was laughing quietly at this. 'The loos are in the main house.'

Sam winked and made his way through some entertainers doing face-painting and a magician – pointless, really, as most of the kids were plugged into YouTube.

Ali rolled her eyes at the Insta-mums. 'He's such a man.'

Moaning about her 'daddy bear' turned out to be a good opener. Hazel leapt in eagerly.

'OMG, yes, Eugene doesn't know how to behave!' She waved over at a short bespectacled man in a suit attempting to kick a football with a young boy while talking into his phone and peering at some complicated-looking document. 'He can't leave the office for one bloody hour. That kid's not even one of ours – not that he'd notice.'

Ali had never seen Eugene on Hazel's Insta and now she could see why. He didn't fit with Hazel's earth-mama-by-way-of-LA-but-actually-living-in-Knocklyon aesthetic. He wasn't an ex-rugby player, like the guy Polly touted around like a beefy prized accessory or a DILF like Dan Devine. Poor Eugene apparently bankrolled his wife's exquisite life but didn't match it and therefore was written out of the whole damn thing.

'Sam's an office man too,' Ali offered brightly, seeing a chance for bonding. 'Though I actually haven't a clue what he does. They get free snacks. I think he's in HR.'

'What do any of them do?' mused Hazel wearily. 'What's Dan doing, Shelly? He is here, yes?' There was something of a challenge in this question. And for some reason, Shelly did look a little startled. Weird, Ali thought.

'He's on to the office as well.' Shelly glanced across the lawn beyond the marquee where, up a grassy verge along the perimeter fence, a dark-haired figure was having an animated phone conversation. 'Asia.' Shelly shrugged by way of explanation. 'So how is the pregnancy going, Ali? Any nausea? I think we're just about the same way along.' She lowered her voice. 'My due date was 9/11 but Amy pushed it out by a week because, well, ya know, you couldn't write that on a post. It'd die a death.'

Polly and Hazel nodded wisely.

'Yeah, I'm around then as well.' Ali found it far easier talking about being pregnant in the comfort of an Instagram Story to thousands of faceless watchers than face to face with even one person, never mind three of the most influential people in the Insta-sphere. 'I've been feeling grand mostly. Sam's really up on pregnancy things and is making me mainline folic acid and stuff like that.'

'Yeah, everyone seems to love Sam, don't they?' Hazel's eyes were steely as she glared over at the hapless Eugene. 'You've done well there. So what else do you have up your sleeve? I see you were touting a few beauty bits during the week – what are you charging for a post?'

Ali felt edgy. This Hazel person was nothing like her Insta-profile. This was the woman who had been talking about her jade yoni egg only this morning on Insta and shiteing on about putting rose quartz in the pot when she was making her weekly batch of bone broth. Ali had the distinct feeling she was being pumped for information and it was giving her The Fear.

The Fear, in fairness, had become an ever-present spectre in the past weeks. Ali was painfully aware that the fake pregnancy lie was at its most manageable in this very moment. At two months, she didn't need to start showing – she had feverishly googled this on many anxious nights secretly slugging wine and tapping on the phone. However, the problem was that people like bumps in their bump content. Faking this for #OOTDs would be fine if Sam hadn't managed to make himself a fixture in her life so rapidly.

Every day she had the unshakeable sense that she was inching ever closer to all-out disaster. And having to make an impossible choice between a fake baby or a real man. But even if she decided that Sam was more important than her #bumpjourney, that wasn't without its complications. However devious lying about a positive pregnancy test was, Ali knew that she couldn't, just couldn't, fake something happening to the pregnancy – that was just too dark, even for her. So Sam would need an explanation. But what?

As the days marched forward and she was booking more and more sponsored content and ever more followers became invested in her story, she had the persistent feeling of detached unreality, as though this was all happening to someone else. When she and Sam were joking around on the couch at night or kissing under the covers in the morning, she could almost forget that a huge problem was looming. These moments of forgetful joy were fleeting, however, and within minutes anxiety could be depended on to return and choke the happiness back out of her.

'Actually, Shelly and Ali, could I borrow you two for a couple of minutes?' interjected Holly, saving Ali from Hazel's probing questions.

Shelly jumped up eagerly, looking a little relieved too. 'Absolutely,' she said as she glanced over at her daughter and the woman who must be her minder. Ali had pored over Shelly's profile since joining Insta and had never seen any mention of minders or nannies. In fact, there wasn't a whisper of childcare on Hazel's and Polly's channels either. They had all the accoutrements of motherhood but their pristine lives rarely seemed sullied by the presence of actual children. These secret minders must be how they could take lavish sponsored family holidays yet also sit enjoying 'a bit of peace with the love of my life' on a sun-soaked Portugal beach, as one vintage Hazel caption read. Only Eugene's left hand had made it into shot.

Ali followed Shelly and Holly over to another out-of-the-way picnic table teeming with colourful mini doughnuts, fruit skewers and an elaborate chocolate fondue, all untouched. As they were taking their seats, Amy Donoghue appeared, looking as gloriously out of place as ever with her tatts and her torn cut-offs, fishnets and Doc Martens.

'We need to wrap up – fifteen minutes, Shelly, max,' she said cryptically. Ali could see Shelly's gaze flick back over to the opposite side of the lawn where Dan Devine appeared to be gesturing erratically and screaming, 'Show me the money!' into his phone in front of a rapt audience assembled just below him. Amy leaned in and whispered something, causing Shelly to relax slightly. Straightening up, Amy said, 'We'll see you in the car park,' and after snapping a couple of pics of the spread for the 'gram, she marched back towards Dan, signalling to Georgie's minder on the way.

Jeez. It'd be so fucking handy to have that. Shelly wouldn't even have to post about the Daddy Bears' Picnic – that's true success, thought Ali: famous for an Instagram account you didn't even have to manage anymore. That was the other thing about her new-found Insta-fame – it was a lot of work. Plotting posts, replying to endless DMs and comments. Ali had devised a master doc of stock responses to followers and that saved some time but, Christ, it was a bit tedious.

As Ali took her seat, a young, pregnant woman with an adorable bump snuck over.

'I am so sorry to interrupt …' she began. 'I just love you so much …'

Shelly seemed to prime herself for the customary receiving of adoration and indeed Ali, who wasn't used to being accosted in public, also presumed that she was there for Shelly. However, the girl clumsily swooped in and hugged Ali. Through the fan's hair, Ali could see Shelly's face. She looked stunned and even … was there a hint of jealousy there?

'Oh, right. Thanks!' said Ali. The proximity of a very real, pretty large bump was freaking her out, as though this girl's pregnancy would make Ali seem even less pregnant by comparison.

'I'm mad into the chicken fillet rolls as well,' the girl offered shyly. 'I can't help myself … As you said, the baby wants it!'

Ali was drawing a blank until the girl prompted, 'Remember? The day you were talking about how pregnancy is like one big nine-month-long hangover?'

'Oh yeah.' Ali had actually been hungover for real that day and then realising the symptoms of early pregnancy were virtually identical to a hangover decided to run with it. It had proved very popular content.

'Anyway,' the girl glanced over at Holly and Shelly, 'thanks for being so real about your life. I was really anxious when I first found out I was expecting and seeing you talking about you and Sam and stuff, it's really, really helped me. Anyway, I'll go now!' She gave Ali another awkward little hug and then, as an afterthought, said to Shelly, 'Oh, congrats on your new baby too, Shelly!'

Ali tried to stay composed as the girl hurried back to her friends but it was too much. Being singled out like that! And in front of Shelly and Holly! Ali was putting everything into not jumping up and dancing a little victory dance. She could see Shelly taking it all in and she didn't look too pleased. She couldn't wait to tell— well, she'd be pretty stuck to find someone that'd be interested TBH.

Kate had dropped off somewhat since Ali's meteoric rise and things had been cool between them on WhatsApp.

Liv would listen alright but then she'd go and type it all up in her thesis to impress Emer Breen. She had, thank fuck, finally stopped berating Ali at every opportunity for lying about the pregnancy. She wasn't happy about it but she was resigned to it. Also, she was now using many of Ali's strategies (Liv called them 'antics') as fodder for her thesis. But Ali was just happy to have Liv talking to her again – Angry Liv was Scary Liv – and what did it matter if some elements of her life were being mined for the thesis. Her name was changed and the only people who'd ever read it were Emer Breen and a few academics.

This, Ali supposed, was the biggest drawback of her Insta-plan: even though she had gained more followers than she'd ever dreamed of, she was losing touch with Liv and Kate and was being forced to keep Sam at arm's length. It was total fuckery, really – typical to get everything you'd always wanted and then not be able to enjoy it because of a pesky little lie. She'd said as much the week before to Miles on her routine visit. His silence felt vaguely consolatory somehow.

She'd taken to confiding in him more and more, especially

since she was short of people who she wasn't feeding some version of a lie, or avoiding altogether – she'd been giving Mini a wide berth. Mercifully, Mini was so far removed from the Insta-world that there was little danger of her hearing anything. Telling Miles seemed to take away the guilty feelings, momentarily at least. Thinking of Miles jolted her back into the moment. She was supposed to be at Ailesend before 4 p.m.

She tapped back into the conversation in time to hear Holly say, 'Holistic Mama Retreat at Fannart Lodge – it's very exclusive'.

Shelly was all ears. 'How long are you thinking?' she asked.

'The retreat is seven days long – the programme is designed for that length of stay. I know it's a big time commitment for you both but, between us, it is truly a luxury experience. Adrienne Mae, the woman who created it, is from California and apparently all the A-listers have gone to her retreats in Napa Valley. Reese Witherspoon, a few Kardashians. They want to launch in Ireland and we've hand-selected the clients who are attending.' Holly dropped her voice and mouthed, 'It's two grand a night.'

'Fucking hell,' Ali blurted, then clamped a hand over her mouth. 'Sorry – obviously I wouldn't say that kind of thing at the mamas' retreat.'

Holly continued, 'You two are the only blog— ahem … mothers of influence who we're inviting. Polly is going but she's paying the full fee.'

Shelly looked keen. 'Did you mention the dates to Amy?'

'She says she can clear your commitments, but you might want to check with Dan first?' said Holly and then, seeing Shelly's disdainful reaction, immediately backpedalled. 'I'm so sorry, my god. I didn't mean that you'd have to check with your husband.'

Ali was intrigued – she'd never seen so much as a slight frown sully Shelly Devine's immaculate features. And this looked like full-on annoyance. Ali flashed back to that night weeks ago when she'd been on her way to meet Tinder Sam and Shelly had been in her hotel room. Something about her faraway shots of Dan had seemed off.

Ali glanced across the lawn to where Amy had headed earlier but there was no sign of Dan now and the place was beginning to empty out. Was he waiting in the car obediently? She could see Sam standing over Polly and Hazel, speaking animatedly, and her stomach churned at the thought of what he might be saying to them.

Ali hadn't felt immediately sold on the week-long retreat but maybe it'd be a good thing – she needed to slow things down with Sam. Soon he'd be demanding to meet her family and come to doctor's appointments. Plus, he was dying to tell his sisters about the baby. Luckily Sharon was in Oz and wouldn't be back for a couple of months, which Ali'd leveraged to convince him to hold off. But it was tricky when she was broadcasting it on her Stories ten hours a day. She'd blocked him once already and he'd texted her an hour later demanding to know why he couldn't see her profile. She'd brushed it off as an accident and he'd seemed satisfied, but it was annoying having him on there. Also why the hell was he on Instagram?

'Straight-man Instagram must be so weird,' she'd remarked the previous night as he uploaded his pic of a burrito and captioned it with the burrito emoji.

'Well, it's no "I've tattooed my eyebrows on to look like a pair of leeches and my highlighter's so bright, my face is glowing green", but it has its own subtle charms.'

'Do my eyebrows look like leeches?'

'Yes, but in the most adorable way possible.'

Later he'd sent her a pic of her with little cartoon leeches drawn on her face. It got eighteen thousand likes. She'd hashtagged it #SamBeLike, as she did with most of her couples content. But she had hesitated right before sharing it. Would Sam mind? Would he think she was using him? The thought had rocked her and she'd felt breathless, her heart stuttering because, of course, this, sharing little texts and gifs he sent her, was nothing compared to the truth.

When the panic attack – though she could barely bring herself to call it that – passed she'd hit the Post button. You're in too deep anyway, Ali, may as well ride the wave. A PR had DM'd an hour later inviting her and Sam to a hotel she repped for a couples' weekend. 'You guys are so cute!' she'd written.

The irony that the one thing she wasn't faking was the thing everyone had latched onto wasn't lost on Ali. Her feelings about Sam were real – she knew this for certain. If they weren't, every kiss and cuddle wouldn't be so marred with regret and foreboding. Some time apart would be good. Ali knew it wasn't a solution – it was just staving off the disaster that she knew lay ahead one way or another.

Going to the retreat would be like treading water on the Sam thing – they could text and Facetime and they wouldn't need to do anything regarding the baby. She'd be a week closer to the Glossies and scoring the Influencer of the Year award – everything else could wait till after that. They'd go away. Or she'd, she'd – god knows what, emigrate? It didn't seem like the worst idea at this point, but it still didn't solve the Sam problem. Her mind was mangled just thinking about it. Stay in the day, Ali, she mantra-ed, reverting to the one thing that had worked to keep her chill since the beginning of all this. Don't think too far ahead, like, beyond tomorrow. Large-scale lying could be so stressful – why didn't anyone ever talk about that?

'I can deffo make time, Holly,' Ali piped up. 'Count me in!'

The marquee was nearly empty by now and Ali, Shelly and Holly started to make their way back under the flower arch and out to the chilly car park, where Sam was waiting, holding a balloon animal and eating a cupcake.

'Ali!' Hazel bustled back over to them. 'We do a gorgeous little get-together every month, a little #MamaMorning. Shelly's hosting the week after next. You should come – it's a great chance to swap tips, give each other's account a little boost, and it's good for us Insta-mums to be seen to be friends.'

'Right.' Ali grinned.

Shelly was quick to jump in. 'We *are* friends, Hazel!'

'Oh, relax, Ali knows what's up.' Hazel winked at Ali. 'She knows you don't get to five digits without a little clever networking, never mind the six digits – though you're getting there, aren't you, Ali?'

'I'm nearly at sixty thousand now,' Ali said. 'So hopefully a few more weeks.'

'Well done.' Hazel smiled a tad aggressively and started herding the kids towards the minivan her driver had just pulled up.

'See you then.' Polly waved in her meek fashion and headed after Hazel.

'Hazel seems so … different to her Insta,' said Ali carefully.

'Hmmm,' was apparently the best Shelly could come up with.

'She seems really nice, though,' Ali added hastily, unsure how close they all were.

'Well—' A commotion at the minivan interrupted whatever Shelly'd been about to say next.

'We've done a head count. This is not one of mine,' Hazel was roaring, shoving a kid back towards the assembled PRs. She hopped into the passenger seat and the car sped away, leaving the PRs to deal with the slightly dazed little girl.

'Well, that makes me less worried about whether I'm actually fit to be a mother.' Ali giggled and Shelly joined in. 'I'd better grab Sam – he's probably off his head on all the sweets!'

'Ali, I hope you're OK after what happened on set. I heard Stephan was being horrendous.'

'Yeah.' Ali didn't want to sound worried. 'Things are going fine so far. I'm picking up lots of bits with the Insta thing.'

'Well, just be careful.' Shelly looked tired as she scanned the car park for her car. 'It can suck you in but don't let it take over. The real things are what's important.' She sighed as a dark car pulled up. 'See you week after next – I'll DM you.'

Ali watched her go, with an eerie feeling in her tummy.

18

Shelly sat in her dressing room feeling apprehensive. The day's filming involved her character, Imelda, throwing one of her regular lingerie parties, which naturally required Shelly to wear the wares. The wardrobe mistress, Dee, was holding up option after sheer, frilly option which Stephan was energetically rejecting while shouting down the phone in a corner of the dreary, windowless room. He vetoed every piece that would cover more than the barest minimum for their primetime, pre-watershed spot in the schedule.

'If we can't have a hint of a nip, can we at least go for some side boob?' He was wrangling the head of drama on the phone and shaking his head furiously at a black silk teddy that Shelly felt slightly better about, seeing as it was pretty close to a nightie.

This is why I need to ditch this, thought Shelly bleakly – she wouldn't be a prude about her body if the role actually meant something to her, but she hated Imelda. She hated having to ham up her Dublin accent, and the stories they gave her were always so weak. Imelda was the slapstick character, always up to stupid schemes like her lingerie parties and that time she and her brother tried to rig the bingo. She was rarely involved in any of the grittier storylines on the show, though Amy was adamant that this was for the best – if Imelda started doing anything too hard-hitting on *Durty Aul' Town*, it could upset the SHELLY audience.

Finally, Stephan appeared to reach a détente with the department head – at least if his parting words were anything to go by: 'Fine! She'll look like she's selling fucking burka-inspired knickers but whatever. Keep your precious family audience happy.' He slammed down the phone and wheeled around to Shelly. 'Looks like you can keep your tits to yourself then.'

'You're making it sound like I was the one desperate to flash them around!'

Stephan snorted at this and Shelly felt a bit better. Aggro Stephan was a nightmare to handle.

'Right, your nips are off the hook, Shelly, but we still want a bit of titillation – OK? Dee? You have the prosthetic nipples?'

'Ah, yes, I have them somewhere – now let me see …'

'What is a prosthetic nipple?' Shelly tried to hide her distress. Why did she have to fight this oafish loon for even a modicum of dignity?

'I'm looking for a very specific look with this scene, Shelly.'

Stephan slipped into his 'serious director' mode, grabbing a chair and turning it backwards so he could straddle it while he talked his special brand of shite. 'I'm thinking a kind of Bernardo Bertolucci feel.' He was making a most unfortunate cupping motion with his hands.

Amy had walked in just in time to catch the prosthetic-nipple chat and was looking scathingly at Stephan. 'What, like Rachel in *Friends*? Total nipple domination?'

Shelly was delighted to see Amy. Stephan hated her and on cue he dismounted the chair and headed for the door. 'Make sure you go for a light-coloured dress, Dee, to show off those nips,' he called back.

Dee looked queasy as she rooted in a large plastic crate filled with Imelda's jewellery and general accessories. 'I put them in with the willy hairbands from that time Imelda had a hen party,' she said, straightening up and proffering the curiously realistic-looking nipples.

'Cool.' Amy feigned mild interest before snapping into business mode. 'Dee, can you give us a minute, please?' Shelly was fussing with the nipples as Amy shunted Dee out the door.

'Shelly, we've got a problem,' Amy began, sounding oddly brusque.

Her tone jolted Shelly out of the nipple reverie. She raised an eyebrow and Amy continued.

'This is awkward.' She fiddled with her iPad cover, opening it and closing it again.

Shelly was immediately alarmed. 'Awkward? I don't think I've seen you looking awkward ever. You sat in on my pelvic exam last week to get shots for the account and looked positively bored.'

'Yeah, yeah …' Amy waved the image away. 'Look, I know this isn't your fault but my pay didn't go through this month.'

'Oh. What?' Shelly was stunned. 'I'm so sorry. I can fix that straight away – just let me get up the online banking.'

'I'm not sure that's going to work, Shelly. I was at the house this morning. I was getting a few pics of Georgie in her new outerwear for that #KidsUnplugged campaign and I ran into Dan.'

The implications were slowly dawning on Shelly. Why had Amy's pay not been debited when it was a standing order every month? It came out of Dan and Shelly's joint account. The same account all the money Shelly made went into. Shelly's only account, as it were. Plum's sage words on the eve of her and Dan's wedding were echoing in her mind. 'Always have a running-away account,' she'd advised, dragging on her cigarette in her worldly Plum way. But Shelly had thought nothing more about it. At the time, she'd made next to no money compared with Dan. Of course that had all changed.

'Oh my god.' Shelly eased herself down into a chair. 'He's … what? Frozen the account?'

Amy nodded slowly. 'Looks like it. He told me that he wasn't going to bankroll me exploiting his family for one more second. He was pretty upset.'

Shelly could feel the tears coming and, even though it was going to mean a trip back to make-up to be touched up, she let them fall.

'Goddamn him,' she whispered. 'I'm so sorry, Amy. This whole thing is turning into such a mess. I have to get on to the solicitor – he can't just do this.'

'Yeah, I'm really sorry it's going this way, Shel.' Amy had never sounded so sincere – it was strange to see her so solemn. 'Look, you never know, marriages go through phases. Like, my mam and dad went through a big phase of fighting with each other after the recession, and it definitely looked really dodgy for a while there, but they're great now. I think Mam was on the verge of kicking him out but then she went to have her cards read, which is her version of counselling, and had some kind of epiphany.'

Shelly sighed. 'I dunno which Dan would hate more: counselling or tarot cards.' She tried to smile but found she couldn't. 'It's just a really difficult time. I can't lose him. Not with this baby on the way. But he can't just expect me to ditch SHELLY after all we've put into it.'

'Look,' Amy's eyes were fixed on the floor to her right, 'I reckon I need to disappear for the foreseeable. I know the money's not an issue in the grand scheme of things, but I think Dan won't ever come around if things stay the way they are.'

'Please don't go.' Doing SHELLY without Amy suddenly seemed as daunting to Shelly as losing Dan.

'I'm absolutely not going, Shelly,' Amy replied calmly. 'I'll just be taking a step back – you need to take over the reins for a while. Luckily, in the early days, I put together a contingency plan for this exact eventuality. I've set daily reminders for all the things you need to post to Insta. There's files with a huge catalogue of

#OOTDs with corresponding captions ready to copy and paste. There's a folder with evergreen content, inspo quotes, #TBTs, attractive acai bowls and charcoal pastries on marble tables. I've set you up with a lot of stock stuff that you can push out as and when you need it. All I ask is that you don't mess with the consistency, Shelly, OK? It's been a while since you've managed this thing and TBH the audience is so much more on it now – like, if I'm three minutes late uploading the Thankful Thursday post, they'll be in the DMs straight away.'

Shelly was slumping ever lower. 'This sounds … so overwhelming.'

Amy came over and put her arms around Shelly. It was so completely un-Amy that Shelly had to laugh. 'Shit, now I know it's a crisis if you're hugging me.' Shelly smiled through her tears.

'Your face is wrecked,' remarked Amy, pulling away and resuming her handover speech. Tapping around the iPad, she showed Shelly the various files and calendars. 'I've emailed you a daily and weekly breakdown of the schedule. Plus a monthly calendar of brand collabs. There're docs with stock answers to pretty much all the comments and DMs. Just keep an eye and make sure you change them up every time or the eagle-eyed Shell-Belles will be all over it, calling you out for not being real. There are a few new features as well – the IGTV is pretty straightforward.' Amy showed Shelly a few more commands on the phone and then pressed it into her hands. 'I've included a little step by step on how to upload. All the photo editing is easy enough in FaceFix.'

Shelly turned the phone over in her hands. It had been forever since she'd really used this phone. She had another that they called the bat phone, for personal calls and texts. The SHELLY phone had pretty much been in Amy's possession since her first day in the job, bar that overnight in Ballinahagh House – and look how that had turned out.

Shelly opened the camera and snapped a selfie of her tear-streaked face. It had practically been years since she'd taken her own selfie! Maybe this was going to be fun. She pretended to upload the crying selfie to Instagram – turning the phone around, she consulted Amy. 'What filter should I put on this, d'ya reckon?'

Amy gasped and made a lunge for the phone. 'Don't even joke. A slip of the finger and that'd be up there for all to see. And there's no deleting posts nowadays, Shelly. Everyone's very fucking fast with the screenshots. You'd delete it and it'd be straight up on Rants.ie within minutes with a dozen wans all bitching about "why did she delete that?" "oh, she must have something to hide". Seriously.'

Shelly laughed but then saw Amy looked perturbed. 'I won't do anything, Amy. It's fine – I can be trusted with my own Instagram account.'

'Look, there's something else you need to know.' Amy glanced back at the door, ensuring it was closed. 'It's—' She stopped abruptly and walked to the door, yanked it open and checked the corridor outside. Deserted. She stepped back in and closed the door.

'OK, you're freaking me out.'

'The night of Dan's meltdown in Ballinahagh House,' Amy began, 'we tracked down every single person who was in the dining room but,' Amy paused and sucked in a panicked breath – Shelly had never seen her so tense, 'we couldn't find one witness, a girl.'

'Kelly's Klobber,' Shelly breathed. She felt her stomach drop. She just knew – she'd had a niggly feeling ever since that night. Even though Amy had insisted all was fine, she just couldn't imagine a hungry blogger like that would let it go so easily without trying to capitalise on it for all it was worth.

Amy nodded, eyes down. 'I'm so sorry, Shelly. I know I lied to you and that was unprofessional. I was just trying to keep it all contained. And I didn't want to stress you out.' Amy looked beseechingly at her. 'I thought I could fob her off, get her onside with a few political likes. You gave her account a shout-out the week after the meltdown and I know she did well out of it – she gained about three thousand followers overnight, I checked.'

Amy looked despairing and Shelly couldn't summon the will to be annoyed that she hadn't told her. Amy had lived and breathed SHELLY for two years. Shelly knew she would've done everything in her power to neutralise Kelly's Klobber. She checked the time – her scene was about to shoot. The timing of this couldn't be worse.

'What has she said so far?' Shelly started pulling on a pair of flesh-coloured control pants to better suck in her first-trimester bloat and was suddenly flooded with pity for this poor unwitting baby soon to be lobbed into this mess – a dad living in a Seomra in the garden and a mother trying to appeal to a potentially psychopathic fashion blogger's better nature. Not to mention the prosthetic nipples. She finished stuffing herself into the Spanx – it's worse than bloody cardio – and put her ivory silk teddy and knicker set on.

'So far nothing at all,' Amy bit her lower lip, 'which makes me more nervous than if she was coming at us with all-out threats. I feel like she's biding her time. I've sent DMs saying how much we'd appreciate her discretion and how much you love her account and that we were giving her shout-outs and stuff, but nothing. I think she's toying with us.'

'What does she want?' Shelly was fussing with the fake nipples and starting to stress about her lines – all thoughts of Imelda and *Durty Aul' Town* had been shoved to one side as she'd tried to absorb the idea that she had a potential blackmailer on her trail, and now she couldn't even remember the opening words of the scene.

'I dunno,' said Amy helplessly. 'It's not Insta-likes anyway, I tried that. I think it's one of two things – a) money, pure and simple. Which is obviously gonna be a major problem given Dan's latest power move.'

'What's b) then?' Shelly was pretty sure she didn't want to hear the answer.

Amy shrugged. 'Destruction? Mayhem? Wreck your life? Humiliate you?'

'Oh c'mon.' Shelly tried for a laugh. 'Is that not a bit OTT?'

'You never know with these internet people, Shelly. To quote *The Dark Knight*, some people just wanna watch the world burn.'

On this unsettling note, a sudden pounding on the dressing room door startled them both.

'Fifteen minutes, Shelly. Thanks!' It was Ruairí the PA doing the rounds, rousing the various players required for the next scene.

'I have to get down to make-up to fix my face.' Shelly gathered the day's sides and gave her perky rubber nipples a final tweak. So typical of my life that in the midst of things falling apart, I'm wearing prosthetic nipples, she thought ruefully. 'Let's try not to assume the worst about Kelly's Klobber – maybe when she knows she's got my attention she'll be satisfied.'

Amy looked doubtful and Shelly hated this new role reversal – usually she was the stressed one and Amy was in control. Nothing had ever got to Amy like this before, even that time they came under major fire for putting a tanning product on Baby Georgie for a #spon post to illustrate it could be used on even the most sensitive skin.

They headed to the door and Shelly paused, hand on the handle, and turned back to Amy. 'Look, stay on set today, please? Maybe we can get more of a plan together between takes?'

'Yeah.' Amy seemed to be returning to her usual efficient self. 'We do have more handover stuff to discuss beyond the bloody Kelly's Klobber debacle.'

'Oh?' Shelly was not in the mood for any more revelations.

'It's just, ya know, it's nothing, but I don't want you getting complacent. Following has dropped off a little since the beginning of the year and you need to keep an eye on that. There's more and more competition, that's all. And they're young and thirsty.

Influencer of the Year is not in the bag yet and @AlisBaba is seriously gaining ground.'

'So,' Shelly grinned, trying to lighten the mood, 'you're saying I'm a dried-up old has-been whose most engaged follower is a stalker?'

'Basically, yes.'

Well, fuck, thought Shelly, a rarity for her. Shelly never said the f-word and she certainly didn't think it too often either. But, god, with the divine Dan putting her money on lockdown, a potential stalker out to ruin her in the wings and Amy going on hiatus, leaving her holding the baby, nothing in her life was looking too on-brand right now.

So fuck it.

19

'Can you just put that thing down for one single episode of *SVU*? You're missing some absolute quality depravity over here.' Sam was looking irritated. 'It's like trying to watch TV with someone furiously wanking in the corner of the room.'

Liv snorted approvingly and Ali sighed and set the phone face down on the couch beside her.

'It's so nice to see you two bonding by ganging up on me.' Ali feigned a huff but actually she loved that they could all veg out together, bingeing Netflix and mocking whatever show happened to be on. It was yet another peskily perfect thing about Sam – Liv actually liked him. And this was no small feat. Ali had rarely had a boy to bring home in the last few years but, on the occasions she did, they hardly ever passed Liv's Knob Test. It was an informal examination conducted by Liv on most people. You couldn't really tell when the test was underway – you'd only hear about the result, a result influenced by myriad nebulous factors only Liv was privy to. Afterwards she'd draw her conclusions and make vague pronouncements in summary: 'He's the kind of guy that thinks he and Vince Vaughn would be best friends.' Or 'Seems to have very limited vocab – he definitely thinks "marmalade" and "helicopter" are "big" words.'

Sam had charmed Liv from the off – which was surprising, as he definitely reckoned he and Vince Vaughn would be besties. Much of their connection stemmed from a shared disdain for Ali's Insta-obsession and, added to that, Sam did a good line in TV-show commentary, which was a pastime of both Ali's and Liv's.

On screen, a highly improbable scenario was playing out in which Stabler's wife had gone into labour while trapped in a car wreck and Benson, Stabler's partner, was being talked through administering the IV drip.

'Not a single paramedic could hop in the window there?' Sam was shouting at the telly incredulously.

'They've lost the run of themselves in this episode,' Liv chimed in. 'I was willing to believe the whole midwife-paedo-ring story arc but this is just a farce.'

Ali settled back against the cushions and pulled the sofa blanky over her. Sam and Liv were now debating about what was the most ludicrous storyline they'd ever seen on *SVU*. Sam was trying to convince Liv that there was an episode centred around a choir that had killed and cannibalised their domineering conductor.

'Jesus, I wouldn't put it past old Dickie Wolf to pull something like that!' Liv laughed.

Satisfied that they were distracted, Ali picked up the phone and began surreptitiously scrolling once more. She'd seen a WhatsApp and several screenshots drop in from Kate and was eager to catch up with what she was saying.

Ali, I'm so sorry to be the one sending you these, but I thought you'd like to know and, as your friend, I felt a responsibility to show what's being said about you.

Below the message were three blurry screenshots of what looked like a Rants.ie forum. The fucking toilet bowl of the internet. If she tapped them they'd come into focus and she could read whatever it was Kate apparently felt was her 'duty' to show her. Well, fuck that. I'm not going there tonight. No way.

She was more disturbed by the thought that Kate wanted to upset her than anything some randoms were spouting on the internet. The pang of upset flared in her stomach and her immediate thought was: wine. Pity Sam was there. She X-ed out of WhatsApp and opened her Instagram. A few minutes scrolling her latest follows, likes and comments settled her, though of course now that the thought of wine had hit, she felt antsy to get rid of Sam. He wasn't supposed to be spending the night anyway – part of her slow-things-down plan. *SVU* ended and Ali spotted her chance.

'Don't you have to be up early for work tomorrow, babes?'

'Oooh, is that a hint, babes?' Sam gave her a little tickle. 'Reckon I'm not wanted here anymore, Liv?'

'Were you ever, darling?' Liv replied with mock pity. Ali made pleading eyes at her behind Sam's back and Liv looked resigned, adding, 'We have some essential girl talk on the evening's agenda, I'm afraid.'

'Well, now I know ye're definitely bullshitting me.' Sam laughed, getting up. 'As if you, Liv, would ever use the phrase "girl talk".'

He leaned down and kissed Ali, apparently not too fazed by being turfed out. 'Enjoy girl time – don't get over-excited now. We wouldn't want a repeat of *SVU* season 44, episode 19, when the pillow fight escalated and the cheerleaders were convicted of manslaughter in the first degree.'

Ali laughed dutifully, hopped up and began shoving Sam towards the hall. Sam being Sam, he attempted to turn this into a reenactment of the pottery scene from *Ghost*, but a few minutes later Ali had successfully ejected him. She returned to the couch via the kitchen, having grabbed a bottle of wine.

Liv cracked a beer and raised a toast to her. 'Congratulations on one of the most impressive acts of self-sabotage I have ever witnessed,' she said snidely. Ali rolled her eyes, but Liv wasn't done. 'No, no, really, I have never seen such an effective and total self-cock-block. Ever. I sincerely doubt it's even been done before.'

'Liv, can you please shut up.'

'Don't be modest, Ali. Seriously, I'm impressed. You've managed to find the hands-down perfect man for you – he loves *SVU*, looks like Louis Theroux's nerdier little brother, seems to adore you – and you, meanwhile, have successfully rigged it so that, no matter what happens, it can never work.'

Ali poured her wine and resisted the strong urge to down it in one. She could drink in front of Liv but she had to keep it in check. 'Please don't you come at me too. Kate already sent me some gloating WhatsApp about people bitching about me on Rants and how she felt morally compelled as my friend to let me know.'

'Well,' Liv sighed heavily, 'they'll be saying a lot worse when this house of cards comes down. Which it will.'

'Please, not tonight, Liv.' Ali was now horizontal on the couch, having been hit by what had become a nightly crushing tiredness – she put it down to the sheer mental exertion of bullshitting so much. Lying should come with a health warning. She was attempting to drink her wine by dribbling it sideways into her mouth. 'Wine straws need to become socially acceptable,' she remarked.

'So what are you going to do about Sam, then?'

Ali had put the glass down and was now rummaging behind her, unhooking her bra and dragging it off through the sleeve of her hoodie – the day wasn't officially over until that bloody contraption was off. 'I've told him we need to slow things down on the whole "relationship".' Ali mimed air quotes. 'Plus I'm heading to that mega preggo retreat next week, which will keep him at arm's length for a bit. So I've definitely bought some time. It could get complicated when the sister arrives back from Oz, though.'

Liv sat with one eyebrow raised sceptically throughout this little speech. 'Sounds totally solid – oh wait, no. You sound insane. Also, this little charade has become excruciating to watch. You realise he is a real person with real feelings, Ali? I like him. It's actually torture watching him fall for you and talk about his "baby".' Liv looked disgusted.

'Liv!' Ali sat up the better to complete the bra removal and yanked it so hard it snapped back and hit her in the face. 'He's not falling for me. He's just being nice because he thinks I'm carrying his child.'

Liv shot to her feet abruptly and loomed over Ali. 'Jesus, will you just listen to what you said there?' She leaned down. Ali could smell her beer. 'What are you doing, Ali? You quit your job, you're ignoring your mum, you're leading this poor guy on—'

'Why do you care so much?' Ali shot back.

'Because I'm a normal person. Because I care that you're lying and hurting people. Because you're going to hurt yourself.'

'I don't have to listen to this.' Ali grabbed her phone and stomped off to bed.

❖

The following day, Ali sat on the edge of Miles's bed mulling over the day's plan. Obviously, the screenshots had gotten the better of her in the dead of night. After Liv went to bed, Ali snuck her bottle of wine out of the living room and had finished it lying on her bed with one foot on the floor to stop the room spinning and one eye closed to focus on the pics.

@peacock44: I do not buy that Sam guy. He seems like such a nerd and she's so desperate to have a baby daddy she just has to fake it and pretend that they're some loved-up couple.

@Mayo_gal: She's just desperate full stop. Did you see that 'bump update' post? Like, calm down, you're about ten minutes preggers, but she's obvi gagging to get in with the whole Insta-mammy gang.

@peacock44: And she announced it before the piss was even dry on that wee stick. Who tells everyone they're preggers when they're six weeks gone? #thirsty

@cassieD: Is she even up the pole at all? She said last week that she was eight weeks along but then I went back and checked the date on her announcement post and that puts her at about ten and a half? I've had two babs and believe me no one gets that wrong.

@Mayo_gal: Oooh juice. Do you have receipts?

@cassieD: See below 🐷

@cassieD had posted a screenshot of Ali's pregnancy-test post with the date circled in red at the bottom of the pic. Below that she'd uploaded a video she'd evidently captured from Ali's IGTV Real Talk series.

Anxiety had pierced the comforting buffer of booze. Feck, she had been a bit sketchy regarding exact dates. It was careless. Honestly, she couldn't believe anyone was actually paying that much attention, but then again, tens of thousands of total strangers were watching her every move – odds were at least some of those were freaks who took screen recordings and bitched on internet forums.

She suddenly noticed the album she'd been playing for Miles had ended. Without the music, the air pump that kept Miles's mattress inflated – a necessity for bed-ridden people – was louder. This made her think about what the air mattress was for, which was not good for her mood.

'What'll we have, Dad? I actually brought you the new Elbow album!' She jumped up to retrieve her bag and swap out the CDs. Then she grabbed the hand cream from her little make-up bag and gently picked up Miles's left hand, watching his face carefully for any sign he was registering her touch. Not even a flicker. The knowledge seemed to thud in her stomach. She forced herself to smile – that was Mini's most irritating advice when confronted with hardship of any degree. Don't like school? Smile! Fake it till you feel it. Dad in a depressing nursing-home room? Smile. It could be worse!

Ali squeezed hand cream onto Miles's cool, dry hand and began to massage his fingers, wrists and forearms. Guy Garvey's sweet voice crept over them and Ali felt soothed by this simple contact with her dad. No over-thinking about being a bad daughter and not loving him enough. No fear of where this was all going, just stroking his pale, parched skin and praying he could feel her love somewhere inside his shattered mind.

'I love you.' She tried out the words. Why were they always so hard to say? They seemed to unlock a terrible abyss of pain that was really better left alone, shored up by everyday faff, rather than confronting the real horror of her dad's illness.

'I'm doing really well on Instagram these days. Nearly seventy thousand people follow me now. I know you probably don't know what that really means but, believe me, it's good. And I have a kind of boyfriend too. Sam. He's sweet. You'd really like him.'

Ali switched hands and squeezed out more moisturiser. She sang along to the music and watched Miles. His eyes were open, as was his mouth. His high cheekbones were more defined every day she came. What would happen? How long could someone go on like this?

A soft knock at the door jolted Ali back to the present. Tabitha, Ali's favourite of all the care team, stood at the door.

'Ali, do you want to go get yourself a coffee? And maybe an ice cream for your daddy?'

This was Tabitha's coded way of saying she needed to change Miles or do some other routine procedure that, mercifully, Ali and Mini were spared knowledge of.

'Yep, sure. Thanks, Tabby. I'll be right back, Miles.' She kissed his cheek and hopped off the bed.

She slipped past Tabitha but, instead of taking a right towards the coffee station, she veered left, heading in the direction of the examination rooms. The screen-grabs had hovered on the edge of her mind all morning. Even the fug of hangover couldn't dull the stab of anxiety – truth be told, the hangover was probably giving the unease an even more sinister edge. That was the terrible catch-22 of alcohol: it dulled the pain and relieved her angst only for it to come back ten times worse, thus requiring more booze to drown out the effects of the last booze. Exhausting stuff.

She looked into the doors on either side of the deserted corridor. There were hospital beds and the usual array of table trays on wheels and nurse call buttons. In the last room on the right, she found what she was looking for: some class of medical equipment. She glanced behind to check she was alone and then slipped in and shut the door. The room was small, with grey rubber floors, pale blue walls and a window looking on to the small courtyard. She closed the blinds partially, in case anyone happened to look in, and proceeded to examine the equipment. It looked to be a monitor of some description. Whatever it was, it should do fine. She just needed a hint of 'hospital' for her purposes. Provided this thing wasn't an instrument exclusively associated with the care of old people – like a soul-catcher for the near dead or something – she was grand.

She stepped out of her boots and took off her jumper. She hopped up on the bed and switched the front camera on so she could talk to her followers. She checked the shot, pulling the monitor closer so it was just behind her in the background, mussed her hair slightly and took a deep breath.

'Hey, gals! Sorry for the whispering but I'm actually in the hospital right now and I've just seen little Ali's Baba for the first time! I was a bit muddled on my dates before – ugh, scatty Ali! – but now they've confirmed I'm eleven weeks pregnant. So that's all straightened out.'

She watched the clip back, adjusting the filter and scrutinising her delivery. This lie was on a new level – she couldn't ignore that – but fuck it. She kept thinking back to Kate and those bitches on Rants. She needed to up the ante. The 'hospital shot' would give it the ring of truth she needed. Plus, she was doing so well. She'd even been invited to design a new Ali's Baba range for a pram company. She couldn't jack it all in now. Not when she was so close. Her resolve sufficiently steeled, she hit the Add to Story button. Then she Google Image searched 'eleven-week-old foetus ultrasound', saved the picture and uploaded it to her next Story, adding a little waving-hand emoji and a speech bubble so it looked like the foetus was introducing itself. Cute. She smiled. She paused for a moment, licked her lips, then hit Post.

20

The entire kitchen was in a complete state. Flour and eggs had combined to form a cement-like paste, coating surfaces, door handles and somehow even Shelly's hair. The fairy cakes were a joke. Shelly took in the carnage and decided to axe the whole post she'd had planned. The segue into food blogger was proving way harder than she'd imagined – especially with her phone endlessly pinging with reminders from Amy about doing posts for #WednesdayWellness and #TanningTuesday. It was less than two weeks since Amy had gone on leave – the admin of the SHELLY Insta was off the charts and unfortunately it was all down to her now to stay on top of it.

She pulled out a soapy sponge and began half-heartedly

scrubbing at the polished cement counter-tops. She stole a glance out the large sliding glass doors that ran the full width of the kitchen. Her gaze travelled past Georgie's toys strewn on the marble patio towards Dan's man-shed-turned-actual-living-quarters and felt again a rush of disbelief. It had been a number of weeks and still they'd barely spoken to one another.

Their solicitor, Bernard Sullivan, had temporarily sorted the money situation. Now each of them had an agreed allowance each week, in theory preventing them from dipping into the joint account until a formal separation was underway. It was galling. An allowance. She was convinced Dan had eked out some separate funds for himself – he was off in Lisbon with 'the lads' at that very moment, and presumably a good time on a lads' weekend didn't come cheap. She still couldn't get over how acrimonious it had become so quickly.

'How is this my life?' she'd moaned to Plum on the phone the night before.

'Darling,' Plum had paused to drag on her cigarette and Shelly wished she could stress-smoke her way out of the situation – she loved the odd illicit cig when she wasn't pregnant. 'It's an adjustment period,' Plum continued. 'Dan is angry – Virginia was the same when Curtis left her. She tortured us for the first couple of years. Always being very controlling about when we could take the house in Antibes.'

Shelly shook her head just thinking of the call. Plum's definition of hardship was worlds away from the average person's. Negotiating six-week summer vacations with your husband's irate ex-wife was a little different to her and Dan's mangled marriage and her chaotic career. Add a new baby into that mix and, well, it was like pouring gasoline over a dumpster fire. Thank god they had an appointment with a therapist before she headed off to the Mama retreat next week – they badly needed some clarity.

Abandoning the scrubby, she picked up a knife and began chiselling at the baking aftermath. Where was Marni? She should be doing this, thought Shelly irritably and straightaway felt guilty. What would her mam say to such entitled thoughts? A nanny-slash-cleaner would've been a completely foreign concept at the O'Briens' house growing up. Anyway, it was probably better Marni'd taken Georgie to the park to keep her out of the way during the set-up.

She picked up her phone: 11.20, forty minutes to get everything in order and do something about her face – at least she still had Amanda – before the Insta-mums arrived for their #MamaMorning (coffee with a side of Instagramming). They had a tacit agreement to promote each other's accounts, tagging all their handles in every post so that followers would follow the other accounts. It was good for boosting following and supplied everyone with dreamy content for the grid.

The host was expected to provide supremely 'gram-worthy snacks; luckily she hadn't been solely relying on the fairy cakes. She'd actually dropped a sizeable portion of that week's allowance on the #MamaMorning feast in Fallon & Byrne. She'd already laid out the seafood platter; crudités and dips; sugar-free, gluten-free, keto-friendly energy balls; and an enormous fruit platter.

She also had smoked salmon blinis for the kids (and frozen pizzas and curly fries to be consumed off-camera).

Shelly trudged upstairs, WhatsApping Marni to finish the kitchen – she could hear them bustling in downstairs but she didn't turn back. Georgie would be excited to see her and she didn't have time for a cuddle and a blow-by-blow of the park. She stopped by Georgie's bedroom and selected an #OOTD for her: a peach pinafore with matching knee-socks and gold glitter high-tops. She was also planning a peach palette for her own outfit for that all-essential #twinning post. How would she fare trying to dress a newborn in keeping with their matchy-matchy vibe? Everything seemed insurmountable this morning, with Amy gone and the perfect Hazel and Polly inbound.

Hazel's brood (five or six kids at last count) were always working some family-wide tonal palette of tasteful greys with muted pink accents. Hazel seemed to be a kind of motherhood machine, delivering post after beautifully lit post of her children running free in sun-drenched fields, wild flowers in their hair and freckles scattered over their adorable little noses. Or family baking sessions in a kitchen that looked to be lifted straight from a nineteenth-century French farmhouse with hints of a contemporary Scandi finish. 'Bogus Bohemia' was what Amy dubbed the Hazel aesthetic.

The house was actually a fairly standard semi-D in Knocklyon. The fields had been scouted by her location manager (that's right) for the express purpose of doing a carefree summer-days shoot – complete with outfit changes – so the shots could be rolled out and give the impression that her free-range kids were off living their best lives on the daily, instead of being locked into an immovable schedule of paid posts, sponcon, forced smiles and gruelling home-school hours with tutors who were paid for their silence as much as their academic expertise.

Hazel had taken the Insta-life to *Truman Show* levels. You had to admire the commitment, Shelly supposed – though it was definitely bordering on psychotic. Any time Shelly felt uneasy appearing at the playground where Georgie would've spent the morning with Marni to do a ten-minute shoot for a new buggy collab, Shelly just thought of Hazel using a stand-in for breastfeeding shots because 'Of course I couldn't feed with a schedule like mine ... but I can't be seen to not be breastfeeding – it'd be totally at odds with my narrative' and Shelly's guilt was assuaged.

Hazel was hugely outspoken about her sustainable lifestyle, the home-dyed linen shirts and her Steiner home-schooling, but she had a veritable army working tirelessly to produce the pared-back, simple life she was devoted to projecting. She employed three minders alone to keep the kids at bay while she endlessly trawled the LA Insta-mums to see what next to be stuffing up her vagina – vapours, crystals, positive vibes. There was nothing she wouldn't shove up there, one of her assistants had once told Amy, who'd gleefully passed it on to Shelly.

Polly, on the other hand, was completely vanilla, striving to be as uncontroversial as possible. Shelly knew that Polly was seen as a kind of budget version of her. She had about half the following and did collaborations with far less salubrious clients – she just didn't have a very strong brand identity. She wasn't cut out for the all-out theatrics of Hazel's Holistic Heaven, and she didn't have Shelly's looks or the acting, which Shelly had to admit was certainly a draw for her followers – they loved a bit of a behind-the-scenes action on set. Polly had a spectacularly dull husband (that she didn't have the good sense to hide from view à la Hazel) and two little boys. She tried to work the #MotherOfSons angle as best she could but there was less to be mined raising boys – even Shelly could see that. It was all about raising girls these days. Every blogger mama with half a brain did at least one 'I'm raising my daughter to be a strong woman' post every week. And having a girl meant you could do one of those posts in the voice of your daughter.

I love when my mama takes me shopping to @MarksandSpencersOfficial to look at the new #AW19Collection #Ad #Spon #Shopping #BornShopper

Shelly couldn't see it landing in quite the same way with a little boy.

'Polly's content is too flaccid,' Hazel had announced at their last meet-up, when Polly had gone to the loo. Shelly winced at the memory.

Hazel was a bitch but she had a point. Ali Jones was already close to overtaking Polly. Maybe even all of us, she sighed, carrying on up the next flight of stairs to her dressing room where Amanda was prepping the perfect, painstaking no-make-up make-up look.

Shelly settled herself on the stool, closed her eyes and Amanda got to work on the primer and base. God, what would Ali make of the #MamaMorning? Last time, Hazel tried to get all the kids to meditate for an Insta-story and Polly's older boy bit her. Shelly grinned at the memory of Hazel's face.

'It's nice to see you smiling, Shelly.' Amanda paused in her blending

'Ah, sorry, Amanda – I know it's been pretty tense around here. It's just so hard with Amy gone and Dan ... off with his pals.'

She hadn't been able to bring herself to tell anyone except Plum about the separation yet. Saying it aloud would make it real.

Amanda gave her hand a gentle squeeze and Shelly got the feeling she knew there was more going on than Dan going away for a few days – how could she not? She blotted Shelly's lips and shooed her down off the stool.

She jogged back downstairs, ducking in to Georgie's room to check that Marni had indeed changed her, and then reached the bottom of the stairs just as the doorbell went.

She opened the door to find Hazel, Polly and Ali, phones held aloft, all facing different directions to get a clear shot and feverishly updating their Stories. Behind them, Shelly counted four bored-looking au pairs just as a swarm of children ran past her into the house.

Marni joined the au pairs in settling the children. They were like car-park attendants, positioning each child near a power point and plugging them into their various devices before settling back to shoot the breeze.

What did the au pairs say about them? Shelly dreaded to think.

'Tea, coffee, wine, gals?' she asked Hazel, Polly and Ali, who were all furiously hashtagging their Stories.

'I brought kombucha,' Hazel called. 'Abigail, bring in the kombucha, please.' One of Hazel's kids detached from an iPad and carried in a straw shopping basket.

'Here, Mum.' The tiny Abigail, dressed in a cream knitted smock and blush-coloured tights – a variation of the rest of the clan's outfits – held the basket out to her.

'Do it again for the 'gram, sweetie,' instructed Hazel, holding up her phone.

'Here you go, Mum,' Abigail obediently repeated.

Hazel captured the moment and replayed it, frowning. 'Let's try one with "mama" – OK, sweetie?'

Abigail was totally unfazed by this bizarre reenactment. 'Here you go, Mama,' she intoned, bored.

'OK, thanks.' Hazel snatched the basket and handed it over. Shelly stole a glance at Ali to see what she made of this little pantomime, but Ali was buried in her own phone and hadn't caught it.

'So how are we all?' Hazel settled herself cross-legged on the sofa in the corner of the kitchen. Her silk kimono jacket was the same blush pink as Abigail's tights and she, like each of her daughters, had a single delicate French plait framing her fine features. Hazel was very pretty – not as striking as Shelly, but she'd nailed a certain surfer-girl-next-door look despite having zero inclination to get her hair wet. Her style directive was Gwyneth

Paltrow-meets-LA-tarot-reader-to-the-stars. 'Ali, I saw you were in the hospital there. All OK?'

'Yep, all good. I was a bit mixed up about the due date but sorted now. I'm … I'm so glad the nausea's over,' Ali concluded – a little hesitantly, Shelly thought.

'You're almost afraid to say it aloud, right?' Shelly grinned. 'I'm the same. I feel like the pregnancy gods will hear me and strike me down with the pukes again if I relax too much!'

'The pukes, ick,' was Polly's contribution as she snapped a pic of the seafood platter.

'Pregnancy is only as bad as you make it,' said Hazel like a wise baby-spawning sage.

Here we go. Shelly suppressed an eye-roll. Now Hazel would be off on one of her favourite riffs about how she'd had six healthy pregnancies and just meditated the babies out when it came time to push. Clearly, she's forgetting the six epidurals and nine private doulas it had taken, Shelly scoffed.

For her last birth, Hazel had broadcast an epic fourteen-hour Insta-live of every grunting, moaning, crowning second of Orca's entrance into the world. For much of that day you could flick over to Hazel, teeth gritted but elaborate braided hair in place, and catch how dilated she was, hear some of the poetry she'd asked to be read throughout or follow the Spotify birthing playlist. A few clever cutaways hinted at some possible trickery in the 'all natural birth' – Amy's theory was they'd staged the whole thing and the baby had actually been a couple of days old at the time of the Insta-live.

Apparently, according to Amy, conspiracy theorists were all over Rants.ie dissecting the footage. Not that that hurt Hazel – all the websites had covered the spectacle and she'd even gone on the *Late Late* to talk about how she'd done it to empower women and not at all to increase her visibility on the international Insta-scene. Tubridy had made a valiant effort to hide that he was clearly struggling to keep his food down during some of the more visceral clips shown.

'Ali, what are you doing about the birth?' Hazel sat up and fixed Ali with a stern look.

'Doing …? Ehm, I dunno. I thought the birth just kind of happened?'

'Only for people without the sense to capitalise on it.' She threw a withering glance at Shelly and Polly before continuing with a hectoring recitation about the myriad ways Ali could be better exploiting her situation. 'You need to get on top of the plan now, Ali, because after that baby comes out, you're gonna be a gibbering wreck – everyone is on their first. Shelly's still a mess, sure.' Hazel laughed and Polly joined in. 'How're you feeling about your impending joy, Shelly?'

She's digging, thought Shelly. Being such a talented bullshitter herself, Hazel had an incredible nose for the bullshit of others.

'Well,' Shelly began, 'Dan's been away a fair bit so that's been difficult.'

Polly nodded sympathetically and Shelly found herself tempted to confide the truth. It was so lonely pretending all the time. Pretending on her Instagram, and pretending to Amanda and

Marni, and pretending to Hazel and Polly, the closest thing she really had to friends aside from Amy and Plum.

'We've been going through a tough time.' Shelly tried out the words, but seeing the horror cloud Hazel and Polly's faces, she backtracked immediately. 'Just spending time apart is so hard. We miss each other,' she explained.

'Christ,' Hazel yelped. 'I thought you were talking about' – she lowered her voice – "marital problems".'

Polly shivered.

'Is that the worst thing that can happen?' Ali was looking confused. 'I mean, we're not living in the fifties – it is 2019.'

'Nothing kills a lifestyle brand like trouble in paradise,' Hazel breathlessly explained, eyes shining with unbridled glee at the thoughts of someone else's life falling apart. 'You're probably a bit young to remember an influencer called @SharonStyleHeaven? It all went completely tits-up for her after she had an affair with her trainer. She told some fairly outrageous lies to try and cover it up but it all came out in the end.'

Shelly felt panicky. Hazel was like a rabid hyena with the scent of blood in her nostrils. One whiff of any real trouble in camp SHELLY would definitely send her digging. Between keeping frenemies and fully fledged stalker enemies at bay, salvaging her relationship was actually looking like a more realistic option. She drained the rest of her kombucha as Hazel picked over the carcass of @SharonStyleHeaven's career – was it her imagination or did Ali look every bit as uncomfortable as she felt?

21

'OK, slow down – the turn is just here.' Ali was leaning back in the passenger seat of Sam's cheery little shitbox of a car, directing him through the gates of Ailesend.

'It's so close to IKEA!' Sam marvelled. 'How do you resist not going up there all the time?'

'I resist,' Ali deadpanned. Though she sorely wished they could ditch this morning's obligations and hit the showroom, or anywhere else, right now frankly. 'The car park's just down here to the right.'

Sam swung into a space and switched off the engine. 'Maybe I should go up. I could pick up a few bits for the Sweet Pea.'

'Ick, I told you to drop the cute name.'

'We can't just call it "it",' Sam argued. 'What about Finn the Foetus? After Ice-T in *SVU*?'

Ali laughed wearily. He's trying to cheer me up. It'd be cute if it wasn't so stressful. She needed him to stop talking about the baby 24-fecking-7.

'I wish you could come in with me ...' She stared, with dull eyes, towards the entrance. It wasn't just any old meeting with the care team. She pulled the sleeves of her hoodie down over her hands.

'You know I would in a heartbeat, right?' Sam drew her towards him, his expression pained. 'I wish I could, Ali. But I'm guessing this is a family-only kind of activity?'

It was impossible to bring Sam in there anyway – too many questions – but she was surprised at how much she wished she could.

'I can call in sick to work and wait here, though,' Sam offered. 'It's no big deal – I can catch up on emails and stuff. I've loads of candidates I need to chase.'

'No, you go. I'm cool. Well, I'm not cool,' Ali laughed quietly, 'but it's probably not even going to be a big thing,' though the squirming feeling in her gut and the jagged beat in her chest told her otherwise.

'I'll come and collect you and we can go on a mega *SVU* bender – how about that?'

Shit TV was their hands-down favourite Thursday-night jam, and Ali felt a bit uncomfortable admitting that after the consultation with the geriatric specialist and Mini, she was due at an event, the Glossie Awards Countdown dinner. Plus it was Liv's birthday. She needed to duck out of the dinner as early as possible and get back to her for cake and prezzies. Things had been so tense around the house and Ali needed to get her back onside.

Why did everything feel so impossible right now? Especially as she was completely knackered lately. She'd been cramping all morning and, with an apocalyptic period evidently imminent, a glitzy influencer event sounded particularly hellish, especially as this period seemed to be gearing up to be a massacre in her womb – she'd never known PMS to be so vicious.

'Sorry, I can't tonight. It's Liv's birthday but I'll text to let you know how this goes. Thanks for driving me.' Ali put her arms around his neck and breathed in his Sam smell for a few moments. He rubbed her back and whispered comforting things to her and her insides wriggled with unease. 'Have a good day.' She disengaged and hopped out.

She waved as the tree-lined driveway seemed to swallow the car, leaving her to turn, dejected, and make her way inside.

Her phone buzzed a calendar reminder – 'Glossies Countdown dinner, 7.00 p.m. Ambassador Hotel'.

The awards were still four weeks away but they really knew how to squeeze every last bit of 'glam spam' out of these events. Ali sighed. It was funny how, before, these influencer events were the Holy Grail for Ali. On nights of a big influencer event, her whole timeline would be overtaken with everyone – wannabes to top-level influencers – who'd got the invite and were desperate to eke out every last scrap of content for it. Updates with the hashtag #GlossieAwardsCountdown had already started clogging her feed by eight that morning with all the Insta-crowd filming their facials, their workouts and even, bizarrely, a visit to the chiropodist. Annabel Stevens, an ex-TV presenter with about ten thousand followers, had elected to make a stab at repackaging some poor unfortunate attempting to angle-grind her corns off as #glamprep.

Now, Ali felt like she would gladly ditch the whole thing if she wasn't so invested.

She signed in at the reception visitors' book, took a seat among other blank-faced loved ones and waited to be called. No sign of Mini yet – she was probably dashing across town shouting down the phone to Erasmus at that very moment.

Maybe her ambivalence about her new-found success was down to her PMS. She'd been happy that morning scrolling her notifications, reading the comments from her adoring followers, though even those had lost some of their sheen. Somehow the words 'you look amazing' really lost their impact after being repeated ad nauseam. Speaking of nausea, Ali could feel a tide of queasiness invading her once more. What is the deal? she wondered. Though she'd been so busy arranging breakfast that morning, she'd actually forgotten to eat any – maybe she was hungry?

She rummaged in her bag and found a bag of Skips. Better than nothing, she thought, starting on them – the saltiness seemed to assuage the nausea – just as Mini walked through the sliding glass doors of the Ailesend reception. Mini was buried in a phone call – she waved, looking hassled, hung up and added her name to the visitors' book.

'What are you eating, Ali?' Mini shook her head as she sat. 'You complain about gaining weight and then you're gorging on crap.'

'When have I complained about gaining weight? You complain about me gaining weight!'

She was obsessed with everyone's weight. Mini'd be happier walking in on Ali smoking a crack pipe than eating a bag of crisps. Ali had once heard her compliment a cancer survivor on their incredible weight loss.

'I'm not getting into a row.' Mini folded her arms, adopting the tone of someone who was a permanent fixture on the high road.

'You literally started it.'

'Ali—'

'OK, OK.' Ali held up her hands in a gesture of surrender.

Mini was crossing and re-crossing her legs. She brushed some invisible lint from her asymmetrical sheer dress, worn over trousers with slim patent-leather brogues. Ali felt bad. Along with avoiding Sam and reality in general, she had been keeping her distance from Mini. She'd tried to still her conscience, reasoning that it wasn't so bad – after all, she was still going up to sit with Miles every second day – but she'd barely spoken to Mini since she'd told her about Marcus. She didn't even know if they'd gone on their date. Somehow she didn't feel so furious about it anymore – in light of the things she'd been up to since then, a date with an old friend seemed fairly innocuous.

'Are you doing OK, Mum?' She reached for Mini's hand.

'Darling!' Mini snatched her hand away, horrified. 'There's some kind of crisp residue on your fingers.'

At this, Ali startled the assembled waiting visitors with a raucous laugh. 'Crisp residue!'

After a moment, Mini joined in.

'These are Skips.' Ali feigned indignation. 'Prawn cocktail is a better class of flavour than your average crisp – everyone knows that.'

Mini wiped her eyes, and her laugh died away but she looked a bit more relaxed. Her fidgeting subsided.

'Dad would've approved,' Ali continued.

'Hah. I've never seen Miles with a crisp in my life.'

'This crisp grudge is off-the-charts snobby,' Ali said. 'Anyway, I didn't mean he'd eat them but the man loved a seafood platter, you can't deny it.'

'Ah,' was all Mini said.

They were getting into tricky territory here. Their unspoken approach to Miles was a careful exchange of information.

Ali would text:

Went to Dad today, we listened to Wilco's last album and I gave him dinner – new levels of gross on that front. Can we not just Deliveroo in something that doesn't look regurgitated?

While Mini might respond something like:

Spoke to Miles's team this morning, they're talking about the morphine patch. Sadly they meant for him, not me.

They were rigid about never veering down memory lane. When, wondered Ali, had her gorgeous dada become such a source of pain? Talking about who Miles had been was like pressing a bruise on her heart. Yet today, perhaps because of the meeting, Ali felt like pressing on.

'D'you remember him and his lobsters?' Ali ventured. She never could've predicted that one day her father's grotesque, near-cannibalistic relish of lobsters would become a source of nostalgia.

Mini was reading her emails, but she smiled and then closed her eyes, her mouth a firm, insistent straight line. Ali realised that whatever hurt she felt thinking about her dad's cruel existence, it was nothing compared with the anguish Mini carried in her very bones.

For many years, Ali had been angry with her parents for being so bloody Irish and refusing to acknowledge his illness. Then she'd just been angry with Mini because it was easier than blaming an ever-more-helpless Miles. And then when her anger just seemed exhausting, it became easier to disappear – online, into wine, anything rather than face reality.

A moment of clarity descended on her then, and her mother's pain was palpable – all the more so for how competently she'd hidden it. All the years since Miles had lain suspended in a terrible middle place, so too had Ali and Mini. Her phone pinged with notifications and she felt hounded. She'd backed herself into a corner where she could neither face up to her life as it was nor escape the life she'd concocted online. She felt jangly. More panic. Ali, this is what you get for lying, she admonished herself.

'Mrs Riordan?' A sweet-faced older male nurse appeared beside them. 'The team are waiting for you both.'

Ali tried to force down the rising dread as they followed him to a part of the home Ali'd never visited before. Upstairs in a large airy office, four different people were introduced but Ali struggled to grasp who each of them was. She studied the plate of biscuits in the middle of the desk – who brings biscuits to a meeting like this? She heard their words, tinny and distant, as though they were coming through a bad phone signal instead of from the lips of people seated just across from her.

'As agreed, there'll be no more interventions.'

'We just want to make him as comfortable as possible.'

'We suggest you come as often as you can.'

Ali couldn't take any more in. Her thoughts were roaring, her heart was charging and she couldn't breathe. She found herself standing before she'd even thought to get up. Everyone stopped talking and looked at her expectantly. 'I'm sorry, I can't stay. I'm sorry, Mum.' She turned to Mini, who sat defeated in her chair. 'I'm not feeling very well.' Ali could barely get the words out.

She grabbed her bag and fled before anyone could intervene. Pushing the door from that airless office, with the shitty biscuits and even shittier words, was like surfacing for air. She hurried down the bright corridor, down the stairs and out through reception into the sunny day beyond. Finally, about halfway down the driveway, she paused, taking huge gulping breaths that didn't seem to quite fill her lungs. He really is going to die – they said as much. That's what all those euphemistic phrases like 'make him comfortable' mean.

She knew Mini would be pissed at her ditching like that but

she just couldn't cope with the enormity of it all. Even though she hoped against hope that Miles would die and they would be released from the agony of counting hours watching his lifeless eyes, she couldn't sit with the knowledge without feeling smothered by it.

Even out here among the trees, with birds singing and the pale March sun shining, she couldn't get far enough from this truth.

She rummaged in her bag for something to put some distance between this moment and herself. She came up with her phone and hit the Story function. She carefully checked her face to ensure she looked OK – her hair was in plaits because she wanted a beachy look for the event later. She shook it out now and touched up her lips.

She checked all around to make sure no one was coming and then stepped off the path into a gap between some trees. She set up the pic, letting a little sunlight drape across her face, accentuating her cheekbones, and took about thirty shots, trying slightly different faces for each. Smile, half-smile, laughing while fixing her hair and looking over to the left. She took some time narrowing down the choices. The final snap was cute – she looked good with her hair in loose waves and her brown eyes open wide, relaxing under the trees. She did some correcting in FaceFix, adding a bit to her lips and losing a bit from her jaw and nose. She could feel her breathing quieting and a calm settling in her chest.

Thinking about how #blessed I've been these last few months. It's been a pleasure to share this journey with you all. I can't thank you all enough for everything you've given me. Without you guys, I wouldn't be doing so many incredible things in my life right now. I can't wait to share some of these with you all soon. #influencer #collab #happydays #loveyouall #AlisBaba #myday #mylife #LittleStoriesFromMyLife #watchthisspace #excitingproject

She hit Post and sat down on the roots of a large oak to watch the likes roll in, refreshing the feed every few seconds and feeling calmer with every 'LOVE you!', 'Looking gorge Ali' and kissing emoji. What the hell did it really matter what was going on, so long as the picture looked good?

❖

'So how are you anyway?' Kate was reapplying her lipstick in the taxi on the way to the Countdown dinner.

Ali did a quick mental run-through of what she was and was not telling people before she cautiously replied, 'I'm good,' as she struggled to steady the card she was writing on her lap.

'Things have been going amazing with your account. Like, I can barely believe it.' Kate sounded more like she could barely tolerate it but Ali tried not to dwell on this.

'Yeah, it's been great. I'm getting loads of work, TG, cos I doubt I'll ever work in TV again!'

'Yeah, that was crazy – that guy was, like, a psycho.' Kate checked her teeth for lipstick. 'And how's Ali's Baba? And Sam, you guys still all loved-up?'

'Yeah, Sam's good, he's great!'

'And are you OK since the Rants stuff?' Kate added a Sympathetic Head Tilt here.

'The Rants thing? Oh yeah … just weirdos with too much time on their hands. Doctors get the dates wrong all the time.'

In the flashing lights of passing traffic Kate looked practically disappointed that she wasn't more upset. 'Thanks for bringing me as your plus one,' she muttered, looking out the window as they cruised down the canal and beyond the city centre.

Ali continued with the card.

Dear Liv,

I am so lucky to have such an incredible friend. Love you so much. You're like my sister.

I hope you have a fab birthday—

The driver veered slightly and Ali's pen jerked.

Crap. She flattened the card – purple with flowers, there'd been a very limited selection in the garage – on the seat beside her and finished by signing her name and adding a few kisses.

She slipped it into the Dunnes bag along with the cake she'd got and the rose-infused face cream Liv liked. It was all a bit last-minute but at least she was prepared. Ali wanted to try and salvage things with Liv.

'Here we go, ladies. Watch your step getting out.'

Ali handed the driver a twenty and they hurried inside Vivian's, the restaurant in Ranelagh hosting the event.

'Oh my god, there's Shelly,' Kate whispered, giving Ali a shove in the lower back as they walked in. 'Let's try get a selfie with her.'

'Sure.' Ali smiled through gritted teeth. It had been such a long day she wasn't sure she was up to mingling, but Kate had been talking non-stop in the WhatsApp about the dinner all week.

'Hi, Shelly! I'm Kate from @ShreddingForTheWedding.' Kate immediately went in for the full hugs and kisses and a power-sell on her Insta-account. 'I'm sure your followers would be so interested in my content, Shelly, if you ever wanted to work together on a collab.'

Ali was looking around the wood-panelled dining room for somewhere to stash her coat when she realised she'd left her bag of gifts and the cake for Liv in the taxi.

Without a word she dashed back to the glass doors but there was no sign of it. Feck. Feck, feck, feck. It was 7.00 p.m. – she'd never get back into town to replace the lost face cream before the Kiehl's shop closed.

She went back over to Kate who'd latched, limpet-like, on to another heavy-hitter influencer in her brief absence.

'What?' said Kate sharply when Ali pulled her aside.

'I left the bag for Liv in the taxi,' she said, stricken.

'Well, what am I supposed to do about that?'

'I dunno, care!' hissed Ali.

'Well, soz.' Kate shrugged. 'I just hailed it, so no idea what company to call. OMG, there's Holistic Hazel, oh my god – she just glows. I really wanna get her for my 'gram.' Kate scurried across to the bar in the corner and Ali watched her hang on the edge of the cluster of PRs and influencers around Hazel, trying to inch her way in.

Ali made her way to the table and glumly took her seat. Her cramps were relentless. The sharknado of periods seemed to be on the way. All she really wanted was to slip out and head home, but she couldn't imagine wishing Liv a happy birthday empty-handed. At each beautiful place setting sat a small jewellery box. Ali cracked hers open. Oh, bingo. Inside was a delicate pendant in the shape of a horseshoe. It wasn't very Liv but it would have to do. She'd snag some cake from the kitchen, maybe, and get home in time to make it up to her friend. It looked bad doing a swag 'n' dash but Kate looked happier bet into these random influencers anyway, and after the day at Ailesend she just wanted to crash.

Kate wasn't thrilled at Ali pulling her aside again to explain. 'It's just I have to be up early to see my dad tomorrow. We had a meeting with his care team and he's really not doing great.'

'But if you go, I have to go,' Kate whined as they stood by the table; the others, Ali could see, were preparing to come over.

'You really don't.' Ali scowled. She could at least feign concern about Miles. 'Have dinner – it's sit-down so you can talk to the people beside you. Or come with me, and we can hang out at mine. I'm just wrecked and I feel bad about Liv's birthday.'

'It's cool,' Kate muttered, suddenly absorbed in the table. She grabbed up two of the name cards and swapped them so that hers was now beside Holistic Hazel's. 'That's perfect – I'm set now, byeee! Have fun with your dad tomorrow.'

And Liv thinks I'm bad, thought Ali, slipping away before she'd have to do any lengthy goodbyes.

❖

'Happy birthday to you, happy birthday to you, happy birthday dear Li-iv! Happy birthday to you!'

Liv was slumped on the couch reading when Ali came in holding a plate of teacakes with a candle stuck in each. She'd lost the nerve to try and score free cake at the restaurant, plus she didn't want to make it too obvious that she'd just come from an event.

'Hey,' Liv said dully. 'Nice of you to show up.'

Ali handed her the jewellery box. 'Happy Birthday, sorry I'm late, I was held up at Miles's.'

'Were you …?' Liv said slowly, opening the lid. She seemed to be smiling as she drew the necklace out by its fine chain and Ali relaxed. She'd pulled it off. Though Liv's smile was slowly turning into more of a sneer. 'Held up with Miles, were you, Ali?'

Ali pushed her hair behind her ear and sat down in the armchair opposite. 'Yeah …'

'So weird, cos this is the same pendant that Kate was just touting on her Instagram. The gift from the Insta-dinner she's been at all night.'

'I can explain!'

'I really don't want to hear it, Ali. Every word out of you since that stupid fucking wild card whatever-the-fuck has been bullshit. And I'm so tired of it.'

Liv stood up and Ali couldn't bring herself to meet her eyes. 'Please, Liv—'

But she was gone, the necklace abandoned on the floor.

22

'I just don't know how to make him see that I didn't do any of this on purpose.' Shelly was trying to keep her voice level and non-confrontational. That's what Plum, a veteran of couples therapy, had advised on the phone the night before.

'Look, the shrinks all say they're not taking sides but they are and, fact is, you want the therapist to be on your facking side, Shelly. So play the game. Don't accuse Dan of anything. Every time you get the urge to blast him for whatever, don't be all "you never give a shit about me" – the key to winning therapy is "I feel". Put "I feel" in front of every damn thing you want to accuse him of. That way the therapist knows you're not there to play the blame game but to heal,' she'd finished triumphantly.

'Right.' Shelly had suppressed a smile. 'And do you feel you've gotten much out of the therapy?' To which Plum had only laughed throatily before hanging up because 'the fit pool-cleaner boy' had arrived.

Shelly had been meticulously implementing the 'I feel' trick, though it backfired when Dan responded to her last one with 'Well, I feel that a lot of what you're "feeling" is BS, Shelly. In fact, bullshit has become something of a speciality of yours.'

The therapy session had been Shelly's idea. She wasn't sure if it was simply that she couldn't face the thought of being a pregnant single mother and the implication that potentially had for SHELLY the brand or if she really wanted Dan back. Maybe she wanted the old Dan back. But when she thought about the last few years of their marriage, it was she who had changed, not Dan, and perhaps that was the root of the problem.

'Shelly doesn't actually want to be with me,' Dan explained to Dr Clarke in a matter-of-fact tone that didn't quite disguise his anger. 'She's put that Instagram account before me – and, worse, before our daughter – every day for two years. And if we're being honest, which I presume is the whole point of us even sitting here, I think this baby,' he gestured at her stomach, which had begun in the last week to swell slightly, 'is all for the 'gram.'

'Dan … how could you say …?'

'Oh, sorry, I forgot,' he made a big exaggerated production out of his apologies, 'I feel you deliberately got pregnant, knowing I didn't want another baby. And d'you know why I feel this?' God, thought Shelly, he's really gotten on the 'I feel' train. 'Because,'

Dan continued, 'all you care about is your precious "content". You should call her Content, in fact. Content Devine – it's got a ring, I suppose.' He sat back, his fists still clenched, though the rant had clearly taken something out of him and he looked exhausted.

'Dan,' Dr Clarke, an intimidating, together-looking woman of about forty leaned forward earnestly, 'a lot of your language is quite oppositional and we need to remember that we're here to resolve this conflict in order to move forward, not make accusations about the past. You feel sidelined by Shelly's career and you feel a sense of betrayal around this baby's conception, but contraception fails and I don't believe it's fair to say that Shelly would bring a child into the world to exploit for business.'

Shelly breathed deeply, relieved that Dr Clarke was clearly on her side. She'd chosen her because she felt she was young enough to respect a woman managing the daily juggle of motherhood and career. There was even a good chance that she followed Shelly, so it was important she didn't see her lose it with Dan now. She realised that maintaining her immaculate front with the therapist was probably defeating the very purpose of the therapy, but she didn't know how else to behave anymore.

'You don't know what Shelly is capable of when it comes to her business,' Dan countered. 'She's a slave to that thing. She hired a man to pretend to be me at some event. Does that strike you as normal behaviour, Doctor?'

Dr Clarke's eyes widened slightly and flickered to Shelly but she remained impassive. 'We don't like to use words like "normal" here,' she said, to which Dan laughed bitterly.

'Excellent, you two will get on famously.'

'I'm feeling really attacked right now ...' Shelly whispered, the line lifted straight from Plum's how-to-win-therapy pep talk. 'I had no choice with the, ehm, stand-in that we used for that event. I had an obligation to fulfil and we weren't speaking at the time. We didn't pretend he was you exactly.' She couldn't bear to look at Dr Clarke's face, knowing she was losing ground rapidly in terms of seeming like the good one in this relationship. 'People might've assumed ... and we just didn't correct them.'

Dan held her gaze, his eyes narrowing, and Shelly swallowed. He pulled out his phone casually. 'Oh, really? No pretending took place at all?' He flicked his index finger over the screen and began to read:

Fun times at the #DaddyBearsPicnic today. Thanks for the LOLs @GreenHilliardMasonPR and so great to keep up with all my international business deals with my awesome @SamsungOfficial handsfree package. Before you ask, the suit's @HugoBoss from @BrownThomasOfficial gifted to me by love of my life @ShellyDevine #ad #spon

'Hashtag blahblah fuckin' blah.'

Shelly cringed as Dan threw the phone onto the low table between them – she could see Dr Clarke twisting slightly to check out the pic.

'If you're going to create a fake version of me online, do I have to sound like such a prick? That's a reasonable enough request, isn't it, doctor? Although, if she gave a shit about what I wanted perhaps she'd listen when I say I don't want to play your dumb little Instagram game anymore. Is it too much to ask for you to stop publishing photos of me and captions purporting to be written by me without my consent? There has to be a legal line being crossed here – it's a form of identity theft, as far as I can see.'

'You said it was OK at the start.' Shelly knew how feeble this protest sounded and Dan didn't even bother to address it.

'Shelly,' he turned around to face her, 'do you actually want to save us? Or are we sitting here because you want to save face?'

This question stopped Shelly cold and she could find no Plum-approved 'I feel' response.

'I … I just … you knew that we were still honouring the @DivineDanDevine posts. You didn't mind before when the money was coming in and you didn't really have to do anything.' She looked down at her hands. Her manicure was perfect; her engagement ring sparkled, almost in defiance of how grubby and mercenary their relationship had become.

'I mind now, I think I've made that clear. And what I really mind is you not giving a crap about my feelings on all this. And,' he was on a roll, his voice getting louder, 'I mind Georgie being trotted out for freebies and to make you look good. You barely even spend time with her when there isn't a camera around.'

This really stung. Deep down, Shelly knew there was truth in it but she couldn't bear the humiliation of Dr Clarke hearing it. They could never come here again. Then she caught herself – as if there would be an 'ever again' for her and Dan in therapy.

'You don't know how hard it was for me when Georgie was born. I was struggling and you just left me to it.'

Dr Clarke was writing furiously in her notes and Shelly shuddered to think of the conclusions she was drawing. She looked up and clasped her hands earnestly in front of her. 'I think we are making progress, even if it doesn't quite feel that way right now,' she intoned in her soothing therapist voice. 'Next week, you'll both have gained some distance from the issues here.'

Dan barked a laugh and stood, grabbing his jacket. 'I'm sorry, I can't take any of this seriously. I'm not coming back after gaining distance or whatever. She can't face reality and I'm done trying to break through her filter. Everything is just a front for her. Even this therapy exercise is probably just a photo op for some faux-revealing post about looking after your mental health – that's very on-trend right now, right, Shelly?' His mouth twisted into a grim smile.

'How dare you. We're here to resolve our marriage.' Shelly didn't feel nearly as indignant as she sounded. It was hard to summon indignation when you knew the other person had a point. Of course she wouldn't be posting about their couple's therapy but she did want them to get back on track. And maybe a part of that was about brand SHELLY.

'I just don't believe that, Shelly. You're living a lie and I'm done with being some set dressing in your weird beige and blush pink life.' He stormed out the door.

❖

Shelly sat in her car eating a bag of doughnuts and feeling uncharacteristically nihilistic.

'First sessions can often be explosive,' Dr Clarke had tried to reassure her as she'd left, head down and cheeks burning. She couldn't believe that woman had witnessed the whole sorry mess of her marriage laid bare.

'Sorry, I think I'm just really hormonal,' Shelly'd offered by way of explanation, as if the woman hadn't just witnessed her husband completely annihilating her.

Now, licking the sugar from her fingers, she felt at a loss, a loss so complete and empty it was frightening. Her phone beeped – an Insta-message. The handle was strange, just @_____.

I know about your lies.

Shelly clicked on the profile, it was private with just two followers. Kelly's Klobber? It had to be.

23

'Morning, ladies! How are you guys? I am so late! I have about a gazillion appointments today but I just had to come on and tell you all about this amazing supplement I've been gifted called Nailed iT – I've linked them here.' Ali indicated the bottom of the screen, before turning serious. 'You wouldn't believe how a woman's confidence can suffer when her nails are all flaky and bendy. Nailed iT are helping women all over the world to love themselves and feel more confident. It's seriously the best thing I've ever used for my nails, like ever. So give them a follow and see if they can improve your nail life! Right, I'm off to get my coconut pancakes cos baby needs her protein.'

Ali played back the video and added the link to the nail-supplement people, hit Post and settled back to finish her coffee.

'It's an amazing supplement, is it? Improving the lives of cutically challenged women the world over?' It was early but Liv was still firing on all cynical cylinders.

'Yes, it's life-changing,' Ali replied happily. 'As is making a grand over breakfast.'

'Fuck off. Not really?'

'Yep,' said Ali, trying to dial back the gloating.

'Shit, the bullshit biz is lucrative.' Liv shook her head. 'Can't put a price on integrity though,' she concluded, making a couple of notes in the journal where she frequently jotted down ideas for her thesis.

'I have used it.' Ali was feeling testy. 'I'm not lying – my nails have improved.'

'Oh, right, you're not a liar. Not at all! If you can't take a little negging, that suggests to me that your conscience is bothering you, darl.' Liv tilted her head and cocked an eyebrow.

God, things had become unbearable between them. Liv had virtually given up all pretence at still being friends. Ali hated fighting with her. She was too good at it for a start.

'Nope, conscience is on board with this.' Ali got up and began prepping the breakfast post flat lay. 'I'm making really good money, I'm not hurting anyone and, if I'm not mistaken, your thesis would be screwed without me, no?'

'Oh, so you're aware of my thesis? Because you never fucking ask me about it!' Liv said pissily.

'Well, you never asked me about the meeting with Miles's doctors.' Ali was relieved to have something to throw back in her face.

Liv ducked her head and looked stricken. 'Shit, Ali. I'm sorry,' she said quietly. She sighed. 'How did it go?'

'It's not good. They seem to think he doesn't have much time left. The last infection …' Ali massaged her forehead. 'I dunno. I don't want to get into it. How's the thesis going?' She wanted to keep Liv talking while she was feeling a touch more amenable; Ali missed her more than she wanted to acknowledge.

Liv sighed. 'My last Google search was "how many people abandon their thesis".'

'Yikes, mine was,' Ali consulted her phone, '"second-trimester pregnancy symptoms".'

'Oh? So how're you going to be feeling in the coming months?'

'Oh, it's a hellscape: leg pains, loose teeth, bleeding gums, pelvic pain, leg cramps, puffiness. You could write a thesis on preggo symptoms. It's a bloody shitshow. Never heard any of the Insta-mums talking about their urinary tract infections before! Lots of material for the 'gram, though. I'm gonna do a whole series on "stuff no one tells you about pregnancy".'

'Oh yeah, you're definitely the right person to be explaining the process of gestation.' Liv's tone was still mocking but definitely warming up. 'How's lover boy? Haven't seen him.'

'Em, he's cool,' Ali said airily, rearranging the flat lay.

'Ah, he's still pissed about the fake visit to the imaginary doctor that he missed out on?'

'Well, he was hurt,' Ali conceded, nudging a bottle of mouthwash closer to a smoothie bowl she'd made by adding food dye to PVA glue and topping with berries and some potpourri – it looked infinitely better than any smoothie bowl she could've made for real and she could use it over and over, just changing up the toppings. 'He's a real "feelings guy".' Ali frowned. It was hard to get the mouthwash bottle to talk to the rest of the breakfast-tray aesthetic. 'It looks a bit off,' she muttered.

'Well, most people use mouthwash in the bathroom,' Liv offered. 'Maybe that's why it looks weird. What's he said?'

'Oh,' Ali sighed, 'just stuff like how it's his baby too and he wanted to be there with me.'

'What a total prick.'

'I wasn't saying that,' Ali protested. 'But he is being weirdly proprietary about the whole thing. Keeps wanting to tell his sisters and, ugh, I just wish he'd get off Instagram. He's always on my Story. I wish he'd be supportive but not so invested, ya know? Thank fuck I'm getting away to the duffed-up-bitches retreat later. I need to get a plan together and I can't think straight when he's around with his lovely arms and nice smell.'

'The arms are very nice alright,' Liv agreed. 'But, Ali, I'm not sure there's any amount of thinking straight that'll get you out of this. One way or another you're going to lose. You see that, don't you? Whether it's followers or Sam. Or both,' she finished grimly.

'I think I need to put the mouthwash into a little jar or something, maybe with a stripy straw.' Ali fussed with the bottle, the familiar quake in her chest at Liv's words.

'Ali?'

'I know it's a tricky situation. I just need to get through the Glossies and I'll figure it out then.'

'But what'll you do?'

'I'll think about it then.' Ali sounded a lot more certain than she felt. 'I don't have the headspace right now. Between Sam and my dad and sponcon, I've too much going on. But I'll figure it out.'

'Sam is genuinely the best thing that's happened out of all this. I think you love him but you need to shut this Ali's Baba madness down and just be real with him.'

'Jesus, can't you just shut up for a minute? I'm trying to get this post up – I have to publish it before 9 a.m. – and then I have a really important meeting. I can't fix this whole thing right this second.' Ali could feel the tide of stress threatening to overwhelm her.

Seeing Liv's face freeze, she tried to backtrack immediately. It'd been the longest conversation they'd had in weeks.

'I'm sorry, Liv, I'm really sorry, OK? I really am – I don't want to hurt Sam. I'm just afraid he'll ditch me if I tell him the truth. I will sort everything out – I just need more time.'

Liv looked like she was about to go on the offensive once more but thought better of it. 'I'm really worried about you, Ali. You ditched your job for this. You're lying to everyone. You're doing sponcon while your dad's getting sicker and sicker.' She came around the table and hugged her long and hard.

'Please, don't. I'll cry, Liv. And then my face'll be wrecked before this meeting.' Ali disengaged from the hug, avoiding Liv's probing gaze. She made a mental note to add Liv to the list of people she needed to keep at arm's length. The list was growing. Miles, Mini, Sam, Liv – anyone she couldn't maintain her pristine façade in front of, really. Avoiding Liv's eyes, she took a final snap of the flat lay and started to clear up. 'I've got to get going. I have a brand meeting.'

Ali started gathering her kit. Now the ring-light and tripod went everywhere with her. With eighty thousand people watching her Stories she couldn't rely on just any old lighting anymore.

Liv stood staring at her and shaking her head.

Ali's phone started buzzing and she could confidently say she had never been happier to see the words 'Mini calling'.

'I have to get this.' Ali started moving towards the door. 'Might catch you before I head to the retreat thingy later.' She hit the green button and mouthed 'Bye' to Liv's stony face as she turned and fled out the door to her car – she needed to get on the road.

❖

Taking the call from Mini had been a mistake. Her make-up had looked pretty dodge by the end of the Liv hug and now, after five minutes on the phone to Mini, it was completely wrecked. Things with Miles were getting worse but the doctors seemed to communicate solely in cryptic euphemisms that made it impossible to establish what they were really saying.

The whole thing was taking its toll on Mini. She barely reacted to Ali saying she'd be away for a few days. Normal Mini would've pumped her for info – where she was going, with whom and why. New Mini had her advantages, of course – at no point had she taken even the slightest bit of interest in Ali's recent Instagram adventures. It was amazing how insular the Instagram world could be and this worked to her advantage. You could be Insta-famous and no one beyond the bubble even knew who you were. It was dangerous too – it made everything on there seem even further from reality.

Mini was clearly lost in her own issues. Her usual all-business demeanour had crumbled in the last weeks. She was even taking time away from the gallery. Eleanor, her younger sister, was staying over a lot. The two were very close, always cackling at private jokes and references no one else got. Seeing Mini transformed in Eleanor's presence always made Ali wish she'd had a sister. Though Liv was nearly as good. Usually. With the way things were right now, Ali was starting to worry they wouldn't get that back. Just a few more weeks. She gripped the wheel, glancing at Google Maps to make sure she was heading the right way.

And then what, Ali? What happens in a few weeks? She hushed the thought.

She got to the business park early for her meeting with Baby Bella Boo Boo Buggies. It was a grim collection of warehouses, tile shops and printing companies on the western edge of the city. She scouted a spot for her next update and found a serious dearth of Insta-worthy locations. Eventually, she set up behind a red-brick block next to what she suspected was a septic tank. The glamour. Careful to keep the shot tight, she babbled for a few minutes about how she couldn't wait to reveal what she'd been working on. Oh, and for everyone asking, her top was from ASOS. No one had been asking, of course – this was just to give the illusion that she was flat out responding to her followers.

It was a curious thing, but the more followers she got, the less engaged they seemed. When she'd just been plain old @Ali_Jones she'd often have the chats in the DMs but now, though there were more people watching, they seemed to say less. It was creepy.

Don't be paranoid, Ali. They're not some giant crowd of faceless stalkers. They're your people. You wanted them and now you've got them. She folded away the ring-light and tripod and headed around the front of the building where Sian, the brand manager, was waiting with a big bunch of flowers.

'Congratulations, Ali! Big day – designing your first collection!'

'Oh gawd, I'm nervous! I've never designed anything. Except maybe the design-your-own at Pizza Hut.'

Sian laughed uproariously. 'That's why we love you here at Bella Boo Boo! You're just so real!' Ali smiled awkwardly. 'So right this way, Ms Designer!'

Oh god. It was always all a bit much with these people.

Ali was shown into a meeting room filled with pram paraphernalia. There was a white board with the word 'ideas' written large. On the vast table were swatches of fabric in different shades of tasteful grey along with a mountain of pastries and fruit platters. A couple of bored-looking men were introduced as the design team, here to 'guide the process'.

The process, it transpired, was pretty simple. Ali was given a coffee. They discussed how structurally there was little to improve on the Bella Boo Boo Buggy but what they needed was Ali's vision – this meant picking which grey she liked best. She also had a choice of three innovative features they could add. She opted for the iPhone holder – great for strolling and scrolling. She practised her signature a couple of times for the new logo, which would be ironed on to the bassinet part of the buggy, and that was pretty much it. The Bella Boo Boo Buggy by @AlisBaba was born. Ali took a few snaps of the process then the photographer arrived to shoot Ali with the buggy for the campaign.

'It's not ready, though, surely?' Ali was flustered; she hadn't expected the turnaround to be literally that day. A hairdresser was already fixing her hair while the make-up artist prepped her brushes.

One of the designers just rolled his eyes and headed out the door. The other one leaned across the table. 'You'll just use one of the normal buggies and then we'll fix the colour and add the logo in Photoshop. C'mon, you're an influencer, you know how it works.' He winked and followed his colleague out the door.

The whole thing was wrapped up by noon and Ali was back in her car posting about her 'exciting news' before lunchtime.

'I've been working on this project for so long and it is so exciting to finally be able to tell you about it.' She paused in her typing. It just wasn't that satisfying to be claiming she'd poured blood, sweat and tears into picking a colour. They'd kept referring to her as the designer, which was fairly awkward given the actual designers were sitting right there.

She X'd out of the post and saved it as a draft. She brought up her feed and found herself face to face with a smiling Kate brandishing her engagement ring. Ali hit the Heart button and typed 'Congrats. Amazing news!' She noticed Kate was also claiming to have 'designed' the ring. She'd picked the diamond and asked for a plain band. That, it seemed, constituted designing something on Planet Instagram.

I should just be owning this, Ali thought. All the times I've seen influencers bring out their various lip kits and #goalsjournals. Now I finally have something with my name on it. I should be enjoying this moment.

She could hear how she sounded but fuck it. She just had to remember how jealous she used to get seeing these exciting-news posts. Now someone else was seeing her exciting news and feeling jealous of her. She went back to the draft and amped up the enthusing to max levels.

'In the planning stages of the new Bella Boo Boo Buggy by @AlisBaba, I thought so long and so hard about what it is that new mamas really need after welcoming their little bundles into the world …' She wrote at length about her 'process', her 'vision' and the nights spent toiling with her sketchbook. She rounded it off with no less than twenty-five hashtags, boldly including ones like #DesignersOfInstagram and #AliSketches.

Satisfied, she hit Post and consulted the calendar app. It was nearly time to hit the road. She just needed to get to the pharmacy and stock up on some pregnancy staples before heading to the retreat. She presumed they'd all have their own private rooms but, just in case, she wanted to look the part. She'd done some research and knew Gaviscon to be an absolute must-have for preggers bitches. She was also going to grab some organic black-bean brownies she'd tried ages ago that had given her mega bloat. Could come in handy for the spa when she'd be in her swimsuit. She was fairly certain she didn't have to be showing yet at thirteen weeks but a little hint couldn't hurt. She'd already bought nursing bras and some maternity workout wear to help her get in the right headspace for the part.

She gave the phone a final check and then started the car. The new post was already racking up likes and comments. She smiled, pulling out of the business park. She'd save them for later, something to look forward to after checking in with Mini and getting an update on Miles this evening. Glancing down at the phone in the holder, she could see a fair few 'oh my god's and 'amazing's rolling in. 'Amazing' had pretty much been sapped of all meaning since the advent of Instagram. Still, it felt pretty amazing to Ali as she headed towards the motorway in the early-afternoon sun. She just needed to stay focused on the good stuff.

24

'Now, mamas, I don't want you getting yourselves all worked up over these letters. Keep them simple. You just want to convey to your baby how much you love them. How you can't wait to meet them. What your vision is for your relationship with them. How you see their place in this world. What you hope they will achieve with their lives – not financially speaking, of course, but on a more profound, spiritual level. Think of what your intentional parenting will look like ...' Adrienne was pacing the forest floor barefoot, gesturing elaborately as she held forth. It was really verging more on an interpretive dance, thought Shelly.

She shifted about, trying to get comfortable. Sitting cross-legged was a special kind of hell, she reckoned. How does Hazel do it? She's forever storying in the lotus pose on sisal rugs that look itchier than a hairshirt. Of course, sisal would be better than the bloody ground. What is this, some kind of hazing? Though tolerating pain and low-grade annoyance would probably be the perfect parenting hazing, thought Shelly, not that any of these women knew that. They seemed to think parenting was going to be all love, light and Liga. Shelly swapped position, tucking her feet underneath her and practically groaning with relief. This attracted a slightly ratty look from Adrienne, which Shelly responded to with a wide smile.

Adrienne continued her spiel about the 'simple missive' they were supposed to be writing as she stalked around the forest clearing among her disciples – fifteen women of various stages of pregnancy all decked out in silk scarves wrapped like bandeau tops around their breasts and floaty patterned harem pants – it was a uniform at the retreat.

'We wear simple garments so we can connect with our mama-earth inner selves' was the explanation during the opening ceremony. It really underscored the cult vibe, Shelly thought.

The other women on the course were, for the most part, fabulously wealthy first-time mums. They had no idea what they were in for. Shelly pitied their ignorance and wished she wasn't so painfully aware of the inevitable fallout coming her way after the sweet-smelling bomb was lobbed into her already tricky set of circumstances.

She was starting to get an idea of the single-parent life in the past few weeks. With Dan practically parenting remotely and

Marni's hours cut back – thanks to the money complications – Shelly had been doing the mum thing more. One upside of spending more time with Georgie was that she'd started to feel less guilty about her.

She was beginning to feel closer to Georgie and the constant self-berating had quieted somewhat. She even found that without Dan around she felt more relaxed. She wasn't second-guessing her every parenting decision in anticipation of his criticism. And when leaving the little girl with her mum and dad so she could come on the retreat, she'd felt torn about going just when they were getting on so well.

Sandra had laughed gently when Shelly made noises about not wanting to go. 'There's plenty of time with Georgie ahead. It's probably no bad idea to take some time to get to know this one,' she indicated Shelly's tummy, 'and find the new you in all this, Shel.'

The new you! Sandra had obviously been bingeing the Oprah podcast but she was right, particularly about having some time to think about the new baby. Even if this hippy stuff was all a bit Enya, it was good to get some time alone to sort her head out.

Her parents had been incredible since she'd finally told them about the marriage meltdown: dropping by to watch the *Late Late* on a Friday night – Shelly didn't quite know how to tell them this wasn't exactly her idea of entertainment – and bringing Georgie to the park when Shelly needed time to work or simply lie down and absorb the crazy shift that had taken place in her life. She was down a husband, an assistant and maybe ten or so thousand followers (the SHELLY account had suffered in Amy's absence) and she wasn't altogether sure if she truly minded this or not.

With a following of her scale, probably only the most eagle-eyed would have noticed the drop in numbers – Hazel, no doubt, was preparing some sort of Machiavellian ambush – but even so, Shelly found she didn't have the will to care about SHELLY with so much else at stake. Never mind the fact that the jarring disconnect between the life she was living and the life she was posting about had become too great to ignore.

There had been that weird DM the week before, but there'd been no more since. Shelly hoped Kelly's Klobber (she was pretty sure that's who was behind it) was just trying to rattle her. She had enough acrimony emanating from Dan's Seomra at the end of the garden at home. With all these issues pulling at her, now the relentless spirituality and good-vibes-only mandate at Mothers of the Earth was really starting to grate. Every time one of the other pregos earnestly professed her love for her unborn child or expressed horror at the thought of ever subjecting said child to such corporal abuses as a fish finger, Shelly felt close to mutiny. They're very easy to love 'in theory', she wanted to scream.

As the pine needles dug into her shins, Shelly found herself glaring at Adrienne as she passed by once more. Is she trying to raise our pain threshold before the birth? She huffed silently, switching back to cross-legged to give her muscles a break. How were the more pregnant ones managing? Shelly stole a glance at the woman on her right who hadn't been happy about her Lululemons being confiscated on day one but calmed when she learned that the harem pants were Stella. She was happily lotusing despite her big round belly, upon which she'd rested the first few sheets of the letter they were all supposed to be working on. She waved Adrienne over, looking a little hyper. Adrienne wafted back towards her, hands clasped behind her back and eyebrows raised.

'Sylvia? Everything OK?'

'Oh yes, totally. It's just I'm a bit worried that I'm being too detailed in the letter. How much is too much?'

'Well,' Adrienne settled herself into a languorous pigeon pose on the ground among the leaves and drew her hands together in prayer, 'it's only natural that you have much to say to your baby. But it is imperative that you don't overburden the baby with your thoughts or she'll be overwhelmed.'

Shelly wasn't sure she'd be able to listen to this without laughing. She pressed her lips together and took in the rest of the circle. Most of the women were hanging on Adrienne's every batshit word – except Ali Jones, who appeared to be shaking with a fit of giggles. Someone sane at least, Shelly thought.

They'd met at Killarney train station en route and wound up sharing a taxi. Amy had tagged along to give Shelly a pep talk on the Kelly's Klobber sitch, and when Ali appeared, Amy seemed all for them travelling together. Shelly suspected that Amy thought it'd be strategic for Shelly to be Ali's friend – such was her current reversal of fortunes.

Amy had been giving Shelly a wide berth in the past few weeks to let her get her bearings with driving the SHELLY juggernaut once more. Once they'd been shown to their separate cabins, all overlooking a small lake at the edge of a wooded area, Shelly filled her in on Kelly's Klobber.

'Well, she sent a DM from another account. She hasn't actually said a whole lot yet and there's been no mention of money – thank god. Imagine if I had to ask Dan for money to pay off a blackmailing blogger?'

Amy didn't smile. 'I hope you're taking this seriously, Shelly. You never know who's really behind a social media handle. You don't want to antagonise her.'

They'd caught up on bits of gossip – Hazel was bringing out a new line of lotions called Holistic Glow that claimed to empower women to 'glow instead of conform to impossible tanning standards'. 'It's absolutely still a tanning product.' Amy had rolled her eyes. Soon after, she'd headed back to the station.

Shelly tuned back in to Adrienne just as she began whispering some kind of incantation directly into Sylvia's crotch. She surfaced and assumed another pretzel-like pose and began to pontificate once more.

'The vaginal canal is our pathway of communication. You must commune with your baby, mamas.' Adrienne demonstrated by parting her legs and swooping forward until she was nose to nose with her own undercarriage. 'Whisper your love, your plans, your truth, your aims for sleep schedules. Commune with your baby.'

Schedules! Shelly suppressed a laugh. As if any baby in the history of babies ever gave a crap about a schedule.

'Eh … Not sure I'm able to get down there with this in the way.'

A nervy-looking dark-haired woman held up an arm tentatively across the clearing, indicating her bulbous belly.

Ali Jones snorted, threatening to set Shelly off as well. Just don't catch her eye, Shelly warned herself.

'Of course.' Adrienne unfurled and began to dispense small mirrors to the rounder women. 'Maintaining eye contact is another option.'

'Eye contact with …?' Ali was looking mischievous.

'With the vaginal opening, Alessandra.' Adrienne could get very stern if she detected the slightest hint that someone wasn't taking her instructions seriously. 'The vaginal opening is the window to the womb. There is a flap in the front of your pants for access or you may practise this exercise in your rooms if you prefer.'

Shelly saw her chance and seized it. She had thought the odd little pants flap seemed ominous and now she knew why. She dragged herself up into standing, the decidedly ungraceful move compounded by a guttural oomph that escaped. The other women looked affronted by her lack of grace, something that ordinarily Shelly would be troubled by, but in the last few weeks she'd noticed a shift in her attitude. Amy would call it no-fucks and she would be most concerned about its effect on brand SHELLY. Shelly, on the other hand, was finding it kind of liberating. Losing your marriage could do that to a person.

'I'm gonna do my vagina-gazing back in my room, thanks, Adrienne,' Shelly announced. She was giddy at the thought of escaping back to her secret stash of chocolate. She gathered her letter and, feeling playful, finished with, 'Wouldn't want a poor, defenceless woodland creature accidentally wandering up there. Things aren't what they used to be after Georgie ploughed her way out.' She gave the group a wink and left them in stunned silence.

Back at her room, a little wood-panelled haven under the eaves, she hopped onto her bed. It was such luxury to be by herself, though her phone was pinging away incessantly. Shelly picked it up to kill the alarms and turn on airplane mode and then dropped it abruptly. Something was wrong. The background of the phone was different. Wasn't it? Shelly struggled to remember the picture she'd had before. She knew it was her and Georgie but couldn't remember the exact photo. She just knew it wasn't this one. This one was taken at the Daddy Bears' Picnic a few weeks ago. She peered closer. It was her and Georgie, taken from off to the side and close up, but now that she examined it, she was sure it hadn't been taken by Amy. Why would Amy be taking pictures off to the side like that? And how had it got on her phone? What the hell was going on? She screen-grabbed the wallpaper and sent it to Amy, who'd gone on to stay with friends in Kerry.

Pretty sure my wallpaper just changed of its own accord? Is that possible? Do you know this picture?

She sat back against the crisp cotton sheets, all delight at her me-time evaporated. She shivered involuntarily. The wardrobe opposite the bed had doors with wooden slats and she found herself unable to take her eyes off the dark gaps. A horrible thought flashed across her mind, an image of herself sitting as she was right now on the bed, knees drawn up to her chest, as seen from inside the wardrobe.

The phone buzzed and she jumped. Keeping her eyes on the doors, she carefully picked up the phone and brought it close to her face so she could check Amy's reply without looking away from the wardrobe. Could she hear breathing? But maybe that was just her own? She strained to listen, to differentiate her fretful breaths and the pounding in her ears from the sounds around her.

What had just a moment ago seemed like a sanctuary now felt very much like a lonely cabin in the woods. It wasn't quite dark outside but the trees seemed to hunker down around the cottage, blocking out the last of the day and compounding the feeling of remote isolation. Calm down. You're getting worked up. There are cottages to the right and more further up the lake towards the retreat centre. There's no one here, she thought firmly.

She pulled her eyes away from the wardrobe to her phone. No WhatsApps from Amy but there was a DM on Insta. She clicked the little paper airplane in the top right of the app and a blurry image filled the screen. A strangled cry escaped her and she scrambled backwards. Wooden slats, darkness, a small light revealing a distant figure on a bed. Shelly moaned, startling herself. A sudden rush of wild energy erupted in her and she grabbed the bedside lamp, ripping it from the wall and flung herself across the room.

Somehow she found her feet and yanked the wardrobe doors open. The hangers clattered as she launched herself in, pushing the hanging clothes out of the way and feeling all the way to the back, fully expecting a foreign hand to grab her wrist at any moment. Nothing.

She staggered backwards until the bed connected with her calves and she slumped down. Her ragged breathing tore at her chest, the roar in her ears continued and she found she was crying. Her whole body was vibrating, coursing with fear. Dropping the lamp, she scooted back to the head of the bed, her shaking hands searching for the phone. She felt sick from the toxic flood of adrenaline. Calm, calm, calm, she whispered. She peered once again at the picture and forced herself to examine it.

They weren't the slats of the wardrobe door. Of course they weren't. She tried to quiet her racing heart. But what were they? And more importantly, where were they? Then it hit her. The Seomra had wooden Venetian blinds. She was looking through the window of the little house at the end of the garden and seeing her husband sleeping.

She dragged air into her body and started to shake, right as the phone began ringing. The sound seemed to rip through the stillness of the room and she quickly answered to silence it, irrationally fearful that she would alert someone – but who? – to her presence.

'Hello?' she whispered.

'Shelly!' A cheery greeting.

'Who is this, please?'

'Hee hee, wouldn't you like to know!' The voice was high and playful.

Shelly checked the screen and froze. Caller Unknown.

'How's Dan? Seeing much of him these days?'

Shelly cancelled the call.

25

Ali woke up to banging on the front door.

'Rise, mama, it's time for our final ceremony,' roared Adrienne from outside as she moved between cottages. Ali rolled over in bed and reached to nudge the curtain out of the way. She could just about see Adrienne's flowing white gown and some kind of vines braided in her hair. She banged on the next cottage with the large staff she was waving about.

Fucking hell. Ali settled back on the pillows. She's so intense. For a place that was supposed to be all holistic, it was a fairly gruelling schedule. Ali had mixed feelings about leaving later. She was averaging one response for every five messages from Sam – she'd told him the signal was patchy so he wasn't pestering her, as such, just endlessly sharing his thoughts, along with snaps of food he was eating and even a dick pic. Though, of course, it being Sam it wasn't just any old dick pic but a dick video of his penis lip synching to 'Fernando' by ABBA. She'd innocently opened the message in the nourishment centre and nearly died laughing. She'd had to pretend she was choking to get out of explaining what was so funny.

Going home meant dealing with everything. It felt like things were accelerating and it was not pleasant. Mini had texted a few times to impart grim updates on Miles, and Ali felt both guilty and relieved at not being there. Of course, hiding in the woods hadn't been the relaxing affair she'd anticipated. For one, Adrienne was completely batshit, an oddly tyrannical hippy, and had leaned on Ali pretty hard for lots of Instagram coverage.

Shelly, she noticed, had barely bothered with anything and was apparently unfazed by Adrienne's snippy comments. Shelly's whole account seemed to have slowed right down, which was interesting. Amy seemed to be taking something of a sabbatical, and several of Shelly's clients had emailed Ali in the past week saying they were on the hunt for a new brand rep. One particularly indiscreet PR said they weren't sure if Shelly was in keeping with their family values angle, which was definitely odd. Ali flashed back on the distant Dan at the Daddy Bears' Picnic. The girl had said there was some talk but she couldn't go into it. 'I've already said too much, but let's just say I'd be celebrating if I were you – you could be poised to clean up.'

Ali probably wouldn't have thought much more of it had

Shelly herself not been acting so weird the whole time they were there. Not even bad weird, Ali realised. She was actually just acting quite normal, making jokes and being quite irreverent, which was of course completely abnormal for Shelly. However, maybe she'd heard about the gossip because in the last day or two her demeanour had shifted again and she'd seemed watchful and nervy.

Ali could hear Adrienne passing back towards her and bounded out of bed and down the stairs to open the door before she could bang on it again.

'Morning,' Ali beamed, interrupting Adrienne's raised staff and giving the guru a start.

'Ah, yes. Morning, Ali. All set for today? Don't forget the personal items but nothing flammable, please. It's going to be emotionally demanding and I'm advising everyone to spend some time centring themselves right now. I'm recommending lots of fluids and being among nature.'

She scooped some sand from a leather fanny pouch and cupped Ali's hands to receive it.

'And this is?'

'Nature.' Adrienne smiled firmly.

'Couldn't I just go outside?'

'This is better nature. It's from Burning Man,' she breathed, kissing her fingers and touching them to her heart. 'Rest, Ali. At noon we journey within to reveal your essence. We will demolish your old identity and through the effluvia of destruction we will birth the new mama-you.'

'Cool.' Ali grinned. What the hell do you say to that? Effluvia? Ick.

Adrienne fixed her with a look and Ali squirmed. All week Adrienne had made much of her 'innate knowledge', as she called it, reading the women's magnetic fields, revealing the sex of their babies and communicating the foetuses' inner thoughts regarding gluten and elective C-sections. It was clearly all very far-fetched but it made Ali uncomfortable nonetheless. Adrienne would catch her alone, fix her with the 'soul stare' and a panicked voice in Ali's head would immediately start up. She can fucking tell you're a fake – she knows!

Then Adrienne would say, stroking her face, 'Alessandra … you have been a mother many thousands of times across space and consciousness, but this time, this is the one that means the most.'

Ali would relax momentarily, until the voice would start needling. She's double-bluffing you!

Adrienne, Ali noticed, was still staring at her. She began humming softly as she dusted herself with some of the pouch sand, holding Ali's gaze. 'Bathe in the dust of nature, Ali.'

'OK,' Ali blurted, anything to stop the staring. 'Gotta go do a bit of Instagramming.'

Instagram was the magic word and Adrienne's razor-sharp focus returned. 'Yes, excellent, do that. My following has really grown since you've been here. It's fantastic. I'll let you get on with it.' She moved closer, and her bony fingers clasped Ali's upper arm. 'It'd be great to get, will we say, six tagged Stories between now and the end of the day? And then one big round-up post after the ceremony?'

'Yep, no probs, absolutely.' Ali could barely hide her amusement.

'Excellent, excellent.' Adrienne casually brought her hands together in prayer behind her back in what looked to be a very uncomfortable pose and began to drift off.

'Adrienne? Your … eh … staff?' Ali called.

Adrienne shuffled back, looking flustered. 'Yes, yes, thank you.' She grabbed the stick and hurried off, turning one last time to aim the staff at Ali's belly. 'That little boy is lucky to have you, Ali. He will bring peace to all he meets.'

'Cool!' Ali called, ducking back inside. Double-bluff or double-bonkers, it hardly matters which, she thought, heading back upstairs to set up her ring-light and get ready for all the spirituality.

❖

The women gathered outside the nourishment centre after an early lunch comprised solely of orange food. Ali was fairly acclimatised to Adrienne's notions by now and didn't bat an eyelid during her speech about the symbolic significance of the orange meal, though the inclusion of an Easi Single did seem to be taking the theme very literally.

'That orange and carrot soup was so tasty.' Helena, a private funds manager, was making small talk as Adrienne filmed the group and talked to her followers.

'Here's my batch of mamas-in-waiting.' She trained the camera on the assembled women, some tugging awkwardly on the day's uniform – an aggressively unflattering co-ord set comprising a hemp bralette and matching shorts.

'Every one of these women has undertaken a journey here in the wilds of Kerry. It was a journey from a state of unconsciousness to one of self-discovery, and today we will complete the process of self-actualisation during an emotional and intensely private ceremony deep in the forest. Tune in on my IGTV to watch in real time as each of these women dies and is reborn … a mama.'

Ali wanted to laugh. If an intensely private ceremony takes place in the woods and doesn't appear on the 'gram, is it really happening at all?

'Glad I'm wearing this hemp nightmare for my Instagram debut,' muttered Imogene, one of the slightly more cynical in the group.

'What was that?' Adrienne had reared back like a premenstrual velociraptor – she didn't take kindly to any dissent among her disciples.

'Nothing, nothing,' Imogene called back airily.

Adrienne began pairing the women off to begin the pilgrimage to the ceremony. Ali and Shelly found themselves shoved roughly together by the sinewy sage as she griped bitchily, 'Don't sign the release form then, Imogene, honey.'

Shelly raised her eyebrows and Ali, checking Adrienne had moved on, whispered, 'She's terrifying.'

Shelly opened her mouth to respond but was interrupted by the sound of a gong and the line began to move across the car park, past Adrienne's brand new Mercedes and towards the edge of a wooded area. The sun was high overhead but only slivers of light reached the forest floor. The women walked with heads bowed, each clutching the personal memento they'd been instructed to bring and listening to the ecstatic ranting of Adrienne.

Much of the rant centred around society's refusal to recognise women as the true mothers of mankind, which seemed like a bit of a reach to Ali. Who was denying that women were the mothers in this equation? The rant veered from society being innately fearful of the power of mothers to ire at the existence of cots. Occasionally snippets of an even more obscure and bizarre personal agenda would seep in. There was mention of nefarious attempts by the Irish media to discredit her teachings.

'Nobody fucking bats an eye at the Happy Pears,' she railed. 'Then I start making a tangible difference in women's lives and I "seem a little whimsical". Oh, fuck you, Mr Middle-Aged Morning Radio guy – stop mansplaining me to me.'

Ali and Shelly exchanged more looks of quiet amusement and Ali felt a flicker of guilt about all the emails currently awaiting answers that could potentially boot Shelly out of a job. What was going on with her?

At last they reached the clearing and Adrienne led them in some sun salutations.

'Is this safe?' Imogene asked as some of the pregnant women struggled to assume the poses.

'You're suffering from societal Stockholm syndrome,' Adrienne barked.

'What?' Imogene faltered.

'Some male obstetrician has convinced you there are things your powerful gestating body can't or shouldn't do. They have medicalised this process to keep women down.'

'But … it's just that … it's just I can't lie on my tummy.' Imogene indicated her bulging belly.

'Everyone back to your feet,' Adrienne shouted over her. 'Now I want you to form a circle holding your offerings.'

Offerings? Ali was confused. She'd brought Miles's watch – she'd thought it was supposed to be something of personal value not something to offer up. She started to feel alarmed and clutched the watch close as Adrienne knelt in the centre of the clearing and lit a fire. This did not bode well.

She wished she had something she could swap for the watch but they weren't even wearing underwear under these hemp monstrosities. Obviously there was no way in hell she was parting with Miles's watch. Shelly, she noticed, was looking similarly disturbed. She was carrying a small wooden box.

Adrienne was stoking the fire with her staff, the rhetoric having taken an unnerving new direction. 'A woman cannot be a mother without first sacrificing her former identity. You must destroy yourselves in order to birth this new life.' She aimed the crook at a woman who seemed about to speak. 'This is not negotiable. You are not you anymore.' Adrienne was getting sweatier as the speech climaxed. 'You must murder the woman you once were. Now, each of you regard your totem, regard the woman you thought yourself to be and accept that she is over.

In your own good time – but not too long because the IGTV has a ten-minute video limit – hurl that self into the flames.' Adrienne started recording.

Well, that escalated, thought Ali, sneaking a peek around to see how everyone else was taking the news that they had to self-immolate just to be a mother. In general, the assembled women were staring with reverence at their chosen objects. Polly was crouched over to the right past Shelly contemplating a papier mâché ornament, evidently homemade. Ali hadn't seen her much throughout the retreat – she obviously wasn't as close to Shelly as their Instagrams suggested. Then Ali's thoughts and the silence were disturbed by a sound that had presumably never been heard before at the Mothers of the Earth retreat: sniggering.

Adrienne marched over to the offender – none other than Shelly! – looking frankly homicidal. Ali felt the rage rolling off her in waves.

Shelly held her hands up in a stance of surrender. 'I'm sorry, Adrienne. I didn't mean to laugh but, like, ya know, it all seems a bit much. We can't only be mothers from now on. You can't lose yourself when a baby comes along. It's hard enough being a mother without trying to make it all that you are.'

Adrienne was incandescent with rage. 'What do you know about it?'

'Well, I am a mother.' Shelly was trying to sound reasonable.

'You only know your own spiritually bankrupt way of motherhood. I am teaching a profound and joy-filled new path,' Adrienne screamed.

The entire circle was now silently staring. Ali wouldn't have bet on Shelly leading the mutiny but there she was looking defiant.

'Joy-filled is the whole fucking problem,' Shelly argued, and Ali nearly died of shock. Shelly saying 'fuck' was big. 'You're making all these women think it's going to be this huge spiritual experience and that's just crap.'

'Don't listen to her, mamas.' Adrienne was verging on hysterical as she covered her own ears. 'She's trying to block your joy.'

'I'm not,' Shelly insisted. 'I'm just saying it's not all what you see on Instagram. Some mornings you're so tired, you just feel like a wrung-out old J-cloth. There's actual poo in your hair and you wish you could just get rid of the baby for five minutes and go for a lie-down.'

Ali couldn't believe the queen of beige was talking like this. Around her the other women looked traumatised.

'You wanted to kill your baby?' Joanna, a Pilates instructor from Westmeath, gasped.

Shelly looked irritated. 'That's not what I said. I did not want to kill my baby – I just wanted a bit of peace. You don't know what it's like. They're sucked on to you round the clock and they don't do anything but scream and shit. I don't think I even loved my baby at first. I just felt this huge sense of obligation to her. And then I felt so guilty all the time because I didn't have the joy. And I was supposed to have the joy and didn't everyone else have the joy. That's why I'm telling you this. Forget about the joy. You're a mother, not a fucking goddess. And being a mother is hard. But it's so, so worth it.' Shelly paused, looking around mischievously. 'Well, it is when they're not chewing the tits off you. Let me just say mastitis is a bitch,' she finished triumphantly and marched back towards the edge of the clearing.

Ali burst out laughing and immediately covered her mouth. A few women gasped.

'Nooo,' screeched Adrienne. 'I would never have invited you here. This is not who I thought you were, Shelly.'

'It's not who I thought I was either,' Shelly threw over her shoulder. 'And maybe that's a good thing.'

Ali watched her go. What was going on? That was the most un-Shelly thing she'd ever witnessed. Did she just say 'chewing the tits off you'? Ali couldn't believe it.

'OK, OK.' Adrienne was desperately trying to regain control of the situation.

Joanna was crying quietly as Helena stroked her back. 'She made it sound so awful,' she whispered. 'Surely it's not going to be like that?'

'She's been against us since the beginning of this retreat,' Adrienne hissed. 'Don't even think about those hateful words.'

'What kind of psycho would want to get rid of a baby to have a nap?' Helena asked, which Ali felt was a little unfair.

'Well, it's not like any of us really know what it's like, though, do we?' she ventured tentatively. 'They do cry a fair bit. Do you have kids, Adrienne?'

'Ali,' Adrienne aimed the staff at her, 'that is not the point. If you want to go all Team Shelly, so be it. But know this, she is a toxic entity.'

'I'm not Team Shelly – I'm just saying she knows, is all.'

'I think Shelly has done enough today,' Adrienne snapped. 'I will not allow her to ruin this ceremony completely. Now, please, your totems. Prepare to fling your former self onto this symbolic funeral pyre and be reborn as the goddesses of infinite wisdom, patience, perfection and nurturing you were born to be.'

Shit. The watch. Ali cast about for something to use instead. There was nothing but leaves and twigs on the ground. Fuck this crazy bitch, Ali! Just tell her you're not doing it. But after the venom Shelly's outburst had inspired, Ali felt wary of pissing Adrienne off further. Plus, she was filming again, and all of Ali's followers would see her arguing on Instagram with the guru.

One by one the women were stepping forward and dropping teddy bears and old jewellery into the flames. One woman tossed in a pair of high heels. Helena, the private funds manager, threw in her datebook. 'All my clients,' she announced proudly. 'I'm so looking forward to my new life as "Mama".'

Gah, it was a fucking cult. It was nearly Ali's turn. As the woman to her right threw in a sexy lingerie set, Ali, dismayed, hurriedly tucked the watch into her waistband and gingerly tugged out one of her strips of hair extensions. She walked forward and threw it into the fire nervously. Would that count?

Adrienne narrowed her eyes but said nothing.

Pissing her off was a small price to pay, Ali figured. She could never have lived with the idea that some mad hippy had peer-pressured her into burning Miles's watch.

She thought back to the last time she could remember him wearing it. He'd been singing her 'Happy Birthday' in the kitchen of the house in Seapoint.

'I hate to tell you but it's not even my birthday, Dad!' She'd tried to sound casual. She'd just arrived with dinner – Mini must've been away.

'I know that.' Miles's clear blue eyes had crinkled as he smiled. 'I'm not that far gone!' He'd come closer then, softly singing 'Dear Ali' before leaning down to hug her. 'I get the feeling that I might not be able to sing it to you some day,' he whispered. He'd straightened up as Ali blinked away tears, pressed her lips together and tried to smile. 'Time's not on our side.' He'd tapped the watch. 'So I'll get a few happy birthdays in in advance.'

Ali felt a drop on her bare feet, bringing her back to the forest. It was starting to rain. Adrienne concluded the chanting and turned to the camera to wrap up the recording with some details about the website and pricelists and then herded the women back towards the centre.

26

'It's Tuesday 26 March. Our top stories: social media star and actress Shelly Devine has come under fire for inflammatory comments recorded in leaked footage that came to light yesterday evening. We go now to Teresa Daly reporting live from the Devine compound – Teresa, can you tell us how events are currently unfolding?'

The *Eye On Today* studio disappeared and was replaced by a harried-looking Teresa Daly, who was positioned in front of the large electronic gates leading to the Devine home. It was 6 pm and nearly dark but in the distance, beyond the gates, the lights of Shelly and Dan's mansion glowed. Teresa squinted into the spotlight trained on her from behind the camera and in fevered, breathless tones she began to relate the minutiae of the day.

'We've been here since early this morning, awaiting any comment from the Devine camp. Family members and supportive friends have entered and exited but as yet there has been no sign of Shelly Devine or her husband, Daniel Devine. The couple lives in luxury, as you can see from the extensive grounds and lavish home behind me. Shelly Devine has a successful lifestyle brand across various social media platforms, most notably her Instagram account. The Shelly Devine account is a destination for mothers in particular, as Ms Devine often documents family life through collaborations with many of the country's leading clothing and homewares brands so it was with shock and dismay that her some 300,000 followers heard her deride mothers in a vicious tirade apparently captured during a wellness retreat in Killorglin, County Kerry.'

'Turn it off, sweetheart.' Sandra positioned herself in front of the TV in Shelly's living room, hands on hips. 'You mustn't watch.'

'It's a bleedin' disgrace that RTÉ are wasting the TV licences on that wan standing out there all day.' Jim came in with the teapot, a pint of milk and a packet of biscuits tucked under his arm.

Shelly sprang up from the couch to help him. 'I have to watch it, Mum. How do I go about pretending I'm not the main subject of the evening news? I need to know what they're saying.'

'Shhh, shhh.' Jim held a hand up. 'Who's that?'

Sandra moved to one side as Jim and Shelly scrambled back to the couch to watch. Teresa and the crew were on the move.

A dark BMW had pulled up at the keypad for the gates. The camera was shaking, veering between ground and sky, and briefly captured the operator's scuffed sneakers running over the gravel. Teresa Daly could be faintly heard growling, 'Get him, get him.' Suddenly the camera found Dan in the glare of the spotlight, looking furious, leaning out the driver's window to press the keypad.

Shelly gripped the arm of the sofa. She'd tried to call him earlier but couldn't get him. In a brief text, she'd asked him to call her but he'd obviously been tied up all day.

'Daniel Devine, can you tell us anything about your wife's state of mind right now? Is she remorseful? Will she be making a statement? What do you think of your wife's comments?'

Shelly could see the gates opening slowly just beyond Dan's car. Open, open. Open! she willed.

'Those gates are terrible slow,' Sandra remarked, hands still on hips, gazing down at her erstwhile son-in-law.

'If he chucks you under the bus, I'll kill him.' Jim was rage-eating the Bourbon Creams and glaring at the TV.

'What are you doing blocking my driveway?' Dan was stabbing at the keypad, apparently trying to hurry the gates up. 'Slow news day or what?'

'Your wife's comments have caused huge upset – are you saying you don't care about that? Do you not care about your wife, Mr Devine?' Teresa thrust the microphone into his face.

'Don't care about my wife?' Dan echoed thoughtfully and Shelly held her breath. Oh god, no, Dan, please, no. She knew she wouldn't be keeping up the pretence of a marriage anymore but she couldn't bear this being how everyone found out. It was too humiliating on top of everything else. She covered her eyes and rocked slightly while Dan's question seemed to hang in the ether for an age.

'Of course I care about my wife.' Dan grasped the microphone and stared into the camera. 'She is taking some much-needed time right now. She'll speak about this matter when she's ready. And it won't be to you vultures.'

Dan put the car in drive, held on to the mic, snatching it right out of Teresa's hand, and threw it into the bushes. The camera panned to Teresa's shocked face and then back to the gates closing as Dan swung up the driveway, giving the finger out the sunroof as he went.

'Well, that was decent of him,' Sandra muttered.

Shelly exhaled. Thank god. She stood and went to the window that overlooked the side of the house. She pulled the curtain back. Dan had parked and was watching something on his phone. It could only be the leaked footage. Shelly bit her lip. Would he come in to her?

He shoved the phone into his suit pocket and massaged his temples, then gathered his coat and laptop and got out of the car. He turned and headed straight for the garden; as he passed close to the window, he started, having spotted Shelly. They stood staring at each other, separated by so much more than glass. As the gentle bickering of her parents receded behind her in the cosy room, Shelly felt the anger of the previous weeks drain away.

Since the one and only counselling session, she knew in her heart they could no longer be together, and her head had told her this would be OK. Eventually.

Dan looked defeated somehow too. She mouthed 'thank you' and he shrugged, his mouth set in a line of resignation. She mouthed 'I'm sorry' and that seemed to crack him. He smiled, if a little grimly, and nodded slowly. She pulled out her phone to text him.

Don't forget mediation on Friday morning. And, Dan, I really am sorry. XX

She watched him read it and nod slightly. He looked up at her. 'I'm sorry too' – his lips echoed hers and Shelly smiled gratefully. He turned and continued towards the garden, but then stopped and turned once more. He tapped on his phone for a moment and then held it up. The video of her rant was playing and she squirmed, but he grinned and made the universal 'you're bananas' gesture before shaking his head and heading on to the Seomra. Shelly smiled with the relief that he wasn't holding it against her. She closed the curtain back over and returned to her parents, who were having a heated debate about the biscuits.

'The Bourbons are a good crisis biscuit,' Sandra was insisting.

'Shhh,' Jim shouted over her. 'They're playing it again.'

The anchor was introducing the footage with a warning that some of the content might be upsetting, particularly to expectant mothers. 'There is strong language and violent imagery. Discretion is advised, especially for younger viewers. We've been advised by our source that Ms Devine is referring to motherhood in these clips.'

''S just crap.' The clip began with Shelly standing, looking exasperated, in the clearing of the forest.

'I was saying all her BS about motherhood being this big spiritual thing was crap! Not that motherhood was crap,' Shelly wailed, all serenity brought about by her reconciliation with Dan evaporating instantly.

'Shhh, Shelly.' Jim leaned forward.

'Some mornings you're so tired.' The camera shook as whoever was filming adjusted the angle. It was low to the ground, as though the person was filming in secret. 'You just feel like a wrung-out old J-cloth. There's actual poo in your hair and you wish you could just get rid of the baby.'

The clip appeared to jump and then resumed.

'I did not want to kill my baby, I just wanted a bit of peace.' The camera swung round to capture some of the assembled women and zoomed in on a sobbing Joanna. Shelly squinted, trying to work out who must've had the camera. The only person she really remembered in the circle had been Ali, who was visible in shot just behind her. Polly had been there, of course. And others whose names she couldn't remember. It was impossible to tell who it had been.

'You don't know what it's like. They're sucked on to you round the clock and they don't do anything but scream and shit. I don't think I even loved my baby at first. I just felt this huge sense of obligation to her. And then I felt so guilty all the time because I didn't have the joy. And I was supposed to have the joy and didn't everyone else have the joy. That's why I'm telling you this. Forget about the joy.'

Shelly crumbled and Sandra rushed over to hug her.

'Mam, I didn't mean it the way they're making it sound.'

'Of course you didn't, luvvie.' Her mother rocked her, and even in her current state, Shelly was amazed how comforting that could be at thirty-four with a daughter of your own.

'I said loads of other stuff about how being a mother is hard but so, so worth it.' Shelly started to shake. Her phone was buzzing endlessly beside her and she couldn't bear to think what was being said about her.

'We've got fellow social media star Hazel Thomas in studio now to share her thoughts on the debacle.' The anchor introduced a heavily made-up Holistic Hazel who was clearly fighting to contain her glee at the situation. She beamed at the camera and then rearranged her features into an expression of solemn concern.

Shelly groaned.

'Hazel, thanks so much for joining us. Can you tell us what the ramifications of this leaked footage will be for a social media star of Shelly's stature? Especially given the Glossies, Ireland's most important social media event of the year, are just days away.'

Hazel opened her mouth and Shelly's whole body tensed.

'My apologies, Hazel.' The anchor cut across her, pressing her index finger to her ear. 'We're getting word that Shelly's making a statement at the Devine compound shortly.' Turning back to the camera, she said: 'We'll take you there now.'

Jim, Sandra and Shelly looked at each other, baffled, then Teresa Daly reappeared looking more composed than during her previous brush with Dan.

'Thanks, Jean. I'm here live, reporting from the Devine compound, where Amy Donoghue, assistant to Ms Devine, will be sharing Ms Devine's statement.'

The camera swung round to Amy, who looked more teenage than ever with her top knot, fishnet body suit, jeans and flannel shirt. Shelly felt like crying with relief just seeing her. Amy blinked, scowling in the glare of the lights, then slipped her glasses on and began reading from her iPad.

'Shelly has been bravely navigating the turbulent early weeks of a pregnancy that has, unfortunately, been fraught with health difficulties. She wishes to extend her heartfelt gratitude to all her followers for their support during this trying time. While some of her comments may appear extreme, they were taken out of context and do not reflect the views of Shelly and the brand and community that she has worked so hard to create. Thank you and, most especially, thank you to all the Shell-Belles out there who know the real Shelly and know that she is being horribly misrepresented by these slanderous and highly edited clips. We will be issuing no further comment and the family would appreciate privacy at this time.'

Amy snapped the cover of her iPad shut and smiled tightly, ignoring the hysterical barrage of questions from Teresa Daly. She slipped in the side gate and started up the driveway.

The shot cut back to studio, where Jean was apologising to a furious-looking Hazel. 'I'm afraid that's all we have time for tonight.'

Sandra turned it off and Shelly ran out to the hall, flung open the front door and threw her arms around Amy.

'You saved us! Hazel was about to have a field day eviscerating me on live TV.'

'God, I know – sure I was watching her Stories. She was all over Insta talking about preparing to speak on behalf of the mummy blogger community to condemn Shelly Devine.'

Shelly winced.

'Don't worry, we'll get a handle on all this in a matter of hours.' Amy had disengaged and was storming towards the office.

'Amy!' Shelly couldn't believe she was capable of smiling right now, but the sight of a fired-up Amy was giving her nostalgia. Amy whirled around, tapping away on her iPad already.

'Mm-hmm?' She didn't even look up.

'You don't work for me anymore.'

'Don't worry, Shel. This is pro bono.' Amy gave a wink and headed on. 'I'll be in the war room,' she called over her shoulder, starting up the stairs.

Shelly ducked back in to say goodnight to her parents. They'd moved on to watching an ad for Brendan O'Connor's panel show *The Cutting Edge*.

'I can't make up my mind about this O'Connor fella,' Jim was muttering.

'I like the look of him,' Sandra said. 'He's a handsome lad, especially for a Cork man. And he's a great singer. I heard him singing 'The Wonder of You' once.'

Shelly said goodnight and gave them a hug. They were going to stay in the guest room and she realised, discomfited, that they never had before. 'I'm sorry if we haven't been that close for a while, Mam.'

'You never have to say sorry to us, pet.' Sandra smiled. 'You've been under a lot of pressure. But we're always here, no matter what.'

Leaving them to it, Shelly climbed the stairs slowly, feeling more #blessed than she had in years. There was no way in hell she should be happy right now. God knows what was being said about her – she was splashed all over the bloody news, for god's sake, and yet somehow she felt oddly lighter. She'd started seeing a counsellor and their sessions were definitely helping to lift the guilt Shelly'd been burying.

She grabbed a towel from the cupboard and stepped into the bathroom where Marni was giving Georgie her bath.

'Mama,' the little girl shrieked. 'Look what I am.' She paddled in the water, sending bubbles into the air like tiny soapy clouds, and let out a series of barks.

'Ah, the puppy is having her bath.' Shelly knelt down to pet her. 'Oh, such a good puppy and so clean!'

Marni laughed, standing up to go.

'Thanks a million for staying late this evening.' Shelly smiled a bit awkwardly. 'I didn't expect all that fuss with the press to be going on.'

'No probs.' Marni stretched. 'I'm glad to help out any time.'

Shelly gave her a hug. 'I don't know if you've seen any of the reports, but I just want you to know, they took me up completely the wrong way.'

Marni shook her head, smiling. 'Of course I know that, Shelly, no need to explain. I'll see you on Thursday night? I'm babysitting for the awards?'

'Em, actually, no, I think I'm going to give them a miss – thanks, Marni. We're going to have a girly night in, aren't we, puppy?' Georgie barked and Marni laughed. 'Can I text you about next week when I know what my schedule looks like? I think I'm going to be cutting back a bit.'

'Sure, no problem, we'll talk. Bye, *chérie*.' Marni kissed Georgie and headed downstairs to run the gauntlet of Teresa Daly and her camera.

Shelly and Georgie played puppies for a few more minutes and then it was time for stories and cuddles in the little pink bed.

'Nighty, night, sweet baby,' Shelly called as she carefully closed the door just the way Georgie liked it.

'Night, Mama … Can I tell you something?'

Shelly grinned. This had become her latest bedtime stalling tactic. She usually allowed her three 'can I tell you something's before getting serious about sleep time. She knelt down by her pillow so Georgie could whisper to her. Her hot breath tickled Shelly's ear but the words buoyed her immeasurably.

'You're my best friend, Mama!'

After several more whispered somethings, Georgie finally dropped off and Shelly made her way up to the office to tell Amy she wasn't sure she even wanted to salvage this SHELLY thing anymore.

She found, to her dismay, Amy looking upset in the corner.

'I'm so sorry, Shelly.' She looked up. She looked so young with half her make-up cried off and her eyes swollen and red.

'Amy, oh my god, please stop. SHELLY's not that important. It doesn't matter anymore. I promise you.' Shelly cradled the girl. 'I was planning to walk in here, sit you down and tell you that I want out!' Shelly smiled down at Amy but Amy only stared back silently. The fear in Amy's eyes as she handed over her phone stopped Shelly cold.

On the screen was an email that just said: 'Shelly is a LIAR.' The sender was imwatchingyoushelly@gmail.com

There were images attached – Shelly smiling but with the eyes blacked out. One was from the Daddy Bears' Picnic – a side-by-side of Dan and the Almost Dan they'd employed for that day with the caption 'Spot the difference!' Next up a side-by-side of baby Georgie and the random stock image of a baby that she'd once used when Georgie was tiny and had terrible infant acne. She'd been banking on no one noticing – newborns all look the same, after all. Once again the words 'Spot the difference!' were typed over the picture. Someone had noticed. Someone had been noticing and watching for a very long time.

❖

Less than an hour later, Shelly was sitting in the police station. Amy was beside her, drawing a diagram, attempting to explain the ins and outs of the Instagram world to Inspector Fitzgerald. Eventually, he sighed heavily and shouted out the door of the interview room.

'Bríd, will you come in here? They're on about selfies and things.'

A younger garda came in, smiling, and introduced herself. 'Bríd Nolan, I'm in the tech division. We handle fraud and identity theft, online stalking, revenge porn, that kind of thing. What's been going on?'

Amy handed over the picture Shelly had taken of her and @KellysKlobber on the night of Dan's meltdown and explained the whole story.

'So this is the woman you think has been hacking your phone? Though, to be honest, I need to look into whether it's possible to change the phone wallpaper like that. It's pretty high-level stuff. There's no way she was there, is there?'

'No.' Shelly sighed. 'I was on a retreat in Kerry. She wasn't there.' She felt utterly drained.

Amy took over then, to Shelly's relief, sliding printouts across the table.

'I've done some digging,' Amy explained. 'I have pretty much everything we need. When I emailed her to tell her to back off, I got an out-of-office. Her address was in the email signature. Idiotic, like. It's straightforward but we just need you to go and deal with her. This has to stop.'

'Absolutely.' Bríd was leafing through the pages. 'This should be totally straightforward – 90 per cent of these people are just bored and never dream they can actually be easily traced or that we're going to show up at their door. I'll update you both as soon as we've interviewed her.'

27

'There are some days that you just know are going to change your life forever.' Ali beamed up into the phone. The best angle was always from above, she'd learned – like, fully overhead. It accentuated cheekbones and eliminated any double chin. 'You wake up one person and you go to sleep a completely different one. I just know that today is one of those days. And I can't believe it's finally here! It's a day that I have waited for for a long time now. It's a day to celebrate and empower Irish women, and I am so honoured to be one of the women being celebrated this evening – and I owe it all to you guys.'

Ali uploaded the video to her Story, adding the hashtag #GlossieAwardsNight, just as the doorbell rang.

Who was that? Liv had already left for college and the make-up artist who was doing her prep for the awards wasn't due for hours. Ali made her way through the detritus of gifts from various brands. She was coming down with baby gear that she needed to photograph and post about. So much to do. In the hall, the collection of porcelain cats in bonnets still manned the table where the long-defunct house phone sat. Stuck to the front door was a note from Liv. The tone was undeniably cold.

> *Ali,*
>
> *I'm submitting a draft of the opening chapters of the thesis. It's due by COB today so I need you to sign the consent form I've left on the kitchen table. It's giving permission for the images I've included from your account that appear in sections two and three. Obviously, I've redacted your profiler and name in the pics.*
>
> *Liv.*

Ali screwed up the note and opened the door to find Sam looking cross.

'Ah, so you're not dismembered by some hippy freaks in a forest in Kerry. Great.' He stepped past her into the hall.

'Hi.' Ali felt instantly wrong-footed. 'What are you doing here?'

'I'm here to say hi in person since you've been ignoring my texts and voicenotes and DMs.'

'I have not.' Ali slipped ahead of him into the kitchen to grab Liv's consent form and shove it under a pile of magazines. 'Tea? Coffee? I told you the signal in Kerry was shite.'

'You've been back six days,' Sam said flatly. 'I feel like you're avoiding me. You blocked me from your Story again. I can tell, ya know. Eamon's girlfriend, Sarah, follows you and she let me see – you were updating last night.'

Ali put the kettle on and rummaged for biscuits.

'I'm sorry.' Ali really didn't have time for this, but things with Sam had to be managed very carefully.

He had become the best thing in her life, but now that the Glossies were here, time was running out on her lies. Still, she couldn't help but hope that she'd somehow be able to style it out. Putting on the blinkers and focusing on the now was the only way she could deal with her mounting anxiety about her various strands of deception. If her mind tried to take in the whole picture it was just too much: instant panic attack. Zoom out and her life was a blazing inferno of chaos and hashtags, but up close it seemed much more manageable somehow.

Like, right now wasn't about trying to figure out what to tell Sam about their imaginary baby. It was about doing some glam-prep for tonight's awards. Then she'd visit Miles and give him ice cream and try not to think too much about what was going to happen to him. Compartmentalising had become Ali's main jam – she just needed to stay focused on the positives.

Sam sat down heavily at the table. 'I thought things were maybe going badly with Miles but then Sarah tells me you're all over Instagram talking about the best cat-milk serum for dry, tired skin?'

Ali squirmed. Things with Miles *were* going badly. She hadn't missed a day with him since coming back from Kerry but it still didn't feel like she was doing enough. 'That's work stuff, I have to do that. And things aren't good with my dad right now. They really don't …' Ali stopped to catch her breath. 'They really don't think he's got long,' she finished quietly. 'I actually have to go up there right now.'

Ali just didn't have the words to talk about Miles anymore. She seized up whenever she thought too far ahead about what was coming. And Tabitha had been different the last few days, as if she somehow was privy to Miles's fate. Yesterday Ali had arrived at Ailesend to find new chairs in the room – not hard plastic like the old chairs but big cushioned ones that reclined. Ali didn't quite know what to make of it.

She'd sat on the edge of Miles's bed, rubbing his forearms and staring suspiciously at the chairs. She got the feeling that she didn't want to know why they'd been changed. When she'd got up to leave an hour later, she'd forced herself to look at Miles for a long time. Some days in that room she barely let her eyes rest on his face for more than a few seconds – it was just too hard. Now she let her eyes roam his face and shock shuddered through her. His mouth gaped, his lips were cracked and dry, his eyes no longer blinked. He wasn't there anymore. He couldn't be. Ali couldn't cope with the idea that he was conscious and trapped inside this mask of a face so she had to believe that he was gone, safe somewhere with no idea of what had become of him.

'Let me go with you then,' Sam implored. 'I want to help. I'm good with sad situations. I can get snacks and say inappropriate things.'

'Like what?' Ali couldn't resist. If she was going to lose him, she wanted to hear him be his sweet, playful self one more time.

'I just can't stop thinking about the cat-milk serum. Are they milking the cats with a machine or are the scientists doing it by hand? Hand-milked sounds posher.'

Ali smiled and tears caught in her throat while regret pooled in the pit of her stomach.

He stood up and put his arms around her. Fuck. It had gone on too long with Sam. How did she let it get this far? Then she inhaled and his smell felt like home. Oh yes, she thought, that.

'Let me come,' he whispered.

'You can't.' Ali pulled away and backed up till she was against the fridge door. She needed to put some distance between them.

'Ali, you're hurting. It's so hard – he's your dad. I'd like to meet him … before …'

Ali clenched her hands into fists. She was going to have to do it. He wasn't going to be fobbed off. She had to finish him.

'I'm not hurting. I just don't want you there. And I don't want you here. I don't want you, Sam,' she said, using his name like the swing of a bat. 'You have to leave.'

He looked stunned and then utterly crushed. She pushed him into the hall towards the door. As she opened it, he seemed to come to his senses. 'You can't push me out of your life. That's our baby.' He sounded shell-shocked. He stepped outside but turned back to face her. 'I … Ali, I love—'

'This is not about that right now.' She couldn't bear to hear what she was giving up. 'My dad is … whatever. You have to go –

leave me alone. I'll get your stuff together and you can come and grab it later. I'll leave a key out.'

She slammed the door shut, feeling sick and off-balance. Breaking up with Sam wasn't actually a solution in any way but she needed to buy time and come up with a plan. For what? Ali barely knew anymore, she felt like she was on a runaway train, unable to stop the momentum of her lies. *After the awards are over I'll figure it all out*, she promised herself.

✤

Ali spent the rest of the morning in the salon, Ellie's Elysium, tensely watching the other influencers' Stories while various beauty therapists added and subtracted hair from her face and body. She'd been late because of Sam, shoving his worn-out T-shirts and novelty boxers into a shopping bag which she'd left in the hall. She'd nearly kept one but he'd definitely notice and then he'd know she was somewhere sucking the smell of him off a grotty old T-shirt.

Ellie, the eyelash technician, chatted while she was refilling Ali's set. 'So, have you heard about Shelly Devine?' Ellie loved the juice – she lived for it.

'Yeah, I was actually there when that video was filmed,' Ali said, trying not to move too much.

'No!'

'Yeah. Though actually, to be honest, whoever did make that video totally screwed her. They made it out to be way worse than it was. Her rant was actually kinda funny.'

The lash technician looked a bit disappointed at this but quickly moved on to speculating over whether or not Shelly would show at the Glossies. 'She's pretty much shut down the SHELLY account. One of the girls heard from a client that she's got a stalker.' She finished the left eye and began on the right.

'Huh, that explains why she was acting shifty at that retreat,' Ali mused.

'I always knew she was too perfect to be for real,' the girl announced knowingly. 'High time everyone saw her true colours. It's the child I feel sorry for.'

Ali squirmed a little. She felt bad not defending Shelly; she'd gotten to like her in the last couple of months. But at the same time, commenting on someone else's Insta-scam was definitely pot-calling-kettle-black territory right now. She snuck a peek at the lash artist – what did she say about her to other clients?

Don't be so paranoid, Ali reminded herself, but it was hard not to be. Being Insta-famous was like being in a very attractive marble and rose-gold prison – you were under constant surveillance. Not for the first time since all this began, Ali wondered if she'd be happier without Instagram altogether. But then what would she have left?

'You're all done, hun, they look amazing! My handle is @ElliesElysium.'

Ali could take a hint but sometimes it was all so exhausting. Plug, plug, plug. She took a selfie and posted it. Within minutes the post was awash with likes and squealing comments. It felt good, and that was undeniable. Ali sat engrossed, refreshing the post every few seconds, as time slipped past. She watched as the likes soared and she felt flooded with the kick of dopamine until Ellie returned with her next client, looking surprised that Ali was still there.

She drove home to meet the make-up artist, feeling the tide of anxiety wash in once more. She wished she could just enjoy herself. The hours of this day were ticking down maddeningly slowly. Why did she just want it all to be over? After everything she'd done to get here? She flashed on Sam's devastated face, everything she'd sacrificed …

❖

After make-up, she ploughed through lunchtime traffic to get to Ailesend, voicenoting with Kate all the way. Even though, these days, Kate barely asked about Ali and seemed much more focused on Ali tagging her in selfies to boost the @ShreddingForTheWedding account, Ali was prepared to overlook whatever cynical motives Kate had for their friendship. This was mainly because, despite having close to a hundred thousand followers now, she often felt lonely in that world. At least Kate was someone real who took an interest in what she was wearing tonight and cared about what was in the swag bag. Though their bitch sessions weren't nearly so satisfying anymore. Now that Ali had grasped that behind every dodgy bit of FaceFix was a real person, she felt guilty swapping screen-grabs and zooming in on dodgy Photoshop.

'Did you see Crystal Doorley's latest?' Kate's voicenote was scathing but Ali just felt bad for Crystal. She'd seen her at a few events and it was obvious she had serious issues with her confidence, even more than anyone else who was editing out great chunks of their bodies on Insta.

'I'd better go – I'm just about to go in to … do a dress fitting, catch you later,' Ali said into the phone, pulling into the nursing home car park. She grabbed her bag and, grim-faced, headed in, refusing to dwell on the fact that she herself was editing out great chunks of her life every hour of the day.

Mini was sitting beside the bed when Ali reached Miles's room – after a quick pit stop in the courtyard to do some more glam content, breathlessly gushing about how #blessed she was to be nominated.

'You're road-testing the new seats, I see.' She kissed Miles on the cheek quickly and flopped into the empty one. 'Much comfier,' she observed.

Mini was about to speak when Tabitha bustled in bearing a tray of tea and biscuits.

'Taby! What the hell? Since when do you make us tea? Are those Kimberleys?'

Tabitha didn't say a word but gave Ali a vigorous reassuring pat on the arm and slipped back out the door.

Ali raised an eyebrow. 'Dad, have you paid her off or something?'

Mini looked pale and watchful and had yet to really acknowledge her arrival. Ali felt something was seriously off. Miles looked more or less the same as ever, though his eyes were slightly more closed than usual and his breathing seemed shallower. She glanced around and noticed a small machine grinding away on the floor by the bed. She peered closer to read the label: OdourAway. Christ. Why was there some kind of industrial air freshener here?

The tea. The biscuits. The reclining chairs. Suddenly Ali wished she hadn't come today, as if her being there or not could affect the outcome.

'Mum, Mum? Mum?'

Mini's head snapped up but she appeared unfocused. 'Ali,' was all she said.

'What have they said? Why is this here?' Scowling, she kicked at the OdourAway.

'I honestly don't know, darling.' Mini sounded utterly lost and Ali felt a chill grip her heart. 'I think they think this is it.'

Her words sucked the breath right out of Ali's body. No, no, no. This couldn't be happening. Not today. Not any day.

'They haven't really said. But I don't think they can say.' Mini was speaking carefully and deliberately. She sounded like a robot and Ali felt like shaking her.

'Why didn't you warn me?' She was up and pacing but pausing between words to listen for Miles's breath. The gaps between each one seemed interminably long.

Mini didn't respond and Ali suddenly felt unbearably trapped in this terrible room, a room with no answers where they had been suspended in this awful limbo for so long. She found herself outside in the corridor without having even thought about taking the steps.

'Ali?' Tabitha looked concerned.

'Is my dada really dying?' Words spilled out and onto the floor.

'Oh, Ali, Ali, Ali …' Tabitha's strong arms encircled her. 'We can't be sure. It's probably not long now. Your daddy has suffered for a long time. And your mummy too. I'm praying for him.'

Ali buried her face in Tabitha's chest. She felt wrung-out. She was sobbing but no tears came.

How can you know that someone is dying, watch them every day as they die a little bit more yet still be completely unprepared when it comes?

No, she couldn't believe it. They had come close before and Miles had always rallied. This wasn't the day, she felt certain.

Tabitha released her from the hug and went to help another resident who had stumbled out of a nearby room. 'I'll be right back, Ali.'

Ali turned and looked through the crack in the door to where Mini was sitting, head down, silent tears falling into her empty hands.

Ali pulled back abruptly; she could feel the dark swell of panic spreading under her skin and filling her insides. Everything around her felt overwhelming and ominous. The beep of medical machinery, the clatter of the ward kitchen down the hall, it was all suddenly roaring at full volume.

She found herself drawn away from Miles's room. A small part of her was screaming, telling her to go back, but she needed to get out. She couldn't breathe. He won't die. He won't die. She pushed through the doors to the ward, through reception and out to her car on autopilot. She would go and get some things from home and then come back. She had time. They had time. Out here in the sunlight, it was easier to believe that he would be fine. Her phone started ringing – 'Mini calling'. She ended the call immediately and squeezed her eyes shut. She just needed a couple of hours. She'd go home, get herself sorted and be back. It would all be fine – she quickly texted as much to Mini and got into the car. The phone started up again. This time it was Liv. Ali bit her lip and hesitated before hitting Accept.

'Ali? Sam called me. He's really worried. Are you OK?'

'Kind of.' Ali started the engine and began to back out of the car park.

'Kind of? Is it Miles? I can be there in an hour – I just need to swing home, drop the thesis to Emer's office and then I can be right there.'

'I think it's OK.' Ali tried to sound calm. 'We have some time – I spoke to Tabitha. I'm heading home myself for a bit and I'm coming back later. I just want to grab a couple of things.'

Liv didn't speak for a few moments and Ali barely noticed. She was absorbed in pulling out onto the main road. She felt numb, like she was wading through a dream.

'Are you sure about going home?' Liv sounded baffled. 'Maybe you should stay. I'll bring up whatever you need.'

'It's cool,' Ali murmured. 'I'll be back.' She ended the call and joined the afternoon traffic heading across town, trying to ignore the mounting dread building in her chest.

✣

Ali walked in to the house and felt like she'd been gone for years. Everything seemed normal yet strange somehow. The shower was going down the hall in Liv's en suite; the brown carpet was still an assault on the senses; the orange lino glowed from the kitchen. Going by her Instagram, she lived in an airy New York-style loft – it was all marble effect and strategic detail shots. Not a scrap of this place made it to her page – too grim for the 'gram. She flashed on the OdourAway air freshener – my whole life is too grim for the 'gram.

She moved through to the living room where the sight of Sam hit her like a blast of heat from a fire on a winter's day. Forgetting her cold behaviour that morning, she rushed towards him.

'Sam, thank god you're …' She abandoned the last of this sentence, hushed by his strange expression. She froze an arm's reach from him. She'd never seen this look before, and she struggled to compute what his narrowed eyes and hardened sneer meant until her eyes fell on what he was holding. The thesis.

Ali stopped dead. 'I—'

'Don't,' he snapped.

'I can explain.'

Sam laughed a long, cruel, hollow laugh. 'Can you? Can you really?'

Ali's hands knotted together and she felt winded. Can I? Of course I can't. It was as though the true magnitude of her lie was only now being revealed to her. Under the scrutiny of Sam's glare, the idea that she'd done this was alien. What the actual fuck had she been thinking?

Sam was shaking his head and leafing through the pages. He stopped at a picture she'd posted of the two of them together at the Daddy Bears' Picnic. 'This is sick, Ali. You're sick.'

'I'm not,' Ali whispered. 'I'm just sad.' As the words dropped, heavy like stones in a well, she knew they were true.

Sam put the thesis down gently on the coffee table. 'I was in love with you. I thought I'd never met a girl like you before in my life.' To her deep, deep shame she could see he was blinking away tears. 'You let me believe we were going to have a family.' He shook his head. 'I never really had a family, Ali. After Mum died. Not a proper one.'

'I'm sorry—'

'Don't fucking say that! This is not an "I'm sorry" moment, Ali. This is so beyond that. You need fucking help,' he spat.

He started towards the door. As he passed her, she tried to reach out to him but he shrugged her off and stormed out of the house, slamming the door behind him, just as Liv rushed out of her room in a towel.

'What's happened? Was that Sam?'

'Your thesis happened,' Ali said simply. She couldn't even find the will to be angry.

Liv's eyes widened. 'Oh my god, no. Holy fuck! I'm so sorry, Ali. I put it down for, like, five minutes while I jumped in the shower. Ali, shit. Shit, shit, shit. I'm so sorry.'

'You really shouldn't be. It's my fault. The whole lot of it. He fucking hates me. He's right too. It doesn't matter now anyway …' Ali dragged in a gulp of air. 'Miles is really bad, Liv. I'm scared.'

Liv stepped forward and held her firmly in her arms. They stood in silence and Ali held on to her friend with everything she had.

'He's going to die and I can't take it.'

Liv started to cry and Ali felt strangely envious. She longed to cry – big, violent, wrenching sobs – to get some kind of release from this paralysing pain. But nothing was coming. She felt like all this was happening to someone else. The many elements of her world had suddenly skipped out of their orbit. It was any old Thursday in the rest of the world, but here in her little sliver of a life everything was spinning out of control. Sam's rage, Liv's tears, the phone buzzing with notifications about the Glossies, Mini's flat, lifeless voice and, beneath it all, Miles's quiet, shallow breaths counting down the minutes, leading her to a precipice, one she couldn't even imagine.

She knew what she had to do.

'This towel reeks.' She unravelled from the embrace and stepped back.

'All towels reek,' Liv said, adopting faux gravitas. 'It's one of life's tragic certainties. Like death and taxes.' She smiled weakly, her cheeks wet with tears. 'He was the best.'

Was.

'I have to get ready.' Ali moved away towards her room, where she had everything she needed laid out.

Liv looked confused. 'Ready?' She wheeled around and followed Ali down the hall. 'You're not … you're not going to the bloody Glossies, are you?'

❖

'Welcome to the third annual Glossies brought to you by *Glossie Life* magazine in association with lip artists Filler Fabulosity and Brown Thomas. How are we all doing tonight?' Blake Jordan was wearing a leopard-print tux and pink dress shirt. His veneers were particularly blinding as he stalked the front of the stage giving shout-outs to the various bloggers and Insta-stars in the front row. 'Look, it's Insta-mum Holistic Hazel, everyone. You've managed to unsuckle the litter and get out on the town.'

Hazel waved her arms in the air and whooped 'Mama is out-out' to a sea of iPhones pointed in her direction.

'And …' said Blake, moving along, 'we've got my fave gal, Crystal Doorley, nominated in the Best Natural Tan category. Don't worry, love, we all need a little help in that department, don't we?' Crystal looked unabashed despite her recent shaming; there wasn't a natural tan in the entire room, never mind that category.

'And here's the amazing Norah Darcy.' Blake had switched to his solemn voice. 'Norah is being honoured in our Best Mental Health Journey category, a new and hugely important category this year. Because, as we all know, it's important to be real sometimes too. Social media isn't this big toxic thing – it's making a difference to people's lives. Well done, Norah – *bualadh bos*, everyone.' Blake clapped reverentially and everyone joined in.

'Now who's this hot bish?' Blake had swung back to bubbly-host mode. 'It's Jess Hamilton, of course. The ridiest ride we've got and nominated tonight for Best Facial Work, a category sponsored by the good people at Filler Fabulosity. Show us those trouty beauties, hun.'

'Not today, Satan!' Liv shouted. Keeping one eye on the road, she slapped the phone out of Ali's hand, interrupting the #Glossies Instagram Stories.

'I'm in distress. Insta is soothing me,' Ali argued as she retrieved the phone, and Liv sighed.

'We're going nowhere fast, anyway – these bloody roadworks.' The car inched forward and she craned to see beyond the snaking line of traffic, leading to Ailesend. 'Three lanes all trying to merge into one. Bloody ridic.'

Ali reinstated the Insta-live, capturing every moment of the awards she'd thought were so important.

Blake Jordan had turned serious once more. 'We do have an important announcement to make before we can commence honouring the women in this room, women of integrity and values. It has come to light that one of tonight's nominees has been less than honest on her Instagram and has been excommunicated from the awards.' As the shot panned the room, the whole crowd appeared to shift awkwardly.

'Uh oh.' Liv had come to a stop and leaned in to check the screen. 'They couldn't be talking about you, could they?'

Ali felt lightheaded. 'I haven't been on much today,' she said slowly. 'But no one told me I was disqualified.' She X'd out of Insta and checked her emails.

'Oh fuck.' The inbox was rammed with brand new unreads, all sent in the last half-hour or so.

'Notice of disqualification' read the subject line of one from the *Glossie Life* magazine editor. 'Termination of contract, effective immediately' said one from Baby Bella Boo Boo Buggies. And on and on.

'Oh, shite.' Liv stared horrified as Ali scrolled. Some subject lines just said 'You're SICK, you fucking BITCH' while others seemed to be dubious offers of help – 'Re your recent nervous breakdown, heal yourself with the power of juicing'.

A beep from the car behind gave them both a jolt.

'OK, OK, I'm going,' Liv muttered. 'We're only after moving two feet – are ya happy?' She gave the finger in the rear-view as Ali flicked back to the Glossies' Insta-live, where Blake Jordan was clearly struggling to be heard over the crowd, who were abuzz.

'The Glossies do not in any way condone or endorse behaviour of this kind.' The Story zoomed in on the circular tables around which nearly every woman held a phone to her ear, many covering their mouths in shock while others were wiping their eyes from laughing so hard.

The person filming the Insta-live could be heard laughing and chatting to someone off-camera. 'I know! What a crazy bitch. OMG, how pathetic can you actually be?'

'We will not be revealing the identity of the person in question,' concluded Blake Jordan.

'As if that matters,' Ali wailed. Fuck. Fuck. Fuck. 'How do they know?'

Liv came to a stop once more, looking stricken. 'You know it's not me, right? What are they listening to?'

Ali shook her head. At the top of her screen, Instagram notifications were dropping in at a ferocious rate. The comment previews were appearing too fast to read fully but the general gist was clear.

Pathetic.

Dumb cunt.

Fucked up.

Poor guy or was he in on it?

Loser.

Bitch.

Stupid ugly lying bitch.

Kill yourself cos we'll never forget this.

Liv grabbed her phone. Ali was numb. Her hands were shaking and she couldn't take a full breath.

'I'm pulling over.'

'Don't, please, we're nearly there. I have to get to Miles.'

'Just please delete Insta, Ali. You can't look at that.'

Without a word of protest, Ali obeyed. She deleted the app from her phone and the violent buzzing quieted. Ali's ragged breathing was the only sound in the car. She felt like she was drowning, fighting for air, her body flooded with dread. Deleting the app didn't really matter – wherever she was, they'd find her. The internet was everywhere.

Her phone buzzed and she squeezed her eyes shut. Please don't be Mini to say I'm too late.

She looked. 'Kate's calling.'

'Don't answer. Look, we're nearly there – this traffic is easing. You can't think about this now. We'll deal with it after.'

We, thought Ali. She still had Liv, even after everything.

A WhatsApp from Kate dropped in and then a voice recording.

'Ali, I don't really know what to say. If this is true, this is completely fucked up. If it's not, you should know what's going around. What everyone's saying. I deserve to know the truth too.'

Ali glanced up – still a few minutes before the turn for Ailesend. What did it matter if she listened now or later? Miles was going to die either way.

'Kate's sent a voicenote that's been going around.' Ali hit Play.

A girl's voice, she sounded young:

'OK so I have something major. I was gonna send it to BU but then the voicenote thing is such craic right now, I figured I'd do it this way! Anyway, here goes – ya know Eamon's friend Sam? So he's been seeing this girl from Tinder for the last, I dunno, couple of months and he was bet into her. And Eamon and all the lads were a bit iffy because she'd told Sam that he'd got her preggers even though they'd only done it one time. Anyway, Sam was crazy about her and now it turns out that she made the whole pregnancy up – like, completely – but you wanna know the best bit? She's a mother-fucking influencer! She's that new one who's been coining it with sponcon, the Glossies wild-card girl, Ali Jones! Can you believe it? And this isn't some high-profile-politician-on-Tinder fake gossip. This is fact. Sam told Eamon, like, two minutes ago. He's devo obvs—'

The voicenote ended there and Ali tossed the phone to the

floor, where it landed by her feet, and leaned her head back on the headrest. A sense of desolation so final it was frightening was spreading through her.

'Jesus, she sounds so gleeful.' Liv had finally come to the entrance to Ailesend and was turning right.

'Well, I guess I would've been too – you know, if it wasn't about me. God, why did I do this?' She closed her eyes. Ali felt flattened – all the fight had gone out of her.

Liv exhaled, looking troubled. 'I feel bad. I should have done more to stop you.'

'Yeah, it is your fault,' Ali deadpanned. 'Just sitting there taking notes on my psychotic break.'

They both managed a weak laugh at this.

They continued up the driveway of Ailesend and Ali was pulled back from the vitriol in her phone and the heinous mess she'd made of everything. She tried to relax her jaw – it had been clenched since leaving the house. He'll wait for you, she reminded herself, though she had no idea why she felt so certain.

'I've never been here at night before. Usual visiting hours are daytime only but now that no longer applies to us.'

Liv pulled up at the door and put on the handbrake. 'I'll be right here. All night, I promise. I'm here.'

'What about the thesis draft? You didn't drop it in.'

'I've sorted it.'

'That fucking thesis.' Ali shook her head ruefully and Liv winced. 'Don't say sorry again,' Ali added quickly. 'I don't blame you. You were right about everything. You were trying to talk sense into me. I blame me. I knew—' The words caught in her throat. Breathe, Ali. 'I knew that I'd lose Miles, but I thought maybe I'd make it out with Sam, ya know?' She started to cry. 'Why am I crying over this? My dada is going to die – why am I crying over some guy?'

Liv looked helpless. 'You loved him too,' she said eventually. 'Maybe it'll work out. Maybe I can talk to him.'

'We shouldn't even be talking about this – it's not the time.' There'd be time to deal with everything, and right now, Ali couldn't bear the thought of screwing one more thing up. She leaned over and hugged Liv. Then she got out and retrieved her stuff from the back seat. Her phone was ringing. 'Mini Calling'.

Ali ignored it and started to sprint through the doors into the home. If Mini was calling to say it was too late, Ali couldn't bear to hear it over the phone.

This could be the last time I ever have to come to this place, she thought as she ran past the empty reception, not bothering to sign in. It gave her no comfort. She realised that, more than anything, she wanted him to stay. She no longer cared that the life he had was no life at all. She just wanted him to stay with her. Through the ward, down past Tabitha, who was engrossed in paper work – she's having a normal day, Ali marvelled. She's just at work right now. She finally got to his door. She peered through a teeny crack, holding her breath. Please don't be gone, she willed silently. Mini was sitting at the head of the bed, clutching her phone and whispering urgently to him. Ali was flooded with relief. She gave them as long as she could and then knocked gently.

She came in and took the chair opposite her mother.

'No change here,' Mini said quietly. 'But it's close, I think. I keep thinking he's stopped breathing and then after an age he does again.'

'I brought a surprise.' Ali smiled.

'Yes, I wondered what on earth you were off doing.'

Ali produced Miles's ukulele, grinning.

'Oh Jesus, that thing.' Mini started to smile.

'Well, I was going to bring lobster for us to eat in his honour but then I thought lobster at a deathbed was a bit … ick?'

'Yes, that's probably why they only serve biscuits – it's all you could stomach at a time like this,' Mini agreed.

'I thought you'd like it, Dad.' Ali strummed a bit, looking at Miles.

'Since when do you play the ukulele?'

'Well, we've been sitting by this bed a long time. I'm not always on the phone, ya know.'

Ali picked out the start of a jokey song that Miles had always played at family parties. Mini would playfully shout him down, pretending to moan about it. 'Why doesn't he play a real instrument?' she'd always say, amused but exasperated.

Mini was quiet for a moment, then she began to giggle. 'You know he brought that bloody ukulele to the hospital when you were born? The nurses thought he was hilarious. So, of course, that really got him going. I was screaming for them to give him the gas and air just to shut him up. Imagine having contractions while someone's playing 'You Are My Sunshine'. I wanted to kill him! After you finally came out, we were holding you and wondering what on earth we were supposed to do now. Everything had finally quieted down, just like it is here now, and he sang to you. 'Dream A Little Dream' it was. And you ...' Mini started to break a little as the tears came. 'You cried along! And you didn't stop for seven weeks straight. Then I wanted to kill you!'

Time stretched and contorted that night. It was the strangest of Ali's life. She was determined to make it beautiful somehow. They played CDs and told stories. The time Miles lost four-year-old Ali at the restaurant and it turned out she was hiding in the dumbwaiter. The time an actor had a fall during an interval and Miles stormed down to the theatre trying to muscle in on the part.

'He'd no shame.' Mini was giggling helplessly. 'There was already an understudy, and he'd walked out of the restaurant in the middle of service. Utter loon!'

'D'you remember when we went to Paris when I was seven and he took me to see the Eiffel Tower and he told me that I mustn't be disappointed but the Eiffel Tower actually only comes up to your knee and all the pictures of it are just an optical illusion? Such odd, pointless lying, Dad! But then when we finally saw it, it was such a surprise – it actually made it more exciting.'

At times in the night the nurses came in, performing checks and making notes. At some point Ali drifted into a strange sleep that hovered just on the edge of consciousness – when she started awake, dawn was creeping in to the room. She leant forward, studying Miles. She put her hand in front of his face and pleaded silently. Don't say I've missed you. Stay, stay, stay. The CD had played out. The room was quiet but for the wheeze of the air mattress pump. She held her breath as she waited for his.

At last, the faintest warmth hit her hand – so gently it was barely perceptible. And she knew the moment had come.

She stood and moved to sit on the edge of the bed. Mini, just awake, reached for Miles's hand. Ali put her arms around him and leaned down. She was surprised that she felt no fear. For the last few months, she had been so afraid of what was happening to him, repelled by the feeding tubes and nappies – the banal yet horrifying facts of a wasting body. Now she held him and began to sing softly, about shining stars and night breezes, her voice cracking on the word 'love'. 'Dream A Little Dream of Me', she whispered. And she searched for the slightest hint that he heard her.

Epilogue

Shelly smiled nervously at Dan as he took a seat across the table. The room was a palette of muted greens with a couple of potted plants. Corporate but projecting calm.

'So have things with the whole televised rant settled down?' Dan grinned, shrugging off his jacket.

'Ha ha,' she laughed softly. Then she paused. 'Maybe we shouldn't talk until the mediator gets here?' She offered up an awkward shrug. She could see he wasn't in a bad mood but she wasn't about to say a word without a professional present. This could get messy.

Dan only raised his eyebrows and began scrolling on his phone. Shelly tapped her nails nervously. Three days since the video had gone viral and things had already somewhat settled down. She felt bad because the whole Ali Jones fiasco at the Glossies had definitely helped. Also, surprisingly, quite a few women had taken Shelly's side and the whole episode had sparked a rash of hot takes in the media, largely commending her for 'bravely' speaking out about the real struggles of motherhood and revealing what goes on behind the filter.

It was awkward being hailed as some bastion of truth-telling, particularly while being at the centre of what looked like a very sinister blackmail plot. The guards had been on the case all week and Shelly was looking forward to putting it behind her. According to Bríd, they were interviewing @KellysKlobber at that very moment.

Meanwhile, Holistic Hazel had ended up with a mini backlash of her own when a few followers called her out for 'tearing down' her fellow mumfluencer.

'What a world,' Sandra had commented, amazed, as Shelly had attempted to recount the intricacies and vagaries of the swings and roundabouts of social-media public-opinion trials. Shelly had zero interest in engaging with any of it, though Hazel's people had been straight on to arrange a 'playdate' to show all was well in the Irish mumfluencer camp. And while Shelly had no desire to be involved in a highly engineered PDA with Hazel, in the interests of playing nice she'd agreed and was heading there that afternoon.

'Hello, Dan, Michelle?' Cliona Ní Dhunta looked supremely competent, just as you'd want a mediator to look. Shelly steeled herself. This was all going to piss Dan off so much.

'So we've gathered together because Michelle wants to update you on some issues that affect the family, Dan. Are you open to discussing it in as rational a manner as possible? And Michelle will be attempting to do the same.'

'I'm all ears.' He sat back, crossing his ankles. He looked so relaxed, and Shelly hated to ruin the civilised détente they'd reached. They'd decided to separate but had agreed that Dan would stay in the Seomra for the time being – a fact she was even more grateful for since the creepy emails, though, as yet, there'd been no more since that one a few days before the Glossies with Amy in the office.

'Great,' Cliona continued. 'Michelle, take a deep breath and go.'

Shelly held her fingertips to her temples and gazed down at the table. 'Dan, I want to say I'm sorry. I know that I let things get out of hand with the whole SHELLY thing. I used it as a way of hiding from being a mother. I was just so scared and lonely when I first had Georgie and I thought I was doing it all wrong. I think I needed help after Georgie. Not just going to the GP and taking the antidepressants – I needed a counsellor. But I'm doing that now. And I'm really trying harder with Georgie.' She finally forced herself to meet Dan's eyes. He looked kind. Which surprised her. With things being so fraught between them for the past year, she'd forgotten that Dan was kind. He wasn't a dick. Well, no more than she'd been a dick too.

'Shell,' he said softly, 'I know. And you are a good mum. I'm sorry, I know there were times when I said some really harsh things …'

Cliona was nodding along approvingly and Shelly wished she didn't have to break this moment with her next revelation.

'Anyway, I asked you here because I've something a bit serious to tell you. I've been receiving weird messages. Someone's been accusing me of faking stuff about you and Georgie on Instagram.'

'Right?' Dan looked nonplussed. 'I mean, "person bullshitting on social media" can't be that much of a shocker though, can it?'

'No.' Shelly shrugged. 'But it's not brilliant that everyone might find out that I used a stock image and said it was my baby—'

'Did you?' Cliona was jotting something down. Jesus, shut up, Cliona! thought Shelly desperately. Luckily Dan was grinning and seemed to be amused by this titbit.

'I feel terrible, Dan. I know it's all my fault. I shouldn't have exposed us to this. I'm thinking of wrapping up SHELLY and the guards are looking into it – we know who it is and they're interviewing her today to make her stop.'

Dan massaged his forehead, looking weary, and Shelly tensed for his reaction. 'Shelly, don't give up everything unless you want to. Don't give up because of this coward. We'll work it out. I'm still in the guesthouse. I'm still Georgie's dad. We'll figure it out. Plus we've got this little baby to think about. I know I've been angry and I was hard on you because I just didn't understand the whole Insta-thing. But we need to stick together. Not together together, but I am here. I promise.'

❖

Shelly drove away from Cliona's odd corporate oasis of manufactured calm actually feeling pretty calm. The time apart seemed to have defused much of the tension between her and

Dan. His concern seemed totally genuine, and Shelly had caught herself wondering if there could still be something between them. A twinge in her belly made her smile. I know you're there, she thought. She headed down the canal in the late morning sun and realised she felt relaxed. Nothing was sorted, as such, but she felt less afraid of the fallout if those pictures did come out. There was something liberating about the fact that her marriage was, to all intents and purposes, over. It'd be embarrassing if people saw her Dan-a-like but she'd live and that was the main thing. Maybe it'd be a blessing – it wasn't like she still wanted SHELLY to work anyhow. Though extracting herself was already proving difficult. Her winning Influencer of the Year at the Glossies, despite her temporary pariah status and not even showing up, attested to how embroiled she was in that world.

'The sponsors need you, the brands need you,' Amy had explained over voicenote the previous day. 'You're part of the ecosystem.'

Shelly turned up towards the familiar road where her parents' pebble-dashed semi-D overlooked an oval green. It was the same green where Shelly had made daisy chains with her friends as a kid and where eventually they'd snuck cigarettes and kisses with the boys from St Finnian's. She pulled over and rolled down her window. Her parents' front door was open and across the quiet road Sandra and Georgie were playing on the grass with a couple of the neighbours' girls a little older than Georgie. It'd be nice to live close to other families, Shelly mused. They'd probably be selling the house eventually. It was too big and isolated behind the electric gates and down that long driveway. Their house, she realised now, had all been for the 'gram. The big kitchen and the biscuit-and-beige floors and walls everywhere. It was a show house, not a home. Shelly tried to picture living somewhere else, just herself and her two babies.

'Mama!' Georgie interrupted her thoughts, hurtling her little body across the green towards the car with Sandra jogging after her.

'Hello, my baby!' Shelly hopped out and gathered her in her arms, cuddling her close. She was getting used to motherhood, which seemed a weird thing to be thinking three years in but there it was. I guess it just takes some people this long to feel OK after having a baby, she thought, marvelling at the acceptance she felt. She was starting to forgive herself. Her new counsellor was helping.

'Well?' Sandra raised her eyebrows.

'We'll be OK, I think.' Shelly shaded her eyes from the sun and saw Sandra smiling.

'Well done. It's all progress, Shelly, not perfection. Remember that when you're going too hard on yourself.' She squeezed her daughter's shoulders.

Shelly loaded the giddy Georgie into the back seat, thanked her mum and started out for Hazel's house for their very-diplomatic not-at-all-awks lunch. She'd spotted notifications on her phone and knew that Holistic Hazel was probably tagging her like mad already, rinsing every last bit of precious content out of the occasion – or, rather, one of her ever-rotating roster of assistants was.

One such assistant opened the door to Shelly about twenty

minutes later. The girl looked haunted. Hazel could do that to a person, Shelly imagined.

'Hi, I'm Jenny – come on through, they're in the kitchen.'

Shelly followed while Georgie charged into the playroom off the hall where the kids were.

About a year ago, Hazel had announced that from then on she was only hiring assistants called Jenny because she was sick of learning new names and updating the contact info every few weeks after another traumatised or fed-up recent marketing graduate saw the light and aced out of Hazel's Insta-sweatshop. Apparently she was so inundated with applications there were enough Jennys in each round that she could actually pull off this bonkers strategy.

'Oh! Look who's here! My fave ...' Hazel was speaking into her phone as she came towards them, swathed in white linen. She held the phone out to the side to capture their awkward hug and air kisses on camera. 'Come sit.' She shared the Story as she drifted back to the low table under the skylight around which lay huge Buddabags and yellow and orange cushions. Polly perched awkwardly on one.

'I see you've got a new Jenny!' Shelly smiled as she eased herself down beside Polly.

'It's such a great approach on all fronts, really, if you think about it,' Hazel explained. 'Those bitch PRs were non-stop gossiping about how I couldn't keep a girl for more than two weeks. Now they don't even realise it's a new Jenny they're dealing with every time.'

'Such a good idea,' Polly enthused.

'Pol,' Hazel sighed world-wearily, 'you're so lucky you don't even need an assistant and don't have these kinds of problems.'

Hazel was a master of the back-handed compliment, and she was going to be positively ecstatic to hear of Shelly's split from Dan. Let her take some skewed pleasure out of it, Shelly thought, smiling at Polly.

'How are the boys, Pol—?' Shelly was interrupted by her phone – it was the garda, Bríd. 'Sorry I have to take this.' She hopped up and slipped out the sliding door into the garden. 'Hello?'

'Hi, Ms Devine? Bríd here from Malahide garda station. Do you have a minute?'

'Yes!' Shelly was so relieved to hear from her.

'I have Ms Byrne in custody – that's, ehm, Kelly Byrne, Insta-handle KellysKlobber.'

Shelly chanced a grin at this as she strolled further down the lawn. It all sounded so ridiculous coming out of a guard's mouth.

'We spent the morning going over her statement and it seems she isn't responsible for the messages and pictures you've been receiving.'

Shelly faltered. 'What? No, it has to be her.'

'I've spent some time fact-checking her story and she's telling the truth. She was actually receiving treatment during the period in which you received the messages. The facility where she was being cared for confirms this, and as the treatment was for a phone addiction, her devices were withheld throughout. We'll keep looking into it, Ms Devine, I assure you.'

Shelly staggered slightly as she hung up the call. A cloud

passed over the garden and she felt a chill that ran much deeper than a simple April breeze. She had never entertained the thought that it could be anyone else. Her phone chirped. An email.

imwatchingyoushelly@gmail.com
Subject: You may be done with Insta but I'm not done with you

The body of the email contained no text, just a link to a Dropbox. She clicked it and a series of pictures appeared. As she scanned them, her terror grew. Each one was more frightening than the last. The images themselves were banal but they were intimate and therein lay their horrifying impact.

Shelly wiping Georgie's face, the camera peeping round a corner in the kitchen. From the angle, the person taking the picture had to be in the utility room and crouched low to the ground.

Georgie and Shelly having their nails done – when had they last done that? – visible through the glass doors into the garden. Shelly felt sickened.

More pictures. Always Shelly and Georgie. Always inside the house. Always so close, so horribly close.

A picture of Dan holding Georgie while Shelly took a pic of the dinner table seemed to have been captured from the garden.

Paranoid, she looked up, her eyes frantically searching every shady corner of this garden. Who else would want to hurt her? She was reeling, like she was on a rollercoaster just peaking at the top of a drop, about to plunge into a terrifying unknown. Who would do this?

She looked towards the house. Through the glass doors, she could see Hazel and Polly both buried in their phones.

❖

The two funeral directors looked as close to death as Miles had the night before.

Ali rubbed her burning eyes after the men stepped out to gather some forms. Mini and Eleanor would be along shortly and Ali couldn't wait to hand over responsibility for this thing.

'Planning a funeral is such a bizarre activity.' Liv was leafing through the coffin catalogue while Ali agonised over the wording for the obituary.

Ali looked up and tried to make a stab at normality. 'I have a theory …'

'Go on.' Liv sounded intrigued.

'The lads,' Ali jerked her head at the door through which Mr Dunville and Mr O'Connor had just exited, 'd'ya reckon they kind of "corpse-up" so the make-up job on the real corpses looks better by comparison?'

'Ali!' Liv looked stern. 'Although,' she conceded, 'it would be a good approach, I suppose. Bit like a reverse of the girls on reception in the cosmetic surgery places.'

They giggled awkwardly.

Then Ali stopped. 'Wait, should we be laughing?'

'I know, I know. But they kind of bait you, don't they.' Liv held up the catalogue open to a floral arrangement made to look like a Jack Russell terrier.

Ali giggled again in spite of herself. 'Is that a toupée on its head?'

'Bizarre.' Liv grinned.

'I've really missed you,' Ali said softly. 'I've really missed us. I'm sorry, Liv. I can't believe I put my Instagram before our friendship. You're like my sister.'

Liv slung an arm around her and replied, 'You, thank god, are not like my sister. She's the worst. I love you too, darl. We're better than family – you know that, right? – cos we chose each other.'

'Right in the feels, Liv. I've never heard you be so sincere! You should be writing this.' Ali shoved the pad and pen towards Liv, who studied what she'd come up with so far: the date.

'Ali, this date isn't even right!'

'I checked my phone.' Ali pulled up the calendar and proffered it to Liv.

'Nuh-uh, that's out by, like, two weeks! How are you living like this?'

'I use the laptop calendar for my appointments. Also, could we be arguing about something more inconsequential right now?' She took back the phone and started to reset the date.

'Miles was a loving father and husband … or should we put husband first? Would Mini mind?' When Ali didn't respond, Liv looked over, puzzled. 'Ali, what's wrong?'

Ali couldn't speak and her vision was weird. She felt like it was zooming in and out of focus, like that bit in *Jaws* when yer man sees the shark at the beach for the first time.

'Ali? Ali?' Liv was whispering urgently.

'The phone's crazy,' Ali finally managed to say. But even as she said the words she knew that the phone was not crazy. Things were lining up in her mind that very much supported the idea that the phone was not crazy.

'What? What is it?' Liv looked panicked.

Ali's mind continued to skip through the recent past. No sex on Valentine's because she'd had her period – though that wasn't the reason she'd given Sam. How long ago was that? According to the phone: too long.

'Ali?'

'Phone says I'm pregnant.' Ali held out the period-tracker app and promptly burst into tears.

At this point, the cadaver-like funeral directors returned.

'Oh jaysus, it's terrible when it hits you, isn't it?' Mr O'Connor slid the tissues across the table to the sobbing Ali.

'She's just … very shocked.' Liv looked awkward. 'Will we be much longer here, do you think?'

'Well, we'll finish these few bits and then we just need a decision on the coffin. Where is the funeral? When is the funeral? That kind of thing. There's actually quite a bit. Is Mrs Jones coming down?'

Ali stood up abruptly, wiping her face haphazardly. 'I'll just pop out and call her. She should be on her way.' As she turned she gave Liv a meaningful look and a flick of her head. Liv got the message and followed her outside, where Ali immediately commenced pacing between two black traffic cones.

'Where do you think they get these?' Ali kicked one. 'I wish I smoked right now.'

'Do you actually think you might be preggers? Is it definitely possible, like?'

Ali scanned back over the past few weeks. She'd been trying to limit contact with Sam but he was very, very cute and what was the point in having a slightly fake boyfriend if you couldn't enjoy the real perks?

'You were careful at least – right, Ali?' Liv was looking stern.

'Well, it was tricky because, with me being pregnant and all, condoms just didn't seem like the right—'

'Ali!' Liv exploded. 'Are you telling me that in playing fake pregnant you've got yourself fully fucking pregs for real?'

'I was using precautions – I was using the period app.'

Liv was now pacing around after her and Ali felt like she was being pursued. 'Ali, that app thing is like the rhythm method and every youngest kid in every family ever might as well be called Little Rhythm Method because that is how effective that bullshit is. And that's when you've got the friggin' date programmed right.'

A passing man looked mildly alarmed, catching the last of Liv's rant.

'Screaming at a crying person outside a funeral home doesn't make for good optics,' Ali shot back at her and burst into fresh tears. 'Please will you go and get me a pregnancy test? I need to figure out whether this day is going to be a garden variety plan-my-dad's-funeral-shitshow or whether there is a legit my-life-is-fucked-and-I'm-up-the-pole-without-a-paddle kind of vibe going on.'

'Yes, yes. You're right. I'm sorry. Maybe I'm having contact hormones or something. You'll be fine. It's going to be fine. Well, not fine but … oh god, I'm shutting up now. I'll be back ASAP.'

Ali slumped down to her hunkers as Liv dashed back to the car.

Ali gazed at the cars driving past. More people having normal days and here she was having a pregnancy scare at a funeral home. What the actual fuck. She tried to detect something, anything in her tummy. Some hint at a new life. Mainly she was just imagining a tadpole with Sam's face bashing into the wall of her uterus. Weird to think she even had a uterus. In all the pregnancy chat of the last few months, it had felt so remote, as if it had nothing to do with her. It was like a story she was writing about someone else's life.

Did she feel pregnant? She did feel gross, but that could be from sleeping in a chair and eating nothing but crap biscuits and milky tea for the last twelve hours. She was shattered but, again, sitting up in a chair all night wasn't exactly restful. She had been tired for weeks. She tried doing the maths, measuring the timeline against her fake pregnancy, which only served to inspire a fresh wave of nausea and terror. Jesus, the Insta-pregnancy.

Ali took out her phone. Even though she'd deleted the app, the email inbox was still jammed with vitriol. She hadn't had the nerve to google her name yet, but presumably the story was already everywhere. It was a strange sensation. She knew that just on the other side of this screen was a tsunami of haters baying for her blood, calling her pathetic and ugly and a weirdo. She still wasn't feeling it, but she knew the anguish, shame and regret were all poised to annihilate her the second this numb daze lifted.

Questions started to bombard her. What should she do? Should she make a statement? A mea culpa post on Instagram? Get Liv to go on and explain that she was 'suffering from stress' like a Hollywood celebrity? Say she was missing? Ill? Mad? A liar? Planning a funeral?

She just had to get through the funeral and then she'd deal with it, whatever that meant.

Ali's thoughts were interrupted by the approach of Mini's trademark heels and clipped phone voice. Ali felt a flash of sympathy for Erasmus, who had, to date, never got a thing right as far as Mini was concerned. Ali could relate. Eleanor was trailing behind looking harried and carrying some of Miles's suits.

'I said no! Not the afternoon,' Mini barked and, peering down at Ali, added, 'What are you doing down there? You look like a vagrant. Not you! I was talking to my daughter! I'm going in now to make arrangements, I'll check in later, Father.'

Ali wearily stood up and brushed herself off.

'Did you just say "Father"?' Ali eyed Mini suspiciously as they all trooped back inside the dim foyer of the funeral home.

'Yes, Erasmus – of all people – found me the most perfect priest for the funeral.'

'But we're not even … Catholic or anything? You just had me specify no cross on the coffin to these lads?' whispered Ali. Since when did her parents have any interest in religion?

'Oh, don't worry. I told him no prayers or any shiteology about god.' Mini waved away Ali's concerns. 'He's just going to do an MC thing. To add a bit of gravitas. He's kind of a showbiz priest.'

To Ali this sounded, if anything, even more concerning than a traditional priest. She raised an eyebrow at Eleanor as Mini bustled in to the funeral directors, who hastily stopped chatting and adopted funereal manners once more. Eleanor leaned close as they took their seats. 'She asked Erasmus to google "burial at sea" but I think we've talked her out of it. She might be in shock.'

'Yeah … me too,' murmured Ali, gazing at the paisley cravat poking out of the jacket Eleanor was holding, Miles always wore it to opening night at the theatre.

Liv appeared at the door behind them, and Ali muttered her excuses and followed her friend to the ladies.

Liv read the instructions. 'Piss on it for at least five seconds, it says.'

Ali weed all over her sleeve as Liv crossed her arms and leaned against the door.

'There has to be a better way,' Ali moaned.

'It's definitely not the most disgusting thing that happens in this place,' Liv pointed out.

And there was the little blue plus sign.

'Confirmed,' said Liv. 'You are up one baby. And down a baby daddy. Remind me where you are with the fake baby currently?'

'Shut up,' Ali wailed.

'I'm just trying to keep it straight in my head,' Liv quipped, but she came over for a hug. 'Is it a good thing or a bad thing

that this isn't even the first time I've hugged you on the jacks?' she asked.

'Well, get used to it,' Ali spoke into Liv's armpit. 'Pissing a lot and generally being gross are the main side-effects of pregnancy.'

'And you think you're going to ... stay pregnant?' Liv disengaged and busied herself gathering up the pregnancy-test packaging.

Ali stared up at her. The madness of the last few weeks meant she'd fucked in her old job, ruined the only good relationship she'd ever had and was a pariah on the internet.

She'd probably be able to go crawling back to *Durty Aul' Town* – what good was a bereavement if you couldn't leverage a bit of goodwill with it, after all?

But Sam was done with her and there's no way the sad-dad card would fly with him – he had the dead-mum card and the you-lied-to-me-about-being-pregnant card. He had the royal flush of emotional upperhandery. But maybe when she told him about the pregnancy test he'd come around? Or maybe he'd lose his shit even more? She flashed back to his cold rage of a few days ago. Sam was evidently the kind of guy who it's hard to piss off but when he finally does get angry, it's apoca-fucking-lyptic.

Maybe it was futile trying to get him involved. Perhaps there's a universally acknowledged number of chances to blindside a man with an unplanned pregnancy – even if one of them was fake. Two strikes and you're out, she thought.

She pulled up her pants and pulled Liv into a tight hug.

'Let's go plan a funeral. And, I guess, a baby shower for some time in October.'

Acknowledgements

As the saying goes, it takes a village to raise a book baby ... I want to thank my village. Thank you so much to:

The early champions of Ali's story, Sarah Gunn, Teresa Daly and Fiona Murphy.

The ledgebags who read the first draft: Liadan Hynes, Louise McSharry, Mary O'Sullivan, Anne Harris and Jacqueline Murphy.

Thank you to Mary McGill and Shereen Martin for help with some particulars of Liv's life as an Indian-Irish academic.

The incredible editor who believed in the book and brought it to a (hopefully) much better place, Ciara Doorley.

The team at Hachette Ireland who have put so much into creating this book: Elaine Egan, Joanna Smyth and my copy-editor, Emma Dunne.

The fantastic, loving women who mind my human babies when I'm working on the book babies: Paola Felix, Lauren Shannon Jones, Virginia De Lucas, Daniella Prates and Iwona Wyporska.

My colleagues at the *Sunday Independent*, *Image*, *Lovin Dublin* and *Irish Tatler*, especially Brendan O'Connor, Gemma Fullam, Jane Doran, Cormac Bourke, Madeleine Keane, Emily Hourican, Megan Cassidy, Dominique McMullan, Lizzie Gore-Grimes, Meg Walker, Ellie Balfe and Sarah Macken.

My pod family, Cassie Delaney and Jen O'Dwyer and everyone who listens and bigs up *Mother Of Pod* and *The Creep Dive*. The VPAKers and the Casual Choir gang especially Soobie Lynch, Esther OMD and Emer McLysaght. The Glenbeigh Massif, Pauline Bewick and Poppy Melia who gave me the magical yard house in which to finish this book. Dee and all of Bill's gang for so much help, love and compassion.

My family, Mary O'Sullivan, Kevin Linehan, Anne Harris, Nancy Harris, Constance Harris, Mungo Harris and my in-laws, David White, Vivianne White, William White, Triona McCarthy, Hilary White and Viktorija White.

Lastly to Sebastian White – the best partner in life and only person as devoted to *SVU* as me – and to, hands-down, my favourite people of all time: Roo and Ari, thank you so much.

Sophie White
June 2019

WHAT'S NEXT?

In *Filter This 2*, our fave Instahuns, Ali and Shelly, return for more boomerangs, bitching and Rants.ie.

Despite Ali's Insta-sham making her a pariah in the Insta-scene, it turns out that followers love a bit of scandal – she's more popular than ever – and when Amy Donoghue steps in to rehabilitate her image, Ali realises she may have to wade once more into the grubby Insta-hole. After all, she needs to cash in just to bankroll this real live bump she's got. With Sam still ignoring her at their prenatal appointments and Mini having a mild grief-induced psychotic break (WTF is she doing on Tinder?), Ali's got little else to cling on to but #sponcon and #bumpupdates.

Meanwhile Shelly is trying to settle into her new life as a single parent while being held hostage by her mysterious Insta-stalker whose sole objective – to keep Shelly on Instagram – is as bizarre as it is alarming. Why do they care? Who are they? With @HolisticHazel immersed in creating the WYND festival (her answer to the Goop Summit) and @PollysFewBits being as non-descript as ever, Shelly must get to the bottom of it herself.

When Ali starts attending Catfishers Anonymous as part of Amy's plan for Image Rehab, she inadvertently stumbles on the key to solving Shelly's mystery …

Now available for pre-order